WARRIORS OF IRON

THE DARK AGE CHRONICLES, BOOK 2

MJ PORTER

B

Boldwood

First published in Great Britain in 2025 by Boldwood Books Ltd.

Copyright © MJ Porter, 2025

Cover Design by Head Design Ltd.

Cover Images: Adobe Stock and iStock

Map designed by Flintlock Covers

The moral right of MJ Porter to be identified as the author of this work has been asserted in accordance with the Copyright, Designs and Patents Act 1988.

Every effort has been made to obtain the necessary permissions with reference to copyright material, both illustrative and quoted. We apologise for any omissions in this respect and will be pleased to make the appropriate acknowledgements in any future edition.

A CIP catalogue record for this book is available from the British Library.

Paperback ISBN 978-1-83617-506-3

Large Print ISBN 978-1-83617-505-6

Hardback ISBN 978-1-83617-504-9

Ebook ISBN 978-1-83617-507-0

Kindle ISBN 978-1-83617-508-7

Audio CD ISBN 978-1-83617-499-8

MP3 CD ISBN 978-1-83617-500-1

Digital audio download ISBN 978-1-83617-502-5

This book is printed on certified sustainable paper. Boldwood Books is dedicated to putting sustainability at the heart of our business. For more information please visit https://www.boldwoodbooks.com/about-us/sustainability/

Boldwood Books Ltd, 23 Bowerdean Street, London, SW6 3TN

www.boldwoodbooks.com

For CS, on the birth of her granddaughter

0   50 Miles

URICONIUM

R. Severn

TOMSA

ICKNIELD STREET

R.

HUSMERAE

BEANSAETE

R. Wye

GLEVUM

STOPPINGAS

FAER

CORINIUM

EORLINGAS

WOCIN

R. Avon

R. Avon

MAP OF C6TH BRITANNIA

R. Trent

R. Welland

GYRWE

SWEORDORA

HERSTINGA

R. Granta

ERMINE STREET

R. Ouse

R. Stour

ENDRICA

HICCA

WATLING STREET

VERULAMIUM

NGAS

WAECLINGAS

S

UPPINGAS

R. Thames

R. Medway

TE

SS WAY

on

CHARACTER LIST

The Eorlingas, a native Brythonic tribe from the west of Britain, close to the River Hafren
Edern, leader of Villa Eorlingas, now dead
Elen, Edern's wife
Gwynmarch, horse
Idnerth, warrior of the Eorlingas
Kenal, warrior of the Eorlingas
Maccus, Madog's son
Macsen, Madog's father
Madog, tribal chieftain of the Eorlingas
Marchell, Meddi's servant and former seeress
Meddi, seeress of the Eorlingas, former wife of Edern
Merin, Madog's father's father
Rhian, Madog's wife

Sian, a woman of the Eorlingas

Terricus, charcoal maker now turned bladesmith

Tudwal, youth, not yet a warrior

Twrch, warrior of the Eorlingas

Urien, warrior of the Eorlingas

The Gyrwe, a tribe from the east of Britain, formerly a *comitatus* invited to Britain after the end of Roman occupation by the sixth century

Bægmund, warrior of the Gyrwe

Bucge, warrior of Gyrwe and seeress

Burnoth, warrior of Wihtlæd

Cenbryht, warrior of Gyrwe

Eastmund, warrior of Wærmund

Goddæg, warrior of the Gyrwe

Heafoc, warrior of Gyrwe

Hygebeorht, warrior of Gyrwe

Maggenræd, warrior of Gyrwe

Nothelm, warrior of Gyrwe

Osfyth, warrior of Gyrwe and hunter

Wædel, warrior of Gyrwe

Wærmund, warrior of Gyrwe and son of Wihtlæd

Waga, father of Wihtlæd

Watholgeot, father of Waga

The Weogoran, a native Brythonic tribe that borders the Eorlingas
Corun, their leader

The Beansæte, a native Brythonic tribe that borders the Eorlingas
Hedrek, their leader
Centus, blacksmith, now dead

The Hicca – a tribe in the middle of Britannia
Boddw, their leader, now dead

The Wæclingas – a tribe in the middle of Britannia
Isarninus, their leader
Iuti, Isarninus' son

The Færpingas – neighbours of the Eorlingas
Prasto, their leader

The Wocingas
Riderch, their leader
Gwener, Rhun's wife

The Husmeræ
Cadwysti, seeress
Padern, leader of the Husmeræ

The Stoppingas, neighbours of the Eorlingas
Ladus, their spokeswoman

The Tomsæte, a tribe in the middle of Britannia
Sennicus, their spokesperson

Within Uriconium
Clynog, trader
Diseta, translator
Eudaf, bladesmith
Gildas, a holy man
Gwladus, of the Wreocensætan
Iamcilla, a holy woman
Katourn, bladesmith

Within the ruined settlement of Verulamium
Cynin, warrior
Dewi, warrior
Eli, warrior
Nyfed, warrior
Rhun, warrior
Veda, trader

LOCATIONS

Villa Eorlingas – based very roughly on the Frocester Roman Villa, but closer to the River Hafren

The home of the Husmeræ – based on the Great Witcombe Roman Villa, Gloucestershire

The home of the Wæclingas/Isarninus – settlement close to Verulamium, now St Albans

Corinium – Cirencester

Glevum – Gloucester

Uriconium – Wroxeter, the archaeology reveals there was a building phase taking place there throughout this period. That's unusual at this time when most former Roman settlements were decaying. I've decided to name it Uriconium and not Viriconium because I came across the name Uriconium first, and hopefully it will prevent confusion with Verulamium

Verulamium – St Albans

Watling Street – Roman road (although evident in the landscape from the Bronze Age) running from Dover to Wroxeter (and further north)

Fosse Way – Roman road running from Exeter to Lincoln

Icknield Street – Roman road running from Bourton-on-the-Water to York

BRITANNIA AD541

Rome's reach disappeared from Britannia over a hundred years ago. In its wake, the sophisticated warrior and political society that allowed a far-distant emperor to govern the unruly province has slowly crumbled with the attendant loss of its currency, skills, political elite and, of course, brave warriors who once fought against Britannia's enemies: the Picts from the far north, long held at bay by the snaking walls crossing the north of Roman-held Britannia.

Quickly, the skills and ideals of *Romanitas* have become subsumed by the basic need to survive amongst those who still inhabit the island of Britannia. Some have taken advantage of the weakness of others, although with the magik of bladesmith and ironworker lost to all but a few, the majority lack the required weapons or the desire to wage bloody wars against their ancient enemies. The blades they have are old and tired, riddled with rust and lacking the keen edge to make warfare possible.

Instead, the men and women of Britannia inhabit the cities abandoned by Rome, forging a living from the soil, reliant on barter. And for those who shy away from the haunted ruins and the lost Roman gods, the even more ancient hill forts of an age before Rome came offer the promise of their protective ditches and ramparts, as well as their familiar gods. Others shelter in the remnants of a once rich and prosperous agricultural landscape doing all they can to grow enough food to survive, daily reminded of all they've lost, as they build ditches and embankments to protect themselves from those desperate enough to risk all for enough food to eat despite the lack of good weapons.

To the east, new tribal warriors have emerged, who were once strangers to Britannia, and herald from the northern lands of the Continent. They're not strangers to war. They have come to protect those too weak to fight but with the wealth to pay them in the immediate aftermath of Rome's departure. With a century of no coinage the *comitatus* now lay claim to that which they were once paid to protect.

This is Britannia, a century after the withdrawal of Rome and a century before the emergence of the kingdoms of the Angles and Saxons.

This is the true Dark Ages.

THE STORY SO FAR

Meddi is the seeress of the Eorlingas tribe. After many, many winters cast out from her home, she's been restored to the ancestral holding of Villa Eorlingas, alongside her half-brother, Madog. He now rules as chieftain of the tribe.

But, in being restored to the Villa Eorlingas, Meddi has realised Madog requires more than the tribe's former renown and her own skills as seeress to maintain their position and hold firm against those with covetous eyes. The Eorlingas need the sharpened edges of new iron blades – a magik long since forgotten in the ruins left by the departing Romans. All that survives are ancient blades, pitted and much repaired; all lacking the keenness to kill an enemy with one strike. None can recall the art of using charcoal to extract fresh iron from ironstone. All think the answer lies in melting down old blades to forge new ones. But they are wrong.

Chance has brought them a man who believes he can forge such blades and who is keen to use his knowledge to aid the Eorlingas. However, a failure to restore the broken ancestral sword once belonging to Meddi and Madog's father has left Meddi feeling angry and impotent. Worse, the two halves of the blade have been stolen away at the hands of Elen, once wed to the despised Edern. Can the new blade-smith and charcoal maker, Terricus, rediscover the lost art and provide keen edges for the tribal warriors? And can he do so before Elen brings an enemy to threaten the Eorlingas, using the sword's two halves as proof of her right to hold Villa Eorlingas, and further emboldened by the lies dripping from her poisoned tongue to turn even more against the rights of the Eorlingas to hold their ancestral villa?

Far from Villa Eorlingas in the west of Britannia, Wærmund, the despised, birthmarked son of the leader of the Gyrwe, has struck out alone with his fellow misfits, some more loyal than others, to make a name for himself as a leader of warriors.

He hopes to cast himself as a *comitatus* in the vision of his forebears who came to the island to protect the locals from the depravations of Britannia's enemies, the Picts and the Irish. He intends to be paid to fight and, in such a way, stay far from any recriminations from his despised father who reviles him for being cursed by the gods from birth with a mark, which some think looks like the depiction of a wolf on his cheek. Wærmund knows his father will not stop hunting him down to kill him in retribution for murdering his favoured son and acknowledged heir unless he gains a reputation to rival that of his father's and the warriors with which to bring that about. He intends to make himself invincible and be known as more than a kin-slayer. He'll prove to all he's not gods-cursed but gods-blessed. That he's a true warrior. A wolf warrior.

However, Wærmund has also realised the key to the strength he requires lies in having access to sharpened blades like those his ancestors first used, and not those forged from second-hand iron which lack a sharp enough edge to kill with a single blow. Now, in the centre of Britannia, and having made a firm enemy of the leader of the Wæclingas tribe, or rather their leader, Isarninus, Wærmund has, by chance, discovered someone who knows those magiks, or at least where they can be found in the ruins of Roman Britannia.

1

MEDDI OF THE EORLINGAS

'Seeress.' The word's snapped and only just respectful. It's more of a question than a form of address.

'My lord,' I reply coolly. Of late, he's been 'brother', not 'my lord', but before the assembled people of the Eorlingas tribe, and with rage pouring from me like heat from the forge after the events of last night, I know to temper my response. My brother sits before me, on his ceremonial stool, his expression difficult to interpret. His familiar wide forehead, drooping moustache and ancestral double-headed shimmering torque encircling his long neck highlight his assessing gaze.

Within the ceremonial room of our villa home,

pale white walls naturally lighting it, he's the centre of attention.

I hope my face is inscrutable, despite the heat boiling within me. I continue to answer the unspoken question the singular use of my title conjures. I take a deep breath. 'The loss of Elen from her captivity is unwelcome. The punishment of Hedrek, once leader of the Beansæte tribe, is a just one. We must now concentrate on increasing the weapons we have to hand and on growing the reach of our tribe. At present, the Eorlingas are much enlarged since you became their leader. Edern was a fool who broke this villa's hold on the surrounding tribes with his ridiculous demands. Already you've reinstated some of our people's prestige. We'll restore all of it, as I always promised.'

I speak to those within the room as much as to my brother. This includes his warriors, steady Urien, young Twrch, Kenal and Idnerth. These are the men who've spent the darkness of night trying to find Elen after her escape was discovered. They've been forced to admit defeat for the time being, the heavy downpour obscuring all signs of the passage of footprints. The women of the Eorlingas are also in attendance: Rhian, my brother's wife and mother of his young son, Sian and even Marchell, the aged seeress of our people, and the mother of Elen. I usurped her position many years ago to become the seeress my brother speaks to now. Every other member of the Eorlingas is also within. I even include Hedrek, the object of our discussion, in that, for he's here, bound and bleeding, allowed inside to listen to our discussion with Terricus a louring presence next to him.

We're gathered within the painted main room of Villa Eorlingas, more likely to be used for ceremonial feasts and welcoming guests than for this debate between seeress and tribal leader. Between sister and brother. We shared a father, not a mother. I knew our father; Madog didn't, our father murdered when he was a baby.

A murmur of approval for my pronouncement rises from those who observe. I've emboldened the Eorlingas to hunger for a return of their stolen prestige. While my brother and his warriors fought the final battle against the remnants of Edern's hold on the villa complex last summer, he only had the men and the desire to do so because I fostered it between my people for two decades. I vowed, after Edern used me and cast me out, I'd take back everything my father once held. How I adored my father. How I railed against his weakness in trusting Edern. How I labour to restore his name to the history of my people.

I turn and note no one looks displeased at my announcement with regard to Hedrek's punishment, even Hedrek looked gratified with it. In aiding the escape of Elen, a captive since the death of her despised husband Edern last summer, and in the process allowing our new bladesmith, Centus, to be killed in a terrible way by the bitch, Hedrek's brought about his enslavement to the people of the Eorlingas. The bloody fool. But it should be enslavement, not death. No doubt that's why he doesn't argue against me.

My brother cautioned me last summer not to have Elen killed when he and his warriors took the villa from her when still in mourning for her dead husband. That was a terrible mistake, leading to this moment of questioning of all we've laboured to achieve. But to kill Hedrek now would be a waste. I've a use for him that allowing Elen to live could never have produced. His assistance and service will recompense the Eorlingas for his unleashing of Elen, who the fool thought would wed him and make him leader of this villa in Madog's place.

Hedrek's servitude to the new bladesmith, Terricus, will go some way to countering the threat Elen poses. Her escape with the broken parts of my father's ancestral sword, carried by every leader of the Eorlingas since the Romans left these shores, threatens to imperil all we've regained.

'See, brother,' I murmur through tight lips, as those who owe my brother allegiance disperse to their daily duties with a gesture from his hands confirming the debate between the two of us is over. They leave with murmurings of conversation but no outraged complaints. None have slept well since last night. But to know their leader and seeress have plans for the future will settle any worries they may have. For now, there are crops requiring tending to, water to be gathered and animals fed. For Terricus, there's ironstone to be melted and Hedrek will pump the bellows to speed the process.

The dark and terrible events of last night remain unfathomable to many. The consolation of returning to yesterday's routine, before all of it happened, will be a comforting reassurance.

'Not one of them is uneasy with your continuing leadership despite everything that's happened. Including the loss of Elen.' Saying her name burns my mouth. How I despise the bitch. She's taken Centus from us. She killed him. I don't doubt she performed the act herself. She'd have taken delight in doing so. She knew what he meant to me. And to the Eorlingas. Hedrek had told her of my plans. Another reason for me to hate him and wish him dead, as my brother does. But no. Hedrek has some use that makes keeping him alive sensible.

My brother makes no reply, expression pensive. Even his wife walks away clasping her young son to her side, a lingering glance assessing what might happen now between me and my half-brother. She knows Madog well, but not me. She offers me her respect as the seeress of the Eorlingas, and the woman who welcomed her son into the tribe and accorded him the honour of being acknowledged as my father's grandson. She understands I ken magiks she can never hope to know. I communicate with the gods of the Eorlingas in a way she can't aspire to emulate.

Perhaps, I admit, she wonders why I didn't foresee Elen's actions last night, but I'm a seeress, my skills are not in prediction. A twist of my lips and not for the first time I consider if Marchell, Elen's mother, might have divined this. Her skills have always been greater than mine where foretelling is concerned. I've questioned her ability to discern the future before. I've dismissed it as something she can see, but not control. I suspect, even if she did know what Elen would do, she was powerless to stop it from happening. Such a gift is perhaps more of a curse from our gods than a blessing.

'Now what?' Madog demands petulantly when all

are gone, and we're entirely alone within the main room of Villa Eorlingas, the precious coloured stone pieces depicting the double horse mosaic in wondrous splendour, pressing into my feet with the familiarity of life-long acquaintance. I wouldn't go so far as to say they ground me to this place, reminding me of all I've regained in the last year, but they reinforce me. I won't deny that. They speak to me of who I am, and not what I once was. A broken husk, denied her daughter, tortured by a man who should have respected her as his wife, and then cast out when the child in my belly was female and not the much-desired male, only to be scarred for life with the marks of his anger on my face and between my legs.

'We return to the task of creating iron blades with sharp edges to defend ourselves. It's even more important now, with Elen on the loose. She'll reap great harm on us. She'll try and win some of our enemies to her side. She's always been a vixen. With her gone and the symbol of the Eorlingas, our father's sword, as well, she'll employ it against us. We must do all we can to support Terricus to perfect the art of forging new blades. We know it's not an easy process. With Centus' death, it's Terricus who'll aid us now. With sharp-edged blades in our hands and not these old copper ones, not even Elen and whichever tribal chief she tempts to do her work for her will stand against us. With or without our father's sword. We'll prevail, brother, I promise you that. Her deceitful lies will encourage others to come against us. We won't allow her to be successful.'

'And then?' It seems he's yet to be convinced. This is the first true test of his leadership. I must remind myself how young he is, with only twenty-one summers to his name. He's not endured as I have.

'And then Elen will finally be called to account for the damage she's caused. It's long overdue. Don't argue with me about this, brother. If we'd killed her last summer after Edern's death when I wanted to do so, we wouldn't face this potential catastrophe now. But, with her death, all of this, this mess, can be undone.'

Madog sighs softly, slouching before me, for a moment the small child I taught to hold a wooden stick and a bark shield sits there, not my fierce and strong warrior brother. The fire's gone from his eyes, although I feel it in my belly. I'm as hot as the blue flames needed to melt ironstone to produce iron to forge new blades. I'm as fiery as the charcoal needed to create white flames to make the iron hiss as it's worked into shape with the aid of hammer and tongs.

'I'll not argue with you about Hedrek, sister. I will

not.' He bows his head in supplication to me, although it sounds as though he tries to convince himself of it. I know Hedrek's immediate execution would go some way to assuaging his anger. But it would be a mistake. I focus on the back of his head, and not on the fear that, somehow, Elen will still prevail against me. It won't be allowed to happen. It can't be allowed to happen.

We are the Eorlingas, the tribe responsible for breeding the finest horses in the whole of Britannia. We'll not be beaten by a woman who opened her legs to the monster who killed our father, the man who forever scarred me and stole my daughter from my arms while she was still bloodied from the passage of her birth, extinguishing the potential of her life.

We are the Eorlingas. We'll better all of our enemies. We'll forge blades to stand as a warning against all who think to steal from us. And we will, in good time, ensure Elen meets her death. Her continued existence is an affront I can't allow to endure indefinitely. I hunger to snuff out her life, like a flame pinched between two fingers. I really do. I know I'm not alone in that. Her mother, Marchell, my teacher and guide, wishes the same. We'll see it done, and then this devastating reverse will not have the impetus it needs to eject us from Villa Eorlingas. My father's legacy will be restored and will continue. I vow it on my daughter's memory.

Finally, Madog looks at me. He must see the resolve writ into my scarred face, and in the firmness of my lips. He must see the spangles of my life's work at my waist, as well as the ceremonial torque I wear as seeress of the Eorlingas. He sits taller, and then stands, shoulders back, neck firm.

'We will see it done, sister.'

I nod. 'We will, brother. I promise you.'

2

WÆRMUND OF THE GYRWE

Not far from Verulamium

I eye my warriors, some giving me more concern than others. My female warriors, Bucge and Osfyth, one almost a seeress and one a huntress, are hale. Heafoc is as well, despite our recent captivity at the hands of Isarninus of the Wæclingas. Eastmund, Goddæg, Hygebeorht and Maggenræd are the four remaining men. We fought a fierce battle not many days ago to escape from Isarninus and his imprisonment on his hilltop location, not far from Verulamium. And afterwards, and I'm still unsure how, we lost Cenbryht. I wish I knew where he was, but it's been two days now since I last saw him. We've not had the opportunity to stop and look for him, but in all honesty, I think he's chosen to leave us. That causes a frisson of uncertainty down my spine. I was always suspicious of him. What his intentions are now concern me. Not that he's the first of my original warriors to disappear. Where Nothelm is remains a mystery.

And this woman who's found us, Elen? I hardly know what to make of her. She has a pale, thin face and dazzling green eyes beneath a mass of dark hair. She's very confident for a woman who's alone. She has an unusual thin copper bracelet around her wrist, which she keeps turning, and she's been gifted with Bucge's new, very thick and well-made cloak exchanged with traders only yesterday. If I didn't know better, I'd think she was our leader, and not me.

She's alluring, but old enough to be my mother. Yet I know she eyes me with evident desire. I find the sensation of her appraisal unpleasant. She'd make a better bedfellow for the older Heafoc than me. I doubt she sees it that way. And, for the time being, and despite my unease, I need her. She can speak the tongue of the old man we also rescued from Isarninus' captivity. Gildas, as we now know he's called, seems to know much I desire to understand. It astounds me, for when we saw him brought before Isarninus to mutter in a strange tongue none of us understood, which I now know is called Latin, he was dirty. His grey beard and hair were so long he almost tripped on them when walking. He was broken but proud. He's perhaps the bravest man I've ever met. He had nothing to defend himself with but his words, and his hands. I admire him. Now his hair and beard are neat – indeed, almost all of his hair is gone. He wishes us to aid him in scalping him further. I suspect we should wait until he has a hat to stop himself getting too cold, or burned by the sun.

'Tell me again,' I direct to Heafoc, who speaks to Elen in a tongue he and she understand, but no one else, not even Gildas. 'Where does Gildas suggest we go?'

'To Uriconium, far north of here. Gildas says we'll find the answers to your questions there.' I nod as Heafoc replies.

I consider this carefully. Although I don't understand the language being spoken between Elen and Gildas, and then Elen and Heafoc, I suspect Elen speaks without malice and truthfully. Indeed, her tone's so reasonable when she tells Heafoc everything Gildas gabbles, I think this place she names is little more to her than a name, just as it is to me. She stumbles when speaking it, just as Heafoc does. It's long and filled with many unusual sounds.

Wherever she's from, and so far she's not made that clear, Gildas directs our steps to somewhere different. I wish I could communicate directly with her and Gildas, but I can't. I can hardly form any of the words Gildas speaks, when he lilts in the strange, almost musical language. It's a wonder Elen and he share a common tongue. They converse in a language they both understand, but it's not Gildas' more natural one. I can tell from the way he occasionally pauses mid-conversation, as though seeking the correct term, and how Elen frequently says something similar but with a different emphasis. It is, Heafoc informs me, a tongue known as Brythonic.

'What will we find when we make it to this Uriconium?' I continue to query via Heafoc, stumbling over the name of the place we must travel to once more. Elen masks a swift look of impatience at Heafoc's question. My enquiries annoy her. That doesn't please me but I prefer to see some sign of emotion aside from the smooth, assessing face she presents with the arrogant tilt of her head. For a woman with nothing, she's assured. I consider whether she's always so confident or if the knowledge Bucge and Osfyth protect her amongst us all gifts her that.

I don't deny Elen intrigues me, not in a way that has me desiring to take her lithe body. Far from that, in fact. No, she embodies much I'm not sure I understand. She's unaccompanied, and clearly previously well fed. Yet she's alone and far from her home. Who's fought for her in the past? Who's kept her clean and well tended to? She's not done so by herself, for all she's now solitary. No one with nails that clean could have done all the required filthy tasks of staying alive herself.

'We'll find the answers to forging blades with sharp edges. We'll find the means to kill our enemy,' Heafoc informs me patiently. I sense ferocity beneath the pallid gaze Elen offers. Does she suspect Heafoc doesn't repeat her words correctly? Does she remain fearful we might kill her despite her arrogance or that I'll allow some of the men to take her as they wish?

Who is this woman? Equally, who is Gildas? He shows no sign of ever having been a warrior. He has no muscle definition. Admittedly, he's been captive for many summers. So why does he know about sharp blades, or rather, where to have them made? I shake my head. This entire situation unnerves me more than the fear my angry father, or an outraged Isarninus, intends to hunt me down and kill me for all I've done to them. Undoubtedly, it was vengeance I sought against both in the first place. I disbelieve they'll see it that way. Any friendship Isarninus and I once shared has turned to a blood feud. Any slight regard my father might have held for me has disappeared in the wake of my murdering his favoured son. I don't regret it. Not that any of my fellow warriors do either. I'm free from my father's begrudging acceptance of me as his son. I'm free from Isarninus' murderous intentions.

'Does Gildas know how to make sharp blades?' I persist despite Elen's obvious ill humour.

'No, but he knows those who do. He's an educated man, in the ways of the Romans.' Heafoc continues to translate Elen's words. There's no sneer on her face, but I narrow my eyes. I sense it in the way she speaks, although I don't know the meaning of the words.

The Romans. They've been gone from these shores since before the arrival of my ancestors to the east, paid to fight the enemies of the British. Yet Gildas isn't that old, although he certainly has many winters to his name. How then is he educated in the way of these long-gone Romans? I don't understand and it's making my head hurt as I try to comprehend what I'm being told.

'The old ways of the Romans endure in some places, far to the west,' Elen continues to speak, and Heafoc to translate, while Gildas answers Elen's questions. 'Surely you've heard of those kings and rulers there? The iron-clad warriors as well?'

I don't like to show my ignorance before Elen and Gildas. I know of my father, grandfather and great-grandfather. What happens to the west of this island is unfamiliar to me. My world had previously been a small one. The people of my birth tribe, the Gyrwe. The traders who visited from our old homeland across the fretful grey sea. Events elsewhere never concerned me until I determined to leave the Gyrwe and forge a name for myself with blade and the shedding of the blood of others. And, admittedly, when I succeeded in killing my despised brother despite myself. I've been forced to travel far to escape my father's wrath, if indeed I've managed to do so.

'Say I haven't,' I counter quietly as Heafoc pauses. I don't wish to sound like a fool. I'm pleased Heafoc nods along, happy to show his ignorance as well. Beside Elen, Bucge and Osfyth continue to hover protectively. They're determined to defend Elen from the appetites of my male warriors. A winter within Isarninus' hilltop settlement has ensured those who wished a warm bed companion at night had one. Now they miss that comfort. Yes, they'd much sooner be free from our captivity beneath the ground where Isarninus put us when we demanded to be paid for our services. Still, there are no women to hold them throughout the night.

I've learned a lesson thanks to Isarninus. Coins up front in future.

Elen questions Gildas once more. He seems content to share his knowledge with us.

'There are kingdoms, to the west, and the south-west, where some elements of the Roman ways of Britannia survive. They speak the language of the Romans. They have kings. They even have people paying their kings taxes to protect them. To do so they must have educated men, and women, who can reckon and write, and keep notices of who has paid and who hasn't. There can be no kingship without the ability to write.' I absorb this, listening carefully to Heafoc as he speaks her words, feeling my forehead furrow as I watch Gildas.

'And they have sharpened blades made from new iron?'

Now her eyes narrow, and she shakes her head, as Heafoc repeats my queries. I notice she doesn't direct this to Gildas.

'I'm unsure about that. They must not, or it would have been easy for...' And here she pauses, as does Heafoc. I think she'll say more, perhaps trip herself up and name the place she's from, but she catches herself quickly. A shake of her head. She resumes, as though her thoughts haven't almost betrayed her. 'They must lack the art, still. Perhaps, though, they trade for what they need with those over the distant sea, to the far south. Do your people not trade?' Heafoc rumbles to a halt as Elen questions us. I'm pleased he waits for my reply, and doesn't give his own answers.

'Not for such blades,' I answer quickly, keen to dismiss all mention of where I came from, and the reminder of my bastard father. We spent all last summer outrunning his reputation. Isarninus threatened me by saying he'd told my father where I was. I don't know if that's the truth. If it is, perhaps journeying to this Uriconium is exactly what we must do. Until we can fight even better than now, I'll not risk encountering my father's lethal blows as he seeks to satisfy our blood feud. With the failure of his warriors to kill me so far, I'm sure he'll be forced to make the effort to murder me himself. A man such as him won't be able to simply forget what I've done. 'So, we go to this place. Gildas will teach us the art of creating sharp blades, or have someone show it to us?' I summarise, or rather Heafoc does, in a language Elen understands.

'I doubt it. You'll need to purchase the allegiance

of a bladesmith, if, as Gildas suggests, there are still men who call themselves as such.' Heafoc's slight stumble shows this answer doesn't please him.

'And then what?'

She shrugs a shoulder elegantly as Heafoc voices my question. Her eyes narrow in thought. Not that she speaks whatever it is she's thinking. I'll need to be wary of Elen. She's sly and not to be trusted. For now, she has some use. If we should find someone else who speaks the same tongue as Gildas, and of us, then I'll have no need of her. I'm sure she realises that just as I do. She's clearly intelligent. What she is aside from that, I don't know. But I'll need to find out, and then, if she's to be feared, I don't care what Bucge and Osfyth want, I'll ensure her threat is contained, even if it destroys our friendship in the process.

* * *

I find Heafoc riding with Gildas as we depart from our overnight encampment to the west of Isarninus' hill fort. I eye the old man once more. I'm astounded he survived his imprisonment at the hands of Isarninus. His skin is so thin, I see where his pulse beats at throat and wrist. He's weak and feeble in body, if not in mind.

I offer him a smile, which he returns, and move to Heafoc's side. Heafoc nods towards me. I know he wasn't speaking to Gildas because he can't. Yet I sense he resents my intrusion. I need Heafoc's advice, though. He's become my stalwart companion. I trust him more than any others who've pledged themselves to me.

'What do you think?' I question softly, mindful Elen's only just out of earshot on the horse she rides proudly. I'm not convinced she's a natural at it. Indeed, she seems wary of the animal.

'I hardly know what to think any more,' Heafoc mutters. 'Everything's the wrong way round. The warrior lord declares himself a *comitatus* and plays us false, while the man with soft hands, educated in the old ways of the Romans, is honourable and without malice, or so Elen would have us believe.'

This really is the problem. I don't understand the words Gildas uses. He doesn't understand mine. Elen can speak with Gildas. Heafoc, with his grasp of other tongues, can't speak with Gildas, however. We're entirely reliant on a woman who's been discovered by happenstance and whom I don't trust, and yet who's proven to be somewhat useful. It's not a situation I'm enjoying as we journey northwards.

'Have you examined the two pieces of the sword

she carries?' Heafoc murmurs. I nod. I've seen it. 'She's clearly as much in need of a bladesmith as we are.'

'She speaks of this place as though unaware of it. Notice how the word doesn't slide easily from her tongue,' I murmur.

'I've noticed that. I don't trust her.'

'I don't trust her either,' I agree, trying not to turn to observe her, where she rides behind us, protected by Osfyth.

'At least we need not ride fast,' Heafoc consoles. 'Isarninus won't suspect we travel in this direction. He'll think we mean to stay close to his settlement and take back the rest of our lost treasure, which is no doubt what Cenbryht intends to do as well,' he ends sourly. I turn then, eyeing the path we've been travelling at the command of Gildas, following a well-depicted road through the landscape we've been informed should take us to Uriconium, eventually. I imagine we also have the Romans to thank for the stone roadway and deep drainage channels lining it.

'Isarninus made a terrible mistake when he held us captive and taunted me with knowledge of my father's quest to find us. We'll need to exact our revenge on him,' I reply, words snapped for all I was the one who argued against taking our revenge immediately, more concerned with escaping than killing the bastard. But bastard he is.

'When news of our triumph over Isarninus of the Wæclingas spreads, our reputation will grow, despite everything,' Heafoc offers with a twinkle in his eye.

'I shouldn't have believed his promises when he found us preparing to defend the Hicca,' I complain.

'No, we shouldn't have. But a roof over our heads and warm food in our bellies swayed most of you. If you recall, I didn't wish to do as the rest of you did. There's something to be learned there, Wærmund.' With that, Heafoc encourages his mount forward, to take Bucge's place, and I absorb his complaint against me. I could level something against him, especially how much he enjoyed being in Isarninus' settlement, but I think we're both wise enough not to voice those words. There'd be no point, anyway. It's done.

I watch Bucge and Heafoc conferring, considering if they talk about more than this place named Uriconium. Certainly, Gildas makes no effort to direct us aside from indicating our horses should be on the road.

I bite my lip.

I'm uneasy with my current course of action, and yet what else can I do? I intended to outrun my father by escaping west, but events took us towards the

south, and now I find I have two enemies where before I had only one.

For now I'll continue to be led where Elen believes I want to go. I hope she at least directs me to
where Gildas says there are bladesmiths, if that is indeed what she's doing. Then I can avail us of fine
blades with which to end the life of my father and
Isarninus. After that? Well, I'll have sharp blades to
hand and can contend with what Elen truly intends
for me to do on her behalf in exchange for helping us.
And if I intend to do what she wants. So far, I've not
given my oath, and the thought of fighting another
enemy whose strength I'm ignorant of isn't that ap-
pealing. But perhaps when my blades can cut the
wind with their sharpness, I'll think very differently.
With a look behind me, assuring myself no one follows our path, I settle in the saddle. I don't know how
long we must travel for. But travel we must. Far from
Isarninus, and far from my father's retribution. However, I'll return this way. I will have vengeance against
them both. And Cenbryht as well, if he does manage
to steal my treasures from Isarninus.

3

MEDDI OF THE EORLINGAS

I watch the flames leap around Centus' body as we honour him with a burial fitting for a member of the Eorlingas tribe. I refuse to look away even though the wind gusts, driving the stink of burning flesh into my mouth and eyes. I don't cry but hold myself immobile, face painted white with charcoal highlighting my eyes and lips to honour the dead. Centus was a good man. He deserves the tears of those who knew him better than I did. He was little more than an extension of a tool for me, but I know there's a woman in the village who sobs for him. Her rounding belly shows Centus will leave behind a child who'll never know its father. I pity the child although it will be welcomed amongst us as we regrow our strength and numbers. Centus wished to recall his father's skills as a bladesmith. That was why he first spoke with Hedrek and came to Villa Eorlingas. He failed in that. His replacement, Terricus, will not. I've avowed that already.

With the new supply of ironstone Marchell bartered for within Corinium when she was absent from the villa, I know Terricus will find success. With our growing supply of charcoal, now we've recalled how to produce it, we have everything he needs to do what must be done. Already, he has more knowledge than Centus did.

I hear the sobs and ululations of the bereaved woman and swallow against her grief. She's a strong woman, but she's already lost two husbands, one to Edern and one to a terrible cough two winters ago when the people beholden to Edern had no seeress to aid them. She has no one to care for her now a child is soon to be born. That child will have to be looked after by the Eorlingas. I vow we'll support her, although the task must fall to Rhian and not me. My role, and that of Marchell's, is to bring each new child into the world safely, kicking and screaming, red-faced and red-bottomed. What happens afterwards isn't my business until the child is old enough to be formally welcomed into the tribe. And even then, the child is left to grow until greeted as a woman or a man amongst the adults of the Eorlingas. Small children are the concern of their mothers. Once they have a use, then they become a matter for me as the seeress of the Eorlingas.

I hear the clank of iron chains and turn to eye Hedrek. His face is haunted in the glow from the funeral pyre. He appears almost skeletal. How he's fallen! Men with such ambitions are always fools to their desires. If he'd not wished to possess Elen then he'd not now be a slave. I won't allow myself to pity him. He's brought this upon himself and now he watches his hopes for the future burn before him. Centus was his man. It's to be hoped Terricus will continue what Centus left undone but Terricus owes Hedrek no allegiance. Enslaving Hedrek to Terricus will cause my new bladesmith no qualms.

But my thoughts return to Elen. The bitch. I've tried to banish the recriminations running through my mind for allowing her to live when I should have ordered her death so she was burned beside Edern. Madog barred me, but really I know I allowed myself to be stopped. Given another opportunity, I'll not be as unwise.

Elen has my father's sword. Well, the two pieces of it I hoped Centus would bind together once more. She knows the potency of such a symbol as well as I do. She will, I appreciate, use it against us. She might well be alone, but that won't last for long. If only I knew where she'd gone. Elen's a woman of not inconsiderable powers of persuasion. After all, how else did she stay at Edern's sides throughout all those summers when no child was brought forth from their union? No. Elen knows how to entice men and women to obey her.

Marchell agrees with my concerns with regard to Elen, for all her rage is more contained. It's been many winters since Elen acknowledged her mother as her mother. But while Elen might have overlooked who birthed her when the truth was inconvenient, Marchell hasn't forgotten. Once we know where Elen is, and we will discover where she is, I'll be hard-pressed to stop Marchell killing her daughter. And yet I intend to do so. Elen's blood mustn't be on Marchell's hands. A mother mustn't kill her child, even if that child is poisonous. It would anger our gods and Marchell has honoured them for so much of her life, I can't allow that to be reversed.

As the blue and red flames begin to collapse on themselves, the body crumbled to ash, I allow myself to turn aside. I blame the ash for the tears streaming down my face, but I know what they're really for. I pity myself for what's happened here. I pity myself for allowing Elen to triumph over me once more. It's always been her way. I can't allow it to define me, as allowing Marchell to kill Elen would also do.

I stand tall, proud, wiping the tears from my eyes, inhaling the smell of death and decay and the promise of an afterlife that provides although I don't sense our gods here, not tonight. I'll send Elen to her afterlife. I resolved to it once before but failed to make good on that. I'll not do that again. I'll not allow the weakness to entertain the idea. Not when I find her. Not when I finally take my vengeance for all she's brought to bear against me, and the Eorlingas.

* * *

I'm once more woken by the clanging of iron on iron, and grimace as my head reverberates with it. Marchell's already awake, the soft shuffle of her feet impossible to ignore. Then Sian arrives, calling a welcome through the doorway, although she doesn't enter.

I rise stiffly, feeling the weight of my many winters on me. I don't know how Marchell countenances it. I grimace at the winters behind me, and at those I have left to me, which must be far fewer. I've much to accomplish and little time in which to do it. I don't believe I'll be blessed with a life as long as Marchell's. I don't believe I truly want to become so old and wizened, anyway.

'What is it?' I call to Sian, aware my voice is husky from sleep.

'It's Rhian, and the new child.'

This brings me to my feet much more quickly. 'Is it time already?' I announce, surprised by it.

'It is, mistress, yes. She's already in much pain.'

Marchell's already bundled together our supplies, including the comfrey, as I creak open the doorway and blink into the bright daylight. The wind from last night has disappeared, but now brings with it the scent of the distant sea as it rustles through Villa Eorlingas.

'Madog's taken the firstborn, your nephew Maccus, to the woodlands, so he'll not hear his mother's shrieks.'

At this, we all share a conspiratorial look. It's well known the men don't like to hear what they inflict on their women beneath the furs.

'I don't believe it'll be long,' Sian offers, hoping to

speed us. I nod quickly, and together we walk towards the main buildings of Villa Eorlingas. As I draw closer, I hear the loud huffs of a woman in her birth pangs and hurry my steps. For now, Terricus' strikes of the hammer obscure the sound for those nearby. Most of the men remain, and I see Urien and another of my brother's warriors guarding the entrance into the villa compound, while others are busy in the surrounding landscape, tending to crops or animals. I notice the mares close to foal, wondering when they too will bring forth new life like the sheep and lambs, already sunning themselves in the pale light of a new day.

Quickly, I allow my feet to settle briefly over the bright mosaic depicting the horses and make my way to where Rhian and Madog sleep. There's no flurry of flustered women. Instead, Rhian's two favourites bend low and step aside as they hear our approach, their work for Rhian accomplished.

It was Marchell who safeguarded Maccus' arrival into this world. Together, we'll ensure this new child benefits from the same.

Marchell moves to Rhian, a smile on her old, lined face, while Rhian greets me, a nod of welcome on her sweat-lined face. I move to add the comfrey to the small fire.

'It began during the night. I hope it will not be long now. Maccus was quickly born.'

I offer no assurances. As all women understand, these things aren't for us to know, but it always behoves a woman to think her time will be quick.

And it is. Before the sun has reached its zenith, a red-faced girl is born, blond-tipped brown hair fringing an angry scowl, and the four of us bend to smile at the babe.

Rhian eagerly takes her into her arms, and her women return to her. Marchell and I finish the birthing, and together take the bloodied remnants away, leaving Rhian with a new babe and little else to show of her labours.

'Send for Madog,' I murmur to Sian, and she quickly beckons one of her small followers to run to the woodlands while Marchell and I return to my workshop to prepare the afterbirth for its many uses. There's power in such and it'll not go to waste.

Only when all that is accomplished do I take myself to Terricus and Hedrek.

The smell of heat shimmers in the air. Terricus sweats with the same ferocity Centus once employed. Hedrek, shackled as I demanded, moves quickly to fulfil all tasks set him.

'What is it today?' I call to Terricus.

He offers me a respectful nod before replying. 'Mistress, today I'm experimenting. Here.' And he beckons me closer to where he works.

I see although the charcoal is burning blue and white at its centre, he's not trying to extract ironstone from its prison but rather to determine the effect one piece of ironstone has on another, which is of a slightly different colour.

'I believe the two metals, mixed together, will form a stronger piece of iron, from which a blade could be forged. See how they merge together.' As he speaks, Terricus works quickly, his hands confident, close to the heat although he wears the leather apron Centus once wore. 'I sense I'm making progress.' Terricus' eyes are flushed with pride as he holds out the tongs to reveal the lump of iron. I squint closely, but not too close. I don't wish to burn my eyebrows. The wash of heat from the metal is unwelcome.

'They melt at the same temperature?'

'They do, yes. Although, I do wonder if that's correct. We will see,' Terricus acknowledges ruefully. 'It's a tedious business, but fascinating.'

I nod, pleased to find Terricus so content without Centus to direct his steps. Centus was stubborn and determined but I'm not sure the thrill of experimenting was one he enjoyed. He was more likely to repeat the process until it worked. It wasn't the correct means to employ.

'And Hedrek? He behaves himself?' I question, lips downcast as I glare at the fat older man. His belly will need to restrict itself if he means to be more helpful.

'He does as commanded, and I don't fear him,' Terricus offers, not looking up from his labours, although I glower at Hedrek. He meets my gaze defiantly, but eventually wilts before my attentions.

'Remember you could die for what you did,' I murmur, the words deceptively soft. 'But, I think death's too good for you, Hedrek. First, you must atone for your mistakes.'

'Mistress,' he mumbles. I turn, recalled to the needs of my mares as a nicker floods the air. Maybe today will be a day of many births, and not just Madog's daughter. It's perhaps a little early, but as with mothers, a horse has no control over when a foal is born. I hurry back to Marchell to gather her, and then we make our way into the enclosure to find the mare. I hope the animal born is as strong as Madog's daughter. While we don't yet have the sharp blades I desire, fine horse stock is just as valuable. It is horses our tribe once grew wealthy on. Now, in a time of barter, it's the one thing we're renowned for. Or rather, what we will be renowned for once more. Edern didn't honour the old way of breeding our horses. I've set that straight, and now the first of a new generation will be brought forth. It's another step on our way to reclaiming all the Eorlingas once had, not just the location of our settlement, but also the source of our reputation.

4

WÆRMUND OF THE GYRWE

We don't rush. Neither do we dawdle. The horses are eager to be free after a winter of containment in Isarninus' hilltop settlement. I watch the landscape as we travel. Here there are some rolling hills, but also open spaces. A lush vista of woodland and growth is clearly visible. I almost taste the crops being grown.

'What is this place?' I call, counting on Heafoc to ask Elen who will relay my question to Gildas. I suspect only he knows exactly where we are.

'It's a road,' Heafoc rejoins while Elen asks my question of Gildas. I shake my head, amusement playing on my lips. The further we travel from Isarninus' stronghold, the more confident I feel we will accomplish our goals.

'And it leads to Uriconium, I know, but where are we now? Are there no tribes here?'

'There are people,' Heafoc offers, his eyes raking in all he can see. 'But it seems they hide away from us.'

I consider that. Since leaving my brother's settlement as a burnt ruin, we've been variously feared or derided by those we've encountered. On one notable occasion, we turned against those we promised to protect. I'll have to make my peace with that as it still sits uneasily with me, but the tribe are dead or under Isarninus' control. Retrieving the survivors will need to wait until we've undertaken this journey to find a bladesmith. Even now, the weight of the treasures I've taken from Isarninus weighs down one of the horses. There's great wealth there, but for now it's merely lumps of heavy iron, previously worked into axe heads and then discarded, or pieces of ironstone, waiting to have the iron broken free from their encasement and put to good use.

I lick my lips, my thoughts turning to the two men who'll seek vengeance against me. My father and Isarninus. I wish I'd killed Isarninus, but it was imperative we escaped as opposed to exact our revenge. It will come, however. Unless, of course, my father does ally with Isarninus. Together, both men might be able to overwhelm my current collection of warriors, which is so much smaller than when I first sought retribution against my brother. There were fourteen of us then. There aren't any more. Wædel, the traitor, is dead. Nothelm is gone. Cenbryht is gone. I don't know where.

Heafoc trained us well last summer but we're still a collection of men and women who've only recently become allies. We've not had time to mould our-selves to one another and to learn the intricacies of the way we fight. It's not like my father's warriors, ad-mittedly, depleted now. But my father's no fool. He'll have been training replacements since they could barely toddle on chunky legs. He'll have others to take the places of those we've killed. He'll not stop until he manages to overwhelm me. I can't allow that to happen. I won't allow that to happen. I'm no longer the gods-cursed boy he mocked and taunted. I have become a man, if not quite possessing the war-rior's prowess I'd like.

As much as I don't trust Elen and her appraising looks, I do want to know all Gildas knows. I want to have a bladesmith who can forge blades as though made by the gods. It's worth this long journey to ac-complish that, but only if we do achieve that.

A gabble of words, and Elen finally answers my

questions, as Gildas labours to speak about all he knows.

'This is the land of the Hendrica. They're a large tribe,' she offers, via Heafoc. This time, when she speaks, I sense she knows something about this place. I'm getting more used to the way she talks.

'You know more about them?' I question before I can stop myself. She arches a shoulder and shakes her head but offers nothing further as Heafoc speaks my questions. I don't believe her. I don't think Heafoc does either, but Bucge rides close to her, eyes fierce as they glower at me. I fear Bucge will believe anything Elen says, even that the sky's yellow and the sun blue. I'll need to be mindful of that development. 'Then we should be wary,' I caution my warriors.

Eastmund rides ahead, alongside Bægmund. Os-fyth is to the rear. Gildas, Maggenræd and Elen are in the middle of my warriors, with Heafoc and I slightly behind them. I like to see where I'm going. I trust Os-fyth to inform me if anything happens behind. But so far we've seen few people other than those with carts of trading goods. They stepped aside from the road, noting our warriors' equipment of spear and shield, hoping we wouldn't steal from them. I felt no compunction to do so, but instead traded for fresh bread and a bowl of pottage from an encampment close to the road, parting with some of Isarninus' treasures to do so. I paid them well but whether they appreciated the axe head, or would have preferred warm food in their bellies, I can only guess.

As the day advances, I'm aware we're being watched, and appreciate the area has more settlements within it than I'm expecting. Not all of them are perched on hills or surrounded by deep ditches. Instead, I see shimmering red atop what I take to be buildings in the distance, and call to Heafoc for answers.

'What are those?' I shout, suspecting all of my warriors share my questions.

He asks Elen and she gives a single sentence in answer, which I detect is dark and filled with foreboding, and which he repeats.

'Old Roman villas,' he mutters.

'What are they?' I feel like a child as Heafoc voices the question.

'Homes and granaries,' he repeats, but I sense her unease with the answer.

'Do many people live here?' Again, Heafoc asks the question, and she directs it to Gildas because while she knows the name of the people who live here, she doesn't know everything about them. The eventual reply is slow in coming.

'Yes, people live here. They grow food and graze their animals. It's the same as everywhere else.' Elen turns to focus on me as Heafoc speaks. I see her eyes narrow. 'Is it not?' he adds.

'No. We have none of these villas, as you term them, where I came from,' I reply, and then Heafoc does.

'What do you live in then? Hovels dug into the ground, no better than the pigs.' Heafoc's voice shows his unease as he translates her words.

Her scorn has me tensing my hands on the reins. I can sense others aren't enjoying her dismissive comments either, even though they're spoken in Heafoc's familiar voice.

'No. We live in circular homes, of wattle and daub, with a hearth at its centre, and behind ditches and ramparts.'

She shudders at this image Heafoc conjures.

'You have no stone walls? No tile roofs?' I realise Elen is unintentionally telling us a great deal about her home.

'No, we don't.' Even with the delay in our conversation because we must reply through Heafoc, I sense her interest and disdain.

'Then you're in for a great surprise. Here, in the remains of what was once Britannia, those who are rich live behind stone walls, and sometimes wooden ones, with good roofs over our heads, and the means to keep warm in the winter by heating the floors.' Heafoc's words rumble once more.

'Heating the floors?' I reply. He again repeats my question.

'Yes, the stone floors are raised above the ground. Beneath them fires are lit and they keep us warm when it snows outside, or the ground's frozen hard.' I see Heafoc shaking his head at this wonder, as he repeats her description carefully. I consider whether she speaks the truth. Is she playing with us to see how gullible we are? I look to Gildas, as though to assess the veracity of her statement, but he's not paying any attention to our conversation.

'Then you must be warm all the time,' I suggest, and wait for Heafoc to translate.

'Perhaps. It depends on the quality of wood for burning,' is the eventual reply.

'So, you lived in a place such as these?'

'I did, yes,' Heafoc replies after Elen answers my question.

'But no more,' I push it. Heafoc again relays my question.

'No, as I told you, I've been cast out, my place stolen from me. You'll aid me in reclaiming it in exchange for taking you to a bladesmith.' Her reply, when it comes, is merely a reiteration of what she's already told us.

'We will, yes,' I confirm, via Heafoc, although once we have the blades we need, my intention is to strike out at Isarninus, and potentially my father, if he chases us. Elen's concerns aren't mine.

Her voice has fallen dangerously low, as though anticipating my wavering. Heafoc adopts the same when he repeats, 'Will you, Wærmund?'

I offer her a small smile. 'Once we have what's needed, it'll be easy to aid you in taking back your villa. After all,' now it's my turn to be dismissive, 'these places hardly seem well defended, despite walls of stone.'

There's something about the way she responds which makes me wonder what else she's not telling me as Heafoc offers an enigmatic, 'Perhaps.'

* * *

We stop that night on the side of the stone road we're following. I've toyed with approaching one of these villas, as Elen terms them, but I've decided not to take the risk. We ride with shields and spears, but accepting the hospitality of anyone has led to too many problems in the past. It's better if we remain outside these small places, no doubt dominated by a chieftain or commander. They can't be entirely self-governing. Men and women rarely manage to get along so well when there's little food and wealth, and therefore much to bicker over.

Osfyth has found us yet more pheasants to cook and she takes charge, while Elen shelters close to her and Bucge.

Elen's continued desire to be with the women surprises me. She's tried to use her appeal on me, and I've refused it, but there are many others who'd happily take her to their bed and, in return, offer her protection. I know Goddæg would certainly appreciate it. He almost drools whenever he looks at her. But it's evident she doesn't want that from anyone aside from me. Perhaps she does realise I'm the leader here despite her disdain.

Gildas sits close to the hearth fire, the flames casting his face into shadowy hollows, assuring me his death is closer to hand than he perhaps hopes. Isarninus' detaining of him has either prolonged his life, or shortened it. I've no way of determining how old he is other than from looking at him. I can't ask him, and I don't want to probe Elen to question him. He's prevailed upon me to scalp him. Now his long

hair is entirely gone, and so is his beard and moustache. When he eats, I see the movement all the way
over his head. It's strangely intriguing but I determine
to keep my hair for as long as I can. And, of course,
my beard and moustache aid me in alleviating some
of the effect of the mark on my cheek.

Eastmund joins me as I tend to my horse. His gaze
is pointed.

'Is this a good idea?' he asks. I'd not welcome such
from many of my warriors, but Eastmund's proven
himself time and time again. And, I like him. That
can't be said for them all.

'We'll see.' I shrug. 'We need better blades to kill
Isarninus and to protect against my father's warriors,
if Isarninus truly did send word to him of our
location.'

'You doubt that?' Eastmund muses.

'I do. It's a perilous journey, through many other
tribes. I don't believe Isarninus would have taken the
risk, although perhaps he has. And, my father may
have sent more warriors to track us down after we
killed the ineffectual ones. And of course, there's the
problem of Cenbryht as well. He might have gone to
find my father.'

'Isarninus could have sent word with a trader
rather than go himself?'

'Perhaps, but while traders have some sort of protection from violence, I'm not sure it would carry one all the way to my father's distant settlement. Do you?'

Eastmund's silent as he muses, while I work my way over to the horse carrying the remaining treasures stolen from Isarninus. Even now, the hoard is close to the fire, with all eyes on it. If any single person should decide to steal from me, the others would see. The only worry is what if all of them decide to profit at my expense. If that should happen, I'll have lost all of my warriors' loyalties. If that should happen, I'll need to collect a new selection of warriors to my cause, which might be difficult without wealth at my fingertips, or a united decision to seek vengeance against my father and his heavy-handed style of leadership.

'Perhaps not,' Eastmund concludes. 'But all the same, you journey to this distant place in search of something missing from our settlement since the first of our kind came to this island. What if it's not there?'

'Then we've lost nothing. We don't have it now. If it's there, it'll be our gain. If not, we'll merely reconsider our intentions.'

'We'll need to find an enemy we can beat for another tribe,' he concludes, eyes alight with bloodlust.

'A wealthy one,' I confirm, thinking of the

sprawling villas we've seen this day. 'It seems to be these people think little of protection and only of growing enough food. I don't see it'll be hard to over-whelm them.'

'Perhaps not,' Eastmund agrees, licking his lips. 'I'd sooner do that than travel to this Uriconium in search of some long-lost art of bladesmithery.'

'And that, Eastmund,' neither of us have realised Heafoc is close, 'is why Wærmund makes these deci-sions, and you merely hasten to do as he says.' For many, this statement might start a fight, but East-mund grins and chuckles.

'Indeed, Heafoc. Now, I'm bloody starving. Let's see if Osfyth's cooked us something tasty today.'

5

MEDDI OF THE EORLINGAS

'Can a day not pass without someone trying to steal away my villa?' I huff angrily, slipping my copper breastplate over my body and reaching for my dagger. Marchell watches me intently.

From outside my workshop, I hear the warriors of the Eorlingas preparing to face our latest enemy to come against us in violence.

'Edern really did piss a lot of people off,' I huff. I know I'm not the only one with a deep grievance against him. I suspect I'm the one with the most intimate of injustices.

'He was always an arsehole,' Marchell suggests, a glint entering her clear-sighted eye. Since Elen escaped, Marchell has begun to talk more often. I find it more pleasant to have someone to speak to than I once thought. I always appreciated her silence in the past.

'Who are these people?' I direct to Sian, standing quietly at the open doorway. Her face is a picture of serenity. There might well be another fight brewing, but she's content Madog and his warriors will be able to overwhelm them. I share her confidence and yet know a slither of fear, as well. There's always the possibility someone will get wounded, and the wound rot will set in. There are occasions when even the most skilled seeress can't aid those who are injured. If such should happen to Madog, with his son still so small and his daughter barely birthed, there could be problems. Although perhaps the men of the settlement would rally around me. They're fine warriors, all they'd lack would be a leader. I could be that leader until Madog's son is old enough to direct them. After all, before Madog became a man grown, I kept the remnants of my people united in our purpose to one day take back all Edern stole from us. The birth of our first foal also shows how I intend to restore the Eorlingas to their wealthy former position. The foal is sturdy and well formed, the mother proud, but wary of all who come close, aside from me.

'They're the nearby Stoppingas,' Sian replies

quickly. 'Their home is towards the hills north of here. Edern stole from them. Admittedly, he did from everyone close by.'

'So why fight us?' I growl angrily, reminded once more of what Edern did to me.

'I don't know,' she acknowledges, and quickly I make my way through the complex of buildings, the bright walls shimmering in the sunlight, emerging to the front of the villa, where Madog's warriors stand ready to fight the enemy, should it come to that, which I'm sure it will.

'Seeress,' Madog greets me curtly, shielding his eyes with a hand to get a better look at the Stoppingas. They're amassed to the far side of the double-ringed defences. I'm pleased we've not thought to allow the cattle and sheep to graze so far out yet. They might have taken them all by now. We've also brought the horses close to the villa. I notice the thin legs of the new foal, standing close to her mother for once. The animal's usually far from her side, running and frolicking. I'd smile to see the product of the last year, but first we face our enemy. 'The Stoppingas come from the west, inland a little, but still within sight of the River Hafren. They say Edern took their women and made them slaves to his demands. He promised them riches and, of course, gave them nothing.'

'Simply return their women to them,' I glower angrily, trying not to grip my dagger tightly as the jeering cries of this new warrior band reach my ears. There are more of them than I'm comfortable with. From here, sunlight flickers on iron-tipped spears and more shields than I'd like to see. The weapons are old but clearly still provide a modicum of protection.

'If only it were that simple,' Madog retorts hotly. 'But Edern used the women hard. They're no longer here. Sian told me Edern took what he wanted from them, and when he grew tired of them, sold them as slaves amongst the tribes to the far west of here, over the sea.'

I shake my head at this, outraged by Edern all over again. 'Did he have no limit to the depravities?' I grumble. 'Can we pay them the cost of the women?'

'What good would that do? They seek revenge, not payment. They want our villa and, no doubt, intend to fire it so all trace of Edern is removed.'

'Then it'll come to a fight?'

'It seems that way,' Madog acknowledges easily. Perhaps he'd welcome another battle to prove his prowess. At some point, his growing reputation will do more work than his blades and warriors. After all, Edern hadn't fought for near enough five summers before his death and, still, everyone knew to fear him.

With a sharp whistle, Madog beckons those of his warriors not already protecting the gate to his side. They try not to meet my appraising gaze, but I watch them. They must know they fight for Madog but with my blessing.

I follow on behind, with my breastplate and dagger, my talisman-strewn hair and spangles of my standing jangling with each step, torque around my neck. My bearing is proud, revealing who I am to those who think to battle my brother. They'll only see me between gaps in the fighting stances of the warriors of the Eorlingas. But the Stoppingas know I'm there. I consider whether I should do more to drive fear into their hearts. I could use my voice to call the gods of our people here, or point menacingly at their leader, while muttering beneath my breath. If these men are as foolish as I believe they are, it will worry them.

From behind me, the taunting cries of the women and children, and those men too wounded to battle or beyond their fighting years, flood the stiff breeze. They're defiant and confident. I walk taller, prouder, carrying myself with the arrogance of someone who knows they'll win, even if, at the moment, I allow myself a shudder of fear. There are more warriors wishing to fight my brother's men than Villa Eorlingas can boast. We could be over-whelmed.

'This villa is ours,' the lead warrior of the Stoppingas calls when we're close enough to hear. He's a wide man, not particularly tall, but advanced enough in winters I see multiple scars on his arms and face. He's a warrior, and has always been so. Or, at least, he's been in many fights. Whom his enemy has been, I don't know. That doesn't concern me. The shimmering edges of the blades to hand does. Do the Stoppingas have a bladesmith? And if they do, why don't we know about it? If they're our near neighbours, we could have reached an accord with them.

I cast my eyes along the row of warriors facing us. They're an eclectic collection of all ages. They carry shields made for Roman warriors. They don't all have spears and daggers as sharp as those the lead man carries. As I realise this, I banish my worry. These warriors of the Stoppingas look the part, but whether they can use the weapons they have is another matter entirely. I don't see horses behind them. I assume the men have walked here, and each step of the way has reinforced their fury and desire for vengeance.

'This is Villa Eorlingas,' Madog rejoins quickly. 'We were restored to it last summer. We've lived here since then. It was taken from us by Edern, over two decades ago. We've merely reclaimed what was always rightfully ours. We are the men and women of the horse tribe of the Eorlingas.'

'No,' the lead warrior calls angrily, his face scrunched with rage, as those behind him add their voices to his denial. 'No. We'll not speak of it or barter with you. This place is ours. We'll take it with force, or you can surrender and leave here, with your lives, if not your possessions.'

I sense Madog's warriors growling uneasily, even Urien who can usually be relied upon to have a calm head. Hedrek was more reasonable when he approached us last year in the immediate wake of Edern's death. Corun wasn't, and he, and his tribe of the Weogoran, paid the ultimate price. The Weogoran are no more. Their men died. Their women came to us and are now Eorlingas. When my brother wins here, as I'm convinced he will, I'll urge him to strike out and attack tribal settlements nearby who might still think to take Villa Eorlingas from us. He must prove his prowess with spear and shield. It will be all the easier when the warriors have better blades made by Terricus.

'Villa Eorlingas belongs to the Eorlingas, not to you.' My brother leaves the words hanging as though our enemy should introduce themselves but they don't. The Stoppingas shout even more angrily, banging shields with wooden spear shafts or on the ground. The sound drowns out the ululations of the rest of the Eorlingas behind us.

I take a deep breath and step through the guard provided by my brother's warriors. Urien and Twrch open the way for me. I sense their tension behind me, although I don't turn.

There's a sharp intake of breath from those of the Stoppingas who've not yet seen me as I run my fingers through the spangles at my waist, eyeing their leader with contempt. I see a frisson of shock, although whether it's from seeing a seeress or looking at my scars, I'm unsure, but he quickly smooths his features. I don't recognise him. Whatever Edern did to the Stoppingas, it was when I'd long since been banished.

'I'm the seeress of the Eorlingas,' I call, ensuring my words are clear and can be heard even above the shouting and banging. Silence falls, as I become the focus of attention for the Stoppingas. I'll attempt a conciliation before my brother and his warriors risk themselves once more. 'Edern did to me as he did to your women, only I survived, and rebuilt my tribe and my warriors. Your women didn't have that opportunity, but know this, Edern's body has been denied entry into the afterlife. His very existence has been erased from this place.' My words are crisp, but angry faces assure me that, while they speak of revenge for their women, they hunger for the blood of the Eorlingas on their hands.

I watch their leader. A flurry of emotions flickers over his face. Then from behind them, another figure steps forward. I don't know her. It's evident she's the seeress of this tribe. There would be no other reason for her to be here when warriors threaten one another with bloody death. It's not the place of our women to fight besides the men.

'You lie,' she spits, fingers running through the objects of her craft at her waist with a clatter of wood on wood, which has me furrowing my forehead in confusion. I've never known another to have wooden spangles as opposed to copper, iron and silver ones. 'Edern sold all he deemed worthless. I saw it with my own eyes,' she hisses spitefully. She's tall and incredibly thin. I fear the wind might knock her over as it gusts from behind. Her hair's cropped short to her head, a collection of yellow wisps. She's younger than I am. Yet she shows just as many ravages, for her hair isn't short by choice but because half of her face has been burned, the flesh angry and red where it's healed, skeletal where it hasn't. I assume Edern wounded her as well.

'I don't,' I offer respectfully. I won't disparage one who shares my position. 'This was my father's home, Macsen of the Eorlingas. And before him, his ancestors also held this place. Edern took the villa, and my body, and did with it as he wanted. My daughter he deemed worthless, and sent to the afterlife when she was but a handful of breaths old. He had no regard for women and the magiks they know.'

A frown touches the other woman's cheeks, or I suspect it's a frown. Her face is slightly lopsided because of her scars. Perhaps she knows of this, but I abruptly doubt it will be enough to stop her encouraging the Stoppingas to wreak their vengeance against the Eorlingas. I don't believe I've had been minded to stop either.

'My warriors will overwhelm yours if you don't order them to move aside,' she shouts belligerently.

I stand haughtily, aware of Madog and his warriors at my side. Urien holds a shield over my chest, as does Twrch from the other side. They'll allow no harm to befall me.

'Villa Eorlingas is restored to the Eorlingas. Now, go home and grieve for your lost women.' But the final word is barely out of my mouth when an arcing spear thuds into the ground before me. A cry of thwarted triumph leaves the mouths of the warriors facing me. I jerk my chin forward, even as Madog hisses angrily. I don't shudder, or shiver. I remain defiant, lips curling, facing my enemy. 'Only a fool would harm a seeress, even from another tribe,' I say softly, so softly I consider whether my words reach the other woman or not. I sense her outrage, which seethes from her at being denied easy entry into Villa Eorlingas.

'None may kill her but me,' she instructs loudly, shouting, and not looking away from me.

I incline my head towards her. 'I believed seeresses had wisdom. It seems you, then, aren't what you appear.'

With an angry shriek, she dashes forwards, unable to contain herself. None of her warriors accompany her, not even their leader, who's been caught unprepared. I sense Urien moving to meet her attack. I force my way through the protecting shields, despite his angry denials, and assess her. She jumps the deep, protective ditch and stands proudly on the crest of the turf rampart. From up there, she'll be able to see the full extent of Villa Eorlingas, but her gaze is fixed on me. She licks her lips, twisting something at her waist, which resolves itself into an ancient dagger, the blade thinned from constant reworking, but sharp. I can tell in how she seems to cut the wind with it as a faint hiss can be distinguished.

She doesn't, however, frighten me. Not any more.

A strangled cry from behind her, and more of the enemy warriors move towards the entrance to the enclosure. She stays high on the turf rampart, as though daring me to attack her. If she had more hair, the wind would jostle it.

'Hold,' I urge Madog and his men, allowing Urien to protect me once more. The seeress' warriors fumble for blades and shields, their leader belatedly hurrying to guard her. A handy spear throw could end her life now but Madog's men will fear to kill a seeress. They're not as foolish as this woman's warriors. They know what they'll unleash with the blood of a seeress on their hands. They will anger our gods.

If she's to die, I must be the one to do it.

With little time for thought, I snatch a spear from Twrch, and rush up the incline, spear outstretched, hoping she'll think I mean to skewer her with it. Amusement glitters in her eyes as she stands evenly on her feet, dagger to hand, waiting to jump aside from my attack.

At the last moment, I thrust the spear towards her, letting go of the wooden shaft, my eyes telling me her warriors are too late to provide the protection she needs. She veers aside from the direct path of the spear, and straight into my advance. My ceremonial dagger now to hand, glinting with the special yellow tinge of copper beneath the sun, I stab into her neck, above the line of her protective copper breastplate. I feel the heat of her blade over my hand, even as her assault falters, the blade dropping to the ground.

I hold her eyes, while all around outraged cries flood the air. Her warriors hurry to engage Madog's. Madog's abruptly at my side. Urien's beside me too, their shields clashing together to protect me while the enemy seeress staggers backwards, hands at her throat as though she could arrest the bleeding. Then she falls backwards. She tumbles down the embankment, into the ditch. I turn my back on her and the coming battle, allowing Madog and Urien to join the fight, alongside the rest of the brave men, as I return to the flatter ground within the twin embankment and ditches.

I exhale quickly, only now allowing the shock of what I've been forced to do to infect my body. I walk on shaking legs, sickened by the hot stink of blood, but refusing to show weakness. Behind me, the battle quickly intensifies. I'd like to think Madog would fight to avenge my death, but these men of the Stoppingas allow their rage to infect them.

They came here to seek revenge for what Edern did to their women but they'll never leave here alive and their tribe will lack a seeress. Their anger will get them nothing. In this, they're too alike to Edern, the man they seek vengeance against. They should have been better than him, but for once, I'm grateful they're not. Madog will be victorious. The Stoppingas will not.

6

WÆRMUND OF THE GYRWE

'How long must we travel for?' It's Bægmund who asks the question, which doesn't surprise me. Heafoc's swift to query this with Elen, who asks Gildas.

The response is quick to come. 'I don't know,' Elen offers through Heafoc, where she rides ahead of him. Heafoc continues to tell us what she says. 'Gildas is the one who knows our route, and the path we must take. We go where he leads.'

I eye the wizened man, perched on the horse so his legs dangle down the creature's sides. We've been unable to make stirrups small enough for him to rest his feet within them. I can't imagine it's comfortable, but he doesn't complain.

'What is he?' I question Elen, keen to distract

Bægmund, while satisfying my curiosity. Heafoc mumbles the query.

'What is he?' He repeats her words. I'm aware Elen fixes me with her bright green eyes and pink lips, tongue licking them before speaking.

'What is he? How does he know such things? Why was he a prisoner of Isarninus?' I continue.

Elen nods as Heafoc speaks. I hear the musical language Gildas understands trip from her tongue. I realise she rouses him from slumber. He sleeps a great deal. More than once we've had to prevent him from toppling to the ground while riding. His imprisonment has left him a tired man. Hopefully, when we reach this Uriconium, he'll be able to complete his recovery. His reply is speedy in coming.

'He says he's a learned man, in the old ways of the Romans. Some might call him a monk. He prays to their god, not our gods. Or her gods,' Heafoc adds as an afterthought, while Elen falls silent.

'And why did Isarninus have him locked up?'

As Heafoc voices my question, she shrugs a shoulder, revealing a glimmer of pale flesh. I sense the eyes of Goddæg on her. She must know what she does. But she asks Gildas on my behalf, and Heafoc again acts as a bridge between us.

'Isarninus was also raised in the old ways, to the

west of here. He was pleased to hold Gildas as his prisoner. Gildas says he once wrote about events after the Romans left our shores. He says he was angry and scared and some of what he wrote was perhaps not very complimentary. Isarninus took exception to it. He delighted in having him as a prisoner and making him repeat the words. It made him laugh.'

I try to think through this tangled reply.

'He wrote something?' I realise this is what confuses me. Heafoc again translates for me, and is swift to reply.

'With vellum and ink. Words, down on a sheet of vellum that others could read,' he speaks quickly. I don't miss Elen's taunting tone, although I somehow doubt she knows how to write. I might not know what she's saying without Heafoc, but it's easy to detect her condescending attitude. And it doesn't stop there. 'Ah, of course, you come from the east where men and women don't read or write but instead claim ownership with chisels.' Heafoc acts out a mason carving. I do know what he means.

'So, it's similar to that? But on something else, what's vellum?' I'm filled with queries. I suspect Heafoc will ask me to stop talking, but instead he voices the question.

Elen eyes me, appraising me before continuing to question Gildas. His reply is quick.

Heafoc doesn't immediately tell me the hurried words, as though he too is struggling with the explanation the old man gives. 'Vellum is the skin of cattle, stretched, dried and then treated. The ink comes from oak galls. The words are then pricked onto the vellum. It's a tedious business. People must really want to write something down to go through all that. It's not the way of Elen's people. They carry all they need to know in their memories and thoughts, aside from when declaring hostilities against others. Admittedly, those who are much older than her sometimes forget.' I nod as Heafoc finishes speaking. I'm still not entirely sure I understand what writing on vellum is, or why they'd want to write, but I'll leave that for now.

'So, he wrote this thing, but what was it about?'

Heafoc articulates my words again and waits for Elen to reply. She questions Gildas. He responds happily enough. He shows no fear amongst us, even though we have weapons to hand.

'About events after the Romans left these shores, and how the Saxon people came here to fight on their behalf but turned against them,' Heafoc states.

I shake my head, still very far from understanding, although curious what Gildas wrote about my ancestors. I wish I could ask the old man. I'm sure he'd be kinder with his responses than Elen's being. I'd ask Heafoc about it, but I need Elen. I can't reveal how much she infuriates me. Not until we reach Uriconium and it's no longer essential to rely on her. But Gildas and Elen haven't finished conversing yet. Heafoc speaks this time as she talks.

'Your people, and by that I mean the *comitatus* you claim to be, came to this island at the request of certain individuals to protect what was here. As you can see, it didn't go well, because in certain areas, to the east, the *comitatus* stayed and settled and took all from the Britons who made this island their home first. And our friend here, Gildas, had a lot to say about that when he was a young man. And he wrote it down.'

I nod at this response from Gildas. I lapse into silence, considering everything Gildas has told me, but it only causes me to ask more questions.

'But your people don't write things down?'

She shrugs another elegant shoulder. 'We don't have vellum, neither have I been to these places Gildas talks about. I've not seen people live as he implies they do. I don't speak the tongue of these Romans. There's little point in learning a tongue only those far away, or long dead, speak.'

'But you live in the buildings they constructed, and use their roads?' It's a laborious process, with me asking the question, and then Heafoc asking it and waiting for a response, before he can tell me what it is.

'Why not make use of what was left? They abandoned it, or left it, or in some cases have merely forgotten what it means to be Roman. It's been many, many winters, long before my father's time, and his father's. And, as so few can understand the tongue, those ways have been forgotten.'

'So, there are vellums containing the knowledge we need to make better blades?'

'He's not said. He merely states the knowledge exists.' Now her tone has grown sharper. She tires of my queries, as does Heafoc.

Eastmund brings his horse to my side. He's been riding ahead, ensuring the way is clear. We've travelled through any number of abandoned roadside settlements, and I know he's eager to start a fight with someone. Further from the road, there are evidently places where people live. I imagine living away from the road does offer some protection from being attacked by those using the roads.

'There's a fine settlement ahead. We should assault it.' I'm not aware of Heafoc telling Elen what he says, but she surprises me by using a single word of my language.

'No,' Elen states, as though she commands here. I eye her, aghast. Quickly, she rumbles into the tongue Heafoc understands. He offers an explanation for her vehemence. 'We ride peacefully. We must find Uriconium, and then we can set about raiding, when it's easier to overwhelm all because we'll have good blades to kill all who threaten us.' She sits defiantly on the horse we've given her. I notice even Gildas tries to understand our conversation. He asks her a question, but Elen doesn't respond.

My eyes narrow. I swallow heavily, while Eastmund looks between me and Elen, unsure what to make of her involvement in our decision-making.

'Elen, I'm the leader here,' I say softly, hoping Heafoc uses the same tone.

'And you act as I command.' Her stance is haughty, and that's with Heafoc wincing to take the sting from her acerbic reply. She's brought her horse to a stop, daring me to ride on without her. I've half a mind to do so.

'We need supplies for the horses, and for us. We can gain that by attacking them,' I explain.

'And what of trade? We've items they'll require if we speak with them rather than skewer them with blades.' Again, Heafoc speaks her words. What he thinks of them is difficult to decipher.

'Why give away what we can take?' Eastmund asks aggressively, his scorn impossible to ignore. Again, Heafoc talks to Elen. I consider what she says. I've traded a few times already, for food and weapons, but I'm wary of Isarninus' treasures getting any lighter. I agree with Eastmund. But Osfyth's belatedly ridden close to Elen, as though to protect her. Heafoc remains at my side.

With my voice low and menacing, I make a decision. 'Eastmund's correct. We must take what we need.'

'No.' Her single word is flecked with fury, even though Heafoc still speaks to tell her my words. 'You'll not disobey me,' Heafoc finishes with a grimace.

'You don't command here,' I offer softly. 'You're not the leader. These men and women of the *comitatus* look to me to direct our steps.'

Heafoc articulates my words again. Elen's eyes flash with fury. Her reply is fast. 'And you have agreed to aid me and Gildas,' Heafoc tells me.

'That doesn't stop us from achieving our own ends,' I explain.

'If you start a fight here, the flames of what you burn will be visible from here to your kingdom in the east. It'll bring Isarninus, and perhaps your father as well, to where we are. They'll fight you and with your poor equipment you'll not be able to prevail easily. Better to do as I command.' Heafoc's tone lacks the fury of Elen's.

'No,' Eastmund interjects forcefully, cocking his head to one side as he glowers at Elen. I appreciate he uses her tactics against her.

I see Osfyth's confusion. She knows what needs to be done, and yet she's given her protection to Elen. She's conflicted and uneasy, as Elen continues to deny my wishes. I can't help thinking Elen's resistance is more to do with her not wanting to be found from whomever she's running from than for any other reason. She uses our enemies against us, but I think she's more scared of her own, despite evidence to the contrary.

'We do as our leader says,' Heafoc interjects, his voice measured, carrying with it the weight of his advancing winters, and his respect for me. He must then repeat his announcement to Elen.

Elen holds his gaze, and her delayed reply, when it comes, is filled with resolve and stubbornness. 'If you do, Gildas and I will leave you,' Heafoc informs me.

'With what? These are our horses. You eat our food. How will you survive without us?' A brief flicker of uncertainty touches her eyes as Heafoc translates, the implacable resolve she conveys shaken by my denial. I consider how often Elen's been refused throughout her life. Evidently, not often.

'You'd rather risk a quick fight that could end in your deaths than the promise of good blades to kill your enemy if you wait a few days more?' Elen's words are honeyed. Heafoc doesn't mirror the tone.

'I'd sooner bloody eat,' Eastmund counters. His face is twisted with fury. By now, all of my warriors have joined this heated argument, Bucge beside Osfyth, the three women facing me and the rest of my warriors, while Gildas continues, oblivious to the fierce debate.

'What do you think?' I question Bucge. She's the hunter. She's been keeping us fed. She knows how much effort it's taking and how much easier it could be to simply take what we want from those who have it.

'We should fight,' she admits unwillingly. 'We need oats for the horses. We lost much when captured by Isarninus.' Heafoc again ensures Elen understands what we're saying. Perhaps I should have told him not to do so.

'No,' Elen repeats flatly, but the argument is lost. I look towards where Eastmund has been scouting. I'm aware of Elen still disagreeing, but Heafoc's concern now is with our intended attack. He ignores her words.

'Tell us all there is to know about the settlement,' I order Eastmund, the promise of what's to come thrumming through my body. I've had time to recover from our capture. With Isarninus still alive behind us, I'd welcome the opportunity to vent some of my aggression, even if those we would face are innocent of making me feel impotent.

Eastmund grins with pleasure, eyebrows arcing high on his face.

'There are no more than five buildings, surrounded by a ditched enclosure. The horses will easily take us over the ditch and banks. I've seen few people and even fewer warriors. We easily outnumber them. There are many new crops surrounding them. They'll be rich in food although, perhaps, not many animals,' he concedes.

'And you're sure there are only five buildings? There's no other settlement nearby?'

Eastmund shakes his head vehemently. 'No, they're alone. It'll be easy to ride through the settlement, take what we want, and be on our way once more.'

'No,' Elen tries again.

I turn to Osfyth. 'Take Elen and Gildas ahead. Keep them close to you. We won't be long,' I instruct her.

She nods, still conflicted by this argument between the woman she intends to protect and me, her leader. I encourage my warriors onwards. Even the horses seem keen to follow our orders. They too were enclosed by Isarninus all winter long. They relish the promise of a gallop with the wind running through their manes. Admittedly, they might not appreciate the bloodshed when that happens. But I bloody will.

7

MEDDI OF THE EORLINGAS

The fighting's brutal, but it's over before it's really begun.

As far as I can see, it's not that these men lack battle skill, or indeed the weapons to bludgeon their enemy to death. But rage drives them. As I show myself to them, sheeted in the lifeblood of their seeress, fury concertinas their faces and they rush against Madog, Urien and the rest of the warriors without thought for how they'll survive the attack.

They don't work as one force, to drive through our gated entranceway and the two ditches and ramparts protecting the rest of the settlement. They come alone, driven on by wrath and, perhaps, fear. Their protectress is dead. I've seen to that. Who then will tend to them when they're ill or shield them from the vengeance of their gods? Who'll stop their women from being killed, or worse, taken as slaves as those before them were?

Bloody fools, I think, but my gaze remains fierce, my lips constantly moving. They won't hear the sounds I mutter to my gods, but they'll understand the intent behind them, as I speak words of protection for my men and warriors, but not for myself. I need not do so. I'm safe from the harm of mere men.

They die screaming for their mothers and wives, praying to their gods, desperately trying to hold in their lifeblood and the intricacies of their severed stomachs. The killing's ruthless. It can't not be. Madog and his men are strong enough to drive even a lump of malformed ironstone into these enemies. At the moment, the men of the Eorlingas don't have the sharp blades I'd like them to have when Terricus completes his task. They don't need them against warriors who have only the same weapons to hand as we do, but who lack the rigidness of fighting without fury.

For now, brute strength wins the day against men blinded by rage. Even as I luxuriate in yet another triumph for Madog, Urien and his warriors, a sense of foreboding ripples down my spine. It'll not always be like this. The urgency to produce better blades must be felt by others aside from me. When someone's clever enough to rework the lost magiks, the decades of uneasy and mainly grudging accord between the peoples of this island who've survived summers of poor harvests will erupt in bloody and brutal war.

When that happens, Madog – or his son, whoever's leading the tribe of the Eorlingas then – must be at the forefront of it all, or we'll fall beneath sharpened blades and spears like wheat beneath the ancient scythes, protected each winter between layers of wool to ensure the blade stays true. They're almost more precious than the cattle and sheep grazing in the fields, if not the horses. They ensure we can harvest the crops with the most efficiency.

Eventually, silence falls, other than from those gurgling their last breaths where they slump on the blood-hued ground.

I turn to Madog with a cold smile. He meets my gaze, chest heaving, blood dripping down his breastplate, his shield, I notice, dented with the sign of another man's flesh and life fluid adhering to it.

'It's done,' he coughs, wincing at some unseen hurt.

'Are you cut?' I demand harshly. There's little point in being successful against our enemy if

Madog's injured and dies from the wound rot. His son will be unable to lead our tribe for many summers yet, and there's no one else I trust to do as he does. We'll fall into bickering, little better than when Edern ruled here.

'No, winded,' Madog explains, shrugging his shoulders and wincing again, while assessing his warriors.

I glimpse Urien limping amongst the dead. There are others showing signs of some hut or other.

'Does anyone bleed?' I demand harshly, grimacing as I try to move only to realise the other seeress' blood has stuck to me, making my skin feel uncomfortably tight. Now, with the heat of battle evaporated like dew from the grass on a warm day, the smell of so much ruin is impossible to ignore. I swallow back bile, and stand proudly.

'I don't believe so. Well, not from anything other than a broken nose or missing teeth.' As Madog recounts this, I watch his warriors, assuring myself of the same. Men are strong until they bleed. They're not used to seeing madder-red leaking from their bodies. It undoes even the strongest of them. 'What will you do with her?' my brother questions, eyeing the dead woman. Now she no longer moves, it's evident she employed artifice to make herself more feared. I see where her flesh has been made pale with chalk, and her eyes rimmed with thick charcoal streaks to draw attention to them. Now she looks like every other dead body I've ever seen. Shrunken and small. Lifeless, not sleeping.

'We'll return her to the women of the Stoppingas tribe. They must know she's dead. If we burn her here, someone will fill their heads with fantasies she yet lives and can help them. Burn the dead men, however, all of them. They deserve no honours for such wasteful deaths. The twelve of them deserve no place in their afterlife.'

Madog grimaces but nods in agreement. 'I'll escort the woman's body back to the Stoppingas settlement.'

'No, you'll remain here. I'll take six of your warriors to perform the task, no more. If you leave here, then Villa Eorlingas won't be protected. She must be safeguarded by you at all times. It's thanks to you we've triumphed as we have. Others will soon realise it's you that makes the warriors of the Eorlingas so strong.'

'But,' my brother begins, and then nods, something behind us catching his eye and driving the defiance from him. I imagine it'll be Rhian, with his toddling son and baby daughter. Such a powerful reminder of all he must protect, aside from those who are his kin, or owe him their spear when attacked by our foemen. 'When?' he questions.

'Today. Better it's done before the flies converge on her, and the stink begins. We'll ride,' I decide quickly, already striding towards where Marchell and Sian await me. Sian has water ready. Marchell peruses me, a rare smile on her thin lips as she sees me so triumphant.

'Take her spangles and other items,' Marchell whispers urgently, as I allow Sian to clean the blood of the dead woman from my face with the water and cloth, while the other women of our tribe watch on. They show no fear of what I've done. Had their men killed the seeress, they'd be worried, but it was me who did so. I took her life and that is as it should be. A seeress to kill a seeress will not incur the wrath of the gods.

'I'll take all apart from her clothes,' I confirm. 'Bring my horse,' I call to one of the youngsters, never far from Sian, and keen to do her bidding, for she has enough prestige within our tribe now to be treated with respect by others. She's no seeress, but my woman. That has power here.

The boy runs quickly. I'm aware of the warriors' horses being prepared for the journey.

'Arrange for food and drink,' I direct to Sian, not quite a command. 'A journey of three days, to be sure we don't run out. Our focus will be on returning the dead woman to her people. Marchell, ensure the dead men are burned as the rites prescribe, and then scatter their ashes at our gateway as a warning and a warding.' Marchell nods, still smiling, even to be given such a gruesome task. It'll be a reminder to those who offer Madog their service and blades that he's a strong warrior, while also serving as a fore-warning to those who think to attack us. News of this will spread. Our neighbouring tribes will see the flames of the funeral pyres. They can't not when the fires must burn so fiercely to dispose of the flesh, if not always the larger bones. Adding some charcoal will no doubt fuel the required inferno.

Another night, another burial. We seem to be sending many to the afterlife. But it's what must be done. The strongest triumph. The weakest must do the best they can in the ashes of all that went before.

My cream-coloured mare is brought to me. I run my hand along her long nose, attuning her to me, and ensuring the smell of blood doesn't unsettle her. I keep my breastplate in place and return the dagger to its sheath having wiped it with some of the tall grasses to remove the blood, although I allow my thick cloak to be slung over my shoulders. The nights might be cold so early in the summer.

I'm pleased Madog and his warriors have quickly decided who'll perform what task. The men who'll escort me prepare just as quickly as I do, after brief exchanges with their families, and another horse is brought to carry the body of the dead woman.

'Aid me,' I order Marchell and Sian, who's also returned with food for the journey. The men don't wish to touch the dead seeress. It'll be difficult for us to lift her alone, but we can cover her eyes, and body, make it appear as though she's little more than a sack of grain before the men are forced to aid us to lift her.

I walk to the gateway where the body lies, lips twisted at the reminder of the wreck of the dead men and women. Already, the warriors are piled to one side, their possessions taken from them by the victors. I doubt they had much, but what they did have is now ours. That's how it should be. They'd have taken everything from us had they prevailed.

Marchell bends with an audible creak of her ancient back, and begins to remove the seeress' spangles and bag of magik items when I'm too slow to do so. Admittedly, I don't wish to take them with me on my journey. In my absence, Marchell will examine them. They disappear quickly into her own dress. When I return, their secrets will have been gleaned and the magiks, perhaps, removed. I'll see. In this, Marchell, as is so often the case, has more experience than I do.

With the aid of Sian, I lay down a spare cloak and roll the body into it, until it's entirely covered. Only then do Madog and Urien assist me in wrapping the cloak tightly and securing it with hempen rope. Then they lift the weight over the back of one of our sturdiest horses, a chestnut mare long past her prime foaling years. She's a pleasant animal, worth keeping throughout the cold months with the stresses on our hay supplies, for she has the stamina to travel anywhere we wish to go and never falter. And she's good with the foals as well. She shows them we're not to be feared, but obeyed, and perhaps even loved. For that, she earns the right to live through every winter season.

'People of the Eorlingas.' I turn to face them when I'm mounted with the aid of Urien, the reins loose in my hands, although my horse shows no concern for the smell of blood and shit. 'Your warriors have protected you, as have my powers to dominate others. We'll return this woman with honour to her people, the Stoppingas, although her death deprives them of much. They'll falter now. Their crops won't ripen. Their animals will not breed. They'll beg to come amongst us, and when they do, we'll treat them kindly. It's not their fault their men and seeress made such mistakes.'

A ripple of unease percolates the group, but it's what we did with Corun's women and oldsters, and also with the Beansæte who Hedrek once commanded. They've lived with us for some time now. They wouldn't wish to be cast out once more.

'All will be well,' I assure them, nodding firmly. 'The gods have done this, and we'll honour them. Now, return to your tasks. Today has been exciting enough.'

At that, Urien leads the way through the blood-dappled entranceway, sitting proudly, eyes keen as he must sweep a glance towards the River Hafren in the near distance before turning to ride inland. Two of my brother's warriors ride to either side of me, the mare with her cargo to the rear. If we should be attacked, we'll abandon the body, but not the horse.

Head high, I ride with poise, but my eyes are just as busy as Urien's. While Villa Eorlingas is the home of my people, we journey through fields that are ploughed and seeded with our strength and animals. Here, the manure from a winter's captivity allows the soil to enrich itself and grow fine barley and wheat. None of our people are outside the protection of the double ditch and enclosure yet, but they'll return to their labours in good time. I gaze at the villa itself. The buildings are perhaps looking tired, some of the roof tiles missing, because Edern never fixed them and we've not yet found replacements, but it's a hive of activity. Already, the women have resumed their tasks with loom and thread, the children being taught the same, or allowed to chase the sheep. A sharp yap of one of the hunting dogs fills the air, as it too frolics. If not for the pile of cold and marbling flesh, visible even from here, and the stink of the burden following on behind me, it would appear as though there'd been no violence this day.

I allow a smile to turn my lips.

Madog and his warriors are brave men. They'll accomplish a great deal with me at their side.

* * *

We stop overnight, seeking shelter beneath a copse of beech trees, their purple leaves just beginning to unfold. The wind rustles above our heads as the warriors secure the horses and then settle for the night, wrapping themselves in cloaks or standing watch. I sit with my back to one of the tree trunks, allowing myself the time to consider the events of the day.

I did the correct thing in killing the seeress, I know that. I gaze at her still form, placed on the ground far from the horses so they won't nibble at it during the night. I'm aware the men are less keen with the dead body. I hear them muttering soft words beneath their breath as they catch sight of the corpse. I know no such fear. The woman is dead, gone to the afterlife, only her physical remains survive. They have no power other than to terrify those who think death will never stalk them. We can all be guilty of that, I acknowledge. But her demise does leave a problem. We'll restore the body to her people. What they do then will be telling.

They can either join the Eorlingas, or attempt to survive alone. No doubt, it'll depend on how many youths didn't join the fight. And on the stubbornness of whoever will lead the Stoppingas in the wake of their losses.

Perhaps they'll walk away from their buildings, maybe even set them ablaze and turn their backs on all they once knew, keen to start afresh, ritually ending all they once were, as is the way of our people. I don't imagine they will. I'm recalled to the events after Edern killed my father and decimated his people, forcing me to his bed with a blade at my throat. Those who survived slunk away. I watched them leave hungrily, desperate to be with them. Only Elen remained, aside from me. Only Elen stayed through choice. I've never understood why, although I suspect it was because she wished herself the wife of the tribal leader, no matter who it was, and what he'd done to earn that position.

When I was cast aside by Edern, and left for dead by him, I carried my wounds with me, but not my child. I was found and taken to my father's remaining people by chance. They were camped out in the remnants of some long-forgotten range of buildings to the south. It was then I met the small baby, Madog, again, and then when I was healed I repaid Marchell's kindness in treating my terrible wounds by taking her place. I had no choice. The Eorlingas had survived, but only just. They needed someone brave to lead them back to what was stolen, and not Marchell. I thought I'd accomplish it quickly, but that wasn't what happened. Perhaps these women and oldsters will do the same. Slink away and seek vengeance. If that's the case, Terricus must work more quickly to produce the weapons we need to prevail over those with the determination to risk all. I know that's what we did on Edern's death.

Unsettled, and filled with memories of my past I'd sooner forget, I roll in my cloak, and find sleep quickly, although my dreams are filled with strange images of warriors and horses I don't understand for, in them, they don't fight an enemy. When I wake, I'm grumpy from a poor night's sleep, and the warriors seem unsettled as an argument ensues between Urien and another of the men.

'What is it?' I demand, forcing my body upright, despite the complaints of bones more used to a soft and comfortable bed these days. I'm grateful I removed my breastplate to sleep, although I'll need to don it once more.

Urien bows slightly, acknowledging me, his expression pained at having disturbed me with the argument, but quickly explains.

'He's convinced there's someone out there. Or something. But, we've not seen anything. I've walked the perimeter. There are no signs of footprints, or tracks left by a bear, wolf or boar.'

With an assessing eye, I scour the area close by. The men are all there, the horses too, and the body of the dead seeress.

'I believe he might be seeing spectres.' Urien comes closer, whispers the words to me. I stand taller, reaching for my copper and silver spangles and running them through my hands. This is what the warrior will expect to see. I witness him shudder as though something touches his skin. His eyes are wild, and his face bleached. He swallows as though bile rises in his throat.

'There's nothing here but the dead,' I call. 'But we should be gone from here, and quickly, before the body corrupts.' Already, putrefaction is taking place. 'We don't wish to be assaulted by flies.' So spoken, I stride into the deeper branches, relieve myself, reattach my breastplate and then hurry to my horse. I approach cautiously, watching the animals. They show no unease, even the animal being led to retrieve its heavy burden.

We're not far from Villa Eorlingas. I've travelled this way before, but so many years ago it's almost as though it was to a different place, not just a different time. The road and trackways are familiar, the height of trees and grasses not so much. And I feel sure there was once a settlement nearby stretched along the side of the roadway, but I see no trace of it. It can be that way, sometimes. Homes and workshops disappearing beneath the soil as though they were never there, ancient stonework being consumed by weeds and grasses, the woodwork disintegrating beneath the onslaught of winter storms. Or, as is sometimes the case, being taken to some new settlement, perhaps with the advantage of an embankment and a steep slope to keep those within safe in exchange for giving up almost all they've ever known.

I shake my head, dismiss the sudden melancholy of a time I can never revisit and mount up. Urien has managed to encourage the warriors to do the same. I do sense that the warrior who fears something close by is still uneasy. I'll keep an eye on him. He can't be running off at the sound of a bird or animal taking flight nearby.

'We're ready, mistress,' Urien calls, and as the day before, we form up, some riding to the front, others to the rear. The wind continues to rustle the branches and new buds, but as we emerge from beneath them, I see the sun bright overhead, clouds scudding quickly by, and relish the fresh breeze keeping the flies and smell of decay away from my nostrils.

Urien leads. He's a firm man. He's a good warrior. He wasn't always so. He was one of the few young boys to survive and escape when Edern took our villa and my body. I find him a steadying presence and a link to that lost time. Edern has much to be blamed for. Once more, I wish I'd manage to kill him rather than him nearly ending my life. I wish even more that it had taken less time for him to finally die, and for my brother to grow to manhood. But a seeress can only control so much. Time isn't one of those events she can command.

I seek out Villa Eorlingas as we crest a steep slope, and see it clearly behind me, laid out in its simple walls and ditches, red tiles gleaming beneath the sun. A cloud of smoke rises into the air from where the dead have been disposed of but I imagine that, instead of worrying about them, the Eorlingas will be busy in the fields, harvesting the early crop and preparing the ground to lie fallow for some time. It never pays to work the soil too hard. Greed often results in more sparsity rather than an abundance. In the distance, the vast river glints beneath the sun, and here it's possible to see the many smaller streams running towards it, so similar to the blue veins beneath my skin.

Before the sun reaches its zenith, Urien calls a halt.

'Mistress, it's ahead.' I look where he points, and see a settlement, half the size of Villa Eorlingas, nestled on the next hillside, surrounded by a single ditch. Within it, there's a small complex of stone-built buildings. This then was also once a villa, but not as large or prosperous as my father's home.

I see people moving around. As our approach is

spotted, there's a flurry of activity. I turn to Urien and the other warriors.

'We'll hope for a peaceful reception, although we can't guarantee it. We bring news of their dead and their defeat. We return their seeress' body to them, although whether they'll want her remains to be seen.'

I've only just come to that realisation. It's possible the seeress riled the warriors of this tribe to war and the women didn't welcome it. That might make our appearance an unsettling experience for them. Will they want back the body of a woman who brought such calamity upon them all?

'Lead on,' I direct Urien, and he does so. The men grip their spear hafts, held rigidly to the side of their horses, but they point upwards. A sign of strength but not immediate violence.

After some shuffling, one of the women steps forward into the entrance of the enclosure surrounding the villa. She's probably my age, but sturdy with it, a cloak covering her dress although a fine, slightly tarnished silver pin holds it in place. My eyes narrow. She looks almost like a seeress but lacks the charms that should be worn around waist and neck. Nor does she wear a breastplate, as I do.

Her words are blunt. 'They failed,' she states.

'They did, yes.' It seems no introductions are needed.

'Are they all dead?'

'Yes, burned and their ashes scattered over our defences.'

She nods, as though this pleases her. 'Then you've acted honourably, despite their intentions. Who is that?' She juts her chin towards the dead body.

'Your seeress.'

Her face twists, and she turns a ferocious glower my way. 'You're Meddi, seeress of the Eorlingas, daughter of Macsen.'

'I am, yes, and who are you?'

'I'm Ladus, healer of the Stoppingas.'

'But not a seeress?'

'No. I don't meddle with such forces. I use what can be freely discovered about the properties of plants and animals to aid people and their livestock. I've no interest in interfering in the ways of the gods.'

'Well met,' I call, finding myself unsettled by how this is unfolding.

'We don't wish her back here. She led our men astray, promising them much and producing nothing but death and destruction on the whim of that witch, Elen. Take her back. Burn her alongside her lost men.'

I startle at the mention of Elen, and see a wry grimace touch Ladus' lips.

'Elen was once wed to Edern, wasn't she? I recall her as she was, all fine clothing and haughty disdain for those he endeavoured to crush, including the Stoppingas. She came here, with wild hair and nails long enough to fix a roof tile in place, inciting hatred from our seeress. I expected her to beg for our aid but instead she promised the men much with her enticing smile and covetous body, once she was clean and given new clothes by our foolish seeress. And then Elen slipped away, leaving the warriors to fulfil her promises. She says there'll be others who'll also attack you, and the warriors of the Stoppingas should move quickly to take the majority of the prizes from the Eorlingas.'

I absorb this unwelcome news. 'She recently escaped from our captivity,' is all I can offer, while the warriors at my back glare uneasily around them, as though Elen might appear before them.

Ladus, seeing this, smirks. 'She's long gone. She knew there'd be no welcome for her from the women of the tribe when the men had ridden out to attack Villa Eorlingas.'

'When was this?' Urien asks impatiently.

'Days ago. She'll be far from here now. She stole a

horse to speed her passage. She pilfered the wits of our men, and our horse. She always was a bitch.' The real venom in Ladus' voice has me nodding. I'm pleased to meet someone who hates Elen as much as I do.

But I'm uneasy with the request to take the body of the seeress away, even while my fingers curl around my ceremonial dagger and spangles. The thought of finding Elen and ending her life, once and for all, is almost overwhelming. I'm sure we could catch her if we knew where she'd gone.

'The woman was no true seeress.' Ladus interrupts my thoughts, indicating the corpse. 'She cajoled them with her wanton ways and promises of more. She thought only of revenge against Edern for all he did to her, which Elen encouraged, filling her head with stories of how he used her poorly as well. I made the effort to discourage her by ensuring she knew Edern was a bastard to all women, but she wouldn't listen. Elen offered the promise of taking the wealth from Villa Eorlingas. The woman was a fool and so were our warriors who believed she was a seeress, even though we knew differently.'

I startle at this statement. I've been driven by revenge against Edern for many winters. Am I no different to the dead woman who clothed herself as though a seeress?

'Never fear, Meddi, mistress. You're one who truly has the knowledge of our gods and the workings of a seeress, and what was done to you was much worse. We know of it. We're pleased you survived to claim your villa once more. It's a pity you'll be forever scarred. You're a beautiful woman. Now, we've much to do. Return to Villa Eorlingas, or seek out Elen. Either way, know we're not your allies, and not your enemies either. We can't risk sending our women and youngsters to find Elen. You'll need to enact your vengeance upon her, and do so knowing we of the Stoppingas stand at your side. We don't seek the protection of your brother. We're self-sufficient, especially with half our population dead, but if we ever need Madog and his warriors, led by these fine men here, then we'll come to you. I promise you that.' There's a hint of resolve in Ladus' voice, and she astounds me by bowing slightly and then turning aside, beckoning the sobbing women to her. She might be stoic about what's happened, but others intend to grieve, and she doesn't castigate them for that. 'We'll make an offering to the gods on their behalf. They died as warriors. They'll be rewarded in the afterlife,' she continues, but I see hateful eyes looking my way. While the promise of no vengeance between us is comforting, I fear not all think the same. But my concern is now with Elen. If she's free to move amongst the various tribes and standing villas and nearby settlements who also hated Edern with the same lies she's shared with the Stoppingas, she'll stir up more and more problems for Madog and his warriors.

I'm torn between a need to return to Villa Eorlingas, and one which has me seeking out Elen in the surrounding landscape. I see clearly now what she intends to do. I curse myself once more for not ending her life when Edern died. I shouldn't have allowed Madog to sway me.

'Come,' I call to Urien and his warriors. 'If we hurry, we can return to Villa Eorlingas before full dark.' The journey, I realise, has been less onerous than I thought. The horses laboured up the steep incline of the hillside, but now we need only go downhill. It'll be a quicker journey to return to my brother and tell him of all we've learned. I won't be hasty in my intentions towards Elen, despite knowing how much I wish to find her. I'll not be wasteful, as the men of the Stoppingas were.

'What of her?' Urien calls, indicating the dead body.

'We do as Ladus suggests. We return with her but

she'll burn this night. There's nothing to fear,' I reassure quickly, sensing the young warrior's unease once more. 'The dead can't hurt you while I'm close,' I assert, running my hands through my spangles and bucket pendants to remind him of who I am. I'd sooner he feared me than treated me with the dismissive attitude Ladus and her fellow women had for the dead woman who claimed to be a seeress, but I banish such thoughts. Elen and her plans towards our tribe infuse me. I'll need to do more than wait for the next warriors to try their luck against Madog's defences. I'll have to find Elen, and finally end her life, as I should have done when Edern died. Will that mistake really put an end to my plans of the last twenty summers. I can't hope they won't. I'll have to ensure it doesn't.

8

WÆRMUND OF THE GYRWE

Watling Street

We don't hide our coming attack. It's bright daylight. I'm not going to wait for darkness to fall. If Bægmund's correct, the settlement won't be able to defend itself no matter when we assault them. I allow a smile to stretch across my cheeks. I've been repeatedly tested since killing Waga, my brother. Those we've encountered have constantly tried to employ us to their own ends, even Isarninus deciding it better to keep us captive than have us escape and attack him.

This island is dominated by weak men, determined to do whatever must be done, to retain their position from any who might think to take it. My brother was a weak man, relying on my father to support him, and the memory of my grandfather, whose name he shared. I refuse to be the same.

Even Isarninus, allegedly the leader of a *comitatus*, allowed himself to forget the skills he'd once used to gain all he had. How I despise the man. He must pay for what he did to us. I'll kill him when I have the prizes Gildas promises us. I'll sever his head from his neck and in the process discover the truth behind his threat about informing my father of where I am.

Now I focus on the way ahead. As Eastmund said, the settlement isn't big, no more than five buildings, with three trails of weak smoke rising into the air, and a small enclosure surrounding it. It's pitiful. It can't be to keep warriors out. It must be to keep the animals inside, I'm sure of it.

'As before, with Dægbeorht's settlement,' I shout to my warriors, realising I've given no other orders aside from the one to attack.

Eastmund turns to me, grinning broadly. My other warriors seem just as keen. Even Heafoc. We stole away from Isarninus when the time came to escape. We hardly bathed ourselves in battle glory. Now we need to restore the faith we have in our newly gained fighting skills.

A sudden shriek from within the settlement assures us we've been seen.

'Hurry,' I call to my warriors, the thunder of the horses loud over the roadway. The hooves of our animals clatter against the stone. It sounds as though there are hundreds of us, and not just seven warriors and horses.

I lead the way, eyes everywhere, as men and women hurry to find somewhere to hide within the settlement. My horse easily crests the banked enclosure. Some of the inhabitants collect small children playing on the hard-packed earth surface inside the ditched compound. But there is one abandoned, ahead of me. I wince, unable to turn my horse aside. But my animal has other plans. I feel him gathering his back legs beneath him, and we soar over the child, who watches us, not moving. Not even seeming to fear us.

'Ware,' I call behind me, warning the men who ride with me. It's one thing to kill a man, quite another to end the life of a child yet to fulfil its potential. My horse stumbles on hitting the ground, and I grip tighter, determined to stay mounted. I don't look behind. I hope the child hasn't been harmed. I'm unconvinced it doesn't lie, head bashed in by a misplaced hoof.

A high-pitched wail floods the air. And then there are a collection of five men facing us, two women standing with them. They have nothing but wood axes and pitchforks to use against us. I grimace. This is hardly a good fight for a *comitatus* to make a name for itself.

A gabble of sound, and I realise this is someone else who doesn't speak my tongue. I don't know what they say, but their actions speak firmly of a desire to fight. I grip my spear and plunge it down towards the single line of seven people who want to defend their village and its inhabitants. Or, more likely, the produce of the early summer crops.

The spear hits fresh air, my horse doing more damage as, this time, there's no chance it can jump the defenders. It crashes into them. I hear the sharp snap of bones hitting the ground too heavily. I gather my horse beneath me and turn, but it's over. My warriors have barely been tested and the seven lie dead or dying on the ground, their gabbled words of hatred flooding the air with wet breaths.

'Is that all?' I call to Eastmund, already dismounted and busy rushing inside one of the buildings. Smoke rises from the thatch covering old stone walls. This is another place once inhabited by men and women who could build in stone, and within which others now try and scratch out their lives, adding thatch or grasses to cover the still standing stone walls.

'There are more in here,' Eastmund shouts. 'Women and children. Those too old to rise from their beds.' I seek out the small child my horse nearly hit. It's not on the ground. I lift my head, a high-pitched voice drawing my attention, and see the snot-faced boy child in Heafoc's arms, mounted on his horse. I open my mouth to argue, but my warriors are busy at their task of taking the food from the settlement.

Goddæg walks amongst us, his horse forgotten about, as he stuffs fresh bread into his mouth, sharing as he goes. Maggenræd erupts from what must be a storehouse, grinning widely as he carries a wooden bucket filled with oats for the horses. Hygebeorht follows him, carrying a round of cheese. This settlement seems rich in good food despite its small size and lack of warriors, but before I can enjoy the still-warm bread, Eastmund's cry of dismay reaches me.

He's being prodded back through the doorway by a crippled man, a spear levelled at his back. There are two others as well, who also have spears, fury on their lined faces.

I shake my head. 'What are you doing?' I call to Eastmund.

He has the good grace to look abashed. 'They caught me unawares. I thought them all weak and unable to defend themselves. I was seeking their treasures.'

I sigh, considering what to do. The spears hardly look deadly, but there are three, and Eastmund's threatened by them. We're too far away to get to the old men before they stab him.

Heafoc brings his horse to my side, keen to see what's happening. A shaken look on the faces of the three men – one hairless, one with a beard almost to his knees and the other with a shock of white hair cresting his head – allows a slow smile to spread on my face.

'Just stay there, Eastmund. We'll take what we need, and exchange you for this child, here.' I dismount as I call the order to him.

'What?' Eastmund gasps. Unsettled at my words.

'Hurry up, my brave *comitatus*,' I call. 'Take what you can carry. Can I?' I take the silent child from Heafoc. He relinquishes his hold on the boy unwillingly. 'It's this child or Eastmund.'

'Ah.' He quickly understands.

I place the child on the ground, gripping one

hand tightly. He walks with me, not seeming to fear me, which does little for my self-esteem, not even lurching away from my wolf-marked face, but at least I need not hurt him.

The three old warriors watch me carefully, occasionally jabbing towards Eastmund with their spears. He shrieks and I'd castigate him for it, but then I'm not the one with three spears at my back. Even as old as the blades are, they could cause a painful injury. It speaks of the value they place on their treasures they allowed seven to face us with little more than farming implements.

I consider whether I should menace the child or not, and decide against it. I place my seax on my weapons belt and hold my hand out in what I hope is a peaceful gesture, even as my warriors ransack the village, taking all the readily transportable supplies of food and oats. Even Heafoc joins them.

The child remains with me. He makes no effort to escape, even when we walk through the blood splatters of the dead and dying. Those seven men and women gave up their lives too recklessly. Perhaps, I reason, they're unused to being attacked for food.

'Are you doing well there, Eastmund?' I question him.

He rolls his eyes, evidently fearful to make any other movements.

'The child for the warrior?' I call, even though they won't understand me. Instead, I point to the boy, and then to my warrior. Fury descends on their faces. They thought to threaten Eastmund and have us leave, but we've something they clearly want. I hold the power in this game of barter, even if Eastmund's far from happy about it. 'The child for the warrior?' I call once more. The three men speak to one another, but I don't understand a word they say. I wince at a loud bang from somewhere behind me, one of the spears jabbing towards Eastmund angrily.

'Hurry it up,' Eastmund calls, the terror in his voice impossible to ignore as he tries to hold his body away from the spear, even while he's surrounded. He shouldn't have entered the building alone. I'll berate him for that later.

I don't break eye contact with the old spear holder closest to me. He attempts to keep his eyes on me, but every so often, they dip towards the boy. I'm convinced this ploy will work.

'We have everything of value,' Heafoc eventually shouts.

Once more, I point towards the boy, but two of the men, watching my warriors mount up with their plunder, are busy arguing. I don't like the sound of it, even if I don't understand the words.

'Heafoc, to me,' I order, keen to have the tall warrior at my side. I hear him dismounting, bringing his weapons.

Eastmund's gaze is fixed on his fellow warriors. I consider who of the others would be content to leave Eastmund here. I can't say they all love one another as warriors of a *comitatus* should. But I know they won't want the boy, either.

The three old men are steely in their resolve. I admire them. They've lost all. The offer I'm trying to make will do them little good, just another mouth to feed when we've taken so much from them, but I'm confident they'd rather have the boy returned to them.

'Hurry this along, Wærmund,' Eastmund calls. I don't feel like being rushed. This is surely a case of who'll capitulate first. Heafoc growls beside me, menacing forward.

I try once more. 'The boy for my warrior.' I point to both as I speak slowly. This is impossible, and yet to my mind it seems very evident what I'm trying to do.

'Just attack them, or kill him,' Eastmund calls in a plaintive voice.

'No.' Heafoc's quick to deny the second option.

'Watch me,' I instruct my warrior instead, encouraging the boy to move forward with me. His hand is hot within mine. It feels small and fragile. Even I feel the urge to protect him. I don't recall my father ever wishing to do the same with me. I don't remember him ever holding my hand. I doubt he'd have bartered for my life, as these people seem keen to do.

The three men hold their spears tight against Eastmund, one to the back, the other two to either side of him. Their stance is rigid, but the lead one, or the one I take to be the lead, keeps his eyes firmly on the child.

I stop before I'm within reach of an opportune spear strike. I offer a smile, which might be more of a grimace with my face marked by the gods. The two other men grimace at the sight of it.

'Go,' I encourage the child. 'Go.' I place my hand on the small of his back, having released the grip I have on his hand. 'Go,' I say more softly, eyes on Eastmund.

The child shuffles forward. Eastmund watches him, as do the three older warriors.

'Now,' I shout, and Eastmund skips forward, the spear on his belly dropping as the lead oldster bends

to gather the child into his arms. The other two oldsters are momentarily distracted but Eastmund isn't.

He bounds free, sliding between the blades, and
rounds on the four.

'No,' I call to Eastmund. 'Get your arse here.'

'They wounded me,' he argues, pointing to a hole
in his tunic. I see no blood. I doubt they've wounded
more than his pride.

'Get here. We've killed enough,' I urge him. My
warriors are all mounted, aside from Heafoc, Eastmund and me. 'We have what we want. There's no
need to kill oldsters using their spears as walking
sticks.' I grab his back, pull him to me, and before
anything else can happen I shove Eastmund towards
his horse. 'Come on,' I shout, aware of bulging sacks
in the arms of my other warriors. 'Come on.' And I
mount up, eager to be gone from the place.

Every time I believe I ride with my men, as warriors who've little to fear because of their prodigious
skills, something quickly proves me wrong. There's
still a great deal of work for us to do. We mustn't get
too self-assured. Here we were confident, and nearly
lost Eastmund, and he's one of the men I would trust
with my life.

Without looking back, we ride from the settlement, towards where I've ordered Bucge, Osfyth, Elen and Gildas to wait for us.

We'll have good food for the night, but then I must return to training my men to be warriors, or I risk losing even more of them. And we're already small enough in numbers thanks to those who proved disloyal to us. Even now, it's difficult for me not to look over my shoulders expecting Cenbryht and Nothelm to be there, leading my father against us.

I look forward to the day I can face them and repay them for such treachery. But it's not yet. No. It's one thing to overpower men and women armed only with pitchforks. It's quite another to face warriors who were once part of my father's *comitatus*.

9

MEDDI OF THE EORLINGAS

We arrive with the sunset, welcoming fires lit to ensure we know our way home because our return has evidently been seen from afar.

Quickly, we're allowed within, through the reinforced and guarded entranceway, and Madog hurries to join me, his eyes narrowed to see the bundle of the dead woman returned over the back of the chestnut horse. Her body is really starting to smell.

'Lay her here, where we burned her warriors,' I order Urien and his men. 'We'll send her on her way this night.'

'Why is she back?' Madog questions, assisting Urien because the other men eye the corpse with unease.

'They didn't want her. She was no true seeress. Instead, she was once one of Edern's discarded women, but more importantly, it was Elen who incited them to strike.' I don't speak with fury but instead with firm resolve.

'Elen?' Madog startles, turning back to me, while others hurry to bundle wood to burn the seeress' mortal remains.

'Yes. She was there. Recently. She stole one of their mares.'

'And you intend to seek her out?' he surmises quickly. Madog knows me too well.

'Yes. She's a menace to our existence with her determination to send fighting men against us.'

'But we're stronger than other villas and tribes. We have defences and warriors, and soon we'll have the best blades as well. We needn't fear what she might do next.'

I nod. I knew he wouldn't understand my decision, but that doesn't mean it's wrong. 'And she has her slick tongue, and tale of our wrongdoing. No. She's the biggest menace to our people and our progress. Not those who think to steal our wealth away. Her desire for vengeance against us, against me and Marchell, will imperil everyone if I don't find her, and finally end her life.'

'Meddi,' my brother draws closer, his words soft now, 'we need only work on the blades and iron, then, when it's accomplished, we'll triumph over everyone else. We already have,' he reminds me. 'Elen will not have access to the same weapons as we will.'

'But that was before Elen was free to interfere and incite hatred amongst the other peoples of the River Hafren. She knows just as well as we do power can be gained by uniting others against her enemy. We're only the Eorlingas. We have only this villa, and our old settlement, little guarded these days although we use the land to grow crops. There are many villas, and many other peoples. It was the Stoppingas first, those closest to us after we overwhelmed the Beansæte and the Weogoran. There are many other peoples. You know that. Edern caused great disruption when he took our villa and claimed to govern everyone else as well. She's told the Stoppingas tales of his wrong-doing towards her, and also of our wrongdoing to-wards her. She speaks the words they wish to hear to come against us.'

'And they all lack weaponry, just as we do. They have only spears and shields as we do. No one can do more than that. Not at the moment.' My brother re-fuses to be dissuaded from his viewpoint.

'Their numbers could overwhelm ours if they

were united. And what if she travels further from the River Hafren? We're only one of many tribes. It's imperative Elen's stopped before she can truly begin to cause insurmountable problems. We'll not lose what's only just been returned to us.'

'What of our people here, and their needs? You think only of killing her because you hate her so much,' he hisses, keen the men and women of the Eorlingas not witness us openly arguing. There can't be discord between the tribal leader and the seeress. Not again.

'I think of doing what's best for our people. Marchell will remain. We both know she's more skilled than I in the way of a seeress. She and Sian can do all that's needed.'

'And what of you? You'll travel alone?' It pleases me Madog already accepts I'm going, no matter his arguments against the necessity.

'No, I'll take two of your warriors with me. They'll protect me.'

Madog shakes his head in disgust, the shadows of the coming night adding age to his young face. It's as though I speak with my father, who was never one to take my advice well while he lived. Perhaps if he had done? No, I'll not consider those dark thoughts.

'You argue we're imperilled but think to take two of my warriors from here.'

'Then no, I'll take two of the youngsters, or one young and one old.'

'What of the other mares? They'll foal soon. It's your skills that will ensure the foals are safely born and welcomed by their mothers.'

'And Marchell will be here to guarantee everything happens as it should. I don't like to admit it, Madog, but she has taught me all I know.'

'She's old,' Madog hisses.

'Being old doesn't make her feeble of mind.'

Madog sighs, rubbing his hand through his beard and moustache, and I think I have him convinced. 'Meddi, sister, seeress, Elen might well be a menace to our people, but you've hungered for Villa Eorlingas for more than half your lifetime. Is it really so easy to leave now it's returned to you?'

I sigh at his adequate summary. 'You're right, Madog. This is all I've wanted for as long as I can remember. But we should have killed Elen when we had the chance. She's already sent warriors against us with little more than a sway of her hips, and slick words from her lips. Just think what else she could do if we don't stop her? If she moves amongst tribes not close to the Hafren, filling their heads with stories of our attack against us, or us stealing what was hers, and she emboldens those claims with promises of the Eorlingas' lost wealth, they'll come for it. She's always been able to convince others to act and fulfil her wishes.'

Madog exhales, the sound heartfelt. And then he gives his agreement. 'You can take one of the older warriors, and one of the youngest. You may have horses each, and food. Seek her out, but for no more than a month. You'll be missed. While we have Marchell, and I'm grateful for that, you're our seeress. The people look to you. It'll soon be time for my daughter to be ceremonially welcomed by our tribe. You must be here to perform the rites. Should something happen to you while you're looking for Elen, it could be our undoing.' I realise it's not simply frustration that has Madog wanting to deny me. It's also fear. I eye him.

'Be strong, brother,' I urge him, conviction rippling through my voice. 'You're a good man, and a wise leader of these people. While I've always stood at your side, they would do anything for you, whether I was there or not. Don't think too little of yourself. I never do.' And with that, I cast a single glance at the billowing fire consuming the body of the dead seeress, and the sharp popping of the buzzing flies being consumed by the heat. I vow there and then I'll not suffer her fate until my time has come to an end. I'll find Elen, and finally end her life. In the process, I'll not prematurely bring mine to its conclusion. As Madog reminded me. The need to reclaim Villa Eorlingas has driven me on through some of the most difficult periods of my life. I'll live to enjoy living here. Once Elen and her meddling presence has been brought to an end.

* * *

The following morning, I check on my mares who are yet to foal with Marchell at my heel. She doesn't argue with me about my task, as Madog did. Indeed, she approves.

'When you find the bitch, bring her here. I demand to end her life as I once gave it to her.'

I nod. I'll not argue with Marchell about this now, although in my heart, I know I can't allow her to kill her daughter. If I've been wounded by Elen, Marchell has been even more fiercely betrayed by her actions with Edern. 'If she's dead, I'll bring her body here as well,' I reassure. 'Now, remember all I told you about the grey mare. She's strong-willed and feisty. Don't approach her while foaling unless there's no choice. She'll bite your hand off rather than thank you.'

'I know the ways of highly strung mares,' Marchell assures me, and I nod. I know she does. She taught me all I know, as I told Madog. In the cold light of day, I confess, I'm regretting my hasty decision of last night, and yet I know my plan is the right one. Elen must be stopped.

'Sian, do as Marchell requests. Please. Assist her and keep the people of Villa Eorlingas hale. There are no women due to birth for at least three months. All should be well.'

'Mistress.' She inclines her head towards me respectfully.

'And aid Terricus if he needs it. And ensure Hedrek doesn't win the regard of any who feel pity for him. He's a slave, and while we're not harsh masters, it's still a punishment.'

'Yes, mistress,' Sian replies. Marchell's running her hand over her lightly downed chin, her thoughts far away. I roll my eyes at this display of inattention, but then she surprises me.

'Terricus will soon accomplish what's needed. Already, I feel more assured in his work.'

I startle at that. In all this time, Marchell hasn't offered such a glowing endorsement of my scheming.

'Good. I'll feel even better when we have better blades and can defend ourselves from whatever Elen means to do.'

'She'll fail,' Marchell hisses, but in this I believe Marchell speaks with more hope than prior knowledge.

'Be well,' Sian states, and I offer her a firm nod.

'And you, Sian. Be well and protect Marchell and the people of the Eorlingas.'

Without pause for further recriminations, I take myself to my cream-coloured mare, and the two warriors. The boy, Tudwal, is thin and lanky, frighteningly akin to a spear shaft. The old man, Kenal, is someone I've known for a long time. He's almost as broad as he is tall, but I know he was once a fine warrior. He'll protect me. The boy, well, he'll be useful for gathering firewood and collecting water, if nothing else.

Madog waits for me at the guarded entranceway. There are men and women in the surrounding fields tending to crops and the soil, or gathering water from one of the many streams, but Madog has insisted on keeping a constant guard after the attack three days ago. He's wise to be cautious. I imagine he'll soon arrange a show of strength to reinforce the might of Villa Eorlingas. I hope he'll wait for my return, but it might prove impossible to do so. If Elen manages to raise another to come against us, he'll need to act.

'Seeress.' He bows low as I near him.

'Brother,' I reply, and he grins like a small child.

'Be safe and go well. Return within one month, as I requested.'

'I will, brother. And, it's to be hoped, I'll have Elen in my grasp.'

'But if not, we'll still need you here. There's much work for you to perform as the summer advances, and I must be able to leave this place, should I need to seek vengeance against another tribe.'

'I know my responsibilities, brother, I assure you. Now, keep our people safe, and your wife, son and daughter. Marchell assures me Terricus will have a breakthrough soon. Help him as much as you can.'

'I will, seeress.' Then he turns to my escorts. 'Kenal and Tudwal, safeguard the seeress of the Eorlingas, and yourselves. I'll hear of your accomplishments when you return. And Tudwal, this will protect you.'

I watch as Madog presents Tudwal with an old and battered willow-bark shield. It's certainly seen better days, but the centre of it isn't damaged so it will still do the required task, even it's not particularly pretty to look upon.

'You had no shield?' I question Tudwal.

He quakes beneath my gaze, but shakes his head, and I think mumbles, 'No, mistress,' although it's so quiet I might just be imagining it. I berate myself for not realising this.

'Then my thanks, Madog, for providing one. Now, we head for the hills.' And I turn my horse to begin my endeavour to find Elen and do what I should have done when Edern died. Killed the bitch and put an end to her constant interference in the tribe of the Eorlingas. I know Marchell welcomes it as much as I do. Madog will come to realise I've done the right thing. In time.

10

WÆRMUND OF THE GYRWE

We stop for the night far from the settlement having rejoined Gildas, Elen, Bucge and Osfyth, so as not to worry about reprisals, although I doubt the people we beat have it in them. Eastmund's shamefaced, and it doesn't help that my other warriors are determined to make much of it.

Elen's furious at what we've done, although I'm unsure why. Gildas can't understand our language, and Elen refuses to speak to him, but he eats the food we offer him eagerly enough so has no compunction with where we've been or what we've done. I consider how little I know about him. I see him doing something each morning and night, taking to his knees and offering muted words, eyes wide open, head cast backwards to see the sky. I'd like to know what he's doing.

I watch him this night, carefully, seeing how he takes himself away from my warriors, who laugh and tease Eastmund, all apart from Heafoc. Heafoc's too quiet. I consider if his thoughts are with the small child I held captive to ensure Eastmund was released. It wasn't my finest moment, but I couldn't allow Eastmund to be wounded. And we needed the supplies they had.

'What's he doing?' I muse aloud. I expect no one to answer.

'He's praying to his god.' Heafoc surprises me by stating. I turn to face him, aware my mouth drops open.

'His god?'

'His god.'

'Not Woden or Tiw?'

'No, not Woden. Some other god. A singular god, not gods. I've seen it before.'

'Seen it before. Where?'

'When I was a young man, some of them came to speak with those of our tribe. Your father's father, Waga, chased them away, but I saw it. They wore an emblem around their neck, as he does.'

'They spoke the same tongue as Gildas?'

'I don't recall if they did. I thought they spoke in the language of the Picts, but perhaps I misremember. I recall the pose they adopted. On their knees, peering upwards.'

'He prays a lot then.'

'He does, yes. This god is different to ours, and I suspect different to the one Elen prays to as well.'

The use of her name earns me a furious glance from her. She sits furthest from the fire, but still lit by the leaping flames, and close to Bucge and Osfyth. I don't miss she's content to eat the food we stole, even while refusing to answer my questions voiced by Heafoc. I remain unsure of her and her intentions. I believe she's devious and working towards her own desires. She promises much, but a woman like her wants to make the decisions. That's not how it's going to work between us. I suspect I should have discovered more about her before agreeing to follow her to Uriconium. But, the potential of what she suggests we'll find within Uriconium – or rather, what Gildas says will be there – was a powerful lure after our failures at the hands of Isarninus. Having damaged our reputation by betraying the people of the Hicca on Isarninus' command, I believed we all needed something new to strive towards. Something promising retribution against my father and Isarninus. The allure of deadly blades to kill our enemies.

'Who does he pray to?' I call across to her, and which Heafoc voices, a question I hope she'll answer, but instead she turns her face aside, nose raised, highlighting the contours of her cheeks and chin. I hear Heafoc tutting at such an arrogant display.

'She means us trouble,' he cautions quietly, rubbing his hand over the scars on his arms from earlier wounds. Heafoc has settled well to our itinerant lifestyle after a winter in the hilltop settlement.

'She does mean us trouble,' I agree. I don't say aloud I believe she's brave to have been travelling alone, the very fact of which is really starting to concern me. Does she belong to someone? Will they be looking for her? Or has she lost all but the clothes on her back and the fine horse she rides, her arrogant charm and ability to speak with Gildas? And, of course, the broken sword. 'She can converse with Gildas. That's her true worth.'

'And what when she demands you fulfil your end of the agreement? We're but a small force, seven men, two women and a holy man. We don't wish to take on those she wants us to defeat. We already have to fear your father, Isarninus and the men who betrayed us and yet live, amongst them Nothelm and Cenbryht.'

'There's time to think about that,' I murmur in response. It's not that I've not considered this. But, to begin with, I felt no unease, no fear we might be the target of someone else's intentions if we added her to our number. Now I'm not so sure. Perhaps that's why she didn't want us to fire the settlement and run off with their goods. 'Where do you think she came from?' I question Heafoc.

'She speaks the tongues of those from the west of Britain. Alone, I don't believe she'd strayed far when we encountered her. And so, somewhere south of here, and towards where the sun sets each day.' I want to complain such a description isn't helpful. But perhaps it is. Or it could be, if we were able to speak directly to Gildas, which we can't.

'Can't you communicate with him?' I huff softly. Heafoc can speak three different tongues. 'Surely it must be easy to learn another one?'

'The tongue he uses is very different to the ones I know. So, alas, it's not easy. But, perhaps, when we reach Uriconium, we'll find someone other than Elen to speak to him for us.'

'Perhaps, but as we go west, we're encountering more and more people who have a different language to the one we speak.'

'Hum,' he muses, offering no assurances to my

troubled thoughts. 'Perhaps you should learn his tongue. It would be good if you could communicate with those you wish to be employed by.'

I consider the wisdom of his words. Not only am I allowing Elen to lead us where she says Gildas means us to go, I realise, in my endeavours to evade my father and Isarninus, I'm also taking my warriors far from all we know. Here, will these people wish to employ others to fight on their behalf? Will they even understand the idea of doing so? I mean, the settlement we attacked revealed there are places in need of defending, but I doubt they could have recompensed us as well as Isarninus promised, before he betrayed us.

I find I have much to think about, and none of it is reassuring. Maybe my father was wise to remain far to the east. Or perhaps not. I'm a man of my ancestors, descended from gods, physically marked by those gods. I'll make a success of this. Or die trying.

* * *

The following morning, while Gildas whispers his words to his god, hands raised and eyes wide open above his head, I slip my way through a thick band of trees, towards the rushing sound of water, lots of water. Gildas' regular honouring of his god has reminded me I've not done the same since escaping Isarninus' captivity.

With a small knife in my hand, taken from our enemy yesterday, I mean to make some obeisance to my ancestor, Woden, god of voyages. I've erred in failing to do this. Perhaps that's why we were undone by Isarninus. I should castigate my warriors, but I lead them. This is my mistake to rectify, if Woden will countenance it.

I allow the sounds of the natural world to overlay all else. Filling my mind with the soft rustle of the wind through the leaves of the trees, the growing thunder of the nearby river to flood my senses. I almost feel like closing my eyes, but not yet.

I don't go without my blades should I encounter an enemy, but my thoughts rest on Woden.

My father always spoke with pride at being descended from one of our gods. I'm aware some would cast doubt on that. I don't. My father, his father and his father before accomplished much more than others of their people. It must have been through the influence of Woden. He made all they achieved possible. He will, I hope, allow me the same.

At the riverbank, running high although there's

been no recent rainfall, I crouch, unheeding of the dampness clinging to my knees.

Now I close my eyes, and I don't direct my head upwards. My god doesn't hover out of sight amongst the clouds and sun, no, he's here, all around me. He walks at my side.

I breathe deeply, the pungent grasses filling me with the scent of the natural world, the occasional sounds of fish jumping clear of the water, only to re-enter it moments later, the only noise. For now. I can't hear my warriors. I'm entirely alone.

My father once sought portents to know Woden was close. I know Bucge aided him in this, until she displeased him by suggesting my father was no longer honoured by his ancestor. I don't do the same. I'll feel him, if he's close.

I consider my journey here. The fact I still live, as do most of my warriors, is surely a sign my actions please Woden, although I've been tested along the way. I allow a smile to touch my lips, and then I open my eyes, and using the small knife, hack through the grassy banks, and place the knife within. I also add a fistful of stale bread, and then close the mound once more. I don't mutter soft words, as Gildas does, but I make Woden a promise in my mind.

If Woden will see my warriors and me safely to

Uriconium, and to the services of a bladesmith, I'll repay him with a bloody sacrifice. I stand, brushing my knees clear of the clinging mud. For a moment, I watch the river, seeing where it surges against the steep riverbanks, and where it runs more slowly. It's a powerful thing, seemingly benign but prepared to cause floods and drown people and animals at will when angered. I share affinity with it.

And now I will follow where Gildas leads. It's him I need. Not Elen. I must remember that. She's expendable. It's the holy man, with his strange lyrical language, whom I need to ensure the safety of me and my men. Elen, it's evident, doesn't know what Gildas does. Indeed, she uses her ability to speak with him against us. One day, hopefully soon, I'll be able to ask him of all she informed him and determine what lies she told him about us.

I vow if Elen causes more difficulties, I'll feel no compunction in angering Bucge and Osfyth and casting her aside. She's no warrior. Really, she brings me nothing but the means to speak with Gildas, and as Heafoc states, we could find a replacement for her, and then converse with Gildas without her. Gildas is the man who knows what I seek, not Elen, and whatever vengeance she desires. And, I suspect, Elen, with her broken sword pieces, hungers for the knowledge Gildas has as much as I do.

I offer a slight bow to the river, to the buried knife and to my ancestor. I don't sense Woden at my side yet, but I know he's not abandoned me. Too much is happening that I desire to think I've been cast aside by my ancestor and god.

'To Uriconium,' I announce, and then move to return to my warriors and their campsite from last night. Somehow, I've not heard the shouts and cries abruptly flooding my senses. 'By all the gods,' I glower, and hurry to a run.

11

MEDDI OF THE EORLINGAS

I travel with a rigid back, determined to show any who watch me I'm confident in my endeavours. I can't say Tudwal manages the same. I eye him as he rides to the side of me. I think he should be behind me, but the horse he's been given has a mind of its own. It's also a stablemate to Kenal's and so, released from the confines of Villa Eorlingas, it wishes to be with its mate. The pair, Tudwal and his grey horse, are so similar in their flightiness, I suppress the urge to giggle. I can't offend him by laughing at his attempts.

'Get behind,' Kenal growls when Tudwal quickly draws level. 'Pull him in or he'll think he's the master, not you.' I'm grateful Kenal offers the advice. If I'd spoken it, I think Tudwal might have fallen from his mount. That would be a most inauspicious start.

We take no spare mount with us. We carry enough food for at least a week. After that, we'll need to barter for what we need. Tudwal is, I've been assured, a fine hunter, for all he seems incapable of not falling over his own two feet. Admittedly, they're huge. I've never seen feet so big. I could fit both of mine into one of his.

Perhaps that accounts for why he rides so poorly. Maybe he doesn't have feeling in his ankles, or his toes to direct the horse.

I amuse myself with such thoughts while pretending to ignore Tudwal's efforts to restrain his horse with the reins, and Kenal's angry complaints when it fails. I could wish my brother had sent me with finer warriors, but the young must learn, and those with more winters to their name than me must also be made to feel useful. Such wisdom as Kenal's garnered in a long life shouldn't be dismissed easily.

And here, with Villa Eorlingas still in sight, we've no reason to fear. Madog's warriors aren't far from us, while people of the tribe are busy with animals and farming. It'll only be once we reach the heights of the Stoppingas that we'll need to be more careful.

Our settlement is one of many near the River

Hafren. Not all look to Madog as their leader, or to Villa Eorlingas as their place of refuge should an attack come. Some would rush to Corinium to the west. Others to Glevum in the north, old settlements with the scarce remnants of stone walls surrounding them, once inhabited by the Romans. There are others who perch on the hillsides, such as the Stoppingas. It's these people I need to be wary of. They'll easily fall prey to Elen's charms and do what she orders them to do when she tells deceitful lies of how we've reclaimed Villa Eorlingas. Not that it'll be couched as an order. No, she'll employ more intelligence. How I despise her.

That night, we sleep in the same place as a few nights ago. The fire's almost still warm in its bed of stones.

'I'll keep guard,' Kenal announces. But I shake my head.

'No, it's the first night, and we're not far from Villa Eorlingas. We should all sleep while we can. There'll be nights in the coming days when none of us may sleep.' As I speak, I pull forth charcoal and chalk from the pouch tied at my waist, moving to the horses and marking them with my protective sigils with swift movements over their bodies. I do the same to Kenal or Tudwal, although Tudwal shudders beneath my hands. He smells of sweat, youth and fear. I hope to make a warrior of him during the next month. Madog would appreciate that, I'm sure.

I do the same to myself. Dusting my cheeks with charcoal powder to allow the darkness of night to hide me. The white demarks only my chin, as it does the two men. It'll allow us to know one another should we be woken in the night. I didn't perform this rite last time. There was no need with so many warriors to protect us.

'Now we'll sleep, and in the morning we'll journey towards where the sun rises. That's the path Elen's taken. I'm sure of it.'

I've given this much thought. Elen has no doubt travelled extensively throughout this landscape. After all, Edern did like to exert his hold over all the settlements he felt owed him their allegiance before he became old and weak. As such, she'll need to travel further than the furthest one she's ever visited to truly find success. I imagine she was merely toying with the Stoppingas because they were the first tribe to welcome her amongst them. I doubt Elen will find allies where Edern acted as some sort of conquering warrior throughout his tenure as commander of these places. She'd be foolish to think anyone owed him any affection. She's always been keen to toy with the lives of men and women she felt were beneath her. Where her arrogance stemmed from, I've never known. Certainly, her mother, Marchell, doesn't exhibit the same trait and I don't recall she did when I was a child either. Elen is altogether different to her mother. I'm grateful she never determined to follow her mother's path as seeress of the tribe. Then she'd be spiteful and imbibed with the powers of a seeress.

Admittedly, in recent summers, Edern had grown weaker. His warriors had died, or left him. He'd become slower to act, more content to grow fat and round on the settlements so cowed down beneath him they wouldn't even attempt to rise up against him. But our people have long memories. The seeresses and leaders of these settlements will not want to do anything in the name of Elen. A pity they won't end her life for me, but I sense it must be my task, as I thought it was over a year ago, but Madog turned my hand aside.

While Madog ensures the well-being of our people, and Terricus labours to forge the perfect blade, I must contend with Elen and the hatred she holds for the Eorlingas, and her mother.

While my thoughts are busy, I sleep soundly, waking only with the crack of a branch as pale daylight floods the landscape.

'Mistress,' Tudwal apologises, but I wave it away. He's busy tending to the horses, and building a small fire. He's attempted to wipe the charcoal from his face, and now only his chin retains the charm I spoke over him.

'Where's Kenal?' I question, standing fluidly, even though my back protests the movement.

'I'm here,' he calls. I realise he's been relieving himself in the undergrowth. I hurry to do the same, while Tudwal works to gut the pheasant he caught. It seems I'm the slowest to wake. That surprises me. I've always been a light sleeper. Better to be, when Edern might make his demands on me at any time, and I've never yet been able to grow accustomed to my safety away from him. Even now he's dead.

We eat and then are quickly on our way. Ahead, the rise that will take us onto higher land is visible, as is, if I squint, the settlement of the Stoppingas, now devoid of the woman who called herself their seeress. I hope the remaining women survive. I'm not convinced they will. Perhaps I should suggest Madog sends a handful of men to aid them during the winter months when it'll be difficult to keep the houses warm and they might need protection from anyone who becomes desperate enough to steal what little they have. I'll think on it. Ladus seemed confident they'd endure without warriors and strong men to aid them.

We follow well-worn tracks in the grass and sometimes scattered amongst the stones forming the uplands. It's too early in the season for the place to be covered in weeds and grasses, but trading routes, and the sheep and cattle tracks, easily guide us. As do ditches cut to the side of some of the better-cultivated land, aiding drainage, or ancient and long since forgotten random bumps in the ground attesting to when the land was once used, but isn't any longer. I've been told there was a time when every blade of grass was under cultivation. I can hardly believe it as I witness the rapid retreat of cultivated fields closer to places offering protection and sanctuary.

We meet few people. Those we see eye us warily but pass by with slightly bowed heads, when they realise we don't travel with violence towards others. I don't ask them if they've seen a solitary woman riding the paths. I don't know any of them well enough to trust with the reasoning for my journey. They'll assume I travel to perform a rite somewhere, perhaps on the hillsides where huge dark stones attest to the magiks once performed there, long before the Romans came to this island. To discover where Elen is, I'll need to question seeresses and tribal leaders, not men and women busy about their daily tasks. They'll fear to speak to me. They'll fear to speak to my warriors.

'Mistress,' Kenal calls to me later that day. We've ridden at a gentle canter when able. I see no need to exhaust the animals on the second day of our journey.

'What is it?' I ask the tall warrior. I can see he's struggling to sit on his beast. He's not spent a full day mounted for many summers. I too am feeling the chafe on my inner thighs. We might need to protect our flesh from burn marks caused by that, and not from the heat of flame.

'Ahead,' and he indicates where he points. Here, the landscape opens up and we can see further. He indicates a large settlement, lying in the dip of a wide valley, smoke billowing from fires, and people and animals busy in the late sunshine, as the hillside lowers itself towards a wide river.

'The home of the Husmeræ,' I announce, absorbing the view before me. I've been here before, but only once. Even then, I was astounded by the opulence of the buildings. Like Villa Eorlingas, it's long past its prime, an age even my father heard about only from his father's father, but this place is as rich as

Villa Eorlingas, and those who live within it know it only too well.

'They had no love for Edern here,' Kenal comments.

'No, they didn't. We'll seek shelter with them this night. I would speak to their leader. Is it still Padern?' I realise I should know this.

'I believe so,' Kenal offers, while Tudwal looks uneasy. He doesn't know Padern, and he's certainly never visited this place before. I fully understand his uncertainty. Such a settlement would be rich in warriors and men able to overpower my two men.

'Tudwal, ride like a proud warrior. There's nothing to fear from these people. They aren't exactly our allies, but there's no need for us to be enemies either. Not now Edern's dead. If anything, I'd say we're equals. We know to keep to ourselves, trading and feasting when we can, and otherwise leaving one another alone.'

Carefully, allowing the horses to pick a path down from the steep hillside, I encourage my animal onwards. Our presence is noted quickly, which doesn't surprise me, and a collection of six warriors blocks the entranceway through ditches and turf banks when we arrive, holding spears and shields before them.

I incline my head towards the tall figure of Padern, who quickly recognises me and gasps in surprise.

'Seeress of the Eorlingas, why are you here?' There's only wary caution in his voice. Perhaps he fears I bring terrible tidings of a coming drought, crop failure or pestilence. It would be correct to share such knowledge, if I had it, amongst people who, as I said, aren't our enemy.

'A fine welcome,' I encourage, grateful he at least bows his head low. Behind him, I see Cadwysti, entirely blind now, eyes milky-white, but still standing proud as the seeress of these people, with her golden torque encircling her neck, and fine spangles at her waist.

'It's unusual,' Padern quickly explains. I don't fear Padern. He's a good man, comfortable in his position. His people respect him. I respect him. Edern didn't but Padern could stand firm against him.

'It is, we seek a runaway.'

'Slave?' he counters quickly, instructing his men to move aside to allow me entry, as well as Kenal and Tudwal. 'They must be valuable,' he suggests, as I dismount and take myself to Cadwysti to be welcomed by their seeress.

'You're welcome, Meddi of the Eorlingas,' she offers in a thin, raspy voice, a young girl at her side offering her support in addition to the wide dark wooden staff she clasps.

'It's good to find you hale and well,' I offer, gripping her one free hand with both of mine.

'And you. It pleases me the bastard Edern is dead, and your young brother, tribal leader in his place.'

'It pleases me as well. I burnt the bastard but offered his skull to the people of the Beansæte when it wouldn't burn. I've no idea what they did with it.'

'He'll be headless in the afterlife,' she chuckles darkly. 'It couldn't happen to a better man. And what of his bitch of a wife?'

'Ah, now you perceive why I'm here,' I reply, Padern almost forgotten about behind us. He waits patiently, as all men must when seeresses speak.

'I suspected, but in this, alas, I'm blinded.'

'Elen lives. She's escaped us and now incites others to attack Villa Eorlingas.' A sharp intake of breath reveals what she thinks of this. 'The Stoppingas men are all dead. The women are staunch in surviving without them.'

'Still a bitch then, and I'm pleased Ladus is finally in a position of such responsibility amongst the Stoppingas. She's a firm woman. But what does Elen have that worries you so much? She'll meet her end, soon. A woman such as her will misstep, hopefully quickly.

I doubt she can hunt and fend for herself. None of her ilk ever can.' I enjoy her disdain regarding Elen, but lean forward to explain more. It's not necessary everyone should hear of the Eorlingas' double shame in losing my father's sword.

'We discovered my father's desecrated body and his sword. She's stolen it.' I feel no compunction in sharing this knowledge with Cadwysti. She's alike to me. We know to keep secrets. Padern, however, need only know we seek Elen.

'Then she must be found, and the sword returned to your brother. Come, we'll eat.' Cadwysti speaks as though she's the tribal chief, but Padern makes no complaint, merely following us like a child, summoned to perform a task. 'He's a good leader.' Cadwysti speaks with pride as I take the place of the girl and support Cadwysti in her movements inside the standing building. The villa complex here is still evident, and welcomes me in with an enticing shape, as though both sides of the buildings embrace me. I know Cadwysti has her own mosaic depicting fierce characters I can't name, which once absorbed her, portrayed in fine detail in a building to the rear. I welcome the trickle of water surrounding us, myriad streams running through the raised terraces, allowing the animals and people enough water to tend to their needs. It's not Villa Eorlingas, but Villa Husmeræ is almost as richly endowed. I wouldn't want to live here though. As pleasant as the constant trickle of water is, I know I'd grow tired of it. And curse it each night when it woke me too often to piss.

The people of the villa barely glance up from their labours now they know we're to be welcomed without fear. I eye them. Some tend to the weeds threatening to clog the many waterways, others see to animals, and in the far distance, even further down the slope, there are small dots working away in the fields. A swathe of green growths sways in one place, another lies fallow, the yellowed earth stark, the promise of new crops hidden beneath it, while the cattle liberally splatter their shit over it. In the final field, the men and women work through the early springing crop, already harvesting the goodness of the land.

Beneath the roof, we move towards the left of the villa complex, through two rooms and then into a much wider one. Here, Cadwysti indicates we should sit. A chair is brought for her by the young girl, but I willingly settle on a lowly stool. My warriors tend to the horses. I'm alone with Cadwysti, her attendant and Padern, although he bows again and hurries away. No doubt, he doesn't wish to listen to two seeresses speak further, when he knows to be respectful and wary of the knowledge they possess.

'So,' Cadwysti's voice is low, 'she's stolen something most precious and now means to act against you. I perceive her intentions are to take back what she believes is hers.'

'I believe the same. Weaken us with these sporadic attacks and then strike us when we're unable to prevent her.'

'But she won't do it alone.'

'No. She'll win warriors to her cause. I'm sure of it.'

'With what?'

I bite my lips at this, and with a glower at the young girl, who steps even further back, I continue. 'We aim to rediscover the lost art of forging iron blades. We have a bladesmith even now learning the craft. We've managed to recall the skill of creating charcoal. Now it's a matter of time before we have better blades. And with the rediscovery of the lost magik, he'll reforge my father's broken sword. I suspect Elen will share this knowledge, if not seek it herself.'

Cadwysti sucks her lower lip at my words, nodding with consideration. She shows no horror at our intentions with regard to iron and blades. 'She deprives you of your father's sword, and will have it re-forged herself, and then come amongst you, using it to claim her place.'

'I believe so, yes.'

'She intends to find the same as you then, the means to restore the sword and start a war such as we've not seen for longer than two lifetimes.'

'Yes,' I admit, sighing softly. I consider my own desire to have Centus, and now Terricus, succeed. Did I wish to restart the old wars that have long since ground to a halt as no one tribe could better another with the poor blades available?

'This wasn't your plan, though, was it?' she questions, facing me. I believe she can see through those milky orbs, although I know she can't.

'I wanted Villa Eorlingas. I wanted Edern dead. I want my brother to be strong. I didn't intend to start a war, only to protect what we have with more than just ditches and rampart.'

'A fine ambition,' she answers without censure.

'It's always the problem when one individual pushes further.' Silence falls between us, broken only when three women appear – well, one woman and two young girls – carrying bowls of food as well as a jug of water, one of perhaps wine, alongside a handy stool to place everything upon.

'Your warriors will eat with Padern,' the older woman informs me, curtseying low, and then meeting my gaze boldly. I incline my head towards her. She reminds me of Sian. She offers me a small smile, while Cadwysti's young helper steps forward to guide the bowl towards her hands.

The cooked fish is good and meaty. I welcome the warmth in my belly, while Cadwysti eats in silence, no doubt musing on what I've told her. I allow my eyes to drink in the walls of the villa, random pieces of adhering yellow paint revealing themselves in the soft glow from the sun reaching into the open windows, the coverings pulled aside to allow fresh air to circulate through the buildings.

If I weren't hunting for Elen, this would be a welcome place to sit and watch the world grow rich and abundant with new crops and animals.

Eventually, Cadwysti speaks once more. 'I'm older than you, and even Marchell, Elen's mother. I'm also well served by my daughters, sons, grandchildren and great-grandchildren here.' At that, she offers a smile to the young girl, quickly reflected on her fresh face, and the fear and terror of behaving incorrectly is wiped from it. I offer her a regal dip of my chin. 'My memories stretch further back than yours. I carry the memories of seeresses who came before me as well. I knew one day, sharpened iron would be used man against man once more. It saddens me, but it was always going to happen, and so I tell you this. The skill didn't die everywhere. I suspect Elen will be focused on reaching one of the larger settlements, where those who live walk each day with the ghosts of the throngs who once made those places their homes. You'll find Elen, I'm sure, seeking aid and a blade-smith either to the north, in the surviving settlements there, or within Verulamium to the east.'

'So far?'

'Yes. She knows the places Edern subdued. She'll avoid them as much as possible, aside from the Stoppingas, where no doubt she first tested her ploy to see if it would work. She's not tried to enter our home. There'd be no welcome for her here. She took a risk with the Stoppingas, but their would-be seeress was crazed in her need to seek vengeance against Edern and had the support of the warriors. Fools that they were.'

'I must consider those Edern didn't subdue to find Elen?'

'Yes, and those where ambitious warriors will hunger for her promises.' A note of disgust enters Cadwysti's voice. I understand what she means.

'Men are fickle creatures, driven by their lusts.'

'They are, yes. It's good when there's an enemy to fight, but not when it's only a matter of pleasing themselves.'

'I should direct my steps towards the north where people akin to our two tribes live?'

'Perhaps,' she muses, uncertainly. 'Stay this night. I'll meditate on it, see if I can find wisdom while you sleep. I so rarely sleep, it'll please me to have something to consume my thoughts with other than aching bones. Now, come, I'll show you the rest of my home. I know you've not seen it all. But now you're a seeress in your own right, I'd like to share with you. I have a tower, of all things,' she giggles like a young girl, the winters driven back from her old and lined features. 'I only wish I could see these days, but I can imagine what you'll be able to view, and you'll describe it all to me.'

She stands, her wooden stick holding her steady, while I move to her side.

'You may tidy away these items,' Cadwysti informs her great-granddaughter, 'and then you too can join us. I'd like Meddi to speak with you of the knowledge she possesses. It's good to know not all seeresses are as I am.'

I realise then the girl has been designated her great-grandmother's eventual successor. She's young to be given such responsibility, but then a seeress is made not born. I only attained my position when older. The girl, it seems, is already preparing.

Supporting Cadwysti, I allow her to guide my steps towards her secretive tower. I've not seen it before, and startle when presented with sagging wooden steps to direct me upwards. Cadwysti grips a rope hanging down the inside of the wall, clearly placed there for such a purpose.

'We ascend upwards,' she murmurs delightedly. 'It's a wondrous location. And, it's all mine,' she offers with a low cackle.

I smile in return, walking behind her, mindful of the strain in the back of my legs, so different to climbing a steep hill, and then stand, able to view the entire villa from one single spot. I confess, I gasp in surprise and pleasure while Cadwysti's smile broadens.

'I see all that you do,' she speaks softly. 'Only as it was before my sight was stolen. But tell me all that lies before you right now.' And so I do, from the shimmering streams to the distant high clouds, to the bundles of small lambs gambolling while some keep a watchful eye to ensure the animals don't come to any harm.

As I speak, I sense a welcome calm washing over

me. As I stumble to a halt, I turn to Cadwysti and grip her shaking hands where they rest on her walking stick.

'You're wise beyond all others,' I murmur gratefully.

'And one day, you'll hold as much wisdom as I do,' she acknowledges, and I feel a lump in my throat. I'll not see Cadwysti again, of that I'm sure. Next time I venture here, her great-granddaughter will be the seeress. She'll never know all Cadwysti does. I almost pity her such youth.

12

WÆRMUND OF THE GYRWE

Heafoc's bellowing cry reaches me before I'm clear from the deep cover of the trees.

'Form up,' Heafoc roars. That confirms my warriors are under attack. I glower, considering Woden's testing me already, and grab my seax from my weapons belt. A thundering noise from ahead, and the horses come tearing towards me, not heeding the branches, or me. I jump aside, seeking shelter behind a wide oak tree trunk, as they streak their way towards the riverbank. For a moment, I'm torn. Should I stop the horses from teetering over the high riverbank or aid my allies?

But it's my warriors who mean the most to me.

Heart thundering in my chest, I work my way towards them. Heafoc's evidently commanding them in my absence. His orders echo, as does the clash of shields and blades. How has this happened? Last night, there were no enemy aside from the broken settlement we overwhelmed. Today, it sounds as though he faces a hundred warriors. Where have they come from? Is it Isarninus seeking his vengeance for us escaping and stealing from him, or my father? Have the deceitful Cenbryht and Nothelm been following us all along?

A shriek, and I face Elen, eyes wide with fright, pulling Gildas deep beneath the trees. She has the fractured half of the sword in her right hand, dragging Gildas with the left. She menaces me with the shattered half of the blade. I veer backwards, avoiding being skewered more by chance than any great skill.

'What's happening?' I demand breathlessly, as she slowly lowers her weapon. I've forgotten she can't speak to me. But she mutters one word.

'Attack,' she shrieks, astounding me, for I'd begun to think her fearless.

'How many?' I question urgently.

'Many,' she again astonishes me by answering. I eye the wizened old man. He shows no fear, which also surprises me as he has no blades with which to defend himself, although I see his lips moving. He prays to his god for aid. I wish him luck with that. My offering to Woden has evidently been too little and too late to win favour from my ancestor.

'Where do they fight?' I demand, the cries of battle urging me to rush onwards, but I know I should learn all I can.

'Spears and shields,' is all she can inform me this time. We must be at the limit of what she can understand and voice.

'That way.' I point, biting my lip, trying to decide how I can help my loyal warriors. 'There's a river, through there.' I point again. Even though she doesn't understand the rest of my words, I can't stop myself from adding, 'Try and stop the horses from falling in. Now go. I'll find you when we're successful.' I turn aside, hurrying my steps, her bitter laughter following me. She thinks I'll fail. I won't allow that to happen. I won't countenance her being proven right. She'd lord it over me, as my bastard father used to do. I growl angrily.

Ahead, the thick tree cover finally starts to diminish. I see chaos unfolding before my eyes.

The enemy, whoever they are, are led by a man bedecked in battle finery, although he remains distant from the bitter fight taking place, sitting atop a white horse, moving uneasily forward and backwards. I see no other enemy horses, but my eyes are focused on the battle taking place.

There's no order to it. My warriors don't clash as one but rather in frantic knots of skirmishing. I realise Heafoc's trying to draw my warriors to him, but he's having little success as he crashes against a wiry warrior, who moves with more speed than a startled hare in the early months of the year.

They're close to being overwhelmed. I shake my head, furious at being caught out by these enemy warriors. I growl low, but hold myself steady. For now.

'What should we do?' a voice whispers to me from nearby. I grip my seax tightly, and only release it when I see Bucge's frantic gaze looking my way.

I still gnaw my lower lip, deep in thought. There are two of us now. We might be able to do something to help my warriors other than me rushing to aid them. My gaze turns to the mounted leader, decorated in finery, akin to Isarninus with his helm of crested boar hair. And too alike to my bastard father. He's the one to tackle.

'We kill him,' I announce, wincing to hear Eastmund's cries, cut off, as though his breath has been stolen from him.

'How?' Bucge doesn't deny my logic.

'We creep up on him. Look. He watches his warriors. He won't expect us to come at him from behind. Now, hurry. The treeline runs close to where he's waiting. The horse is already unhappy and unused to the blood and screams. It's no seasoned warhorse. We can unsettle it further.'

'Come on then,' she agrees, a glance into the trees as though she knows that's where Elen has gone. I see she does at least have her shield and spear. I've nothing but my seax. I should never have left the encampment so ill prepared. I shouldn't have felt so comfortable in this land which owes me nothing, and through which I ride with violent intent besides my warriors. We're the enemy to these people. Will I ever have enough wisdom to deserve the loyalty of my warriors and to steer them safely to what we want to achieve?

Breath huffing through my tight chest, I follow Bucge. We're not at the treeline. We stay back, constantly avoiding tree branches and roots, the one which tries to knock us over, the other which attempts to trip us.

Only when we're behind the enemy warrior do we stop. Bucge's breathing as heavily as me, her eyes wide with fury, as she holds her talismans strewn through her hair to stop them from knocking together. She intends to be quiet.

'We go together,' I urge her through panting breaths. 'We split up when we're behind him. We kill him or spook the horse. Better to kill him,' I glower, wincing at yet more cries of pain and fury from my warriors. I can hear Heafoc bellowing with battle rage, but I've not been able to detect Eastmund's shouts again. Osfyth's higher shrieks can also be discerned, and Bucge winces.

'This better work,' she replies. I can't determine if her anger is directed at me or the enemy warrior. I'll find out. Provided we live through this.

'Come on,' I encourage, finally moving to the treeline, allowing the brightness of the day to temporarily blind me after the darkness of the tightly packed branches overhead.

She dogs my steps. I glimpse my warriors, fighting ferociously. I try to count them, to assure myself the six men and one woman all still stand, but I have to watch my feet and focus on the warrior. He's an arrogant bastard. He sits alone, with only his horse for company. I can't see any other horses. The man must only have the one. His warriors have run here. Perhaps, then, they wanted the horses we ride. Maybe, then, the animals were purposefully sent crashing through the trees by one of my warriors with more wits about them. It does once more beg the question of how they've caught us so unprepared. Did we not keep a guard last night? Was no one watching our rear when we left the attacked settlement? I feel sure I assigned the duties but now I doubt myself.

We move as silently as possible. Bucge has her spear poised to strike in one hand, her hair tied back tightly with a strip of leather. I have my seax. She could jab from further away than me, but I want to kill the arrogant bastard. I hurry to get closer before she can begin the attack.

At the last possible moment, our foeman must sense we're there. He turns towards us. I push Bucge to his blind side with me, but while he can't see me, his restless horse skips sideways, almost giving us away.

'Arse,' I glower, and hurry my final steps, flinging myself towards him. Only he's not there as I stab with my blade. The horse sidesteps, and I can't reach him. Bucge jabs forward with her longer spear, coming up right behind me. She also misses.

A florid outpouring of words I don't understand greets our actions, as the warrior finally sees us, a deep scowl evident even beneath the helm. Another torrent of words, perhaps the tongue Elen can speak, and he has a sword in his hands, the edges glistening with bloody menace. It seems he's drawn blood. Whom he's wounded, I don't know.

'Come on,' I urge Bucge. 'We must overwhelm him.'

The warrior stays mounted, the animal, shrieking in terror, struggling to obey his commands, as he turns the beast's head. I feel the heat of its breath over my face, desperately trying to hold back my blade so as not to kill the animal.

'Coward,' I howl. He puts his horse before him. That's not the way of a good warrior. He should have dismounted and let the horse run free.

Bucge's prodding with her spear, doing her best to miss the horse. The animal's shrieks are wild, and as far as I know, we've not wounded it yet. But the warrior digs his heels tight to the horse's belly. It must hurt it, and my rage pools within me.

I launch myself against the warrior as he tries to turn the animal, flailing with his sword. I catch the shiver of the sharpness of the blade, and know a moment of fear. If that cuts my skin, it'll run deep, possibly too deep to live through. I dismiss it. Perhaps this is my test. Maybe I need to prove to Woden I deserve his regard by facing a warrior who fights with a blade worthy of a god.

At the last moment, the horse spins. My blade skims along its backside, a shrill neigh accompanying the movement, as I wince in sympathy. Blood pools against the animal's white coat. It bucks, desperate to be rid of the man determined to fight from its back. I skip aside from the flailing hooves, Bucge to the far side, her spear wavering with the movements of the mounted warrior, who's committed to staying in his seat.

Hurriedly, I reach across, and slit through the leather holding the saddle in place. His leg slips down the animal's back, his balance lost. Before the animal's hooves are back on the ground, I grasp the warrior by the arm with which he holds his reins. I yank, hopeful he'll fall from the horse's back. But he doesn't. He spits into my face as I growl angrily. Then the horse, level once more, gathers its hooves beneath it, and tears off, towards the knot of fighting.

'Bollocks,' I exclaim, breathing hard. Bucge still has her spear, and she rushes after the animal. It takes me longer to control my own legs, but then I'm streaking after as well. The rider bounces in the saddle, forced to bend low to grip the horse's mane to stay seated, but it's not going to be enough.

I catch sight of Heafoc's astounded expression as he stands, heaving air into his body, the man he was fighting a bloodied mess on the ground. The horse rushes towards the gap between Heafoc and a limping Eastmund.

'Get out of the way,' I bellow, fearing my men will be crushed by the animal, even while I'm relieved to see Eastmund fighting.

Before my eyes, the mounted warrior loses his grip on the horse as the animal bunches its legs and soars over the back of a warrior bent double to retrieve his weapon. He stands, not aware of the animal's approach. His chest is knocked forward by the beast, while the warrior on the horse's back finally slides to the ground.

'Hurry,' I urge Bucge, eyes on the horse, which staggers but then rushes away to where there's no fighting, chest heaving.

Both men are our enemy. The mounted warrior stands unsteadily, thinking nothing of using the other man as the means to right himself. He's lost his sword in the fight, and he grabs the other man's seax, even as he rounds on me, lips compressed in a snarl beneath his shimmering helm.

'He's mine,' I shout, but Bucge's had enough. She launches her spear at him, as though a javelin. The shot's a good one, piercing his foot, as he thinks to rush against us.

His other warriors are oblivious to what's happening, even though he roars for them, or at least that's what I believe he's doing. I don't understand his words.

As Bucge recovers from pausing to aim her spear at our enemy, I overtake her, and while the warrior endeavours to free his foot from where it's stuck to the ground by the spear shaft, I rear up before him, out of breath, seax pointed at his throat.

He gives me a twisted grin, and moves his back foot to provide some balance, as he thrusts the seax towards me. I notice he wears a breastplate of dented iron. He has thick padding on his arms, but I'll still kill the bastard.

I jab out with my seax, and curl my other fist, ready to punch him. It'll hurt, impacting the iron covering his head. In the heat of the battle, I feel nothing but pleasure as his head jolts backwards, revealing his neck. I slice with my seax blade, but he recovers too quickly. He stands with one leg on the man his horse knocked over, and so he's higher up than me, even with the reach of my seax, and his one foot skewered to the ground.

'Will you just die,' I mutter angrily, once more bunching my fist. He keeps his gaze on me, but with his free hand works to release the stuck spear. Sweat beads his face, his eyes wild with pain, as he screams for his men.

Eastmund redoubles his attack on the one warrior I notice who looks to aid his leader. He thinks to turn, but Eastmund lands a blow against his back, and his knees buckle. He's not dead, though. Eastmund launches himself onto the warrior's back, stabbing furiously, although blood coats Eastmund's face and his actions are laboured.

The man below the enemy foeman must be dead not to try and topple the weight from his back. I jab closer. He veers backwards, the spear shaft twanging as it curves as far as it can. He releases it rather than risk it snapping. I move aside at the last moment to avoid being hit. Bucge has no weapon now other than her seax, and she mirrors my movements from the far side.

The warrior gabbles something else, his seax swaying from side to side before him. For a moment, I allow him to continue. He'll tire soon enough, as blood leaches from his skewered foot, turning the ground slick.

A movement to the left and I realise Bægmund's fallen foul of his opponent, who lurches towards his leader.

'End this,' I order myself through narrowed eyes.

The next time he sweeps his blade towards Bucge, I launch myself forward, blade extended, fist clenched once more. I punch upwards, knocking his head back, and thrust my seax into the gap between his chin guard and neck. With all my weight behind it, the blade pierces his flesh. I ram it even deeper, my foot now on the dead man as well.

His lips twist with disgust as my blade severs his neck and he gargles his last breath with a loud hiss of expelled air.

'Bastard,' I huff, ensuring my blade erupts through the back of his neck.

He dies, staring at me, holding my gaze, as I smell the rankness of him and the other dead man.

'Move.' Heafoc's words startle me. I leap back as the horse rushes once more through the fighting, eyes wild with pain, its rump sheeted madder-red.

'Bloody bollocks,' I exclaim, assessing who needs my help, as I labour to release my seax from the dead man. It's an effort. Bucge's already wrenched her spear free from his foot.

'Bægmund,' Bucge calls to me. I rush to the man he fought who's escaped his clutches. He howls with rage at seeing his leader dead, but isn't prepared to die himself. Not yet.

His shield comes up before him, daubed with

blood, but undamaged in his fight with Bægmund. Behind him, Bægmund slips on the blood-drenched grass, and hurries to aid me. I lash out with my reddened seax, a flicker of blood landing on my face with a warm splatter, although the warrior ducks aside from my attack.

He rounds on me. I'm forced to turn back, pivoting quickly, my balance compromised. I see Bucge in the distance, aiding Osfyth, who fights a tall man using his fists against her. I can hear the heavy impacts on her body from here. She won't be able to absorb that for long.

I hold my seax outstretched, sucking in much-needed air, assessing him in the blink of an eye. He might have his shield, but he's wounded. Bægmund's done half the job of killing him already.

I jab towards him. He thrusts his shield between us, which is just what I wanted him to do. I run at it, turning my right shoulder to absorb the impact. He goes down, trapped beneath the shield he thought would protect him. I wriggle my way up the shield, as he bucks beneath me, flailing with his weapons arm. I lash out, stabbing into it, and then I'm above him, straddling his shield. I stab into his chest, pinning him with my weight and my blade.

He howls in pain as I withdraw the blade, and stab again, and then again.

My sweat drips into his open mouth, but after three cuts are opened on his chest, he stops trying to wriggle free, blood welling quickly. I stab three more times, ensuring all of his chest is open before me, and only then do I push myself upwards. Fatigue slows my movements. I feel as though I try to stand with the weight of five shields on my shoulders.

My chest hurts from my deep breaths, my shoulder throbbing with the force of the blow, my fisted hand catching my eye as I realise the knuckles glint redly.

I turn, surveying my men, catching sight of the bloodied horse as it rolls on the ground, as though it can stop the stabbing pain in such a way.

I count my warriors. Osfyth and Bucge have killed the warrior between them. Heafoc's triumphed against his. Bægmund huffs to a stop before me. 'Bastard,' he spits down on the dead foeman.

But others of my warriors still fight. I assess who needs my help, and stagger towards Hygebeorht, but my body is spent. My left leg buckles. I struggle to correct my balance. Bægmund grabs my shoulder to keep me upright, his fingers digging into the ache there. I grimace, but thank him all the same.

Red-haired Maggenræd's also struggling against two warriors.

'I'll go,' Bægmund assures me, ambling to a run while Bucge supports Osfyth, who's bleeding from a jagged gash on her upper thigh. I consider if it's Osfyth the dead leader wounded with his sword. The pair come towards me. I turn to survey the rest of our former encampment. One body lies half in and half out of the fire, smouldering gently. I hobble towards it. I recognise the shock of dark hair and grimace as I find lustful Goddæg, dead, his face white and eyes staring, his clothes slowly blackening beneath the flames. He was forced to abandon his unborn child at Isarninus' hill fort, but vowed to return to reclaim it. Now the child will never know his father.

I grip Goddæg's lifeless arms, and yank him clear from the fire, sorrowful at his loss. I hope I've not lost more warriors. There were few enough of us as it was to counter the threat posed by my father and Isarninus.

'Is he dead?' Bucge calls wearily.

'He is,' I try to say, but all that comes out is a dry, hacking cough. I try again. 'Yes, he's dead,' I acknowledge.

Sorrow clouds her face at the news. 'By all the gods,' she expels, releasing Osfyth to sit beside the fire now it's no longer fuelled by Goddæg's clothing. 'What a bloody mess.'

I can't but agree with her, and prepare to take the blame for what's happened in my absence. But then she surprises me, lips twisting.

'It's Elen's fault,' she announces. 'Where's the bitch?'

13

MEDDI OF THE EORLINGAS

As we prepare to leave the villa of the Husmeræ the following day, Kenal and Tudwal restored to me from where they've spent the night with the warriors of the villa, all eyes turn upwards where the path runs. Padern inclines his head from where he waits to bid me goodbye.

'Traders,' he advises. 'A collection of men and women we welcome into our villa twice each year. There's nothing to fear from them.' And then he pauses, his face pensive. 'They may have news of the person you seek. They travel the route from Glevum to Corinium, and further afield, using the stone roads.'

I nod, watching them come closer. Some walk in

front of two heavy-looking wooden carts, laden with all sorts of shapes and sizes, and pushed onwards by a collection of small yet sturdy-looking horses. The animals gleam with health, as do the men and women who come with them. We step back, allowing them to be greeted by Padern – although not Cadwysti, who I've already bid goodbye to, her determination firm that Elen is to be found in Corinium – and then Padern makes an introduction between us.

I don't know the men or women. I've not seen them before. But the leading man is quickly named for me.

'Meddi, seeress of the Eorlingas, this is Veda,' Padern offers. Veda eyes me with interest. He's grey-haired but sprightly. His eyes are bright with curiosity.

'Seeress.' He bows low, as the women behind him all curtsey, although the collection of five children pay me no heed. 'I know of you, although we met when both of us were much younger. I doubt you remember. We ceased trading with Villa Eorlingas when Edern took control. He wasn't a man to trust or with whom to trade. I held your father in high esteem. I mourn his loss still.'

I incline my head, and indicate the women should rise from where they hover close to the ground.

'Then we're well met once more. I'm grateful you mourn my father, as I do.' I consider whether he speaks of my father because Elen has recently come across him, or whether he's simply honouring a man he once knew. I certainly don't recall Veda.

'I'm pleased you and your young brother are in control of Villa Eorlingas once more. But what brings you here? It's a time for cultivating plants and animals, not visiting neighbours. After all, that's why we traders travel during the growing season when the markets in the old settlements are sparsely attended.'

'I'm seeking a runaway,' I explain. 'Perhaps you've heard of such. A woman. Alone, but with a horse.'

Veda's eyes narrow at this explanation. He turns to assess the women with him, as well as those men who had weapons to hand but have now stowed them away, carefully wrapped so as not to tarnish.

'We hear nothing of a woman. There's some unease about a *comitatus* to the east, latterly made welcome in the home of the Wæclingas. I believe there may be women amongst them, but I've not seen them with my eyes, alas.'

'Where did you journey from?' I question, intrigued by news of a *comitatus*. Not since my grandfather was the leader of our people have we been plagued by those who live in the distant east. We're more likely to face problems from the west and the Irish. Have those settled to the east, easy with their holdings for two or more generations, decided to incite war as well? Have they rediscovered the path to make fine blades, just as I hope to do with the aid of Terricus? I find such news unsettling. I don't wish to be beaten to my intentions.

'Only amongst the local area. We wintered in Corinium. Our path will take us towards Glevum and then north. We'll return to Villa Eorlingas when our trading is done in those places. But, we heard word of it from other traders we met at Corinium who had latterly travelled from Verulamium.'

'My brother would welcome you visiting Villa Eorlingas, if I'm not yet returned. I thank you for sharing all you know,' I offer, aware Kenal and Tudwal are eager to start the day's journey, yet curious about the *comitatus*. Perhaps, if they've rediscovered the lost magik, once I've found Elen we should seek them out. But I return my attention to Elen, for now. She's the immediate problem. We must make our way up the steep hillside to find the road we seek. I'm not looking forward to it.

With a final goodbye and murmur of promises from Veda he'll visit Villa Eorlingas, and with thanks for the night's hospitality directed to Padern, we move through the gated enclosure, and begin the steep trek. We don't ride. It would be cruel on the animals, and with our ultimate destination still unsure, I won't risk them.

The day turns hotter, sweat beading on my back, and we stop for water before finally cresting the rise once more. Here we pause, catching our breaths, ensuring the animals are well.

'I don't like the sound of this *comitatus*,' Kenal murmurs to me, far from Tudwal's ears. The youth is already flighty enough.

'They won't concern themselves with us. We're no challenge and have no wealth for them. If Veda spoke true, they're far from here.'

'But they may threaten Villa Eorlingas, eventually,' Kenal persists.

'Madog has the warriors to protect Villa Eorlingas.' I sound confident, and I feel it. Madog, with the aid of Urien, has done much since retaking the villa to ensure it can be well protected from all who think to attack. His warriors are staunch fighters. The defensive ditches will make it difficult to mount a strike. Even without superior blades to meet any attack.

'Mistress,' Kenal acknowledges, as we turn ourselves to follow the line of the steep hillside. While this villa is one of the finest and most richly endowed, there are others, not far away, who'd welcome what Elen promises: wealth, riches and Villa Eorlingas itself. We must find her before she can do more harm. It's her who's the real threat to my people, not this random collection of warriors, the *comitatus*, although I'd like to know if they have better weapons and blades than us. If they do, I'd invite them to Villa Eorlingas, to share all they know with Terricus. Perhaps we might trade or barter with them. Maybe.

I glimpse the River Hafren shimmering in the far distance, and I hope all is well within my home. All I've wanted for so long is my home returned to me, and for us to live peacefully. But Elen's escape imperils it.

'We'll journey towards Corinium and the people of the Wocingas. They've always had covetous gazes. And Elen knows that.'

'But we'll be riding into trouble,' Kenal complains.

'Perhaps,' I confirm. 'And it's possibly too obvious a place for Elen to go, but that doesn't mean I'm wrong.'

* * *

Our greeting by the Wocingas isn't welcoming. Instead, a collection of warriors guard the entrance to their hilltop site, the spear shafts misshapen, the blades themselves so thin with being reworked I fear they might fall to pieces instead of wounding anyone.

'Why are you here, Meddi of the Eorlingas?' The voice is cold with malice, lips downturned, allowing the long, drooping moustache, clearly carefully cultivated, to touch his chest.

'And a warm welcome to you, Riderch. How fares Gwener?'

'She's hale,' he admits grudgingly, eyeing Kenal with unease, while Tudwal he seems perplexed by. 'You're not welcome here. None of you are,' Riderch continues, not indicating his warriors should stand down, even though we merely speak. Indeed, he holds his bark shield before him as though Kenal or Tudwal might leap forwards and try to stab him.

'We didn't ask for a welcome. I'm seeking someone. I ask for news.'

'Who do you seek?' he questions, filled with suspicion.

'Have you seen a woman in these parts? Perhaps living wild. Or perhaps,' for I've noticed his eyes widen at my words, 'seeking aid from you, and filling your head with pretty tales of riches to be gained if you do as she bids.'

But Riderch's already shaking his head in denial,

his moustache ends reaching up to touch his ears as he does so. I find it most distracting. I should be watching his mouth to determine if his words are truthful or not, rather than considering why he doesn't cut short the clearly annoying moustache. He scratches his ears without seeming to notice the action.

'We've seen no one, or welcomed anyone within our settlement. We trust no one.' He stands staunchly, the shield unwavering before him.

'Then, we'll leave you. It's been most pleasant to speak with you.' I arc an eyebrow, keen to be gone from Riderch. I've never liked him. Age has made a ruin of him. Perhaps that's why he keeps his moustache so luxuriant.

'And if we did see someone? What would the Eorlingas give to us?' He surprises me by asking.

'If you brought the woman to us, we'd reward you. It would depend if it were the right woman and how many parts she was in.'

'I'll remember that,' Riderch confirms, but doesn't move.

'Come on,' I encourage Kenal and Tudwal, aware we'll need to turn our backs on Riderch and his warriors before they relinquish their guard. I'm grateful I wear my breastplate beneath my cloak. Not that I believe he'd attack me. He's too fearful of the knowledge I possess. And of what Gwener would do to him when she discovered his disrespect.

'This is a waste of time,' Tudwal mumbles when we're out of earshot of Riderch and the warriors of the Wocingas.

'It's not,' I assert. 'We act for the good of our people.'

'It's been five days and we've discovered nothing. I doubt anyone would tell us even if they knew of Elen's whereabouts.'

'Perhaps,' I confirm. 'But we've time yet. Another nine days and then we'll turn for Villa Eorlingas.'

The two men acquiesce unwillingly. I control my anger, and frustration. I was convinced we'd have found Elen by now. I believed she'd incite one of the local leaders against Villa Eorlingas, despite Cadwysti stating she'd be in Corinium. Perhaps Elen has, and my home is even now a wreck, but it feels to me as though she's simply disappeared. Is she already dead? Was she wounded when trying to escape and has long since succumbed to those wounds? I will it to be so, but instead I feel only an absence, as though she's been plucked away by someone, perhaps in the claws of an eagle, and is far from here.

I'd give up and return home, admitting this has

been fruitless, turning my attention to the mares and their foals, the women and their as yet unborn children, and to the prosperity of my people, but that would be foolish. Elen means us all harm. It would be wrong to think, because I can't find her, her malevolence has disappeared. I know the bitch far too well. And she still has possession of my father's blade. It must be restored to my brother.

We've journeyed for many days away from Villa Eorlingas, towards Corinium, as Cadwysti suggested. We've followed the road towards the rising sun. But I no longer believe she's gone that way, towards Verulamium. Instead, I consider turning north, the other option Cadwysti suggested. So far, no one we've met has been as welcoming as Cadwysti and Padern of the Husmeræ. We've slept outdoors, using the trees to protect us, and on two occasions caves. There have been few people other than traders on the roads. As Veda said, this is the time of year to be busy with crops and animals, and not trade. It's a difficult time of year for traders, when they must seek for transactions from the tribes as opposed to waiting for them to find them in the ancient settlements.

Those we've met and who've spoken to us have had no news, aside from caution against the roving *comitatus* they've also heard about. They've told me the group moves northwards, using the road running from Verulamium towards locations I can't even name. We're not following that road. It would take me longer than the days I have left to track them down. I've only Kenal and Tudwal to protect me. I fear they might overwhelm us after all. Especially if, somehow, Elen has attached herself to them. That thought plagues me. It would answer much about why I can't find her if she's found a roving warrior band to protect her.

Pensively, I turn my gaze north, to where I know a large settlement lies to the west. It's somewhere known to the Eorlingas, although its name isn't. It's nowhere I've ever travelled to before for it takes many, many days to reach it, passing through many tribal regions which aren't always friendly. Instead, the people of the Eorlingas are more likely to visit Glevum or Corinium. In those places peoples inhabit the abandoned buildings of the old way of life, when warriors encased in iron ruled this land. There are other such places, to the south as well as the east.

Perhaps that's where Elen went. Maybe she went to hide away amongst the ruins of these other former huge settlements that had protective stone walls. Perhaps she's decided to cause the Eorlingas no more problems, merely pleased to be free. But no. Elen has never lacked for ambition, and she's always been bold. When I was cast aside by Edern, and replaced by Elen, I returned to my people, gave myself time to heal and then took the place of Marchell, for no man would have me, damaged as I was. And I wanted no man to touch me. Elen has no such hesitation. She's alluring. She is, I admit, beautiful, and her attraction has always been strong. She perhaps cast her net too shallow when she set her hopes on joining with Edern. I consider if she thought he'd amount to more than he did. Did she dream he'd make her a lady, or an empress, as used to happen long ago, when Britannia's wealth went straight into the coffers of our distant overlords?

She's always been too ambitious. Not for her the spangles and magiks of a seeress. Oh no, Elen always hoped for much more. Now I hope she grovels in the muck and filth, living hand to mouth, desperate for succour from anyone who might offer it. But I'll not have my wish. That's not the way Elen conducts herself. Somewhere, she'll be restoring herself to the ascendant, using my father's blade to tempt warriors to her cause.

'We'll travel to meet Icknield Street,' I inform my two guards. The words mean nothing to Tudwal, but Kenal looks uneasy. 'Then,' I speak before he can

voice his worries at travelling even further from Villa
Eorlingas, 'we'll be able to follow Watling Street
home, if we don't find her.' Kenal meets my gaze at
that. I offer him a nod of agreement. The use of the
word 'home' works. He doesn't think of the vast distance still to travel, only that, eventually, we'll turn
homewards once more.

14

WÆRMUND OF THE GYRWE

'Why do you say that?' I hurry to catch Bucge as she stamps her way through the bloody slaughter field of our fight. Heafoc bends to check his foeman is dead, but Bucge's eyes sweep more quickly than mine, almost frantic with her desire to find Elen. 'Why do you say that?' I grasp her arm as I repeat my question, but she swings aside from me. She's been so accepting and protective of Elen, I can't understand this rapid change.

'Where is she?' Bucge asks, growing frantic when she can't immediately find her.

I shake my head, mindful of the dead below my feet. I should be rifling through their belongings to add to my treasure, not arguing with Bucge about Elen.

'She went that way, with Gildas.' I point towards the thickly packed trees, realising it's the only way I can get her attention.

'I just bet she did,' Bucge growls.

'Bucge,' I demand, as she strides that way, anger writ into the lines of her body. Suddenly, I'm too exhausted to follow, cuts and bruises starting to throb or pulse, depending on what they are.

'Are you coming, or not?' She rounds on me, her face angrier than I've ever seen before, fists clenched tightly at her waist. I step back, even though I'm no closer to her than a spear shaft.

'Where?'

'To find the bitch.'

'Explain why you say she's responsible?' I hurry to catch her, now she moves once more, but Bucge's beyond all reason. I think I could hold her down and demand answers and she'd still refuse. 'Heafoc, Eastmund,' I call to my most trusted warriors. 'Ensure the enemy are all dead and our allies are helped to the fire,' I command.

Heafoc's expression is puzzled as he turns his head in my direction. I consider whether he's taken a knock to the head, because his eyes seem to be looking everywhere but at me.

'Eastmund,' I call to the other man. He pivots from pulling boots and a weapons belt from one of the dead, to nod wearily in recognition of my command.

'Aye, Wærmund,' he responds.

Osfyth raises her drained arm in acceptance of what I'm doing, as Bucge disappears beneath the trees.

'I thought you liked her?' I shout with growing frustration.

'I did,' is all Bucge offers me in reply, as she slips and slides her way through the densely packed tree trunks. This woodland's ancient. Aside from close to the treeline, I don't believe it's ever been coppiced. It would be impossible to chop through the thick branches with the poor-quality axes the woodspeople have available to them. Perhaps, in time, once I have blades with which to slice and kill with a single blow, we might be able to build strong buildings using the thick wood. I suppress a smirk at the thought, and hurry after Bucge. I've no idea what she's going to do to Elen. I've no clue as to why she's so angry with her. What she's done to Bucge is beyond me knowing, until Bucge shares more than the hissed word 'bitch' when I ask about her.

Beneath my feet there are lumps of horse crap, assuring me I'm following the horses, if not necessarily Elen. I wipe the sweat from my face, noticing the blood marring my arms and hands. My nails are caked in the stuff. I sniff, disgusted at the stink of my body and the smell of death. I hope Woden's happy with me now.

The branches slap and crack into my face when I forget to hold my arms before me, and I forget a lot because my arms are tired, and throb with exhaustion. I've not had anything to eat or drink yet this day. But Bucge's determination hasn't faltered. I need to follow her and see what she plans for Elen. As much as I've been considering how much easier it would be without Elen, for now we do need her. She's the only one capable of communicating with Gildas, and he's the only one who knows the solution to what I want to achieve when we reach Uriconium. I hope she's still with Gildas. I can't lose him, either. He's the most important member of our *comitatus*, and he doesn't even have a blade with which to fight.

The thunder of the nearby river floods my senses. Ahead, I catch sight of my horse, kicking at the ground, but unharmed. There are a few of the other horses with him, but I can't see Elen or Gildas.

'Go softly,' I hiss to Bucge. 'The riverbank's steep. We need the horses.' A frustrated growl erupts from her, but she does take more care with her footsteps, avoiding the twigs that might snap and crack, startling the horses to run onwards to a watery death. That would be a terrible waste.

I reach out and touch my horse's nose with a gentle finger.

'There you are,' I whisper. The animal stills beneath my touch, as do the four other beasts with him. I see some of them have whiplash marks on their coats, blood already congealing, where the branches have been vicious during their gallop beneath the trees.

Bucge's already past them scouting the riverbank. Her face is tight with fury, her hand resting on her weapons belt. I fear she'll kill Elen should she find her, and I still have no idea as to why.

'Bucge, what's this about?' I try again. She turns, face twisted with fury.

'She saw them, and didn't warn us.'

My forehead furrows at this. 'How do you know?'

'I just do. I was watching her to make sure she

wasn't assaulted by Goddæg or any other of the foolish men. She was on the viewpoint, to the east of the encampment. From there, she abruptly hurried towards where we'd sheltered for the night, grabbed Gildas, and scampered beneath the trees with no thought for warning us.'

'I...' I open my mouth to say something, although I'm unsure what, only for Elen to materialise from beneath the branches, the severed half of the sword in her hand. She's poised to stab at Bucge, who doesn't realise she's there, so consumed with her fury. Where Gildas is, I don't know. I reach for Bucge. 'Ware,' I shout at the same time. Bucge spins with the speed of an eagle on the hunt, and holds her blade towards Elen's throat, moving backwards towards me, arm fully extended.

Whatever Elen thinks she's doing in threatening Bucge, it comes to nothing.

'Bitch,' Elen spits, while Bucge appraises her angrily over her menacing seax.

'Did you see the enemy?' I demand, although she won't understand my words. Like Bucge, my anger has been stoked. I know some of my allies are dead. Despite my absence when they were attacked, my warriors would have defended themselves, had they known to do so. Aside from a few scratches on her cheeks caused by branches, she shows no injuries.

Elen crows, voice too high, screeching like the eagle I was considering, although I can't understand the words she shrieks. I feel my lips twist in disgust, even as she thrusts the shattered half of the blade she holds towards Bucge. If she somehow managed to land a blow with that, the wound would be terrible. I'm not convinced Bucge would be able to heal herself. That fills me with fear.

'Where's Gildas?' Bucge's suddenly thinking more clearly than me.

Elen screams at the name she recognises. I wince against the sharp sound, even as the horses move, uneasy once more. They thought to have run from the danger, not into it.

'Where is Gildas?' I threaten slowly, stressing Gildas' name, gripping my seax intimidatingly. Elen can't hope to defend herself against the pair of us. What does she believe she can achieve?

She shrieks again, and then mutters one word, 'Gone.'

I shake my head angrily. 'Where?' I retort hotly. I want to get back to my warriors. I want to ensure, aside from Goddæg, the others live.

'Why didn't you give a warning?' Bucge menaces.

Both of us are forgetting Elen can't speak more than one or two words of our tongue, although she perhaps understands more than I previously thought.

'Where's Gildas?' I challenge, temper starting to fray, my arm straining uncomfortably from being held towards her. 'We want him returned to us.' There's no need to tell Elen the enemy are all dead and the danger contained. Let her think of us what she will. My warriors triumphed, all apart from poor Goddæg.

'Mine.' Elen arches an eyebrow. 'Mine,' she hisses, tapping her chest with her free hand.

'He's our friend,' I mutter. 'We rescued him from his captor.'

'Mine,' she shouts once more.

'This is useless. We should have brought Heafoc,' I explode. 'Take us to Gildas, and we'll let you live,' I intimidate, all the same.

'No,' she snarls, turning wild before me. I do nothing but blink, and when next I focus on the spot where she was standing, Elen's gone. I can't hear her fleeing beneath the branches, the roar of the river drowning out all other sound.

'By the gods,' I exclaim, but Bucge's already moving, her gaze unwavering as she crashes through the spindly plants growing so close to the riverbank, and beneath the sheltering embrace of the much taller trees. 'Wait,' I shout after Bucge's receding back.

I reach for my horse. The animal will move more quickly than me. Exhaustion threatens to mould me to the spot, unable and unwilling to move my feet at all.

'Come on,' I encourage my mount when I labour onto his back. The other animals startle. As I direct the horse towards where Bucge disappeared, I'm aware the other four horses follow on behind. I can't make them stop. And, I reason, we might need them when we find Gildas. What has Elen done to him? I feel protective towards the frail old man. Isarninus treated him poorly. Does Elen plan to do the same?

I'm perplexed by what she's done. I thought she wanted our aid to retake her settlement. It seems she believes my *comitatus* too weak to do that. Yet she didn't want to ally with the helmed warrior either, or attack the settlement of yesterday. I don't understand her intentions.

Bending low over my horse's head, I direct him where I hope Bucge's gone. There are pieces of broken-off branch, the shimmering white or green of the split bark providing some means of tracking the pair. Admittedly, it could have been caused by me earlier, or indeed by any animal able to stand tall enough to

pretend to be the shoulder height of a man or a
woman. But it's all the information I have to aid me. I
can't allow Bucge to face Elen alone, and I must find
Gildas. He's the important one. Even without being
able to speak the same tongue, I'm convinced he can
get us to Uriconium and the bladesmith. Once there,
surely someone else will be able to speak his tongue
when we kill Elen? Surely.

15

MEDDI OF THE EORLINGAS

We find the road that will lead to Icknield Street easily and it's in a good state of repair. The three horses move swiftly. Even Tudwal's mount has become used to its rider at long last. I can almost allow my mare to choose its own path rather than directing with heel and reins. Ahead, Kenal's stoically silent, also used to riding once more. Behind me, Tudwal's all mouth agape at finding himself so far away from all he's ever known. I snap my jaw tightly shut to prevent myself from looking as witless as him. I've not been here before either.

'What if she's not gone this way?' Tudwal surprises me by asking as he rides at my side.

'Then I'll have to admit defeat and return to Villa

Eorlingas,' I reply unhappily, having considered my options since our latest failure to find Elen.

'What if she is with this *comitatus* from the east?' he further questions, again astounding me. Perhaps he's not as slow of thought as I've suspected until now.

'We'll act when we know the truth of that,' Kenal announces from ahead. His gaze is fierce as he scours the landscape. The road's dusty, for all the summer isn't far advanced. I cough aside the grey cloud threatening to envelop me from where it's being kicked up by the passage of Kenal's horse and carried on the slight breeze. Some rain would be welcome for the growing crops, although not for the three of us travelling in search of Elen and my father's stolen sword.

'At least we'll see the *comitatus* coming,' I mutter unhappily, eyeing the landscape we travel through, which is flatter than I'm used to seeing.

Kenal's intense visage turns to rake me in. 'It's a blessing of the gods,' he suggests. 'It'll aid us.'

I don't deny that, because he makes a very good point. It will help us if there are others on the road. We'll know about it sooner than we would if there was no dust.

We traded for some fresh supplies within Corinium when we visited there, seeking Elen to no avail, so I know we don't need to speak to any we encounter along the way. But if we don't, then we won't know if Elen has come this way, either. Not that I need worry unduly. We don't meet another person until we come to a confluence of two roads.

The smell of meat cooking forces a rumble from my stomach. I don't miss Tudwal and Kenal lick their lips hungrily as we draw closer to a collection of ramshackle dwellings. Nothing disturbs the deep silence settled over the dwellings. I see where houses once extended all along the joining roadways, north, south, towards the rising sun and the setting, the telltale signs of abandoned walls and collections of hay revealing where animals were once stabled. But now there's only three stray buildings, and none of them look to be connected to the others. There might also be some sort of abandoned shrine to the gods the Romans once worshipped if I interpret the broken-down lump of stone and roofless walls correctly. I've seen such before, in Corinium and Glevum where they're still put to some use. But not to offer prayers to the Roman gods. Instead, they often house chickens.

There are firm wattle fences defining each dwelling. The clucks of hens can be discerned. From somewhere, a sing-song voice can be heard as we draw closer, perhaps from a child or a young woman, but no one comes to see who we are. The noise of the hooves over the stone road attracts the attention of no one.

'We carry on,' I call to Kenal, but even I detect the question in my voice. Everywhere seems quiet, almost too quiet, although I sense no malice here. Perhaps we could barter for cooked meat?

'Yes, we carry on,' Kenal responds quickly, while Tudwal groans. I direct my mare to follow Kenal's path along the road that will take our path towards the north. From nowhere, a small four-legged creature rushes across the road barking ferociously, startling Tudwal's easily upset horse.

'By the gods,' I hear Kenal shout. Tudwal grips tightly to his panicked horse as it gathers its hooves beneath it and surges to a gallop. 'Stay with me,' Kenal commands. I prepare to obey, but become distracted when I realise the small thing is a squat, grey-haired dog, chasing something to the far side of the road with ferocious barks, perhaps a rat or other unwanted vermin. There's nothing to fear here. But Kenal's already gone.

'Awen, come here,' a voice calls. A young woman emerges from behind the wattle fencing of one of the houses. Her hair's intricately plaited down her back, a dress skimming her ankles, held to her body by two bright copper brooches close to her shoulders. 'Oh,' she gasps, frightened eyes taking me in, as she hesitates, unsure whether to follow her dog or not, evidently not having heard the horses.

'I mean you no harm,' I reassure. 'Your dog startled the horse of one of my attendants.'

Relief flashes on her face, even as she looks where we can both see the tail end of the horses surging onwards.

'I better be going,' I suggest, keen to return to my warriors.

'Indeed, seeress,' she disconcerts me by offering, bobbing quickly and lowering her head respectfully. 'It's best you go before the few who live here realise who you are. They'd seek your aid, and I perceive you're in a rush.'

'I...' I start, but realise I don't know what to say to her. I don't want to ask her about the *comitatus*, mainly because if I've divined their intention correctly, they won't have come this way. 'Good day,' I instead state, encouraging my horse onwards.

'And to you, seeress,' she rejoins, before hurrying to collect her yapping dog, who's broken the quiet of the settlement. I hear a male voice shouting, and the woman lifts her voice to reassure it's only her dog.

As I ride away, encouraging my mare to join Kenal

and Tudwal, I turn back to assess the few dwellings. A sudden fear thrums deep within me. If, or rather when, Terricus manages to forge blades once more, a young woman such as her, perhaps living alone, won't be safe. I can't deny, despite my ambitions, the realisation saddens me. Do my ambitions to make the Eorlingas safe threaten those who already live without great fear of being attacked? I've much to consider as I hurry to join my guards.

16

WÆRMUND OF THE GYRWE

With the river to my left, the horses and I continue onwards. I quickly lose all sense of time beneath the trees. It could be full dark above my head, but I don't think it is. The temperature drops, the smell of dankness tickling at my senses, while I try not to scratch and jab at the wounds I can feel prickling all over my body. Even the brush of the leaves over my flesh makes me want to itch.

I worry I'll never find my warriors again, and it'll be me and Bucge, and the horses, and no one else. I can't believe Elen can move so quickly, but then she disappeared between one blink and the next. She, I believe, has some skills akin to those Bucge possesses.

She's not a witch, or a seiðr as I'd know it, but she's something other-worldly.

I consider my dead warrior, Goddæg, and my wounded men and women, and realise if we don't find Elen, and Gildas, we'll be much reduced. I was overly confident when I trounced my brother and defied my father's restrictions against me. That success made me think I could accomplish a great deal. Then we grew wealthy in iron and food, further emboldening me. Subsequently, Isarninus took it all from us, and now I know, as never before, how feeble my hopes for the future are, and how tenuous my grasp on the loyalty of my warriors is. I hunger for better blades to exact vengeance on Isarninus and my father, but I can't do it alone. I need warriors to make me the leader of a *comitatus*. That number declines in every battle I fight. Which concerns me. How can I have vengeance without warriors? How can I become the man I want to be when so much keeps going wrong?

A noise ahead, and I pull my horse to a halt, straining to hear where it came from. Sound moves strangely here. The leaves shush above my head, as though it's windy higher up. I grimace, bat aside a questing branch and turn my mount once more towards the river. I've not truly lost it. It's the only means of knowing which way I travel. I keep it firmly to my left. It'll restore me to my warriors, when Gildas is found.

What I'll do with Elen remains to be seen.

Another shout, and I think it's Bucge's voice. I wish she'd stayed close to me. My progress has been slow. I've been using the horse's legs to move me, but we've not managed speed much above what I could manage had I not had the horse.

'This way,' I decide, diverging from the riverbank and questing beneath the trees, head bent low. I lick my dry lips, cursing the sound of the running water and wishing the riverbanks were shallow enough it would be easy to quench my thirst. But they're not. And then I emerge into a wider space. It's here I find Bucge and Elen.

Thankfully, I see Gildas, off to the side, sheltering beneath a spreading branch, on his knees and praying once more. I'm reassured he seems unhurt. Bucge and Elen circle one another like vixens after the same carcass. It won't end well, although for whom, I'm unsure.

Eyeing the two women, I direct my horse to Gildas. He doesn't seem to notice my arrival.

'Gildas,' I call. His expression shows his great relief as he tries to stand, only to stumble. I dismount quickly, all my hurts making themselves known, and go to his side. He gabbles, but, of course, I don't understand his words. Well, none of them apart from one.

'Witch,' he hisses, eyes fearful, looking to the two women.

Elen menaces Bucge with the two halves of her sword, the hilt half tipped with sharp spikes and the other little better, although Elen's grip is less tight without a hilt to grip. Bucge gives as good as she gets with her single seax. Neither appears eager to engage the other as they circle out of easy reach of one another, but when I look closer, I realise they're both sweating heavily, faces bloodied, arms as well. This fight has been ongoing for some time. I'd expect Bucge to have already overwhelmed Elen, but similar to Gildas, Elen mutters beneath her breath. I consider what her words mean.

'Witch?' I question, just to be sure. Gildas nods fervently, ensuring he keeps close to me, eyes wide with fear. I realise I don't know if he speaks of Elen or Bucge.

'Witch,' he confirms in his soft tone, pointing at Elen.

'Here, get on one of the horses,' I encourage, indicating what I mean, as he won't understand me. While Elen and Bucge menace one another, I actually have what I came for. If Gildas is so fearful of Elen, he won't worry if we leave her behind. But I need Bucge to come with me.

The old man's stick-thin. I almost boost him entirely over the back of the pliant animal that once belonged to Goddæg, head down, nibbling at grasses growing in the lush open space in the clearing. Here there's no need for coppicing and management. Here the trees are seeing it done themselves, almost respectfully staying clear of one another's branches.

A harsh crash, followed by a crack, and I see Elen on the ground, bucking and twisting as though mortally wounded.

'Bucge, leave her, come, I have Gildas, we need to return to the others before it's dark.'

Bucge's eyes flash dangerously as she turns to glower at me. My words of caution come too late, as I'm forced to dash across the open space to intervene in the bloody fight, as Elen takes advantage of Bucge's distraction. I curse myself even as I watch everything unfolding before me.

Elen veers up ominously, jabbing with the jagged edge of the sword, holding the edge of the blade with a hilt and tang. Bucge buckles, a cry of animal rage pouring from her mouth as this part of the blade impales her upper thigh, blood sheeting blackly over her trews.

Bucge staggers. I fear she'll fall but she still seeks revenge for Elen's treachery. Despite the way she wobbles, taking the strain for her wounded leg on the other one, Bucge stabs Elen with her seax, punching with her other hand. Elen, believing she's the victor, hasn't retreated as quickly as she should have done. With the deadly seax wound, Elen drops to the ground, unmoving.

Too late, I reach Bucge, breathing heavily, her hands wrapped tightly around her wounded leg, where she pants over Elen's unmoving body.

'Tie it above the cut,' she gasps, face sheeted in sweat. 'Do it bloody quickly,' she urges me. Suddenly, I'm all fingers and thumbs, ungainly as I hurry to aid her.

I bend to rip the bottom of Elen's dress, where she's lifeless on the ground, a huge swelling red patch growing close to her left side where Bucge landed her deadly blow with the seax. The fabric gives, my arms straining with the effort, and I do as Bucge orders. Her face is turning pale, her breath more frantic. She yelps as I tie the cloth tight, trying to prevent more blood from flowing. I eye the projecting blade and its tang in her leg uneasily, again licking my dry lips.

'Leave it,' she urges me, as my hands flutter close to it. 'Leave it, or I'll die here and now, and I refuse.' Her lips are tinged blue.

'What?' I gasp, and then I realise what she's saying. 'You need fire to seal it,' I huff, a desultory glance towards Elen assuring me the 'witch', as Gildas termed her, is definitely dead. A thudding hoof, and I see Gildas bringing the horses this way, a gloating look on his face at seeing Elen motionless.

'You'll have to mount,' I caution Bucge.

'I know. But keep the blade inside the wound. If it tumbles free, I won't be going anywhere this day alive.'

Hurriedly, I pull my tunic from my back, and use it to secure the visible part of the blade to her flesh, even though she gasps. She's trembling beneath my hands. It's taking her everything to stay upright.

'Horse,' Gildas huffs, offering his advice on how to aid Bucge. He's learning more of my tongue than I have of his.

'Yes. Take my animal. It's wider than yours. You'll be able to keep your leg lifted up more easily.' I may have stumbled and been aghast when Bucge ordered me to apply the cloth above her wound but I'm no fool, despite my father's thoughts about me. All warriors must know how to prevent a wound from killing them. I'm remembering much of what I witnessed before. I know how to help Bucge. We just need to get her somewhere with a fire to seal the terrible injury, and then I have to hope she'll recover.

It will all depend on how deep the cut is and what appalling damage it's done within her upper thigh. I hope she'll walk again, but for now I focus only on what needs to be done.

'Come on,' I urge her, pulling her to the side of the horse and aiding her with a cupped hand to lift the leg that has most movement. It takes four attempts, and she's almost lost all sense by the time she's mounted on the horse, her wounded leg extended to the side. 'Now, where by all the gods are we?' I shout, angry the day which began with my offering to Woden has descended into such chaos. But Gildas leads the horses on, taking an unswerving path across the open expanse and once more through the trees. As he passes the lifeless figure of Elen, he leans over and spits on her cooling corpse.

'Witch,' he states, and then a further gabble of his words erupts from his mouth.

'Witch,' I hiss as well. I think Bucge would say the same, but her eyes roll in her head. I manage to grab her before she slips from the horse. If she falls, I don't think she'll rise again.

Dismounting in a flurry, calling for Gildas to wait, I bind Bucge to the horse, her hands around its neck, her head along its neck. I look to her leg, which now hangs too limply for my liking, but I can't risk securing her any more tightly there. I must hope she stays mounted.

'Come on,' I urge the horses, one of them keeping close to Bucge's far side as though it knows she might fall, while another horse also stays nearby. Ahead, Gildas, who stopped when I called to him, turns and resumes directing the animal onwards. I wish, in my brief glance, I hadn't seen the man's eyes were shut, his hands held before him in supplication, as he must allow his god to guide him out of the woodlands.

I swallow the bile and nausea in my throat, my failures of today threatening to undo me.

I thought to start the day with an offering to Woden, to my ancestor, to the very deity I claim descent from when he walked on this land, and ruled his fellow gods, but he's abandoned me. Or so it feels. Unless, of course, as all good men who worship him must be, he's testing me once more, to see if I'm worthy of being his descendant and of claiming to lead these warriors through him.

I close my eyes, and offer a swift prayer towards him.

'When this is done,' I affirm, 'I'll gift you more than a small blade and a bloody sacrifice. When this is done, I'll gift to you the finest blade, of the best iron, and with the sharpest blade. When this is done,' I barter, hoping, despite everything, Woden isn't above that most basic of transactions.

17

MEDDI OF THE EORLINGAS

I catch Tudwal and Kenal easily enough, Tudwal's horse now subdued, while Kenal berates Tudwal for not keeping better control over the animal.

'It's not his fault,' I murmur, remaining unsettled by my thoughts within the small settlement. 'Come. We can still travel a good distance today,' I hasten the pair. With a pointed look of admonishment, Kenal's quick to turn his mount along the roadway again. Silence falls between us, aside from the regular sound of the horses' hooves over the stone road.

I allow myself to be wide-eyed, watching the landscape as we pass through it. I'm convinced we journey through the remains of more and more settlements, not all of the shapes making sense to me. Few lack good defences. Even fewer seem to be very large, just stray houses or dwellings, some close to the road, and others much further away. There are no villa shapes as I'd recognise of my home and that of the Husmeræ people. There's little to no horse shit on the surface either. This place feels abandoned. That might account for why the road we follow is in such good repair. If no horses travel this way, the stones can't become dislodged beneath hooves, although, I imagine, come the end of the growing season the drainage channels will easily become blocked by weeds and crisp brown leaves, floating free from their summer home.

We sleep that night close to the road. Tudwal's still in trouble with Kenal, despite me cautioning him to leave the lad alone.

'He can't help what happened with the dog,' I chide, and the two fall moodily silent, although Tudwal flashes me a quick look of gratitude. He's growing increasingly confident the more time he spends in my company and the more new experiences he encounters. But Kenal's doing exactly the opposite. His unease sits upon him like black clouds obscuring the moon. 'Sleep tonight,' I order both of them. 'I'll keep guard watch.'

'Seeress...' Kenal opens his mouth to argue but I

shake my head in the light of the leaping flames of the campfire.

'I've much to think about. It's been months since I last spoke with our gods.'

He subsides but it's obvious he's uneasy. Before he rolls in his cloak to sleep, he slips his seax into my hands. 'Better to have two blades than one,' he mutters. I acknowledge him with a dip of my chin. Soon, both men are sleeping. I gaze up into the cloudless sky overhead.

I've not stayed awake all night for some time. I've often found the darkness to be a comfort, rather than something to fear. Alone, with only me and the moon and the stars, my eyes growing accustomed to the shadows and the sight I can achieve when I've spent enough time in the black of night, I allow my thoughts to tumble.

We're far from home, but it doesn't overly concern me. I run my hands through my spangles and bucket pendants, seeing if I can seek my god here. This has long been Marchell's particular skill. No matter how often I've tried, success has always been denied to me. But, I perceive, soon I might be able to achieve the unobtainable.

Eyes wide open, my breathing even, I listen for the sound of the sky, and for the sense I'm not alone here.

I consider Elen, and how much I hate her. I think of my father, and how much I mourn him. I banish an image of Edern when he enters my mind. He's no place there.

I consider my brother, and focus on the future, and all I've ever hoped to achieve. Madog will be the one who makes everything right, but he can only do that when Elen is gone.

Abruptly, my thoughts skitter and divert, myriad ideas coming together, only for one to scatter aside, and another to replace it. My breathing grows quicker, my hands worrying more and more at the spangles I wear around my waist, as overhead clouds twist and turn, the wind growing stronger, and the scent of rain coming to me. My hand seeks out the blade Kenal gave to me, as abruptly I feel I'm no longer alone.

I'm panting, sweat beading my face as I struggle to my knees. It's as though I've summoned Elen here, as well as the spectre of Edern. I peer into the darkness, blind now because the moon and stars are entirely obscured by thick clouds. A pair of glowing yellow eyes appear before me, the low growl flooding my senses.

I gasp, as the huge shape forms. I shake my head, hoping to dislodge the image, but it remains. The knife is in my hand, but I know I'll never be able to beat off the monster before me. The horses nicker unhappily, and not just from the wind and promise of an approaching storm. I swallow against my sudden fear.

A bear. It's rare to see one these days, my father said the Romans once hunted them, but of course, we're far from home. Perhaps we've stumbled into a bear's lair, or we're sleeping where it might spend the night.

Another growl and rumble from deep within its chest. I appreciate any moment now it'll lumber to a run and come against me.

'Kenal,' I call, trying not to open my mouth too wide for fear of startling the animal. 'Kenal,' I whisper again, growing desperate. How can the men not hear the bear? How can they not hear the terrified shrieks of the horses? Why aren't they disturbed by the promise of the approaching storm which makes my skin prickle with unease?

But they aren't. I begin to rise slowly, a blade gripped in both hands, preparing for the bear's attack. Its face is forming before me. No longer just eyes, but a snout as well, saliva dripping from its open mouth.

It watches me. I watch it, barely daring to breathe.

Any moment now, I know it will come for me. It'll think me nothing more than an animal to devour. It has all the advantages of size and strength against me. It sniffs the air, the sound sharp and grating.

And then, from overhead, the loudest crack of thunder I've ever heard rumbles forth, and the bear freezes, terror writ into the quivering lines of its face. It runs from me. Overhead the sky blazes with staggered lightning, and the crash of heavy rain hitting the hard surface.

I look upwards, allowing the forceful rain to thud onto my face. Only then do I take a deep, shuddering breath, refusing to relinquish the hold on my blades.

I might be concerned about a future of strife and war, but with decent blades to hand no bear would ever threaten me. With sharp iron and lethal edges, all would be safe from unwarranted attack, and that's also what I crave.

Slowly, I retreat beneath the sheltering branches of the tree, allowing them to take the force of the rain from my face. I breathe deeply, and calm my shuddering body, while all around me the sky is lit by slashes of white so bright I have to look aside. The rumbling thunder quickly dies away, but the rain and lightning remains for a long time. Through it all, my warriors sleep and the horses grow calmer, but I remain awake long after the storm has moved away, gripping both seaxes, so in the morning, when Kenal wakes he eyes me aghast.

'Mistress,' he speaks softly. 'Mistress, be careful or you'll bleed.' And I realise my hands are gripping the blade and not the hilts. The skin is white, and remains uncut, and that merely reinforces how desperately we need Terricus to succeed in his quest to make better blades.

I don't tell them of the appearance of the bear. I know we won't see it again.

18

WÆRMUND OF THE GYRWE

As darkness begins to fall, our view becomes dulled and then brown, edged with shadows, and the threat of being knocked aside by branches increases. My body aches all over, and I bite my lip, fearing for Bucge, wanting to urge Gildas to hurry – but, of course, we don't share the same tongue. Would he even know what I was so desperate for him to do?

Still, he moves without faltering. I'm astounded when he brings us to another collection of our horses. I hurry to rope them to the four we have, while Gildas waits. He shows no impatience. He does wince to see Bucge so badly wounded. He of-fers to do nothing to help her. I would suspect him of a lack of knowledge to do with healing. But per-

haps it speaks to a great deal of understanding. As
Bucge stated when she was still sensible. We can't
remove the embedded blade, not without having
what we need ready. And what we need is fire and
heat. Something to seal the cut, and hopefully allow
her to live through the violent attack Elen visited
upon her.

I banish thoughts of Elen from my mind, for fear
I'll grow too angry, and want to return to desecrate
her body. I talk myself out of it repeatedly. It's better if
we leave her to be eaten by the animals of the woodland. It's Bucge whom I must think about. Not Elen.
Elen played us for fools. I was so pleased she could
tell us what Gildas was saying I never truly considered she'd abandon us at the first sign of danger, or
indeed visit that trouble upon us.

Just as I'm about to call to Gildas and indicate we
should stop for the night, frustrated when I almost
lose an eye to a sharp, slim branch, we emerge from
beneath the sheltering cover of the trees. I squint into
the bruised sky, where the sun's setting in a welter of
dim colours. I don't know where I am. Once more,
Gildas is the one to direct our steps. I follow, because
I'm unsure about what else to do. And then I see it. A
good distance away, there's a single fire, the flames
leaping merrily, almost enticingly. I hope it's where

my lost warriors are. I hope it's not yet a pyre for God-dæg, but it could be.

Suddenly, I'm grateful Gildas can't talk to me. I'm exhausted, stifling yawn after yawn, threatening to fall from the horse as Bucge did, but there's no one here to tie me to the beast. It's an effort to sit straight, to use my heels to direct the animal where I wish to go.

'Who's that?' a rough voice calls to me when I'm still far distant from the fire. I recognise Osfyth's angry tone.

'It's us – well, it's me and Gildas, and Bucge, she's badly wounded.'

Osfyth emerges from the gloom. I'm unsurprised to find Heafoc beside her. The pair of them are shadowed, but I can still see where they're bruised, and carry cuts and injuries. Heafoc's limping, but holds his spear firmly as though he'll skewer me should I prove to be an enemy. Osfyth's not much better. She also limps, I realise.

'What's the matter with Bucge?' Osfyth demands, rushing to her, while Heafoc questions me as well.

'Where's Elen?'

'Don't,' I shout, as Osfyth reaches out to touch Bucge. 'She has a blade, embedded in her thigh. We can't remove it or move her, until we have heat to seal it.' Osfyth's face turns paler. I hear her swallow heavily. 'She still breathes,' I reassure, for I've checked. 'Elen did it to her, but the witch is dead.' I sense confusion from Heafoc at this abrupt change in the relationship between Bucge and Elen, but Osfyth understands well enough. 'Mount a horse. We'll move more quickly,' I instruct the two. 'Aside from Goddæg, are any others dead?' My urgent question isn't immediately answered, which worries me. It falls to Heafoc to speak once he's mounted.

'We've lost two men, Goddæg and Hygebeorht.'

'Bollocks,' I exclaim, closing my eyes in sorrow, and anger. We're so few now, I can hardly term us a *comitatus*. We left my father's lands with fourteen of us. Two died at that first battle which I didn't believe I'd win, but I did. Wædel was a traitor and I killed him. I still don't know where Cenbryht or Nothelm are. Now I've lost another two warriors. And Bucge's badly wounded. Aside from her, there's me, Heafoc, Osfyth, Eastmund, Bægmund and Maggenræd. Our number is half what it once was.

'Maggenræd's injured too.'

'Bollocks,' I explode. The horses barely move faster than we'd have done, but we're drawing closer to the fires.

I see Eastmund's familiar shadow against the flames of the fire.

'It's me,' I call, so he knows not to attack.

'Where by the gods have you been?' he demands, but already he's moving amongst the horses.

'Don't touch Bucge. Not yet.' I repeat my earlier order. He obeys without questioning me about it. I can hear him greeting his horse with joy.

I slip from my animal, and lead him to the side, away from the fire, where the enemy horse waits. I see two others have also returned from where they ran into the woodlands when the fight started. I definitely have more horses than warriors now.

'You found Gildas, I see. But not Elen?' Maggenræd huffs from where he huddles close to the fire, his red hair seemingly aflame. I see his leg extended before him, and caution myself not to trip over it in my haste at being reunited with my men and women.

'What have you done?' I question instead.

'A long wound, along my calf. Bloody hurts like a bastard,' he complains.

'He lost a lot of blood,' Osfyth clarifies for me. 'He needs to learn to move more quickly,' she adds acerbically.

'Elen's dead. She attacked Bucge. Elen saw the coming attack and warned no one,' I inform the two men who don't know, with resignation, and an uneasy silence fills the space.

Gildas has dismounted and already sits beside the fire. He's found food from somewhere. He eats and drinks happily. I'm reminded of how brave he is. Alone, with only us, and none of us able to communicate effectively using words, only hand gestures and the occasional word we all understand. And us with more blades to hand than men and women to wield them. I don't think I'm as courageous as he is.

'We need to help Bucge. Do we have more wood for the fire? We must get it really hot.'

Eastmund ambles to his feet, and moves far to the side of the flames. I see now there's a pile of wood, but it's not for our fire, but rather to send Goddæg and Hygebeorht to the afterlife as we won't bury them here, far from their homeland. Our Gods wouldn't find them here. Better to send them on their way with fire and heat. I sigh unhappily.

'It's more important to help those who live.' I voice what we're all thinking.

'You need to eat and drink,' Heafoc instructs me, going to aid Eastmund. 'You'll be no good to anyone if you fall over. Over there, by Gildas.' I look where he points and see our water skins, more of them than we now need, as well as a sack from which Gildas is pulling more food. 'The enemy were determined to eat well,' Heafoc mutters. I sense him moving aside. In the glow of yellow flames, I feel entirely exposed.

'Who were the enemy?' I question, aware none of us know that.

'It doesn't matter. They're dead,' Osfyth counters, crouching awkwardly beside the fire with one leg extended, busy with some task I can't quite determine because her back is to me.

'Another enemy to hunt us down,' Maggenræd suggests wearily. I know what he means. We've left a trail of foes behind us. My father, Isarninus and those we killed on the first few days we formed a *comitatus*.

I sigh wearily, as Eastmund and Heafoc feed the flames with their collection of deadfall and broken-off branches they must have gathered from the nearby trees. I don't think they've been busily coppicing in my absence.

The wind rustles my hair, bringing with it the scent of the dead, mouldering on the slaughter field. At least Goddæg and Hygebeorht aren't out there. All the same, the food I eat tastes like ash in my mouth. The water's stale and hardly refreshing at all.

'Is there water for the horses?' I suddenly remember they have needs as well.

'There's a stream, over there.' Maggenræd points

with all the confidence of a man who's not going to be made to stand up and lead the horses over. A hand on my shoulder, I startle, and meet the gaze of Gildas. He points to the horses, and then to where Maggenræd indicates, inclining his head questioningly. I nod, and he walks to the animals, but not the one with Bucge still tied to its back.

'My thanks,' I offer while Osfyth faces me. I see she's placed a collection of seaxes in the flames, allowing them to warm before yet more fuel's added to the fire. The heat makes me itch, the sweat of my exertions already dry on my skin, and now demanding to be wiped clear. I eye where Gildas walks, taking five of the horses with him. I should go as well, but for now I couldn't stand even if my trews were on fire.

'You can communicate with him?' she asks accusingly.

'No. Nothing more than what you saw. Oh, and he named Elen a witch but nothing else.'

Her lips twist in thought. 'But Bucge has some knowledge of the arts of being a seiðr,' Osfyth comments, perplexed.

'Not like Elen. I thought he liked her. It seems not.'

Now the flames are leaping more merrily, already

threatening to burn superheated blue at the heart of the fire, we need to tend to Bucge.

'How do we do this?' I ask of no one.

'Where exactly is the wound?' Osfyth questions. Her words are thrummed with concern. She shows no remorse Elen's dead, surprising me because she's protected her so much until now. I consider if she had suspicions or if the news of what Elen did to Bucge has overshadowed earlier, warmer thoughts.

'Upper thigh,' I answer. 'Close to where she might bleed her last if she were cut there.'

Osfyth grunts. I take it as another sign of her concern. 'We bring the horse as close as possible, and then slide her to the ground, and immediately cauterise the wound,' she informs me. I'm pleased to hear her taking responsibility for this. I should be the one to do it, but my head pounds and it's difficult to think with much clarity. I drink more, scrubbing at the blood on my face, feeling some of it drop away from where it's dried in my beard.

'We need everyone to help, aside from Maggenræd,' I clarify quickly. 'Although, does he need the same treatment?'

'We've already done that to him. The wound was bad but not too deep,' Heafoc reassures, while

Maggenræd listens dispassionately. 'And Osfyth also had her wound sealed.'

'I imagine that hurt.'

'He's not long since regained his senses,' Heafoc retorts quickly, before Maggenræd can brag about how he endured the pain. I offer him a grin.

'Heafoc, you and Wærmund take her weight. Eastmund, you cut the bindings, and move the horse aside.' Osfyth's all cool command, treating her friend and ally like no more than an animal to butcher, only in this regard we need to fix her, not slice the meat from the bones. I wonder if Osfyth knows how to do that.

I stand wearily, and hobble towards where Heafoc waits beside the horse, offering soothing words to the weary animal. My legs and back throb, my arms as well. I fear I'll drop Bucge. She has the build of a warrior. She'll be heavy and I feel feeble.

'Now, we do this quickly and carefully. Don't dislodge the blade, or this'll be for nothing.'

I lick my still dry lips, and reach out towards Bucge. Heafoc's opted for her legs. I get her head and upper body, although Osfyth's also there. I realise she'll help us once we've released Bucge from the animal's back. Even away from the light of the flames, the shadowy black patch down the horse's side assures me Bucge's bled a great deal, even with half of Elen's special sword still in position.

'Now,' Eastmund huffs, standing from beneath the animal, and holding it still, as we lift Bucge free. Osfyth supports the weight of her wounded leg, but even so, I stagger.

Osfyth hisses angrily. 'Be careful,' she urges through tight lips. Sweat once more beads on my face and I grimace, the strain in my shoulders and legs almost too much. Only then it increases as Eastmund moves the weary animal and I have to support all of Bucge's upper body while Osfyth and Heafoc share the lower load between them.

'I can't hold her.' I shudder, staggering closer to the fire. The heat of the fire is like ice on my sweat. I hear the harsh rasp burning through my throat. I'd close my eyes, but it's no help.

'Just a moment longer,' Osfyth urges, and then Eastmund's beside me, bending to support Bucge's upper chest as my legs falter. I think I'll fall but somehow I don't, not until Bucge's laid on the ground, a blanket of cloaks to cushion her. I stagger to my knees, feeling nausea rise in my throat. I can hardly breathe. My arms shake. My legs have no substance to them.

'Well done,' Heafoc murmurs, sounding as spent

as I am. My heart thuds so loudly in my chest, it's all I can hear. But Osfyth's busy. She's either stronger than I thought, or for now the desire to heal her friend drives her onwards.

Maggenræd is up on one of his elbows, watching what we're doing through the dancing flames, as he's to the other side. I'm also curious as to what Osfyth will do. All know of the need to seal wounds with heat to prevent the wound rot, but whether that will be enough for Bucge, I don't know. I consider Woden, and my promise to him. Perhaps, I realise, it should have been more concerned with ensuring Bucge lived. But then, Bucge isn't descended from Woden.

'Heafoc, when I say, remove the blade,' Osfyth orders. I should be doing that, but perhaps Heafoc's a better choice. 'Eastmund, when he pulls the blade away, hold the severed flesh together. Watch your hands, though. I don't want to burn you.'

The sizzle of flesh reaches my nostrils, and I gag and swallow down my nausea.

'Now,' she orders, and Heafoc emits a loud grunt, while Eastmund grips Bucge's severed thigh tightly between his huge hands.

'Careful,' he urges, as Osfyth must get too close to his hands with one of the blades.

A loud thudding sound reaches my ears. I turn,

grappling for my blade at my waist, but then Gildas appears, leading the horses. He watches Osfyth and Eastmund with interest. I notice he carries something in his hands. It looks like some sort of plant, the roots extending past the reach of his hand. I consider what they're for, but he simply places it close to the fire so it won't be trampled.

He wrinkles his nose at the smell of burning flesh but moves forward to get a better view of Bucge's wound. Osfyth's ripped her trews so her entire leg is revealed. Bucge doesn't even stir as the seax is applied to her flesh with Osfyth's hand wrapped in another cloak. Neither does she stir when the action is repeated not once but three times in total before Osfyth's happy. But Bucge still lives. I can hear her breathing, and see her chest rising and falling.

Osfyth's forehead's sheeted in sweat. She licks her lips repeatedly, while examining the wound. It's so long it takes those three seax blades to fully seal all of it.

'She'll have a fine scar when she heals,' Maggenræd offers. I can't help but think he's disappointed his scar is already being rivalled by that Bucge will carry.

'She will,' Heafoc affirms.

I realise none of us dare say 'if', only 'when'.

'I'll stand guard, but I doubt anyone will come to see what happened here, not with all of the enemy dead,' Heafoc grunts, already gathering his spear back to his hand to act as a walking aid. 'All of you, get some bloody sleep. In the morning, Bucge will wake and she's going to howl like a vixen in heat and be a grumpy bitch as well. Prepare yourselves for that.'

Without waiting for me to offer instructions, or argue he needs sleep as much as the rest of us, he disappears into the darkness of night, and I confess, I lie back where I am, too exhausted to move. Sleep claims me, although for a long time I dream of fire and blood, of iron and rust, and Woden's wolf stalks me at every turn, saliva dripping from an open mouth, sharp teeth threatening to savage me.

19

MEDDI OF THE EORLINGAS

I sleep in the saddle during the day, exhausted from my sleepless night. It's as though we've been transported somewhere entirely different after the storm.

The ditches to either side of the stone road rush with water, and the air's sweet smelling, rich with damp plants and the promise of new life. Kenal's astounded by how much it's rained.

'There was a huge storm,' I comment, yawning. 'The sky was lit by lightning, and there was terrible thunder.'

'And yet, we heard nothing of it,' he muses. I nod, thick-headed from last night, eyes itching with exhaustion.

'We could do with somewhere behind walls to

sleep tonight,' I suggest. I've not warned them about the bear. I don't believe the animal will do anything to us now, but its appearance has reminded me there are other creatures out there, in the night, that could attack us. A wolf is much more likely to try and savage us than a bear. Wolves know no restraint.

'We've seen few enough dwellings throughout the day,' Kenal comments. 'We might be able to find walls, but no roof, and I think it'll rain again shortly.'

My cloak remains damp, despite the strength of the wind in the wake of the storm. I've been cold for much of the day after getting so wet during the night. There was no fire for warm food when the men woke, either. The rain had ensured the stone circle was too wet to spend time attempting to coax a flame when I was eager to be on our way.

'Then whatever we can find,' I murmur, not wanting to argue with him, but desiring the promise of walls tonight. I will have to sleep. I can't remain awake for another night.

'Mistress,' he agrees. Tudwal's silent behind me. Both men are quiet today. With every loud clatter of hooves over the stone road, we move further and further away from Villa Eorlingas. It's an unsettling sensation when there are only three of us, and three horses. We'd not be able to put up much defence if we were attacked, whether by person or animal.

Eventually, Kenal pronounces a location where he's happy for us to stop during the night. It's little more than the remains of a building, lifted slightly from the ground, and into which we'll need to climb, leaving the horses on the ground nearby. It reminds me of a grain store, but there's not been any grain within it for a long time. It has half a thatched roof, dripping even now after last night's rain.

'We'll need to stay away from the puddles,' he comments.

Quickly, there's a fire smouldering in the damp remnants that have fallen into the dwelling. The wind outside's really starting to gain in intensity. I sense the horses are unhappy outside. I look to Kenal, and he nods unwillingly.

'It'll be better if we can get them within,' he confirms. He jumps outside, landing heavily. I hear him moving about while Tudwal's tasked with ensuring the fire catches alight. I help him, scurrying below the damp layer of grasses and twigs to find dry pieces of kindling. As flames leap, replacing the grey smoke of previously, I hear a clatter from outside, and glance upwards, startled to be looking up into my cream-coloured horse's face.

Kenal brings the other two animals within as well, and while it's a much tighter fit now, and the horses don't welcome the fire as we do, it means we manage to eat some cooked food, and stay out of the wind. The walls of the dwelling are surprisingly sturdy, although they can't stop the chill breeze tumbling within through the open roof.

As darkness swirls, I glance upwards while checking on my horse, and see the moon's obscured once more.

'It'll be a dark night, and filled with rain,' I mutter. Tudwal grimaces, but Kenal nods.

'At least, here, we can all sleep through the storm, if that's possible.' He seems pleased by this, as he blocks the entrance with a long piece of wattle wall. 'When we douse the flames, no one will think of looking within. No one.' He sounds content with his preparations. I run my hand down my horse's long nose, and bid her goodnight.

I lie down and wrap myself in my still slightly damp cloak. I allow sleep to claim me, and tumble dreamlessly while outside the storm rages. Every so often, I stir at the heavy rain and sound of drumming water, but it's the sound of voices outside that wakes me, as bright watery daylight floods our temporary shelter.

The voices speak a tongue I recognise, and have me turning to shake Kenal and Tudwal awake as well. The conversation sounds far from happy. Indeed, I reach for my blade, fearful that having evaded the bear the night before last, we might now face an enemy more alike to us.

Kenal rouses, and instantly he's alert. Even the horses sense something isn't right, as Tudwal and Kenal stand to either side of our makeshift door.

I swallow, tasting my fear, wishing we'd not stopped here, for the walls prevent me from seeing who's outside. There are evidently more than three people and their horses.

I look to Kenal and Tudwal, ensuring they have all they need to protect us. I also cast a quick glance towards the horses, but it's not possible to mount up and burst through the doorway, not with the steep drop to ground level. We'd break the animals' legs. No. I straighten my shoulders, run my tongue around my dry lips, and only then speak.

20

WÆRMUND OF THE GYRWE

A cry of rage wakes me, heart thumping, eyes squinting against the too-bright sunlight, the crackle of the fire urging me backwards on my elbows, as though it might burn me.

I blink, and blink again, gritty eyelids arguing against my desire to wake.

I look around, fearing we might be under attack, already reaching for my blade, which I've foolishly removed from my weapons belt so I don't roll on it in the night.

Belatedly, I make sense of what's happening before me.

It's Bucge who shouts, not in pain, but fury. Osfyth bends close to her, still awkward with one leg held straight, trying to examine the wound, while Heafoc snores loudly from the far side of the fire. At some point, he and Eastmund have exchanged their roles. I'm grateful Heafoc didn't have to keep watch all night, but am aware it should have been me, not East-mund who thought to replace Heafoc.

'What is it?' I huff, eyes also alighting on Gildas, who once more sits contentedly, eating from the sup-plies our enemy brought to the fight, no concern on his placid face.

'That bitch,' Bucge rages, trying to stand upright, although she can't manage it and Osfyth works to re-strain her.

'Bucge, calm down,' Osfyth instructs, while Maggenræd groans with a thousand hurts. At the sight of him, struggling upright, face white with pain, I realise I'm not much better. Everything throbs, even my little toes where I scrunch them tight in my boots because I've lost the sense in them. I grimace, and groan, collecting my seax and then forcing myself to stand.

I need to check on Bucge and Maggenræd. I must drink, eat, piss and tend to all the horses.

'Where's her body?' Bucge rounds on me, twisting from her seated position. At least she's not trying to stand any more.

'What?' I huff, aware my mouth threatens to drop in surprise at such a request.

'Where is she? I've not finished with her yet.'

My forehead furrows. 'We left her. I couldn't wait to haul her corpse onto a horse. She's dead, Bucge. She's very bloody dead.'

'No,' Bucge rejects. 'We'll go and get her. I'll see her cold body with my own eyes.'

I shake my head, while Osfyth tries to placate Bucge. 'First, we get you well again, and then we'll talk about Elen's corpse,' I glower, aware I need to take command here or Bucge will undo the healing that's begun. I peer closer. Her upper leg is a mass of dark scabbed blood, but pink where the seaxes have sealed the gaping wound with fire and heat. The smell of burning flesh still emanates from her. I gasp at the size of the wound. I knew it was huge but it covers all of Bucge's thigh, almost to the mound of her sex.

'Where's the blade?' Bucge demands. 'I'll see the bloody thing.' I've not given much thought to the weapon that wounded Bucge since Heafoc extracted it from her leg.

'Here.' Osfyth hands it to her. It shimmers with the maroon of Bucge's lifeblood, but it's the terrible nature of the severed sword that makes me appreciate how much danger Bucge's still in. We hoped to find someone to make sharper blades for us, but this old thing, broken in two pieces along a jagged edge, is truly terrible. It offers no neat wound that could heal, but instead the promise of unevenly severed flesh, some elements digging deeper than others.

Bucge handles it with care, running her blood-stained fingers over the haphazard edge of the blade, her eyes narrowed with interest. The blade's a fine one, even in such a state. I consider whether the other half of the weapon is, but it doesn't matter. Bucge could kill anyone with the blade in its current form. At least, I realise, the hilt survives enough she could get a firm grip on it. Perhaps she might even have it replaced, and the jagged tip smoothed to make it more pointed.

The blade's irregularly serrated, the iron tarnished and in need of a good clean, and what remains of it is decorated, the bladesmith working a swirling pattern into it either before or after forging, I'm unsure. I reach for it, to examine it more closely, but Bucge snatches it back, her actions making her wince as her leg moves. I open my mouth to ask to see it, but Gildas is there. He also inspects Bucge's wound, and then offers something to Osfyth.

She nods quickly, eyes brightening at the item

pressed into her hands. I consider if it's the plant Gildas brought here last night, but it's not. It's a long patch of green moss, perhaps also from the stream nearby. In his other hand, he holds something else, yellow in colour and more fluid, the sweet smell making me hungry. Bucge shows more interest now. Of course, she has some knowledge of healing as part of being a seiðr. She licks her lips, which I notice are cracked from thirst, and she smiles. I've no idea where he found this precious pot.

'Thank you,' she says to Gildas, while bracing herself for Osfyth to pour some of the honey onto her leg and then cover it with the moss and a long strip of cloth no doubt taken from one of the dead men. Thoughts of the bodies lying nearby have me striding to my feet. There are two warriors to burn and send to their afterlife. I must do that before they start to corrupt. Already, the smell of the enemy dead is rife in the air, the harsh shrieks of carrion crows and their sharply snapping wings easy to hear in the dawn stillness.

I bend and retrieve a long stick from the edges of the fire, and stride to where the two dead men are laid out over what wood remains from the pyre. I look at their faces, pale and lifeless as the warmth of the day starts to infuse my tight shoulders. I fix Goddæg and

Hygebeorht in my mind, as a means of remembering them. Eastmund joins me, his face mournful as he deposits more wood close to the bodies. Maggenræd can't stand to join us and Osfyth's aiding Bucge.

'They were brave men,' I offer. 'I'll mourn them, and drink to their afterlife, when we have ale with which to do so.' Eastmund nods, and I consider if he thought of either of these men as his friends, or whether they were just allies. I wish I'd known them better than I did.

'They were brave warriors of the *comitatus* of Wærmund,' Eastmund surprises me by stating loudly. 'They'll go before us. We'll join them when we've avenged their deaths, and spend the afterlife recounting tales of our military might.'

I swallow, wishing I could be as eloquent as Eastmund, and then I jab the flaming brand into the wood, moving it towards the clothing of Goddæg, aware it will catch much quicker. I step around the pyre repeating the action, only standing aside when the smell of roasting flesh becomes too much. I swallow against my revulsion, as Goddæg's hair flares brightly, and the skin on his face begins to blacken and burn. And still I stand there, a guard to watch them being consumed by flames. I couldn't save them, which burns as fiercely within me. They were my warriors, and now they lie dead. There'll be no physical way to mark their lives as they've died so far from the place we called our home. Our people will not mourn them. If anything, the men and women of the Gyrwe will delight in knowing the traitors of their people are dead.

Temporarily, grief consumes me rather than self-pity. I watch them, as the flesh bubbles and bursts, as the terrible stink permeates everything. It'll take me days to get it off my flesh, but still, I stand the guard and watch them on their way to the afterlife. I aid Eastmund in collecting more wood to replace that taken to build the flames that have, I hope, saved Bucge's life, when the fire threatens to gutter with half of them still intact. It takes much of the morning, and only eventually do I turn my back on the smouldering fire, the embers so hot I'm sweating.

I return to my warriors, and slump beside the other fire, which is little more than a bed of cinders.

'We need to leave, today,' Heafoc informs me. He's woken from a long sleep. I see his gaze switch towards the funeral pyre, an unreadable expression on his face. 'The enemy will be missed when they don't return.'

I nod, and yawn, and look to my lacerated warriors.

'Can you ride?' I question them.

Bucge nods, although sweat shimmers in her hair. I worry she's already fighting off the wound rot. Maggenræd sighs but grunts his agreement as well. I hold Osfyth's eyes but it's as though she's forgotten she too carries a wound.

'I want to see Elen's body,' Bucge repeats, but I'm shaking my head, fixing her firmly with my gaze.

'She's very bloody dead, Bucge. Believe it. We should eat another meal and leave,' I confirm, although the thought of food when the smell of the funeral pyre is so strong turns my stomach.

'Where are we going?' Osfyth questions, her pensive expression resting on Gildas.

'To Uriconium, as we intended,' I confirm quickly, eyeing Bucge. 'We still need to find the key to such strong weapons. If that old sword, even severed as it is, can do so much damage, then think what a new forged blade could do. And we need good weapons to defeat Isarninus. Only then can we exact our vengeance against him.'

'If we go to Elen's body, we'll find the other half of the blade,' Bucge argues with me.

I shake my head. 'I don't even know where she was killed. It was far from here. We move towards Uriconium. We can't risk people coming to see what happened here. There are few enough of us anyway and now two of you can't fight. No. We leave this place.' I don't feel I need to remind her of my father's vengeance, of Isarninus who might be hunting us down, or of the people's village we ransacked for all their goods. With a growl, she subsides.

'You sure Gildas knows where to take us?' Maggenræd juts his chin towards the holy man, who seems to be doing something with the plant he found last night. I watch as he pulls leaves from it and offers some to us all. I sniff it, and then recognise it's mint. Gildas smiles and places it in his mouth, chewing the plant. It's one way of telling us our breath stinks, I suppose.

'Let us hope he does,' I reply, fatigue weighting me. I can't shake the sense of failure stalking me. There are so few warriors forming my *comitatus* now.

'Will there be others who'll join us?' Heafoc voices my concerns. 'There aren't enough of us to fight off any who might not like us.'

'I really don't know, Heafoc, I really don't. But what other choice do we have? I refuse to return to my father and beg for forgiveness. Let's hope there are warriors within Uriconium who would welcome fighting at our side.'

'Your father wouldn't give his forgiveness,' Bucge

states angrily. 'Not after what we did.' Unconsciously, I rub my hand over my face. Although the purple mark of my birth feels the same as the rest of my skin, I know too well where it is. It's stained me more than anything else since I was born. Wihtlæd's first child, a boy child, and yet an immediate disappointment to him. I grimace. At least, I console myself, Waga, my brother, is dead. A pity I couldn't also murder my father, but my father is a man who can kill with great skill. I didn't possess that then. I might never possess it. He truly walks this earth with his god, Woden, guiding his steps. One day I might be as great a warrior as he was. One day.

'No, we continue to Uriconium,' I confirm, taking the offered piece of stale bread from Osfyth. 'We must hope to find someone else who can help us communicate with Gildas.' The old man bobs his head as I speak, as though he understands what I'm saying, but I know it's just the use of his name that occasions the response.

'And if not?' Maggenræd asks, using the aid of Eastmund to try and stand upright.

'Then, we'll have to take the time to be able to say more than his name to him, won't we?' I retort. I don't have the answers to everything. I wish I did. 'We'll get what we need,' I announce, realising my demeanour is far from reassuring. 'We're the best of my *comitatus*, that's why we live when our allies don't. We might be few in number, but we have much wealth in horses and battle equipment, including the horse the leader rode yesterday and all of his battle gear. When we get to Uriconium, people will want to trade with us for what we have. We'll use that to get what we require. There may even be others who wish to join us, and enlarge our ranks once more. And this time,' and I fix my warriors with a firm gaze, 'we'll have the benefit of being able to pick and choose, as opposed to relying on any brave enough to anger my father and his warriors.'

I force a grin to my lips, and meet the eyes of those I still have with me: Heafoc, Eastmund, Maggenræd, Bægmund, Osfyth, Gildas and Bucge.

'We might be small in number, but we're mighty in our intent,' I reassure, mindful my voice wavers, but none of them comments. I'm grateful to them for that.

21

21

MEDDI OF THE EORLINGAS

'Who are you?' I shout.

'Who are you?' a grizzling voice demands. 'If you're the bastards that left our men dead, then I assure you, you'll be next.'

I furrow my forehead at the words, while Kenal shifts his stance to try and get a good look outside.

'We've killed no one,' I reply. 'We sought shelter from last night's storm, nothing else.'

There's a buzz of conversation from outside. I'm trying to decide how many people I can hear, but then Kenal holds up both of his hands, fingers splayed. I appreciate he can see ten people from where he peers through the wattle screening.

'Then who are you?' the same voice questions.

'I asked first,' I counter, wishing there were more than three of us.

'We're from the Tomsæte, a tribe who live beside the River Tame. I'm Sennicus,' I'm told, after a hurried conversation. A prickle of recollection stirs in my mind. I'm sure I've heard of them. They're a tribe from the east of ours. Not neighbours. They're too distant from our villa to be called that.

'Open the door,' I instruct Kenal, and gathering my seeress' spangles into my hand, I peer through the doorway. A figure startles at my appearance, but I can see the collection of men and women have no blades drawn. 'Well met,' I call. 'I'm Meddi. Seeress of the Eorlingas.'

'Then you're a long way from home,' a figure announces, walking around the only person I can see, to reveal a tall man, with long hair, worn loose, and littered with talismans clacking in the gentle breeze.

'As are you,' I counter, stepping down onto the ground with the aid of Tudwal. Kenal jumps to stand at my side.

'We are, yes. We seek murderers of our warriors, to the north of here. But, I can see that's not you, seeress.' The man's respectful as he bows towards me. I really look at them now. They're evidently not warriors, because they lack fine blades and shields, but menace thrums through them.

'Where were your people killed?' I question, alert to the possibility the fight will lead us to the rumoured *comitatus*.

'North of here, where this road joins with Watling Street. An ally called upon them for aid against an enemy who stole all their supplies and left their warriors for dead. They were a poor tribe, but allies all the same. They're left with little but three oldsters and young children to keep them safe now. However, whoever this enemy was, they overwhelmed our warriors, so now we're in as poor a position as our allies.'

'Who was the enemy?'

'That, we don't know. But we'll find out. They had horses, but lost some of their own men in the battle.'

Tudwal's leading the horses from their night's lodging. I sense the interest of these people who lack mounts to hurry their steps. But I also don't think we're in danger. All the same, I run my hands through my spangles, drawing attention to them so they'll know to be fearful of the powers of a seeress.

'We've travelled this road from the south and seen no one,' I inform Sennicus and the rest of the Tomsæte. 'Wherever your enemy are, they've not come this way, I assure you.'

For a moment, I consider if they might reject my words, but Sennicus nods unwillingly, evidently unhappy. 'We fear they've travelled west. We don't wish to go that way, even to seek vengeance for those they killed, and to reclaim our lost weapons and fine horse. There are too few of us. And that way leads to the lands of the Wreocensætan, who are a warlike breed. Alas, our leader has always been too keen to prove himself against enemies he hoped to overwhelm. He's fallen far short once more.' The stance of the Tomsæte shifts slightly at the admission. I consider if they all think the same. Certainly, no one complains at the stark summary.

'How many enemy dead were left behind?' I question quickly, because I'd certainly welcome knowing if Elen has been killed by these people.

'A funeral pyre was lit. Perhaps two or three of them. We'll need to return to dispose of our dead. We thought it more important to find those who did this to them.'

'What will you do now?' I ask.

'We'll return to our depleted allies, and inform them we're unable to find those who attacked them. I'll suggest they come with us. There's safety in larger numbers. Along the way home, we'll return to the site of the slaughter field to honour our dead. You should come with us. There's nothing to be gained from travelling alone, just the three of you, not if there's an enemy war band nearby.'

I grimace. These people have no horses. I wish to cover more distance before turning home. Our time to find Elen is growing short. 'I thank you for your offer, but we've somewhere to be, and little time to reach it.'

'Then, Meddi of the Eorlingas and her warrior protectors, we wish you well. Should you come upon the enemy, take your horses and gallop away. You'll find protection amongst my people, if all else fails. Simply follow Icknield Street east, and you'll find them. Tell them my name and you'll be welcomed, if you arrive before we do.'

I incline my head towards him, grateful for his offer, despite my rejection of it. 'I wish you well,' I murmur, and the ten men and women nod, anger once more written into the lines of their faces. 'Now, we'll leave you and resume our journey.' And with that, we mount and are quickly on our way. I encourage my horse to ride quickly until those on foot are out of sight, and then slow the horses.

I look to Kenal and Tudwal.

'This sounds like the work of the *comitatus*. Let us

hurry to find them, and then we'll know if Elen is with them, or not.'

22

WÆRMUND OF THE GYRWE

Uriconium

Our arrival to Uriconium goes unnoticed, or rather, no one stops us. Perhaps, I realise with a grimace, they can tell we're no threat. Bucge's unwell. Her wound, even with the aid of the cauterising, honey and moss, has turned red and angry. She sweats constantly, and is often incoherent. Twice during the night stops, I've woken to find her gone, wandering away from us, hobbling on her leg, although we've ordered her not to stand on it more than necessary. In the end, our guards were there more to ensure Bucge didn't walk away from us than to ensure we weren't attacked by another enemy seeking vengeance against us. It's fortunate no one has trailed us here. We aren't able to do more than protect Bucge from herself.

Maggenræd's fared much better with his wounds gained when we were attacked by the arrogant warrior. He's almost back to fighting fitness in the days it's taken to reach Uriconium. Osfyth no longer limps either. The journey has been slow and laboured, bedevilled by the extra horses we need to keep under our control after the death of two of our men, and the white horse we gained as a reward for the loss of those two men. And by Bucge's wound.

I would sigh with relief as Gildas points onwards, a smile transforming his face as grey smoke billows into the sky from a large collection of hearth fires. I hold my hand above my eyes, keen to stop the sunlight blinding me. I sense we're being watched but not from those within the stone buildings lining the roadway we're following towards a gateway cut into a stone wall consisting more of sporadic pieces than a concerted whole. I look upwards, and discern one of the nearby hills seems to be populated, another hill fort, similar to that Isarninus lived within. There's no other explanation for why smoke billows from amongst the oak and beech trees hugging the hilltop.

I sense unease prickle along my spine. Abruptly, I realise I know nothing about where we're going and what we might encounter. I look at my fellow warriors. We're such a small group. There are only eight of us, including Gildas. But Gildas rides confidently, his lips even lifting in a grin as he mumbles in his strange tongue. I've become more used to it but I still can't decipher the meaning of many words. However, he's been taking the time to understand more of our speech. We can now, I hope, speak competently about food, and directions. Not for the first time, I appreciate Gildas has made a great deal of effort to communicate with us. Much more than he ever did when he was held captive by Isarninus.

'Be wary,' I urge my warriors – well, aside from Bucge. She's managing to ride, but the familiar gait has deserted her. She'd be better in a cart not on horseback. Osfyth growls angrily at my warning. Her temper has worn thin. I've tried to intervene as much as possible in caring for Bucge but Osfyth won't allow us to perform some of the more intimate tasks required. I've cursed her, but she's been belligerent. Perhaps, then, it's her own damn fault if she's exhausted and fractious.

'What now?' Heafoc questions from ahead, where he keeps Gildas company.

'We see what our guide does.' I swallow, uneasy about all of this. No matter that Gildas seems happy, I fear we're riding into a trap, and one of our own devising. But we need food for the horses. We need somewhere Bucge can rest. These tumbled-down walls offer some semblance of protection. Provided those living within don't turn on us, and we've not been beaten here by my father's warriors or those of Isarninus.

There's no one guarding the entranceway. The horses continue right through, the occasional loud *thunk* ringing out as they walk over cobbles and stones. I try and absorb as much as possible, but Gildas moves with unerring speed along the road running through the settlement. I smell food cooking, and even hear singing from close by. A collection of dogs and cats watches us ride past from their places in gutters and on rooftops bowing low to the ground. I consider if the place is overrun with mice to have so many damn cats. They're bloody fat cats as well.

'Where is everyone?' Eastmund asks uneasily. Clothing dries on collapsing walls and it's evident people live here. Where they are, I don't know.

And then we have our answer. Gildas leads us onwards and suddenly we're enclosed inside a sort of structure with four imposing walls, and in which we seem to be disturbing some sort of gathering.

'A market,' Osfyth quickly surmises. There are many people milling around, and the shouts of sellers peddling their wares are easily heard, even if I don't understand the words being used. I narrow my eyes. These people don't speak as Gildas does.

'Do they speak the tongue "she" spoke?' I ask Heafoc. He nods immediately. I sigh. My assumptions are incorrect. I thought these people would converse as Gildas does, but they don't. As I'm reconciling myself to this, our arrival's abruptly noticed by all. I imagine it's the collection of horses marking us as different. No one else is mounted as they move from market stall to market stall, a gabble of voices busy bartering for their goods.

Ahead, Gildas quickly dismounts, and hands his reins to Eastmund. Eastmund takes them without thought. I watch with mounting horror as Gildas slips through the crowd watching us and disappears, no matter that I shout his name.

'Follow him,' I urge Eastmund, but the crush of the crowd makes it impossible. He's dismounted but now can't make it through the press. They present an immovable force, unless we want to start a fight. And here, where the men and women are evidently not warriors, they still have knives to hand. They might lack all battle skill, but they vastly outnumber us, and I'm wary of warriors descending from the hill fort. Any moment now, I expect to hear the shout of warriors coming to stop us. Perhaps it's simply taken them some time to ride from their eyrie to counter us.

'Now what?' Heafoc questions angrily.

'Come back,' I urge Eastmund. I feel my lips twisting in thought. As I'm still mounted, I can peer over the heads of those surrounding us, but I can't see Gildas at all, even with his bald pate, so out of place here.

'Wærmund,' Maggenræd calls. I turn and narrow my eyes. A collection of three people approaches the horses. Their gaze is appraising, and not at all violent. They come closer, reaching out to greet the animals which have no riders, speaking excitedly to one another, especially at the sight of the white horse. I grimace.

'They might think to trade,' I offer weakly, having no idea how to communicate with them. They don't speak the same tongue as Gildas.

'I can understand them,' Heafoc mutters, and quickly dismounts. 'Find Gildas,' he orders me heatedly. 'That's why we're here.' I turn to look where I'm sure Gildas has gone. I can see something standing proud on the near horizon. I think it's a building. Has he gone towards that?

'Here.' I turn to offer Bægmund my horse's reins. He nods quickly. 'Heafoc, do what you can,' I urge him, wishing I'd given more thought to this. But then, how could I have ordered Gildas to stay with us when we don't share the same tongue? I don't know his word for 'stay'.

'What is this?' Osfyth questions me, unease in her voice.

'A market.' I repeat her earlier words, surprised she questions it. We have markets in my father's kingdoms. Traders from across the sea, and from neighbouring tribes. Even those who simply travel long distances by land, bartering and trading between the different peoples.

'No, this.' And although it's hard in the press of people, who show no fear at having us walk amongst them, Osfyth lifts her hands to indicate our surroundings. The walls that once encircled this place might not be fully standing any more, but within there are many stone buildings, rising high, with red-tiled roofs glinting beneath the sun, or yellow thatch. But it all seems calm and orderly.

'This must be where the Romans lived,' I suggest. 'This must be what a city looks like when it's not been abandoned.' I stumble over the unfamiliar word for city. We've nothing like this where I lived all of my life until killing my brother and leaving the territory of the Gyrwe. It makes my skin itch to be enclosed like this.

'It's not like where Isarninus kept us captive,' she mutters. 'Or what we escaped through to evade him.' Osfyth's eyes are everywhere, but no one does more than pass an appraising glance at us now, as we try to forge a pass through the swell, with the cries of bartering, barking of dogs and shrieks of small children. If anything, they're more annoyed we knock them from where they're perusing what goods are available to purchase. There's even the shouts of someone standing on a raised piece of stonework. Whatever his intentions, the crowd are largely ignoring him. I consider what the man's doing, and then narrow my eyes as he lifts his arms upwards, in a way very reminiscent of Gildas. Perhaps, then, he's a man of Gildas' faith, although his clothing is very different. The fact the crowd pays no heed confuses me. Does Gildas not share a faith with all those here? Perhaps not, as he speaks a different tongue.

And then a strange sound bellows through the place. My hand's on my seax before I can stop myself, Osfyth doing the same. It's a hollow noise that vibrates through my feet and up my neck, making me scrunch my shoulders with unease.

'What's that?' Osfyth asks urgently. I shake my head. Again, no one else seems concerned by it.

'Whatever it is, these people are used to it,' I surmise quickly, removing my hand from my seax handle, after I've surveyed those present.

'Does it mean there's an enemy nearby? I can't think why else they'd have something everyone could hear.'

'Seemingly not,' I mutter. 'No one shows any concern.' And finally, we push our way through the crowd and emerge in front of a building with tall pillars of white stone holding a tiled roof aloft. There's also a walkway beneath the roof, but to the outside of the walls of the building. I'm confused why there's a walkway under the roof, that runs around the building but isn't blocked off by a wall. I narrow my eyes. Again, in all the places I've visited since last summer, I've never seen anything like this. I swallow my unease, the strange sound ringing out periodically.

'What is that?' I demand, but of course, Osfyth doesn't know.

I stand, unwilling to risk walking beneath the roof supported by the rounded stone pillars. Admittedly, this roof has perhaps stood for many hundreds of winters, if it was raised by the Romans, but I'm not sure I want to risk it collapsing on my head by walking within.

From inside, I hear the hum of people talking in an incomprehensible tongue. I believe the deep, booming noise is also coming from nearby. I look to Osfyth. She looks to me. I turn, slightly, gazing back to where I've left my few remaining men and Bucge, to the horses, to all I've ever known. And then I stand proud, chin jutted out, and force myself beneath the red tiles and into whatever is within the building. All the same, my chest feels tight, my lips narrowed so I feel as though I'm not getting enough air. It's too reminiscent of being within Isarninus' prison for my liking.

Within, it's darker than I expected, and a hand on my shoulder has me reaching for my seax again, before I recognise the voice gabbling to me.

Gildas grins broadly, showing me a mouthful of uneven teeth, as he talks even though he knows I won't understand a word he's saying. He pulls me onwards. I turn to make sure Osfyth's following me through the room. Now my eyes have adjusted, I can tell it's not that dark inside. The walls are white, allowing the few candles to lighten a larger space than I might expect. There are several men and women in there, some watching us, but mostly they seem to be arguing, arms raised, voices high so they echo beneath the roof, causing me to wince at the sharp tones from some of the women.

I see two men, dressed similar to Gildas, although their robes are much cleaner, but then I'm outside once more. Here, there are more of the stone pillars, holding up the red-tiled roof, and there's a strange object in the middle of this open space, with shapes on it. They're formed of the same stone as the building's pillars, I think, because they don't move as I'd expect them to. I sniff and smell water, and consider why they have a pond here with a naked image of a woman depicted in stone. I shake my head, entirely perplexed. Gildas urges me onwards. His feet flap against the tiled floor, his stick-thin ankles visible as he moves hurriedly, the long material hitching along his calves. I don't know where he's taking me, but I've little choice other than to follow.

The toll of the loud sound floods the space. I feel it as a dull throb through my body. Gildas forces his way through another door, this one much smaller, and into a room seemingly deserted. Here, he pushes me down onto a wooden stool, a smile on his lips. He holds up his hands to me, palms flattened, perhaps indicating I should be quiet. I look to Osfyth, who stands in the doorway. There's no stool for her.

A shuffling noise and I startle, turning to face a figure emerging from a shadowed corner of the room I thought was empty.

The face that greets me is covered by a thin piece of material, so I can't truly see many of the features. I consider if they're old or young, male or female, and then I have my answer.

'Welcome,' the voice states softly, in words I can understand, 'to Uriconium. Wærmund, Osfyth, we would thank you for returning our lost brother, Gildas, to us.' The woman speaks without hesitation, not even stumbling over our names. There's an edge to the words, making it clear our tongue isn't her usual way of communicating. 'He's been missing for many, many winters. He tells me you aided him in escaping from his captivity. We thought him dead, along with his brethren. It's a miracle he's returned to us. The bell rings to welcome him home.'

'Bell?' I question, realising it shouldn't be my first question, but it is.

'The noise you hear. We ring it to welcome home our lost brother, Gildas.'

'That's the noise?' Osfyth asks. The figure nods her head slowly.

'What's your name? You know ours.'

'I'm Iamcilla, a holy woman.'

'Like Gildas is a holy man?'

'Yes. We pray to our God. I imagine you have many such gods?'

'I'm descended from Woden,' I say proudly, unsure why I share this with her as one of the first things I speak. My words don't unduly concern her.

She's also talking to Gildas. I imagine she's sharing what we say with him.

'There's much you and Gildas wish to speak about. I'm here to aid you. I can't always be with you. I have other duties, but I'm not alone in being able to speak your tongue. I'll find you someone else to keep you company while you remain within Uriconium.'

'That would be most welcome. But one of my men can speak the language of those outside.'

'Then that's good. But for what you wish to know, I think you'll need my aid as well. Gildas informs me you wish to find the service of a bladesmith. Or at least, you did. He tells me there was a woman with you, a witch, Elen, who wished to have a blade repaired.' She speaks the word 'witch' with surprising vehemence.

I nod again, trying not to reveal my frustration

Gildas has spoken so freely with Iamcilla. I should have realised he'd do so.

'She's dead,' I announce firmly. 'She tricked us, I believe. But still, we'd welcome the services of a bladesmith, as well as the opportunity to trade. We've good horses, and once we have what we want, we'll seek vengeance against Isarninus for all he did to us, and to Gildas, of course.'

'Yes, I understand you have good horses. Taken from another enemy.' I'm not sure if there's a hint of reproach in her voice. 'We live peacefully here. There's little need for blades and warriors as there are to the east of here, where I suspect you're from, but I know of settlements where you'd be welcomed. And so, I'll not refuse you access to the bladesmith. But his price is very high. All the horses in all the world might not be enough to recompense him for what you want. And know Gildas seeks no vengeance against Isarninus. And neither do we.'

My lips twist at this, as she repeats this to Gildas. He nods quickly, in agreement to her, but I can't deny the desire for revenge against Isarninus remains a prime motive for us.

'But he kept him captive for many winters? In terrible conditions.' I question, eyeing Gildas as I speak.

'That may be,' she murmurs, 'but Gildas says it's

made him a better man, more staunch in his faith. As such, he seeks no vengeance.'

I consider that. I think of my father, and others who've betrayed me, including some of my fellow warriors. Isarninus has my brother's sword. I must reclaim it. I must have my revenge against him, even if Gildas doesn't desire it.

'This land isn't peaceful, and we require good blades to defend ourselves,' I restate my intentions.

'Perhaps not, but it's more peaceful than it has been for many summers. Here, within Uriconium, we're safe and well protected by those living atop the hill which overlooks us. We've built a place of worship, where we can continue the work of spreading the word of our Lord God.'

'And so you don't seek to employ the bladesmith to make weapons for you?'

'Not members of this holy community, no. We've no use for such deadly weapons. But we protect the bladesmith. His skills are important to preserve. He does much more than forge blades. If we don't safeguard him, and provide him with a space to forge his nails and other items, his skills will be entirely lost. And too much has already been lost. We seek to preserve him, as we do our faith against the religions of others, such as yourselves. Not that we have an issue with your gods. They're simply not our God.' Her tone's even as she speaks. I feel I should trust her, even though I've only just met her. 'And, we have no argument with you, or where you come from, far east of here. However, we also have little or no contact with the new tribes who've settled there.'

For a moment, I'm uncertain. Is this a threat or a mild rebuke? I don't know of this place. I can't imagine my father does either. Is she telling me we're safe here? Before I can ask more questions she continues speaking.

'Now, return to your people outside. Bring them here. I'll have someone show you where to stable the horses. Don't be too hasty to sell the animals on. There are those who'd welcome a fresh bloodline for their breeding stock. There are few able to breed good horses these days. There was once a tribe, south of here, but alas, they have, I'm assured, fallen on difficult times, riven by internal strife.' As she speaks, a young woman enters the room – well, more a girl on the cusp of womanhood. She inclines her head towards Iamcilla, and speaks quickly to her in Gildas' tongue. Whatever passes between the two, the girl looks uneasy and eyes me aghast, eyes frightened. She wears no cloth over her head. I can see her features easily. She's slim, and surprises me by having blond hair. I've learned, travelling through this island, it's rare for others aside from my own people to have blond hair. Unconsciously, I run my hand over my marked face, aware, despite the beard and moustache, it remains visible. 'This is Diseta. She can also speak your tongue and will help you. I trust you'll keep her safe, as you have women amongst your number.'

'We will,' Osfyth offers, challenging me to deny her words. I don't state aloud I hope she's less treacherous than Elen.

Another gabble of words, and Diseta focuses only on Osfyth. 'Come,' she says softly, and then repeats the word more staunchly. 'I'll show you where to keep the horses.' Her tone is smooth, and show no hesitation. I consider how she can speak my tongue so well, but offer her a small smile instead. 'We need to hurry,' she continues, when I make no effort to move. 'Or there'll be a crush within the marketplace.'

Osfyth goes to follow the girl, but I turn to Iamcilla. 'What of Gildas?'

'Don't worry for Gildas. He's home, where he should be. We'll care for him and tend to his wounds, and get him clean. In the meantime, go with Diseta. She'll show you what you need to see, and there'll be lodgings for you as well. Oh, and I understand you need the aid of a healer. Gildas has told us of the woman who's wounded. I'll send for our best healer. He'll know what to do and we'll pray to our God for her to be restored to health.' I'm not sure Bucge would like that, but I incline my head, and follow Osfyth from the room, aware Gildas speak excitedly to Iamcilla in my absence.

It appears I've much to be thankful to Gildas for. If only I could speak those words myself.

23

MEDDI OF THE EORLINGAS

The smell's the first thing I notice. I wrinkle my nose and try not to gag, while Tudwal's forced to bend and expel the contents of his stomach noisily onto the ground. I'm not far behind him and Kenal's just as pained. I share a conspiratorial look with him, both of us determined not to do what Tudwal's done, although it'll be hard.

'This is it then,' I say quickly, hoping I don't need to get too close to the remains of the warriors who fought here. The sharp snap of birds taking to the air rings loudly. My lips twist. I can see the carrion creatures have been busy at their tasks. All the juicy bits, I notice, are already gone. Great gobbets of decaying flesh are visible beneath the clothing these men once wore but nothing else.

'I can see why the people of the Tomsæte were unhappy about losing all of their warriors,' Kenal comments sourly. We've left the horses behind us. They don't need to be unsettled by the unmistakable stink.

'Indeed. I perceive why they seek vengeance, but perhaps they should have buried the dead first.' These men have been left with almost nothing. Whatever blades, shields or horses they once had have long since disappeared.

'How long?' I question.

'Seven days,' Kenal replies. I see him bending low to gaze at the bloodstained tunic of one of the corpses. He rears backwards, no doubt at the collection of pale maggots infecting the skin.

While Kenal just stops himself from backing onto another of the carcasses, Tudwal continues to heave up everything he's ever eaten, if the sound he's making is anything to go by.

'She's not here,' I conclude quickly, surveying the dead bodies, my hand raised to stop the bright sunlight from blinding me. I shouldn't have expected Elen to be here, and yet, I confess, I suspected the only way she could have avoided us and every other tribe we've visited while seeking her, is by her joining with the *comitatus*. I've brought Tudwal and Kenal far from home on a foolish whim I hoped would explain how she managed to disappear so completely when she was a lone woman – alone aside from the horse she stole from the Stoppingas.

I realise I shouldn't have pursued Elen here. This trek has gone on for too long. No doubt my brother worries about where I am. And yet I feel rage driving me on to find Elen and the two pieces of my father's stolen sword.

'No, she's not,' Kenal unwillingly admits, having carried out his own assessment of the dead. I know he feels it too. But my eyes alight on something else. To the side of the slaughter field is a long and thick stretch of trees, their boughs hanging low to the ground, but what catches my attention is the two very evident paths someone, or something, has forged through the trees. Not just opposite where the fight took place, but lower down as well, to the far side of the stream gurgling away as though this was a bright and sunny day and there weren't a pile of mouldering bodies to foul the air.

My curiosity piques, and despite my words to the contrary, I can't give up on my quest to find Elen. Not yet.

'I want to go through there,' I announce. Kenal looks to where I point, his eyes narrowing as he also shades his eyes from the glare of the sun.

'We take the horses,' he agrees. I'm pleased Kenal doesn't waste precious time arguing with me. 'We'll get Tudwal away from all this.' With his other hand, he indicates the corruption of the bodies.

Mounted once more, but directing my horse around the area where the most bodies lie, I take her towards the obvious remnants of a fire. Or rather two fires. I dismount once more, sifting my hands through the ashes of the larger fire, which I convince myself still maintains some heat. It might have been seven days since the fight, but it's not been seven days since this fire was blazing. I reach into the ash and pull forth what's undoubtedly the remnants of a small bone that's escaped the heat of the flames, somehow – a finger bone, I suspect. Some of the enemy died here. They've been burned and, it seems, their ash allowed to scatter on the breeze. Was this honourable? It wouldn't be amongst my people. I bite my lip.

Kenal examines the other fire. 'They bled a great deal.' His eyes appraise the ground when I turn to look at him, and I see a deep red stain, even now, clearly visible where windblown ash has partly covered it.

'So it wasn't an easy victory. Warriors died on both sides, and some were wounded. Whether they live or not remains to be seen. Come, we'll go through the trees. I suspect we might find the survivors beneath them, taking the time to recover from what befell them.' Again, I sense Elen must be close, if she's with these people. Increasingly, I convince myself she must be here.

Mounting again with half an eye to poor Tudwal, who looks wretched and almost as pale as these corpses would have done before the animals ate what they could, I take my horse towards the furthest collection of broken branches. Quickly, we pass from the light into darkness. I feel my fingers reaching towards my dagger but I don't grip it. Beneath the trees, the busy activity of birds and animals floods my senses, the smell rich and dank. If there are people here, the animals and birds don't fear them, and neither will I, even though I've seen what they can do with their blades, and suspect I should be worried. How many of them were there? How many still live?

Bending low over my horse's head, I encourage her onwards. The path is easy to detect if you know where to look. There are snapped-off branches and churned leaf litter from hooves that have slipped or kicked roots sticking out of the ground. I also hear the

thrum of rushing water. I understand why the survivors came this way. My eyes are focused on where
I'm convinced I see the shimmer of water through the
trees, but Tudwal, now he's away from the decaying
corpses, is alert, making use of his young eyes to see
much more than me.

'Mistress,' he calls, having dismounted and taken
himself to something shining on the ground in a rare
break in the thick trees.

'What is it?' I shout, foot twitching on my horse's
side, keen to be on the way.

'You should see this,' he calls. There's something
about the way he speaks that has a shiver running
down my spine. Even the spangles around my waist
click together softly, and there's a residual warmth
around my torque that feels as though it might burn.

Kenal looks from me to where Tudwal squats on
the ground, and then reaches for his dagger. I dismount quickly, lifting my skirt above the dew-covered
grass. Beneath the trees, it's unlikely to ever have the
opportunity to dry fully, even in the pleasant,
warm day.

'What is it?' I question, but then I see it. I swallow
down my rising unease, gripping my dagger hilt, as I
peer into the deep undergrowth surrounding us. The
birds still sing merrily. There's the distant scampering

of hooves or paws over the spongy ground beneath the trees. There's no one else here but us, or so everything tells me. Yet I remain suspicious.

It's evident there was a fight here. The ground's disturbed. A deep maroon coats a specific area where the grasses lie compacted, shimmering not with the see-through quantities of water, but with something else, madder-red. Blood.

'Is this...?' he asks, eyes focused on something on the ground. I watch where I step, not concerned by the bloody remains, but not wanting to wear it either, and then a half-strangled cry rips from my mouth at what Tudwal's found and I almost rode straight past.

I reach out, and then retract my hand again, bending at my knees to really look at it. I've held it too much, and lived with it for so much of my life, or rather, the memory of it, that I'd know it anywhere.

'It's the shattered point of my father's sword,' I whisper reverentially, eyes already scanning the surrounding area for the other half of the lost blade, the end with the tang. If I can't find Elen, then having the two pieces of the sword returned to me will suffice. At least that way Terricus can repair the blade, and it can be restored to Madog's son. It will be a symbol of the Eorlingas. It won't be possible for any to use it against us. 'Where's the other half?' I demand urgently, aware

Kenal continues to hold his blade in hand, but he's also searching the ground. I see now I'm looking properly, and not distracted by the noise of the nearby river, there are hoof marks here, made before we came this way. There's also lots of flattened grass and the compressed outlines of previously made footprints. 'Who died here?' I question, not expecting an answer. Kenal's bent over, walking towards where the river thrums, following a trail in the grass.

'Someone pulled themselves towards the water,' he announces confidently. 'I can see where they left hand imprints, and a trail of blood.'

'Who was it?' I demand, again reaching for my dagger, and not yet touching the half of my father's blade. I can't tell whether it's been used to kill, or whether it's merely slipped from Elen's possession as she perhaps fought for her life. I'd like to think she died here. Why else would she have abandoned the blade? But perhaps I'm not that lucky. 'The other half isn't here,' I decide unhappily. I've looked everywhere, and Tudwal's scouting the banked grasses where the trees once more take prominence. 'It's just half of it,' I muse, returning to my horse to find a cloth to gather the severed spine of my father's sword to me. I don't want to touch it with my hands. Not yet. I'll need to cleanse it of Elen's foulness, even if I only have this half. I'll purify it with fire and herbs when I return to Villa Eorlingas. Marchell will aid me and be pleased to do so. She too will hope her daughter is dead, as I do.

'It could be through here,' Kenal proclaims eagerly. He's standing upright to peer through the trees. 'We should go this way.'

I nod, carefully placing the blade into the saddlebags on the horse's back. I remain uneasy, but I realise it must be because of what happened here. I've been drawn to this location. I'll offer thanks to my gods when I return home. They've ensured this happened.

'Tudwal,' I call.

He seems absorbed in something else. 'Mistress.' He stands quickly, a guilty look on his face.

My eyes narrow. 'What have you found now?' I stride towards him. He moves aside. I peer to where he points, and realise immediately why he looked so guilty.

There, lying on the ground, is an object of old bronze, the sides pitted and far from smooth, even the marks of its casting in heat and flames smoothed away at the join by its age.

'This belonged to Elen,' I assert confidently, noting the irregular shapes of the thin bracelet she once wore around her slim wrist. I thought all traces of her wealth and position had been taken from her when she was incarcerated, but evidently not. 'Pick it up,' I instruct Tudwal. Like the broken sword, I don't wish to touch it with my bare hands.

'Mistress?' he quails. I'm not surprised.

'Pick it up with this.' I hold out a strip of cloth I'd forgotten I was holding. 'And then add it to the horse's saddlebags.' He seems happier to do this, and I watch him carefully handling the bracelet that once marked Elen as Edern's wife. Together, we walk towards the horses, my thoughts a riot of confusion, trying to make sense of what we've found.

'Mistress,' Kenal calls, his voice unusually filled with fear. I hurry to join him where he's disappeared under the hanging boughs of the many trees. Beneath them, all is darkness once more. A premonition of what I'll discover ripples along my spine. I'm almost smiling with anticipation of finding Elen's body, cold and marbled, but the grin leaves my face before it can truly take hold.

Beneath the boughs of the trees is no body, but remnants of bloodstained clothes, as though someone ripped fabric from their tunic to staunch the blood. There's the sure sign someone dragged themselves this way, handprints outlined in the mud.

'Follow them,' I urge Kenal. 'No.' I change my

mind just as quickly. 'We'll all follow them. If she's here, I want to find her. We can take her body back to Villa Eorlingas and assure everyone her interfering is at an end.' It would bring me great delight to have Elen's body. I know it would also reassure Marchell her daughter was truly dead.

Kenal nods, and we make our way back to Tudwal. He already waits with the horses.

'This way,' I direct him, reaching for my horse's bridle. The animal's grown placid. I consider if the smell of blood has gone away or if now she knows there's no dead body, she's dismissed the worry.

Bending low, and pulling my horse's head to the same height as mine, we follow Kenal. He leads with unerring ability, never faltering, as the sound of the river grows to a roar and he emerges from the treeline. Only then does he turn to me, confusion on his face. He's risked peering over the steep bank of the river, and I know what he's going to say long before the words leave his mouth. 'She's simply gone. There are no other prints.'

I growl angrily. I thought this was to be all over, but it's not. However, I have half of my father's sword. That, at least, after all this time, is some progress in my quest to find Elen and bring her meddling to an end.

24

WÆRMUND OF THE GYRWE

Diseta might be slight, and little more than a child, but she knows her way around the settlement, and what words to shout to force people aside from our path.

I'm aware of curious gazes on us, now Diseta accompanies us, although I'm unsure why that's more exceptional than our appearance here. Perhaps these people often trade with *comitatus* but don't often see those of Gildas' faith walking with them? I really don't know.

Osfyth's silent at my side. I sense the tension boiling from her. She's not comfortable here. I can't say I am.

Quickly, we return to the horses and the rest of my

warriors. Eastmund watches our approach through narrowed eyes. Heafoc's doing his best to communicate with those interested in bartering for the horses. Eastmund's making little effort to assist.

'This is Diseta,' I inform them quickly. 'She's to help us because she speaks our language. Gildas has arranged it.'

'Come this way,' Diseta instructs, and then speaks heatedly in the language of the men and women who are too interested in our horse stock. I almost grin to see Heafoc's narrowed eyes as he tries to keep up with her rapid speech. Then to us she states, 'I've told them to seek you out tomorrow, when you're more settled. The horses as well. Watch that man there. His name's Clynog and he strikes a hard bargain and then sells the horses for much more. I can make sure you get the best prices for the animals. Agree to nothing without me being present.' I open my mouth to comment, but Heafoc chuckles at the slight girl telling us what to do.

'I'm Heafoc,' he offers, when the traders have finally moved away now we have Diseta to speak for us in more fluid tones than Heafoc has evidently mustered. 'I'm pleased to meet you.'

Diseta runs her warm blue eyes over the warrior's face without fear. 'Come,' she repeats, rather than replying to him. She directs us back much of the way we've come through the settlement. The roadway remains strangely quiet for a short while. Then I hear the familiar lowing of cattle and the aggrieved baaing of sheep trapped within. 'This is the market for animals,' Diseta assures, turning to face us. 'Here, there are stables for your horses.' Ahead, I see more of the decaying wall surrounding the settlement, and I'm pleased to find the sharp smell of animal piss and crap fading with the gentle breeze. 'If you'd entered through this gate, you'd have found the stables first,' she suggests, with the faintest trace of a smile on her lips. 'But, of course, Gildas was keen to reach the forum and his brethren, and so led you through the northern gates. It makes sense to me.' Her words flow naturally. I consider if she's one of my people by birth, after all, Iamcilla knows of my kind. Is she perhaps, I consider, a slave to the holy men and women? If she is, her clothing's good quality and she moves with surety. Maybe she's no slave after all.

A woman with knowing eyes watches us approach a collection of wooden shacks, her hands on the pouch hanging from the belt around her ample waist. She speaks very quickly, and I startle, because this is yet another tongue I don't know.

'This is Gwladus of the Wreocensætan. She's also

one of those who'll protect us from any possible attack. When not here she's to be found within the hill
fort above our heads. She owns these stables, and will
allow you to use them. You'll have to barter for your
animal feed, but that can be discussed when you're
more at home here, within Uriconium.'

I nod, and meet the gaze of the woman. She's
older than Bucge and Osfyth, and her wide waist assures me she's used to living comfortably, even if
Diseta claims she's a warrior. As she assesses the
horses, she startles, and then nods, coming forward to
meet my animal, and offering what sound like nonsense platitudes to it. I dismount, and walk to
greet her.

'I'll introduce you to Gwladus,' Diseta offers, and
then speaks in this other tongue as well. I sense
Heafoc's scrutiny. This then is something he doesn't
know. I consider how many different languages can
be spoken on this island. Evidently far more than I
ever thought possible. 'Wærmund,' Diseta says, and
holds out her hands to indicate I should greet the
other woman. But I don't understand what she's
asking of me. With a soft huff, Diseta grips my
forearm with her light fingers, while Gwladus holds
out her hand. She clasps my unwilling one, and only

as her grip tightens do I realise what I'm expected to do.

I return her grip firmly, but not as firmly as I could, and she nods.

'I'll stay with you and ensure the horses are settled, and then I'll take you to your lodgings,' Diseta explains.

'What? We're not to stay with the horses?'

'No. This is a stables. The animals will be quite safe here. Gwladus works for the good of Uriconium. She'll ensure no one touches your horses, and they'll be well cared for, while you're prepared to meet Iamcilla and Gildas again. There's to be a feast of thanksgiving for returning Gildas to his people.'

Gwladus releases her hold on my hand. 'Gildas?' she questions Diseta, although there's a harsh crack to the way she speaks his name. Diseta must hurry to clarify Gildas has come home. Gwladus looks at my warriors and I with a nod of appreciation.

'She's pleased you've aided Gildas. He's been much missed. She thought him dead,' Diseta explains.

I'd like to know more about Gildas and why everyone knows his name, but now isn't the time. At a shout from Gwladus, three younger men tumble from within the wooden buildings, and then come to a stop on seeing us. I sense their scrutiny as they see my pur-ple-marked face in the bright daylight, but it's evident Gwladus is in control here. Her orders are quickly spoken. The three youths hurry towards the horses, hands outstretched to take control of them. I keep hold of my mount, and so do the others. Gwladus huffs softly, and once more speaks to Diseta.

'They can be trusted. I assure you. Gildas would say the same, and you've helped him home. He's most grateful to you and wouldn't wish you to be inconve-nienced now,' Diseta says with a smile on her face.

Bucge's the first to dismount, with a huff of pain that has Gwladus walking towards her. Another flurry of words from Gwladus, and Diseta speaks.

'She's the one who's wounded?'

'Yes,' I reply. 'Iamcilla said there was someone who could help her.' I don't miss that I stumble over Iamcilla's name. The sounds are so harsh.

'Ah, yes, of course. She means the surgeon. He's been summoned for when we return to Iamcilla. Now, leave your horses. We can see to your comfort.'

With a confidence I'm not sure I'm feeling, I turn to my warriors. 'Come. We're welcome here. Let's not repay that kindness with our customary wariness. These people are grateful to us for restoring Gildas to them.' I don't deny the words almost pain me. We're so used to being unwelcome, and outsiders. I hope our ready acceptance here won't result in a similar situation as with Isarninus.

Osfyth's the next to dismount, and slowly we're all standing beside Diseta, allowing our horses to be led away. I wish I'd thought to bury my treasures, but it's too late to consider that. I grip the sack containing them tightly. Diseta and Gwladus watch us. I'm sure humour continues to play on Diseta's lips. I consider how often they must welcome strangers amongst them. Certainly, it seems to be more often than in the lands of the Gyrwe, where my father rules.

'Aid me with Bucge,' Osfyth calls, recalling me to Bucge's difficulties if she doesn't have a horse to transport her. Perhaps I should have ensured Bucge was delivered to Iamcilla and this surgeon first. But Bucge shrugs aside my aid.

'I can walk on my own,' she growls, which we all know isn't true, but I bite my tongue. I don't want to reveal any more of the possible divisions running through my small band of warriors.

'This way.' Diseta strides ahead. I fix Gwladus with a look. She inclines her head towards me, which I take to be a sign she's conciliatory. I hope that's what it means. She calls something to Diseta. The other woman shakes her head, a smile on her thin lips. It seems the two know each other well. Does Diseta act as a go-between often for those not sharing Gwladus language? I wish I knew more, but I don't want to reveal my underlying unease by asking too many questions.

Quickly, we retrace our steps to the market, Bucge hobbling along, while Maggenræd limps. Thankfully, Osfyth no longer limps. We hardly look like a mighty warrior band, while I clutch my sack, my two warriors limp, and the rest are dust-stained and sporting their own bruises and cuts. Before we cross the roadway dividing the settlement, Diseta strides down another street. I wrinkle my nose, unsure what I can smell. It's hot, but damp. I shake my head.

'Here.' Diseta steps aside, and indicates where she means with a sweep of her hand over her body. 'You'll be able to get washed and there are clean clothes being brought for you.'

'What?' I question, totally perplexed by what she's saying.

'This is a bathhouse. Within, you'll be cleaned, and your hair cut and nails trimmed. It's not what it once was, but our visitors enjoy it. I know Gildas will appreciate it. I imagine he's already within. Come. I'll show you.'

I look from Bucge to Heafoc, to Eastmund and Osfyth, and then shrug.

'How bad can it be?' I question.

'Bad,' Eastmund mutters, but in no time at all I appreciate why we've been brought here. Our clothes are taken from us, even the women's, although we're all provided with something to cover our cocks and mounds. Unwillingly, I relinquish my hold on my sack of treasures, but watch them placed within a small space on the wall, with a wooden door to keep it secure. Then Diseta, staying fully clothed, leads us into another room. Here, it's hot and steamy. I startle at the feeling of warmth under my naked feet.

'The floor's heated, as is the water,' Diseta reassures. She's accompanied by three other people, faces red with heat, appraising us and pointing towards a wide expanse of water, from which steam rises.

'In there?'

'Yes, slowly. Use the steps,' Diseta offers. We all stand there, none of us prepared to be the first. Frustrated, I take a deep breath, and lower myself into the water. The heat's immediately pleasant, even though I can feel the water running over cuts and bruises I've forgotten about. I can understand why there are others in the water, eyeing us with no surprise, and indeed not even halting their conversations.

I lower myself up to my chin, and then sneeze. Diseta giggles softly, but Heafoc's already moving to join me, dropping his covering at the last possible moment. There are men and women within the warm water. Not a huge number of them, but then it's the middle of a market day. I imagine many are bartering for goods, while a few are taking advantage of the quiet here.

'It's quite pleasant,' I assure my warriors.

Osfyth aids Bucge to lower herself into the water and joins her, while we all avert our eyes, although I see the angry red mark of her healing wound. Then there's only Maggenræd, Eastmund and Bægmund who aren't submerged.

'Honestly, it's nice,' Osfyth reassures, her surprise clear to hear, and then we're all up to our necks in it. The three attendants collect our coverings, and move to the side. One of them beckons for me to go to the side of the pool. I go warily, especially when I see a knife in his hands, but he mimes his intentions and so I follow his instructions, provided by Diseta, and soon have a shaved face and a lot less hair on my head. Heafoc's undergoing the same, as is Eastmund. In no time at all, we're all bathed and have had our hair cut.

'Now, let them trim your nails, and you can get dressed. You'll have to leave the water for that,' Diseta suggests. I see her wince away from me, and appreciate that with my beard and haircut, the vibrant mark of the gods on my face is much more clearly visible.

Once more, I lead my warriors, allowing myself to be sat down on a wooden bench so my nails can be clipped and then, squeezing my toes together, I relish the feeling of not having toenails imbedded in my skin. I'm taken away, to be dried and dressed in clean clothes. They're not mine, I notice with surprise. The colours are far too bright for my liking. I consider arguing about it, but realise my clothes probably stink. Soon I look similar to the others I've seen within the settlement.

'You can wait here,' Diseta informs me, showing me to another seated area, beneath a tiled roof, and which has benches against the wall. I settle and find myself watching the activity around me. When we walked through the gateway, I thought this place was largely deserted, but it's not. Perhaps just the side of the settlement we initially entered through is less densely settled. I allow my eyes to rise, and rest on the puffs of smoke from the nearby hillside, where Gwladus usually lives, according to Diseta. With my hand above my eyes, shielding them from the bright sunlight, I see there are what look to be ditches and embankments. I consider the settlement I'm within. It has walls made of stone, not turf, and the means to keep feet warm when they walk over tiled floorings, but even here that's not enough to safeguard these people. If it was, they'd have no need for warriors to guard them, offering the protection of the difficult-to-attack hill fort above our heads. I imagine from there the enemy could be seen approaching from a long way away. They must have known of our arrival for perhaps days. That's why I felt as though we were being watched.

It's something to consider carefully. I can't imagine they have need of more warriors, or a *comitatus* to fight on their behalf. Indeed, they seem to have settled on an arrangement allowing people to live within the old walls, but with the promise of somewhere to run to for shelter, should it be needed, from the hill fort.

Quickly, the rest of my warriors join me. Our belongings are restored to us, including my lumpy sack of treasures, as well as our weapons, if not our clothes.

I smile to see my men so clean-shaven, and the women with neatly trimmed hair. Their faces are flushed with heat.

'Not bad,' Bucge offers, wincing as she sits with her wounded leg extended before her.

'Not bad at all,' Osfyth confirms, yawning widely. And then Gildas is before us, grinning broadly, clothed in a new tunic and trews. He looks unrecognisable with his clean face and bright clothing. He smiles with delight.

'Food,' he suggests, hand rubbing his belly. Once more, our fate is entirely in the hands of someone else, as we follow him back through the rapidly clearing market to where I met Iamcilla. The day's so advanced, I expect the market is finished for the day.

'I could get used to this,' Eastmund suggests, as he straightens his weapons belt so his new tunic hangs more comfortably.

'Well, don't,' I caution. 'Don't forget our true purpose is to find a bladesmith so we can seek vengeance against Isarninus and protect ourselves from my father's warriors.' But I must admit, I could probably get used to this as well. Perhaps being a warrior and leader of a *comitatus* isn't my true path, after all. Maybe I no longer need to consider revenge against those who've deceived us, or my father. Here, so far from where I began our journey, I feel as though I've travelled to a strange new land, where nothing is similar to anything I've ever known, and it's certainly somewhere my father would never think to seek me.

25

MEDDI OF THE EORLINGAS

We retrace our steps and emerge once more from the woodlands. The view greeting me is little changed. I'm conflicted about what to do next.

I intended for us to return to Villa Eorlingas to ensure we didn't overextend our month-long journey. It seems evident to me Elen has been badly wounded in whatever fight occurred beneath the trees. Why else would the severed half of my father's sword have been abandoned? But where she is now, if she still lives, which I suspect she does, and where the other half of the sword is, I simply don't know. I need to see her to know she's dead. Or alive.

I'm aware Kenal shares my unease. He and Tudwal were to escort me and protect me, but we're far from home. I can't imagine Madog ever thought I'd travel such a vast distance.

'What now?' Tudwal questions me as we squint in the dazzling bright daylight now we're free from the tree cover. I don't immediately reply. I've been considering it but I'm not yet sure.

'First, back to the road but avoiding the decaying bodies,' I order, mindful Tudwal needs to not spend the next few moments vomiting noisily. Luckily, the wind's blowing the stink away from us. For now.

'And then what?' Kenal persists, directing his horse close to the treeline, but not beneath it.

'I'm considering that,' I announce without heat.

'We should return home, so as not to anger Madog with our prolonged absence,' he suggests, but before I can reply angrily, he contradicts himself. 'We should continue to hunt for her.'

'Isn't she dead?' Tudwal questions, being careful to shield his eyes from the ruined bodies.

'There was no body,' I complain. 'We can't be sure she's not survived.'

'But there was so much blood, and her bracelet was there, and the sword tip.'

'The blood wasn't necessarily hers,' I mutter unhappily. If I knew she was dead, I'd have no problem with returning to Villa Eorlingas. But, understanding only too well what's possible even when she's so badly wounded, I'm unconvinced. No doubt, she meant to encourage the warriors who've triumphed here to attack Villa Eorlingas. What she'll do now, I don't know. I don't know if she's wounded, if she's dead, or if she's simply hiding from us.

'It can't be many days travel to the Wreocensætan the Tomsæte spoke about,' Kenal admits grudgingly. 'Might that be where the *comitatus* are going? They could have the other half of your father's sword?'

I consider this. I know my brother will be growing frantic with worry at our lengthy absence. But whether that's enough to have us turning for home, I'm uncertain.

'We'll continue north for a little while longer,' I eventually decide. The thought of returning to Villa Eorlingas without knowing Elen's fate is unpalatable. 'It's to be hoped we find her body, and if not, the other half of the sword.' But even as I say it, I know it's impossible. Wherever she is, and if she lives, she'll have the sword piece I desire, or, if she's dead, she'll have cast it into the raging river as some sort of offering to the gods before she breathed her last. I'd do the same.

'Mistress,' Kenal acquiesces, no hint of argument in his voice. Even Tudwal seems firmly resolved to what I propose. I'm the only who's apprehensive with the decision. We've travelled a long way from home. We're going to be gone for longer than the month Madog allowed us. Soon, we'll enter an area so far from Villa Eorlingas and her neighbouring tribes I fear the customs and possibly the tongue spoken will be entirely different. If we continue on this path, I'm unsure who else we'll meet, but know it could become increasingly complicated for the three of us. These people may have no respect for a seeress, worshipping different gods. I don't wish to place myself in any greater danger. But the pull of finding Elen and the other half of the sword is strong.

'Another day, no more. If she's not found, we'll return to Villa Eorlingas. I'll not risk encountering those of the brutal Wreocensætan, the Tomsæte feared.' So resolved, we continue on the stone-built road, and yet, with every step my horse takes, I suspect we're travelling further from Elen not closer. I curb my frustration. Two more days. And then we'll return to Villa Eorlingas. Madog won't be dissatisfied with me, but I will be, and I'll have to live with the disappointment.

* * *

Of course, we see no sight of Elen throughout the day and the one that follows. At midday, with a line of hills coming ever closer to the west, I call Tudwal and Kenal to a halt.

'There's nothing. We return,' I instruct them. The pair have been riding with spears to hand, unease growing as we move through this familiar but un-known landscape. We've seen few people, preferring to either not approach nearby settlements or being roundly rebuffed by those we have encountered when the road ran through villages. Then we were greeted by nothing but closed doors and wooden shutters, even the animals hidden away from us. I was almost pleased those who felt so threatened feared only the three of us. Certainly, having called out for news of a wounded woman, or a *comitatus* who didn't speak our tongue, I stopped asking.

Now we'll do the same but in reverse.

'Mistress,' Kenal confirms, again dipping his head low as he turns his horse around, kicking up a small cloud of dust. I feel a prickle down my spine, as though we're being watched, but we're nowhere near a settlement. Unless someone's staring down at us from one of the hilltops, there's no one to witness as we give up our quest and turn for home.

At the beginning of our search, Kenal looked for

splashes of maroon on the dark surface of the road, but quickly I told him not to do so. It was impossible to tell what was horse piss and what was something else. Not even encountering the river I'm convinced travelled through the woodlands offered any clues as to Elen's location. Certainly, there was no handily discarded body on the river's meandering curves or washed up on the riverbank and suspended in the water by weeds and green plants, as food for the fish.

Our returning pace is faster. Before nightfall, we make our way back to the slaughter field, and discover that in our absence the Tomsæte have lit fires and the bodies now burn. The air's scented with crisping flesh, but it's better than what was here before.

'We'll seek somewhere else to stop during the night,' Kenal urges me and Tudwal. I nod in agreement.

Only when it's fully dark and the stars glitter in the night sky does Kenal decide on a location for us. It's not one we used on the way north.

'We'll be safe beneath the tree,' Kenal assures me confidently. 'It's dark, but the moon's bright. I can see there are no beasts who live here. Or people.'

Wearily, I dismount, as does Tudwal. We remove

the horses' bits, but using the reins keep them close to us, loosely tied to one of the branches.

'We've some bread left, but it's hard. And also some cheese.' It's too late to be considering a fire, and beneath the tree we'd risk it spreading. 'Tomorrow, we'll find hot food,' I offer as a reassurance, but I believe my guards are too tired to truly care what they eat. I take pity on them. 'I'll keep a watch for some of the night.' As exhausted as I am, I know I'll not sleep straight away, my thoughts too consumed with my failure. I may as well put my wakefulness to good use.

'Mistress,' Kenal tries to argue.

'Rest, get some sleep. I have my dagger. I'll wake you if I hear anything.'

He subsides unwillingly. I wait until the horses, as well as the two men, are asleep before emerging into the dark night once more. The wind's grown stronger. A chill breeze has me shivering, but I don't return to the protection offered by the branches of the tree.

Instead, and carefully, I carry the severed blade once belonging to my father to an open area, halfway between the road and where my warriors sleep. The blade's still covered by the cloth I first used, but rather than cleaning it of Elen's blood, or what I take to be Elen's blood, I've decided on another purpose.

I sit cross-legged on the ground, careful not to sit

on some animal leavings, and then close my eyes. The sound of the leaves soughing in the breeze quickly fills my hearing, as I breathe slowly, deeply, looking for the connection with the landscape around me I usually feel.

I realise my thoughts are disordered and so it takes some time to accomplish the serenity I'm searching for. I must banish all thoughts of the disappointment I feel, and of the frustration. I must stop blaming myself for failures I perceive are mine. I have to focus only on the blade I hold in my hand and the tangible connection it gives me to my father, and Elen.

I sense every part of my body as I slow my breathing, relax my shoulders, and allow myself to sink into the substance of the ground surrounding me. This is as it should be. I'm connected to it, and I welcome it within me.

All sounds fade, and yet I feel no fear we'll be attacked while I'm inattentive. Rather, I perceive I'll be given a warning. Perhaps my horse will nicker, or an owl will hoot. Until then, I think only of what I hope to accomplish. I must find some peace within myself.

The mystery of where Elen is can't be allowed to bedevil me, as Edern did while he lived. I'll not live another twenty summers consumed by worries she'll appear before me, or berating myself for losing half of my father's sword. Perhaps, when I return to Villa Eorlingas, Terricus will have managed to produce iron of a good quality so we don't even need the symbol of my father's sword. Instead, the part of the sword we do have could be returned to my father. He could forever rest with it.

My breathing deepens further. My thoughts skittering. Elen remains a problem for me. I've hated her for so much of my life, I realise, as I sort through the tangled skeins of my feelings, I need do more than accept I'll never know what happened to her. I must make my peace with everything she's done to Marchell. And to me. For Elen is much more than the woman who replaced me when Edern cast me aside for failing to birth a son for him. She's much more than Marchell's daughter. She is, and always has been, my sister, just as Marchell's my mother. But Elen always lacked loyalty to the Eorlingas and our shared father. Madog is her half-brother, as he is mine, and that's why he baulked at killing her. He believed no kin should kill kin.

I'll have to forgive him, and her, and that might prove the most difficult thing I've ever had to do.

I sense tears sheeting down my face as I recall my shock when I discovered, when I was sensible once more after my terrible wounds had begun to heal, how Elen had betrayed me.

It was Hedrek who brought the news to us, where I lay in Marchell's hovel, the screams of young Madog, always a hungry child and denied his mother through her death at his birth, ringing loudly through the small enclosure, reminding me of all I'd lost so recently.

'Mistress,' Hedrek had spoken to my mother outside. I'd not wished to be seen. I'd not wanted others to see the terrible scars I could feel inflicted on my face. Or to know of the more personal ones between my legs. 'I hope she's well?' Perhaps I should have been pleased he worried about me. Perhaps. After all, he'd long been an ally of my father. He'd known me for more of my life than even I could remember.

I'd not been able to hear Marchell's response, turning aside to allow the tears that fell from my eyes and stung the healing wounds on my cheeks, to fall onto the soft fur beneath my head. All around was the smell of Marchell's healing herbs and the clatter of her talismanic spangles at her waist. It had, despite everything, made me feel safe.

'I bring terrible news,' Hedrek had stated, perhaps reassured of my health. Perhaps not. Again, I'd not heard Marchell's response. I think now she didn't wish me to hear. She'd spent so much time trying to heal me, to assure me I'd be restored to myself one day, she'd not wanted me to learn of her worries. I realise now they must have been great.

Edern had forced me to his bed only the year before. He'd killed my father, and stolen me away from my people. He'd made me open my legs for him and he'd filled me with his seed. And when that seed produced only a girl child, his anger had been terrible to behold. I'd held my daughter, weeping to see her so tiny, so perfect, after two days of constant pain and blood. I'd smiled, perhaps for the first time since my father's death, to behold such beauty.

She'd been ripped from me, nameless, her head collapsed between his huge hands, and Edern had taken his dagger to my tender places, no one able to stop him. No one even trying.

Bloodied, bruised, weak, but still living, I'd taken myself to my workshop with the shattered remains of my beautiful baby, and interred her within, while others thought I was weeping in my room, perhaps dying slowly from my bloody wounds. My belly had hurt, my breasts had ached, and under the cover of darkness I'd swaddled my daughter, as I'd never been allowed to do in life, and buried her within the only space I'd been allowed as mine since Edern took Villa Eorlingas. My mother's workshop.

Then, as the sounds of snoring had filled the air, I'd crawled from that place. No thought for where I'd go, only the need to escape. My hands had bled, my feet as well, and I'd been aware of night-time denizens sniffing my trail and following me, sensing I'd die soon, and they'd be able to devour my flesh. I'd welcomed the thought, too dry to cry, desperate to drink, head spinning. But that hadn't happened.

Instead, at some point, I'd collapsed, and been found by Hedrek and his hunters. I had no memory of what happened next. I'd woken to find Marchell hovering over me.

She'd smiled softly.

'Welcome, daughter,' she'd offered.

I'd wept to see her.

'Elen has united with Edern, to ensure his claim to the villa remains strong.' I'd wanted to howl with grief, in pain, in horror at what she'd allowed to happen.

'It was willingly done,' Hedrek had confirmed. My sister had seen the ruin I'd been turned into, and still, she'd taken herself to Edern's side. Her ambitions had always exceeded her abilities, but she'd one thing that

Edern wanted. Well, two things. Her beauty and her place as our father's child.

As the tears drip down my cheeks, the one still pitted and scarred from Edern's terrible retribution for failing to birth a son, I feel my breathing hitch. It's too much to come to terms with in one moment. In twenty summers, I've never been able to reconcile myself to it. How, then, can I do so now?

A gentle touch on my cheek. I feel my eyes open unbidden. I don't shriek in horror, or even in shock. Somehow, I expected this to happen.

There's something before me, not quite a shape, not quite a person, but something all the same. I squint in the gloom, my cheeks tight with shed tears, and peer at what's come to me. It wouldn't be my father. He was lost to me because of the nature of his burial. Instead, I sense something else, and then there's a soft lick on my hand. I smile broadly, tugging my cheeks tight and, for once, not wincing at the unfamiliar action.

'Horse,' I whisper. The shape before me remains indistinct. However, I know the sensation of a horse's tongue on my hand. I've known many in my time. The animal, of course, can say nothing, but eyes wiser than time appraise me for a long time, as my breathing slows so much it's almost as though I don't need to breathe air to live. I feel grounded to the earth surrounding me. 'Hello,' I speak, the sound coarse after my outpouring of sorrow and grief. The animal's squat, the face too bulbous, the legs almost stubby, but as I squint, trying to allow it to coalesce in front of me, I know a moment of recognition. I know this animal.

There's a jangle of something distinctly metal from close to the horse, or rather, the representation of a horse, for this is no true animal. It couldn't be, with such grotesque limbs and head. The rattle of metal draws my eye, and something else appears before me. Somehow, I've dropped the slither of sword remaining to me, and now, next to it, rests something else. Old eyes watch me, as though they've seen everything this world has to offer and nothing can surprise or shock them. The head swishes from side to side, from side to side, between my father's broken sword and the small object I was examining on the day my brother told me of Edern's death. It feels like a lifetime ago.

I gaze at them, sensing there's some connection here, something that will make everything whole once more. I feel my eyes narrow, my tongue poking through my lips in concentration. This then is something else. It's the answer to all I've been fearing. It's the way to make my father's sword whole, to make sharpened blades, and to finally banish the spectre of Elen forever.

Again, the rounded nose sways from side to side, a pointed reference to the two objects beneath it. I wish the animal could speak and explain what it's trying to show me. Only then a fresh image forms in my mind. I don't know where it comes from but my mouth drops open in an 'O' of shock, as I reach forward, weight on my knees to gather the broken blade to my hand, although the other object seems to dissipate because it is vaporous, not real at all. But I nod. I know what it is. And I understand what needs to happen.

My tears dry, my anger towards Elen disappears, at least for now.

It's time to go home and stop searching for her, because I understand what will aid Terricus, and what will make my brother, and his precious son, invincible in the coming summers and winters.

I know, somehow, the secret to make the iron blades to protect Villa Eorlingas and ensure no one can ever steal her away again.

A voice calling my name breaks through my reverie. I turn, startled to find Kenal watching me, his face filled with concern, for daylight has arrived between one blink and the next, all trace of my visitor gone in a swirl of early morning mist.

'Is all well, mistress?' Kenal questions, his words soft as though he knows not to startle me.

'It is, Kenal, yes. Now, we must hurry home. I've information for Terricus, and I've missed my people. Wherever Elen is, she's no concern of ours any more. We must think only of the future, and not the past.'

A small smile plays on his bearded face, and he nods, his eyes showing the wisdom of his summers on this earth.

'Then we've accomplished a great thing,' he suggests, aiding me to stand upright after a night, cross-legged on the ground. My feet are numb, my legs are tight with the unfamiliar position. I welcome his support as I stagger to stand.

'We'll eat and make haste,' I inform him, even as Tudwal stumbles free from the tree, confusion on his face to have slept so late. I incline my head towards him, offering him a rare smile, minded my face doesn't hurt when I do so. I lift my hand to my cheek and startle. My eyes furrow, and it's Tudwal who assures me I'm not mistaken.

'Mistress, your scars have disappeared,' he gasps in fascinated surprise.

26

WÆRMUND OF THE GYRWE

The food's good. And there's a great variety of it. Some of it I've seen before. Some of it I've never tasted. The meat leaves a pleasant buzzing sensation on my tongue. The drink we're given is spicy. Gildas eats with enthusiasm, as we're arranged around a low table, on cushions we can recline on, and with people to bring us drink whenever we empty our beaker.

Gildas is accompanied by Diseta and Iamcilla. The two speak to us, and also to Gildas. It's a strange way to hold a conversation, but one I'm accustomed to now. There's also three other men and a woman, dressed in a similar way to Iamcilla. Before we began to eat, words were spoken, and they all bowed their heads. I met Heafoc's gaze above those heads, and his shrug assured me this was all new to him as well.

'We praise our God,' Diseta explains, reaching for a bowl of small round shapes I've never seen before, to pop one in her mouth. 'These are good,' she offers. But it's the roasted pig I feel most comfortable eating. Bucge's more inclined to try the new foods. She was tended to by a man who examined her wound with curious professionalism, nodded his appreciation for what we'd done to her, and slathered the reddened flesh with some sort of greenish ointment. Through Diseta, he told Bucge to keep the ointment on her leg, but to remove it at night, and allow air to cool the hot flesh. He handed her a container with more of the ointment. 'And then cover it when you dress,' Diseta had interpreted. 'He'll look at it again in two days.' Bucge was filled with questions, but the surgeon disappeared before she could ask them. Perhaps next time.

'Your animals are well?' Iamcilla questions.

'I believe so, my thanks,' I reply. Diseta inclines her chin towards me, while Iamcilla simply looks content.

'They'll fetch a good price. Now, I've asked our master bladesmith to join us after we've eaten. He knows about your arrival,' Iamcilla states.

'And he'll help us?'

'Not so much help, but he may take your commission.' The word confuses me. 'He might do what you want in exchange for barter or coin?'

'Coin?'

'Yes, we don't have much of it these days. Small circular discs of silver, sometimes gold, often just silver. It's more likely to be lumps of precious metals, or perhaps you might have something he desires. You'll talk to him about it. We'll not be involved in whatever agreement you reach. But, I will assure you, he's an honourable man. He can be trusted.' As Iamcilla speaks, I suddenly understand what some of the treasure was I stole from my brother. I wish I'd known they were coins before I gave them to Wædel.

'I'm convinced we've something he'd welcome,' I offer, although I'm suddenly not so sure. I sense Bucge's assessing gaze on me, although Heafoc shows no concern. 'Will we receive coins for the sale of the horses?' I clarify.

Iamcilla shrugs and her lips flatten into a line. 'Perhaps. Perhaps not. There are many ways people buy and sell things. The bladesmith will inform you himself.'

I nod, and bite down on the many questions I still have. I suppose I'll know soon enough.

Finally, when we've all eaten more than any of us are used to, all of it good, and I'm aware Heafoc and Eastmund might have had too much of the wine and ale, Iamcilla stands, as do the others with her, including Gildas.

'We must retire to our church,' she states. 'We'll pray and, perhaps, see you on the morrow. Diseta will remain with you to aid you with the bladesmith. Again, on behalf of Gildas, I thank you for returning him to us. He has much work to do now he's restored to his brethren and sisters.'

'It was nothing,' I reply, standing suddenly as they've done, aware I might have imbibed too much as well, because the room sways alarmingly. 'But please, can you ask him what it was his captor made him speak before all?'

I've been curious about this ever since I first met him.

A sharp glance directed towards Gildas assures me he has made no mention of this. Iamcilla speaks in his tongue. I watch a flurry of emotions cover Gildas' face; one of them, I'm sure, is embarrassment. Eyes cast down, he replies to Iamcilla, who startles me by laughing, the sound rich and musical.

'I'm afraid venerable Gildas was once a young

man with lofty ideals, and his captor, this Isarninus, knew of his transgressions.'

'Transgressions?'

'When Gildas was no older than you, young man, he wrote something intended to embarrass the kings of the day into acting against the invasions taking place to the east of here. It was this that Isarninus had him recite whenever he was so inclined.'

'So, it was a means to embarrass Gildas?'

'It was, yes. A reminder not everything we believe when we're young is always correct.'

'So, now he wouldn't write such words?'

'Gildas has learned much humility since then. Alas, there are copies of his work in many places. Gildas is still blamed for them by those he denounced.'

'Denounced?'

'Oh yes, he castigated many of those who thought they were warrior kings and were protecting the kingdoms to the west of here. Ah, here he is,' Iamcilla interrupts herself, and I turn to see a man being shown into the room we've eaten within. He's squat, with fierce eyes, dressed in a serviceable tunic, but with a silver chain around his neck, and even silver glistening from his ears.

He bows to Iamcilla and Gildas, but then fixes his

gaze on my warriors and me. He speaks. It's Diseta who offers the translation.

'He wishes us all a good evening. His name is Katourn.'

'If you'll excuse us,' Iamcilla speaks in my language, and with a phrase towards Katourn vacates the room, leaving Diseta with me and my warriors.

Katourn sits quickly, his hands folding one over the other, and then meets my gaze without flinching.

'Katourn is pleased to meet you, but states his services can't be purchased cheaply.'

I already feel stung by the man, while my warriors mumble unhappily to one another. I hold his gaze, and then turn and pull forth half of the blade from my sack of treasures. His eyes sparkle at what I lay before us, and he stands, and with a searching gaze runs his hand over the remnants of the sword, and the fractured section of the blade. Immediately, I detect a change in his demeanour.

When he speaks next, his words are slower, and I suspect more respectful.

Diseta gives voice on his behalf. 'Where did you get such a blade? It's a fine piece, despite its break.'

'It was used to wound Bucge,' I reply, pointing out whom I mean.

Katourn licks his lips, looking from Bucge to the blade hungrily.

Silence falls, and then he speaks again, and now Diseta's tone reveals her surprise.

'He asks you to meet him at his workshop in the morning. He'll be happy to show you some of his skills.' This is clearly unusual.

'My thanks. We'll be there.'

Katourn nods, once more caressing the surface of the blade, flickering in the light from candles and the lowering sun. He speaks once more.

'Would he be able to keep hold of your blade until tomorrow? He'd like to study it more.'

I nod quickly – after all, the blade is little use to us as it is, and Katourn's interest is obvious. I feel a flicker of triumph. It seems, despite everything, we've found a bladesmith who might be able to provide us with what we want. That pleases me more than it should.

Katourn eagerly scoops the tanged blade into his hands, and bows towards me and Diseta. And then he's gone. It doesn't take Diseta's next words for me to appreciate we've already won Katourn's regard.

'He never does that,' she whispers as he strides away, whistling softly, seeming to shake his head in astonishment.

'Until tomorrow,' I call after the bladesmith's re-treating back. Diseta doesn't repeat my words for him, but he lifts his hand in acknowledgement, as I look at my warriors. We're all smiling, and not just because some of us have drunk too much ale and wine. Finally, it appears we might have what we desire in our reach.

27

MEDDI OF THE EORLINGAS

I ride proudly through the double-ditched enclosure, my hair flung back from my cheeks. It feels good to sense the gentle warmth of the sun on my face, and to know people no longer look at me and shudder. I don't understand how it's happened. I welcome it, however.

Urien acknowledges me with a respectful bow, words of welcome dying on his lips as he notices the change. He offers me a bright smile. I return it. That perhaps startles him more than the lack of scars.

'It's good to see you, mistress,' he offers. 'You have five fine foals. They're all doing well. Marchell ensured they were born without issue.' This pleases me even further, and my smile broadens, only to slip from my lips.

'Seeress.' I wince to hear the fury on Madog's lips. I knew he'd be displeased with my prolonged absence. He hurries towards me, the hoe still in his hand. My brother performs all tasks within our settlement, just as I would do. We're all one in the attempts to keep us fed. 'Seeress.' He huffs, his eyes sweeping Kenal and Tudwal, no doubt to reassure himself we're all well. 'Seeress.' He states somewhat more calmly, relief at our return overshadowing his anger we've been gone for much longer than we should have been. 'It's good to see you.' Only now does he truly look at me. A broad grin stretches upon his lips. 'I didn't believe her,' he murmurs.

My forehead furrows. 'Believe who?'

'Marchell.' And now his grin broadens even further. 'She told me you'd return much changed, perhaps even happy, when I complained at your long absence. She didn't explain to me why that would be.'

'Then it'll not be a surprise.' My anticipation dims a little. Marchell, I can't deny, has always understood the path of a seeress better than I have.

'It'll be a surprise, Meddi, I'm sure,' Madog consoles, assisting me to dismount. We've been in the saddle since before daybreak, the thought of finally being home encouraging us to push the horses from north of Glevum towards home. 'We'll feast this night,' he assures me. 'But come. You should meet the foals, and see all we've accomplished in your absence.' I find it strange he doesn't ask me about Elen, but perhaps Marchell also told him we'd fail in our attempts to find her.

'All is well?' I question, just to be sure, as my horse is led away. Kenal still stands at my side. I'd tell him to leave but I feel we've developed a friendship, and I welcome him being there. Tudwal has been tasked with the horses, but even that will no longer be the burden it once was. Tudwal has become a man in our absence. He'll soon have younger boys to instruct in how to care for the animals, and how to hold a shield and spear.

'All is well. And with you?'

'We didn't find Elen,' I complain. 'It's possible she's dead. We did find half of our father's sword.'

'Half?' he questions, perplexed.

'Yes, just half. Abandoned on the ground beside a bloody streak and with a river nearby. She may have died in the river. I hope she did.'

Madog nods, leading me to where the mares and their foals are grazing. I note with delight the ungainly animals, observing them keenly. Our horses are mostly dark, blacks and browns, occasionally a patch of white here and there, but one of the animals is entirely grey, from head to hoof, tail flashing almost white against its backside.

'We've named him Gwynmarch.'

'He'll be a fine mount for your son,' I acknowledge, smiling at the name, which is very much what the animal is: a white horse.

'He will, yes,' Madog confirms. I walk amongst the mares, reacquainting myself with them, and also offering soft words to their foals. Some of them are frightened of me, but not the grey one. No, he's bold, and I laugh as he tries to eat my hair.

'Aptly named,' I suggest, greeting Gwynmarch. Madog nods. I notice his son has joined us. He also strokes Gwynmarch with a proprietary look. It's evident he knows the horse will be his. I bend low, and look at Maccus. He's over a year old now. He's well formed, the excesses of babyhood already starting to drain from him now he's active every day.

'Well met, Maccus,' I speak.

'Seeress,' he lisps, which delights me, and then his eyes narrow and he reaches towards me. His fingers remain chubby. I sense their stickiness as he touches my cheek. I find myself smiling. Even young Maccus sees I'm changed. Maccus' fingers are warm. I feel their touch, almost feather-soft over where the dips and scars used to be, where my cheekbone was too visible, as though it lacked all flesh. Maccus chuckles, the sound rich and filled with joy. 'Better,' he suggests, appraising me. I consider when he learned to speak so well. He's still only very small. Madog's gasp of shock has me tilting my chin, to eye him.

'He's never said that word before,' he confirms, and I nod, somehow suspecting that. Only when his hand moves do I make to stand, as I do so, I pull Maccus' heft into my arms and dangle him high in the air, something I've never done before.

'Now, Maccus, to win the love of Gwynmarch, you must also win the love of his mother. Come, I'll introduce you to her.' I chuckle as well, eyes alight with joy as my favourite mare lifts her long head to watch me. Her eyes are soft, glowing with an inner light. I'm reminded of the small object within my workshop. I'll need to take it to Terricus.

There's something about it that will ensure Maccus will, one day, be feared by all, although I hope it also means he can live in peace. I find I'm no longer terrified of the future of Villa Eorlingas. We'll accomplish all Edern tried to take from us. And all Elen also tried to steal away.

* * *

'Marchell.' I incline my head towards her as I step beneath the lintel of the workshop, running my hand along its comforting stone groove.

'Seeress.' She speaks more clearly than she has done for a long time. Abruptly, I recall all she promised me about Elen, and how we'd have our revenge against her. That promise can no longer stand because we don't know if Elen lives or dies. 'I see you're healed, at long last,' Marchell states, hobbling towards me, although her gaze is searing. 'It's taken too long.' Now her old and gnarled fingers run across my cheek and she smiles. 'Daughter.'

I startle to hear her speak of our relationship. I've denied it for a long time, too angry she couldn't foresee what would happen to our people and that I'd borne the brunt of Edern's attentions. I realise now perhaps she did see it, but what was the point in alluding to it? Those events had to occur as they did.

'It's good to see a smile on your face. I know of Elen, the bitch. I'm sure she's dead, but alas, like you, I can't be certain. She's always had the means to foul my visions of the future.'

'I have this.' I reveal the sharpened point of my father's sword, a man Marchell bedded for many years, until she determined her life's work lay else-where. My father was reluctant but he honoured her enough to allow Marchell to replace the then aged seeress, and in turn took Madog's mother to his bed.

'It's good to see half of the sword come home to the Eorlingas. I take it you will now inter it beside your father's remains.'

'I suspect I will, yes. It's little use to us now. I won't allow another hilt to be forged for it.'

'You're wise to do so,' Marchell confirms, holding out her hand to take the blade. 'I see it's coated in blood. Is it Elen's?'

'I believe so, yes,' I answer. Together, heads bowed, we consider what we suspect was once a part of Elen. She betrayed me, but she also deceived Marchell, which of us she betrayed the most is difficult to fathom. Perhaps Marchell and I have always been more similar than I like to consider.

'She's the only reason I became the seeress of the Eorlingas.' Marchell meets my gaze frankly. I feel as though, in my absence, the curve of her back has re-leased. She stands tall towards me, no longer wrapped in rags but in fine clothing. I sense Sian's hand in this. 'On her birth, the old woman warned me Elen's future would bring us nothing but grief. She said the only way to stop it was to take her place as seeress. I fear she was less than honest about that, but certainly, it's been easy to try to consider Elen as just another child, and then just another woman, rather than think she came from within me. She's the darkness and you've always been the light.'

I nod, tears once more running down my face. I've treated my mother poorly and for many long years, and yet she doesn't seem angry about it.

As though she can decipher my thoughts, she nods. 'We both had our wounds to carry. We might have treated one another ill, but we needed to survive until this day. Now,' and she places the sword tip on the work surface without further thought, 'I believe you have need of this, and a meeting with Terricus to arrange.'

She places the small object into my hands I was examining on the day, last year, when my brother told me of Edern's death. It seems a lifetime ago. The bulbous legs and head of what I now know is a representation of a horse appears even more grotesque after having been reunited with my finest breeding mare and her grey-coated foal.

'Go, take it to him. Explain what he must do, and have him forge the finest blades to protect our people from this day onwards. Maccus will never know the sorrow his father, or his aunt, knew. Maccus will be a man of the Eorlingas, a fine leader, and someone who ensures peace will prevail for us. After all this time, we've earned such a respite from near-constant fear.'

The small but heavy object, forged of precious metal, is no longer than my thumb and yet it carries the hopes of the whole Eorlingas people. How, I consider, did I never realise its secrets before? Something so small, and yet so heavy, unearthed by Urien at our former home, called to me then, but there was too much else to consider. I should have paid more attention to it at the time. Perhaps if I had, Elen would never have deceived us, and escaped. Perhaps then, my brother would be assured in his position as chief over the Eorlingas without fearing attack from other tribes. I feel a tinge of guilt at the knowledge, but then I remember my healed scars and know something else. I was being tested, by my gods. I have, I hope, earned their regard now. And with that regard, the Eorlingas will grow from strength to strength, and the problems Elen has caused us will quickly dissipate. We'll be the strongest of all.

28

WÆRMUND OF THE GYRWE

We sleep that night in a room close to the building we ate within, but not the same one. We're offered beds to sleep upon, complete with furs to keep us warm. Not that we need them. It's warm. The summer's beginning to advance.

For once, Bucge doesn't wake us with her shrieks of pain and terror. As such, it's even more of an effort to wake than I think it should be. I've grown used to sleeping lightly, stones and grass pressing into my back.

'Come on.' Heafoc touches my shoulder. I squint up to see him dressed and ready for the day. 'Diseta said she'd be here early. Come on,' he urges. I hear groans from my other warriors now. Eastmund flings a pillow towards Heafoc. But then I hear the soft tread of Diseta's approaching steps.

'Do as he says,' I call, and stand quickly, stretching and reaching for my clothes. I've not slept without my tunic on for many months. It's almost pleasant to pull the colourful tunic over my head, not having to hold my breath to stop the smell of my body making me want to gag.

Bucge's the slowest to rise. We wait, impatiently, as she and Osfyth ensure the ointment's coated over her skin before she pulls her trews up. Only when she's ready does Diseta actually appear. I consider whether she's been waiting outside for our complaints to lessen. I suspect she has been.

'There's food and drink,' she advises. 'Of course, you've found the latrines.' We have, and they're an interesting experience. I don't look at Heafoc. Our antics of last night don't need to be discussed. It was embarrassing, but provided only he and I know how we misinterpreted the use of the sponge in the communal latrine, it need go no further.

'We wish to see our animals and Katourn.'

'Of course,' she agrees. 'Food, horses and then Katourn? He's not allowed to begin his work until after prayers have been spoken within the church. If he does, a fine must be paid to the holy men and women.' The way Diseta speaks, it's evident she expects us to know more about Gildas' faith than we do. I look at Osfyth. She shakes her head. None of us know much about Gildas' prayers and rituals.

'Food. Yes, and then the horses, and then Katourn.'

'Very good,' she confirms. 'This way.' Quickly, she takes us outside and leads us to the same room we ate within last night, but there's no long table within, only small stools to sit upon, and a big bowl of pottage from which people can help themselves. There's a small quantity of honey, and we eat eagerly, aware of the curious eyes of others who live here. They're evidently not all followers of Gildas' faith because from nearby we can hear a low murmur, which Diseta explains is caused by the holy men and women praying.

'The Christians must say their prayers many times a day,' she explains.

'Christians?' I question.

'The name of Gildas' faith is Christianity, so he is a Christian. You, I believe, are a follower of Woden?'

'Yes, I'm descended from him,' I reply quickly. I don't miss the small smile on her lips at my assertion. I think she might be laughing at my statement.

'These Christians don't claim descent from their

God,' she murmurs. 'They revere their Christ as you do Woden.'

'We don't all worship Woden,' Bucge interjects.

'I understand. You have many Gods, Woden, Tiw, Frigg, I know of them all,' she murmurs. 'But Christians worship Christ, a man who once walked amongst his adherents, similar to how you believe Woden was once your ancestor.'

I consider this, and shrug. I suspect it makes sense, if not to me.

'They are followers of this Christ?' I question, just to be sure. She nods, and then encourages us to eat and leave to check on the horses.

Gwladus greets Diseta cheerily when we appear. She swings open the stable door and beckons us within. I'm relieved to see all of our horses, and extend my thanks to Gwladus.

There's a rumble of conversation between the two.

'Gwladus will continue to tend to your horses, but she reminds you it's not from the goodness of her heart. There'll need to be payment.'

'I understand that,' I comment, running my hand along the noses of the horses, while at the same time sniffing the air. The stables are redolent with the tang of the animals, but they don't stink of shit or piss. 'Let her know we'll discuss once I've been able to forge a bargain with Katourn.' The words are relayed, and Gwladus inclines her head in agreement. I suspect, in our absence, she's discovered a great deal about us from examining the horses we have. I don't miss that the animal we took from the dead warrior leader when Bucge was wounded particularly interests her. I'm also aware the men who tended the animals yesterday have been joined by others. Despite the way they hold spade and broom, I suspect they're some of the famed warriors from the hilltop because stable boys don't tend to have such large builds. All seems welcoming, but we're being watched. We have fine horses. Soon, I hope, we'll have the blades to go with them to become the *comitatus* I've been hoping to be. Not everyone might be pleased about that.

We're then led away by Diseta once more, but not towards where we were bathed, but rather deeper into the heart of the settlement, past where Gildas lives, and beyond. I absorb all I see. There's no busy market today. Indeed, there are few people about, and those we do see seem to be suffering from aching heads, faces pale, groaning as they shuffle around.

'They always enjoy themselves too much,' Diseta explains, her voice rich with disdain, and then comes to a stop. There's a sharp smell in the air of something very hot. She wrinkles her nose at the aroma. 'Stay away from the fires. They're so scalding they'll incinerate your skin if you touch them, or take your eyebrows if you get too close.' With that firm caution, we round a wall of wattle and daub, and immediately I appreciate the warning.

I feel the heat from where I'm standing, and the fire is at least four horse lengths away. It's beneath a roof similar to that running around the building we first met Iamcilla beneath. Katourn stands there, wearing a thick leather apron, and banging something with a huge hammer so the resultant clang throbs through my head. I imagine he didn't drink too much last night.

On seeing us, Katourn offers a brief smile, but continues to work. He calls something to Diseta.

'Excuse him. He won't be long.'

'What's he doing?' Heafoc questions. Diseta scrunches her face, but doesn't immediately reply. It's hard to see the details. The flames from the fire he stands close to are so hot as to be almost white. While Katourn thrusts the item he's banging back amongst the flames, another person is doing something with a strange contraption that opens and closes. I don't know what it is.

'It makes the charcoal burn hotter,' Diseta explains helpfully, even though we've not asked her.

'Katourn's aided by Eudaf. They both know how to use iron to make objects. They're skilled men.'

In silence, we watch as Katourn removes his object from the heat and continues to hammer it until he's happy. He places whatever it is into a waiting stone trough I realise is filled with water when the air sizzles. Only then does he stride towards us. He's speaking quickly. Diseta hurries to explain what he's saying to us.

'He says the sword remnant you have is good. The iron's excellent quality, but it can only be put to use if melted down and forged into a new sword.'

'It just needs a new tip, surely?' I retort, astounded by his statement.

'No, no, no,' Diseta comments, shaking her head as Katourn does. 'An object like that would be no use to anyone. It would fracture at the first stroke. Instead, he'll melt down the remnants and make a new blade, by adding more iron to the mix to have enough to produce a sword of the object's original length. You need not worry, the hilt can be removed, and then replaced, once the work is done. It's simple to remove the hilt.' It's obvious Diseta is just telling us what Katourn's saying. She has no idea of the process either.

'Remove the hilt?'

'Yes.' She nods, as does Katourn as he extends the

severed blade towards us, with the remnants of the hilt extended. 'See here,' and she speaks his words. 'You tap this aside, sometimes it can be stubborn, and then the whole material of the hilt will come free. Shall he show you?'

I look to my warriors, uncertain, but we're all curious. Not one of us doesn't lean forward to see what Katourn intends to do.

'Should we discuss the cost first?' I ask quickly. What if we don't have the required means to barter with him?

'He says this will be his way of showing you what he can do. Then, he'll discuss costs with you, if you require more blades. He's enthused about this project,' Diseta explains. Katourn's excitement can be heard in the way he speaks, and seen in his quick hand movements, as he evidently tries to explain everything to us.

I cough, look down at my feet, but then nod. 'He has our permission to do as he says.'

Katourn offers me a slight bow as he receives my agreement, and takes himself back towards the heat of the flames, calling for Eudaf to join him. The two talk, and then I stifle a cry as Katourn thrusts the hilt into the flames. Heafoc's hand on my arm assures me he's as worried as I am. But it's not the whole hilt being plunged into the flames, rather the very end of the hilt. I consider what Katourn's doing, and quickly have my answer.

With the rest of the blade held firmly between two pieces of iron, attached at one end, which Diseta tells me are called tongs, he collects a very small hammer and begins working away at the area he's heated. I try to see what he's doing, but don't want to get too close. Katourn bites his lips as he works, an intent expression on his face. Whatever he's attempting, it takes a long time. He has to replace his hammer with a file, which he works in and out of the hilt of the sword. But, eventually, a huge grin splits his face at whatever he's achieved.

He holds the hilt towards us. I see there's a raised area now. I feel my forehead furrow. I've no idea what he's doing. It looks like very little to have pleased him so much. But quickly, he uses the hammer to bash the upper and lower guards of the hilt, between which my hand would rest if it was my blade. Abruptly, the tang of the sword slides free from the body of the remaining blade.

I nod then, making sense of his actions. Katourn carries the blade towards me. I see the tang where the hilt once sat, and realise he's managed to remove it intact. Now we have the remains of the blade only. At this point, he and Eudaf have an intense conversation, one or other of them holding the fragment upwards, running their fingers along the metal, and either nodding or shaking their heads.

Diseta shrugs her shoulders as she turns to us. 'They're talking of things I don't understand, of iron content and other matters. I don't believe it's relevant. It's their secret art,' she explains. I'm aware Katourn directly addresses her. Perhaps he's asked her to be vague as she translates for us. Not, I realise, that I have any intention of ever being able to forge my own blade.

'Now, they'll melt down the core of your sword, and then add it to more iron. That way, they'll be able to produce the blade and hopefully restore the tang afterwards. They warn it'll be a long process.'

I nod. 'I'm not leaving.' I turn to my fellow warriors. None of them are unsettled. 'Can we stay and watch?' I ask. Diseta directs this to Katourn. He nods willingly but absent-mindedly. His focus is on what he means to do, but then he speaks again.

'You can, yes, but today the sword will be melted down and then tomorrow he'll begin the process of combining the melted-down bar with another one.'

'So, it's just going to be watching a fire today?' Heafoc quickly realises.

'Alas, yes. But, you can stay, or go elsewhere.'

The thought of watching a fire is not how I'd like to spend my time. Perhaps there's something else we can do instead.

'Tell me,' I question Diseta. 'Would we be able to visit the hill fort?'

My question startles her, and she shakes her head. 'No, but I'm sure Gwladus would happily talk to you about it. She might even share some of her knowledge with you.'

'Then, we'll do that,' I announce, but Bucge shakes her head.

'I'll stay here,' she calls. 'I can rest my leg and learn some of these secrets as well.'

Now Diseta looks torn, but Bucge quickly realises the problem.

'I'll merely watch. You can go with the others and I'll find you, later.'

So spoken, Bucge settles herself on the only available wooden stool, and the rest of us turn aside. Diseta explains what's happening, but Katourn hardly notices, waving a hand in acknowledgement.

'We'll see you shortly,' I call to Bucge, but she's just as focused on Katourn as he is on the fragment of the blade. I shake my head. I thought the process of forging a blade would be exciting, but it's far from that. Indeed, everything takes far too long. I'd rather learn what I can about the local inhabitants of the hill fort. I'm hoping I might discover something that could help me in the fight against Isarninus. Perhaps the men we saw in the stables might even aid us in becoming even better warriors. I'd welcome learning how they fight one another. If they have different skills, I'll employ them against Isarninus and any of my father's warriors who still think to hunt us down and, in that way, win my father's regard. Soon, we'll have better blades, and then, well, then we can begin to reclaim what was stolen from us.

29

MEDDI OF THE EORLINGAS

I find Terricus where I expect to, Hedrek not far away either. I see how Hedrek's lost some of his fat belly in my absence. A bit of hard work has made him a better man, not, I'm sure, he'd say as much. Sian glances up at my footsteps, and offers me a bow of her head. I consider why she's here, but she seems to be busy. Perhaps Marchell has sent her here in preparation for my arrival.

'Mistress.' Terricus looks up from what he's doing, a wary expression on his face. Hedrek, I notice, also takes the opportunity to stop his endeavours and look at me. I offer him a stern stare. His eyes narrow in confusion.

'Good day to you, Terricus,' I offer, and now his

forehead furrows. I notice Sian's mouth open in surprise as she gets a good look at me, and only then does Terricus perceive it as well. Self-consciously, I run my fingers down my healed cheek, and offer a smile to Terricus, mindful, on the periphery of my vision, Hedrek's also noted the change in me. I consider whether I should be kinder to him. After all, as I've remembered, if not for him, I might have died from my wounds all those years ago. 'I've something for you.' I hold out the small object.

Terricus walks towards me, his smell overpowering, but not noxious. He's a man doing honest work. If he sweats as he does, it must be because he works hard. 'What is it?'

'It's a horse, of course,' I offer, my tone light.

His eyes narrow, turning the small object in his huge hand to examine it from all sides. 'And why do I need it?'

Now, I feel my mouth widen in a huge grin. 'I've been assured this is the answer to your problems of forging good iron for sharp blades. I imagine, although I don't know everything, if you melt this small creature down, and add some of the material it's constructed from to the iron you have, you will, at last, be able to make a blade that doesn't shatter on impact.'

'How do you know this?' he queries, sceptically. I

don't blame him – after all, this is not the first time we thought to have the solution to our problems, only for it to not prove to be so.

'My face was restored at the moment of realisation,' I inform him. He looks from me to the horse-shaped object, and then back to my face. I see his thoughts whirling in his mind. I promise much with little proof, and yet it's evident something has happened to me in order for me to stand here, before him, healed.

'I'll examine it carefully,' he assures me. Behind him, I'm aware Hedrek has returned to his task.

'Yes, I can't imagine all of it must be used, but once we know what it is, we'll need to find more.'

He nods, his thoughts already on the object and not on me. He weighs it in his hand, eyes narrowed, before collecting something else to counter the weight in his other hand.

I'm grateful not to have to explain more to him. The workings of the seeress of the Eorlingas must remain secretive. I don't wish to have to admit I don't fully understand everything I've endured either.

Sian watches Terricus keenly. 'It's good to see you, mistress,' she comments. 'And looking so well.'

'It's good to see you as well, Sian. I hope Marchell hasn't worked you too hard.'

The older woman shakes her head fiercely in denial. 'Not at all. But, am I to return to you now?'

'When Terricus no longer needs your services, yes,' I confirm. She smiles, evidently pleased to continue her task. 'What are you doing?' I ask, confused by her presence here. After all, Hedrek's the slave, working for Terricus. Why does the bladesmith need another?

She glances at Terricus, but he makes no attempt to speak. 'I sort the charcoal and the iron pieces. We've learned not all pieces are worth the effort of either burning, or adding to the furnace. He says I have an eye for such detail. Hedrek's tried to help him, but he doesn't see the pieces as I do. Here, look.' And her black-coated hand unclenches to show me something balancing on it. 'See,' she continues. 'This charcoal won't burn well, but this piece will.' She unclenches her other hand. I look from the one to the other. She nods. 'I understand your confusion, but I see it easily. This piece here will burn for a long time, this piece will be consumed almost as soon as it's touched by flame.'

'Then you possess a great skill indeed,' I murmur with approval. I realise she has two piles of small, round pieces of charcoal before her.

'These will aid with the cooking. They do have

more heat in them than wood when they burn. These pieces here' – and I'm unsurprised the other pile is smaller than the first – 'will sustain the furnace for much longer.'

'It's the same with the ironstone,' Terricus calls, evidently paying some attention to our conversation. 'She sees the pieces best to add to the furnace. It's a wonder,' he concedes, his face showing respect for her ability to aid him.

'Then you make quite a pair,' I offer with a smile. I sense a trickle of unease in my belly. It's been hollow for so long, but now I feel a stirring, as though I were with child, but it's excitement.

'Between you, and Hedrek,' I indicate the other man with my chin, 'there will be success.'

'Yes, Hedrek works well. He causes no problems. He's better at the heavy lifting, digging new holes for the furnaces and clearing away the waste material. But, did you find the sword?' Terricus asks. 'In your absence, I've given it much thought. I'm confident I've the means to join the two pieces together.'

'The sword pieces have been separated. I only have part of it now, unfortunately.'

'That is regrettable,' he concedes. 'However, I can melt down the part you have and forge a new blade afresh with the iron contained within it. In that way, the sword will live once more. The sword of your fa-ther, of the Eorlingas, will still be powerful.' He sug-gests this quickly. I feel a frown on my face. 'I've been considering it,' he offers. 'I think the two pieces could never be reworked together in such a way as to be strong enough to kill a man, although if the item were merely for show, it would suffice. But separately, well, separately, I could make two blades from that one, one for Madog, and one for Maccus.'

I consider my intention to return the sharp point to my father's grave, and to the barrow beneath which the people of my tribe have their ashes interred, but that would be a waste if Terricus speaks the truth.

'When you've obtained the solution to sharp blades, then you can melt down the half of the sword I have, and make it into a new blade.'

A grin touches his cheeks. He nods quickly, biting his bottom lip in thought. 'It'll be even stronger than the original blade,' he offers, and while I suck in a shocked breath, he's already turned aside, unheeding of my reaction.

'It need only be well forged,' I counter, but he's shaking his head, the small horse-shaped statue in his hand.

'Oh no,' he muses, almost too softly for me to hear. 'It'll certainly be much better.'

30

WÆRMUND OF THE GYRWE

We have only one horse each, and a spare one to carry our food supplies, as we leave Uriconium as the summer nears its end. However, we're richer despite exchanging so many horses for the blades we now possess. Around my weapons belt, I carry the sword made using the remnants of the blade Elen tried to kill Bucge with. At one point, I believed I'd gift it to Bucge, but she wouldn't allow it. Now it's mine. It's a finer blade than anything my father possessed.

Bucge's healed, although she'll always walk with a limp, while Maggenræd struts as though he's never been wounded. Bucge's foul-tempered about it. Maggenræd, obviously, is not. Even Heafoc looks better than I've seen him since we left our homeland far to the east. Our stay within Uriconium has done us all good, although I was never able to entirely relax there. Too many people visit Uriconium, coming from every corner of this island. I fear word of our presence will make its way to my father and Isarninus.

While parting with Gildas is painful, he's made it clear in talking to Diseta, he understands what we're doing. He doesn't berate us, although Iamcilla made some small attempts. But that's all they were, small attempts. Perhaps, despite all their praying to this god I don't fully comprehend, at the heart of it, Gildas and Iamcilla can appreciate the blood feud and desire for revenge we hold against Isarninus. Maybe Gildas, in his quiet moments of contemplation, hungers for what we plan to do. I bloody would if I'd been a captive for as long as he was. Isarninus stole ten summers of his life. That's a heavy price to pay.

'I take it you're sure about this?' Heafoc questions, when we're once more on Watling Street, as we now know the road is called, riding east towards where Elen, who was either a witch or a bitch, probably both, deceived and betrayed us only to meet her death.

'We've no choice. Isarninus will spread the story of what he did to us. Perhaps, even now, my father's warriors hunt us down. Maybe with the aid of Cenbryht. Isarninus isn't a man to treat as a friend. We all know what he did to Gildas. And we know that in doing it, Isarninus broke some form of contract between the holy people and his own. Gildas told us they should have been free to move and visit the burial of this martyr to their religion in the ruins of the settlement of Verulamium beneath Isarninus' hill fort.'

Heafoc grunts, but not with unhappiness. We've finally learned what Gildas was made to do when Isarninus was so minded. The words he was forced to speak were a complaint against people such as Isarninus. There was some irony in having them performed before him, when he was so triumphant. It speaks to a man who understands much more than we do but made no good use of it. Or rather, used it against others. I consider who Isarninus was before he became the leader of the Wæclingas. He must have been someone important to understand Gildas' Latin. After all, Diseta assured us the language is only spoken far to the west of our island these days, and by the Christians.

'We return to him, and exact revenge,' Heafoc asserts. I'm not the only one to cheer. Isarninus played us for fools. It's time the wrong was set right. I can never restore the lives of those who died when I ordered us to turn traitor on the Hicca, but I can take advantage of our fine new blades to end Isarninus' life and ensure he can't play such games any more. The people protecting Uriconium have shown us all how loyal warriors can aid those who don't fight. I might still wish to be a *comitatus*, but certainly I'll be more careful in choosing whom I fight for in future.

'We will, yes. And then we'll decide what to do next.'

'Return to Uriconium?' Osfyth questions hopefully.

'We'd be welcomed there, yes,' I admit somewhat grudgingly. We might be received there, but as our extra horses have been sold, we've nothing else with which to trade. And, of course, we have many good blades now. We can be *comitatus*, as I first hoped. 'But that isn't where my future lies.' Osfyth holds her tongue. If she decides to think her future lies elsewhere to mine, I can't stop her, although I'd miss her steadying presence and hunter's skills. But we couldn't be further from home, not really. And we've all learned the world is wider and bigger than we ever thought, when my father's sometimes illogical decisions governed our lives. I'll never allow myself to be held so in awe of anyone again. Never.

'If we return to Uriconium, we'd have to bathe

more often,' Maggenræd mutters. I can't decide if it's a complaint or not, especially as for now we all smell fresh. Not at all like the people we were before discovering the joy of the bathhouse, as Diseta termed it. Or the convenience of the latrines. As Heafoc and I discovered together.

* * *

The journey to Isarninus' home, to the east and then south, is much quicker than that which we took to reach Uriconium. Gildas showed us the distance we travelled, picked out on one of his precious vellums, stored in a well-ventilated and often warm room. Within it many others worked over other vellums, the scratching sound of the ink, as he called it, moving over the vellum, or dried and stretched calfskin, as he told me vellum was, making my head itch as though lice-infected. It seemed to me from studying the map, we'd missed many of the settlements in between we could have visited. But then, Gildas had been concerned with returning to his people, not in befriending, or stealing, from others.

Far from Verulamium, the settlement below Isarninus' home, and where Gildas and his fellow religious were travelling over ten summers ago to take part in a special religious ceremony, I rein in and gaze towards the glowering hilltop, cowering beneath thick clouds. Like the people close to Uriconium, Isarninus lives high on a hillside, able to see for a great distance, if he so chooses, and the weather allows it. That'll make it difficult for us to get close without being seen. But we've learned much within Uriconium. Perhaps we've even learned things Gildas didn't intend for us to know from the people of the Wreocensætan, who protect him with their warriors and blades, including Gwladus. Not that Gildas evidently likes to consider such. But, for the holy men and women who live there, devoting their lives to this single 'God' figure they praise, I can see they need others to keep them safe from the 'enemy'.

'We do what we decided. I suggest we adopt those identities now. We wouldn't want the bastard to know we've returned, and we must also be wary in case Cenbryht's still close.'

Hastily, the distinctively coloured and woven cloaks we've purchased from Uriconium are pulled forth from our supplies. We swirl them around our shoulders, shrouding ourselves in the identity of the Wreocensætan, and not the Gyrwe. The cloaks aren't noticeable for anything other than they fully cover us from head to mid-calf, and allow us to ride in dis-

guise. The settlement below Isarninus' hilltop home
might be all but deserted, but it's put to one very important use, and we mean to take advantage of that to
exact our vengeance against the bastard. For us. And
for Gildas. I mark myself as lucky we weren't captive
for anywhere near as long as he was.

'Be sure to use the correct fastening for the
cloaks,' Osfyth reminds us. I'm not alone in removing the cloak fastening I was going to use,
which marks me as from the Gyrwe, and replacing it
with a different one. We might still only speak our
own tongue, aside from Heafoc, but at a cursory
glance, we can certainly pretend to be something
we're not. For the time being, we're traders from Uriconium, with the promise of good knives for sale.
Admittedly, the knives are far from sharp, and the
bone handles not the best, but that's because I speak
with the critical eye of one who has a blade in their
hand forged from the weapon Elen plunged within
Bucge, trying to end her life. It, our friend the
bladesmith informed us, was made from far superior metal to even that which he used to make the
other weapons. The others have blades just as good,
but not better. When Isarninus is brought before us,
to examine the blades and weapons we have, which
I suspect will be quickly, we'll kill him easily. The

blades will cut with a precision I've never known before.

'Here.' Bucge takes my cloak fastening and expertly secures it with twin brooches showing some strange emblems I can't quite decipher so the fabric won't come free and reveal my warriors belt. It's not as though I'm going to put aside my warriors belt when I'm willingly taking myself into such danger.

'My thanks,' I offer, watching her to make sure she's content with our intentions. It does feel as though we're walking into a trap of our own devising. I've even had to regrow my beard and moustache, and my hair, to cover the distinctive purple mark on my cheek. I did enjoy being shaved and free from a beard. Now I struggle with it. Once Isarninus is dead, I'll shave again. I've grown used to people's shock at my birthmark, shaped like a wolf, covering my cheek. I don't wish to hide it any more. Here, these people don't see it as a bad thing, or despise me for being so branded. It's a pity my father was so adverse to doing so.

'There you go. Even I'd not recognise you.' Bucge assesses me critically. We continue on our way, quickly merging with others on the roadway who have carts and supplies to trade with the men and women who come to this place, despite Isarninus' presence, to offer their prayers to their martyr. Gildas has told us of this festival, as he called it, before the summer draws to a close. Through Iamcilla, he stated Isarninus had often taken him there, to show off his captive, and have him perform, although few had understood his tongue. It had certainly ensured Isarninus was offered exclusive exchanges by those who visited the site, especially the Christians amongst them.

I'm not alone in being covered and having altered my appearance. We've all darkened our hair, using plant dyes offered by Gildas. When that didn't work as well as we'd liked, we dabbed dust into our hair, and for the men, beards and moustaches. It's difficult to entirely mask who we are. We considered bringing others with us, to masquerade on our behalf, but I decided against it. Gwladus was keen to aid us. She said it's been many years since Uriconium has been attacked. I heard the anguish in her voice at being denied a good battle for so long. This is our fight, no one else's. Enough men have died. I won't countenance others ending their life so I can have my vengeance. If we fail, it'll be our fault, and no one else's.

'Come on then,' I murmur to my warriors. Diseta advised us how to change the roll of our words. After many days in one another's company, she admitted her identity was not as one of the Wreocensætan, but rather a member of a tribe close to our home in the east, but a little further north. Now we speak like she would do, if she were at home, and not in Uriconium. Well, it's not always possible, but we try our best. Eastmund and Bucge are the best at masking their origins. Heafoc, for all his skills with different tongues, is poor at it. I'm passable, I've been grudgingly told. It'll be Bucge and Eastmund who do most of the talking. By pretending to be something we're not, I hope to ensure our true identity remains hidden.

Together, we ride through the few standing remains of Verulamium, past a strange construction I don't understand, with banked stone walls in tiers. I'm curious as to what it is. We must have passed it when we escaped, but that was in the dark, and the fear of being chased had us looking only forwards, to where we could flee and evade Isarninus and his men.

Verulamium's ruins aren't as impressive as the standing and serviceable buildings remaining within Uriconium. But then, few if any people live here. It does, however, provide a place where many can meet together to trade and attend to their religious needs. Already, there's a swell of people entering and making their way towards a central location.

Head bowed, but with my eyes everywhere, we follow others. There's a babble of voices, and so many tongues it makes my head spin. How can there be so many people upon this island who speak a different language? It astounds me. I even hear some who speak as I would, and indeed I'm sure some share a tongue I've only rarely heard from the few maritime traders who visited my father's settlement, bringing with them white and brown furs from creatures I'd never encountered or even heard of before.

With fresh eyes, accustomed to Uriconium, I'm sure I can trace the outlines of what buildings once stood here, although much of the stone and tile has been robbed away. I marvel to see it all. We're in an entirely different location to Uriconium, many days' ride from it, and yet, if I took the time, I'm sure I could walk through it with the same confidence as within Uriconium, perhaps even finding the remnants of the bathhouses. I'm astounded so much is the same although different people live here now. The reach of those who first constructed stone buildings and walls upon this island has gone far.

Even the marketplace, so busy within Uriconium, when we first took Gildas home, is the same. Admittedly, there's no building under whose roof we could gain protection from bright sunlight or the coming rain, but a few of the pillars that once held up the roof running along the open sides can be seen.

I'm aware the others also observe with more intent. I consider if we could use this new knowledge to further aid us. Maybe, somewhere, there are locked rooms we could employ to sleep in at night, or gaps beneath the floor, once used for heating, beneath which we could hide. Perhaps.

'We should get as far into the marketplace as we can,' I murmur, and feel Heafoc's sharp gaze on me. He wants to be close to the entrance so we can escape quickly should our plan fail, or some of my father's warriors find us before Isarninus comes to us. I want to be far enough in the market Isarninus will have to make a special trip to visit us, perhaps even right out at the edge, where most hope to avoid because, without passing traffic, it's the least profitable area. Those with food to sell want to be the first stall reached, or else their goods will sell more slowly. If my father's warriors find us, I feel confident our better blades will end their lives quickly.

'As you wish,' Heafoc agrees unwillingly. After all, we've made all of our plans never having set foot within this place, reliant only on Gildas' hazy memories. We were Isarninus' guests within his hill fort. We never descended to the settlement. To my eyes, it seemed mostly abandoned.

It's tedious, with slow-moving oxen and unruly sheep either crawling forward or darting all over the place. The animals are being herded towards the far side of the market, opposite to where I want to go. I squint against the glare of the sun, and see there are some wooden lean-to buildings squatting against the remnants of a stone wall, and also some open areas, clearly marked out by piles of loose stones.

'Here,' I suggest, when we're in danger of leaving the marketplace and entering what was once, I see, a row of houses running beside a roadway that's no longer level, but rather bucked and twisted by weeds and the movement of stones. The walls of the former houses are mostly down to about waist height. There are no roofs to be seen, although some of the wooden beams which would have held the tiles in place remain in position. The resemblance to an animal's ribs is a reminder not even the great Romans could build things that would last forever, not when others could so easily dismantle them. As could the passage of time.

We dismount carefully, not needing to pretend to our aches and pains. It's been a long summer, and much of it hasn't been spent on horseback but as guests within Uriconium. We've practised our fighting skills against those of the Wreocensætan but we've not ridden a great deal. Bucge hobbles a little, stretching out her thigh. We lead our horses to a small, shady area beneath the sagging remnants of a grass roof, but it will prevent them from being uncomfortable during the heat of the day.

There's even a channel in the stony remnants of the floor into which clear water runs. I bend and drop my fingers into it, tasting it and deciding it's good enough for the horses, even if we'll need to find another source of water.

'Let's get set up,' I order my warriors. Quickly, the supply animal is divested of wooden trunks and sacks, as are the rest of the animals.

Heafoc appears with a long piece of slightly buckled wood he's found and, with the aid of Eastmund, constructs a flat surface upon which we can place the small collection of blades we have to help us in our guise as traders. They're not that heavy, but they make an unmistakable metallic sound as they're placed on the wood. Already, I sense people looking our way.

'We need to start a fire for cooking,' Osfyth announces, not as interested in the blades as in eating. I'm hungry too.

'I know where there's more wood,' Heafoc confirms, and ducks into the abandoned dwellings, returning quickly with the twisted remnants of weeds
that have grown in the ruins, as well as some of the
crisp, browned grasses that once covered the homes.

In no time at all, we're prepared, and people start
to visit us. Eastmund and Bucge stand to either side of
the supply of knives, talking when they can, and other
times using hand actions to discuss the knives we
have when those interested in trading don't speak the
same tongue. We've been watching how those within
Uriconium perform the task. It is, I've discovered, surprisingly easy to barter without words.

Heafoc wanders through the gathering collection
of other traders, and returns with a grin on his face,
and a well-made loaf of bread that's hard as a rock.

'I'm not eating that,' Eastmund complains.

'It's not to eat, you bloody fool. Look.' Heafoc
thrusts one of the knives into the bread, and shaves
the almost blackened crust from it. 'We can show
them how good the blades are.'

I narrow my eyes, resting my back against the wall
of the building in which the horses have been stabled.
'In another life, you'd have been a good trader,' I offer.

His eyes flash with fury, but then he relaxes and
grins. 'Maybe.' He shrugs, before pulling another loaf

from beneath his cloak, and tearing the end from it hungrily. I smell it from here, and combined with Os-fyth's fire and pots, my belly growls angrily.

'Are you sharing?'

'Depends,' Heafoc counters.

'On what?'

'On whether I feel like it.' Maggenræd makes a wild grab for the bread. Heafoc skips away from him, easily evading his reach. I shake my head, laughing as well, until Eastmund, with his greater stealth, steals the bread and helps himself to almost half of it, before handing it back to an outraged Heafoc.

Eastmund shares what he has, while Heafoc complains, but then Bucge stamps heavily on my foot in warning. Immediately, all of my humour evaporates as a collection of five men, all large and bulky, shoulder their way to our knife display.

I watch them carefully from beneath my cloak, the hood pulled once more over my hair as much as possible. I'm not sure I recognise them, but they certainly look like the sort of mean bastards Isarninus might have at his side. I calm my rapidly beating heart. I can't give away our identity when we've only just arrived. I must have my vengeance against Isarninus. I must have my brother's sword back. Now I understand the power in the old blade, I know that with it I'll be possessed of the regard I need to survive with no tribe to name as my own.

The first two, both broad-shouldered and stocky, observe the blades with eyes hungrier than I am. Huge calloused hands reach out to run fingers over the longer of the knives, shimmering with intent beneath the bright sunlight. They could be used in combat. Some of the knives are smaller, more useful for eating with, and we have more of them than the true battle blades.

They speak to one another in low voices, the three behind trying to peer over their shoulders. I can't decipher the words from where I'm standing. I don't move closer, leaving it to Eastmund.

He cocks his head to one side, his ear closer to the men, and then they turn to him. My breathing's grown more rapid. They could easily just palm one of the knives and use it to threaten us rather than discussing payment.

'These are good,' the tallest one states, using words I understand, which pleases me. 'How much for two of them?' We only have ten altogether, and they cost a great deal, almost all of the treasures we managed to steal from Isarninus, but this isn't about growing rich. Well, for me it's not.

'I doubt you could afford them,' Eastmund states

combatively. This is how all spoken barter in Uriconium began. Even when it was for bread and cakes. I
keep looking behind the men, determined to be on
my guard should Isarninus appear, arrogant and
cocky, but I don't believe these men are anything to do
with him.

'We won't know unless you tell me the price,' the
man states without inflexion. He's good at this, I realise. He knows how to barter. 'My name's Dewi, well
met.' He decides to be more friendly. 'We have these.'
And quickly, a waist pouch I've not seen is revealed.
He dips his hand within and reveals a motley collection of old metal brooches, tarnished, and others that
are potentially much newer. I see a few of them flash
redly, perhaps with small pieces of garnet, which are
costly indeed. Not that we want garnets and brooches,
but we need to make at least one sale so word of our
presence will make its way to Isarninus in his eyrie.

'One knife will be five good brooches,' Eastmund
announces confidently.

Dewi assesses Eastmund's words, and then grins
broadly. 'A fair bargain,' he comments. 'So, for two
knives, nine good brooches,' Dewi decides.

I see Eastmund open his mouth to argue, but then
think better of it, snapping his lips shut. And just like
that, we become, for the time being, traders not war-

riors. I watch the exchange, confident we're one step closer to our intentions.

'One will be for me,' Dewi asserts, and then turns to assess his fellow warriors, who lean forward eagerly, eyes running over the new blades. 'Eli will have the other. The rest of you, Nyfed, Cynin and Rhun, you'll need to earn yours.'

The men who won't have a blade sigh dramatically, but accept Eli's good fortune without rancour, as far as I can tell.

'We may return,' Dewi states confidently. I've no idea if he will or not, but certainly he and Eli are pleased with their choices, both men trying a few of the handles before deciding which knives to take, depending on how the hilt aids the balance of the blade. These men know what they want. And thanks to Katourn, we all know much more about the blades we need to fight best with.

The knives have been sold, not cheaply, but for a fair exchange, as Dewi stated. Now we need only wait for Isarninus and his greed to hear of this. Then he'll be here, demanding better terms than we offered Dewi and his men. When that happens, we'll kill him, overwhelm those within his hilltop fort, and reclaim my brother's sword as well as the rest of my stolen treasure. The realisation thrills me. Once that happens, I'll know if he truly has informed my father of where we are. And if he has? Well, I can seek vengeance against my father if I so desire. Or we'll return to Uriconium. With our blades, we're in command of our destiny. When I once more have my ancestral blade, a blade of Woden, I'll be even more assured in who I am, what I've achieved, and the future of me and my warriors.

31

MEDDI OF THE EORLINGAS

'Mistress.' Sian beckons me to join her ten days later from where I'm tending to the six foals. It's important they know me as their mothers do. If not, I'll never have the control over them I require to ensure they obey the commands of whoever rides them.

'Is it done?' I question. I've seen much less of her than I might like, but now Marchell and I are entirely reconciled to one another, perhaps I need her less.

'Terricus has something to show you, yes. Madog's also to join you.'

I nod, and with a final pat on the back for my favoured mare, I turn and follow Sian towards the main villa building, dazzling beneath the bright sun. It's been a warm few days, but the mornings are turning cooler. It'll soon be time to think about which animals should be culled from amongst our stock, and which can be kept throughout the long dark times. Then it'll be an occasion to feast with our neighbours. I know Madog's already considering whom to share our largesse with, perhaps the Husmeræ. I'm wary. We've many animals to cull. If we aren't careful, I fear such fortune throughout the summer months will make us fresh enemies. Although, perhaps, when we have new knives to defend ourselves with, it won't really matter. Or, it will compound the problem. I wince to consider that possibility.

I stride confidently, eyes keen as they take in the activity of those nearby. Marchell and Madog did well in my absence. The people are more and more settled, and keen to labour towards our shared goal. Those who came to us from the Beansæte and other defeated peoples have intermarried and become Eorlingas. Next year, Madog informs me, he intends to have the drainage systems surrounding five of the least productive fields re-dug. It'll be a huge expenditure of time and labour. It speaks of Madog's ambitions to make the Eorlingas even more prosperous while we have good weather on our side. All too often, droughts can blight such hard-won prosperity.

Terricus, with the aid of Hedrek and Sian, has been busy since my conversation with him. I've left him alone, and purposefully not asked him to tell me how he fares. He'd inform me soon enough, or so I've reassured myself.

'Sister,' Madog calls to me. I chuckle to see him, mud on his familiar face, his boots caked in yet more of the brown substance.

'What have you been doing, brother?' I question. He shakes his head ruefully.

'There was a blockage in one of the small streams. I've removed most of the detritus, but I got very wet and muddy feet.'

'You do have people who'll do that for you,' I retort.

His grin broadens. 'But where's the fun in that?' he chuckles. 'Ah, Terricus,' he calls to the bladesmith as we emerge into the shade provided by the villa buildings.

'My lord, seeress.' Terricus inclines his head towards us, but I detect a sparkle in his eyes. 'I've something to show you. You'll be pleased to see it.' At that, he produces two blades, one in each hand. The one shimmers brightly. The other is duller. They've no hilts fitted to the bare tangs.

I gasp in pleasure, and Madog's muddy hands are outstretched as though to touch them.

'Here,' Terricus states, 'is a blade made in the way Centus and I thought iron should be forged, complete with marks where the iron's been cold-shorted. And here's the one produced with the addition of some of the metal found within your horse-shaped object.' I see immediately why his eyes gleam. The difference in the blade is impossible to deny. It glints brightly. There's no sign of where the two sorts of iron have been merged together. It's as though they're one and the same. 'This one,' and Terricus offers the naked tang of the blade to Madog to hold, 'is lighter, and sharper.' As he speaks, Hedrek, his eyes as bright as Terricus', comes forward with a whole chicken, roasted in the flames of the hearth. 'Try it,' Terricus offers.

With a slight furrow to his brow, Madog bends to slice into the chicken with the blade.

'No, no, stab into it,' Terricus advises quickly.

'Very well.' And Madog does just that. I see his shoulder tense. He places all the weight on his front foot and jabs forward. And immediately overbalances as the blade pierces the cooked meat with no effort at all. I reach out and steady Madog, who looks down at the blade, astounded. 'Well, that's much easier than I thought it would be.'

'And it will continue to be,' Terricus assures, new-found confidence writ into the lines of his face. 'Mistress, you were correct. Not just one sort of ironstone, but two. That small object there is cast with a different sort of iron. It reacts exactly as the ironstone found nearby. The two can be used together, but it gives the blade the sharp edges I believe we've been hoping for. Look.'

Madog's observing the point of the blade, and the iridescent edge of one side of the knife carefully.

'Be careful. Don't run your finger over it, as you might do this other blade here. You'll lose your finger, as we've learned to our cost.' I see then Terricus has a number of healing cuts on his fingers, scabbed and reddened, but not infected, of that I'm sure. Sian has evidently ensured we don't lose our bladesmith due to the wound rot.

'So now we need to find more of this other substance?' I can't deny I'm excited Terricus has finally achieved what I've been hoping since Hedrek first brought Centus to us, but already I'm busy considering the consequences of this development.

'We do, yes, but it's not urgent. It only takes a small amount to change the effectiveness of the blade.

And now, if I have your permission to do so, I wish to melt down the sword fragment and forge a new blade. I believe it too possesses these two different types of iron, if not multiples of different sorts of iron.'

'But you'll make more blades as well, like this one?' I interrupt him before he can focus too much on his plans for my father's fractured blade.

'I already have.' And now he pulls aside his cloak which, I'd not realised, has been doing more than just resting on a wooden barrel close to him. 'Look.' I see Terricus has produced fifteen blades to the same design as the one Madog held. 'All I need do now is attach hilts so they can be used by your warriors.' I'm astounded, I can't deny it.

'By the gods,' my brother expels reverentially. I swallow heavily. I could never imagine such success as this. I'll need to make an offering to my horse god in thanks for bringing me such knowledge.

'And Hedrek here believes he knows the skills to add hilts to the tang.' My joy evaporates immediately, as I scowl at Hedrek.

'You need bone,' he assures me confidently, ignoring my sudden fury. 'And the hand of the man who'll hold the blade. That way, the hilt can be weighted correctly.'

'And how are they attached?' I ask aggressively.

Hedrek has borne his enslavement well, but if he means to evade it now by suddenly becoming useful to us, I've got other ideas.

'I'll show you, mistress.' Hedrek inclines his head towards me, and reaches for a bone handle he's evidently already prepared. 'Like this.' Quickly, he slides it over the tang of the blade, so the hilt rests level with the blade. 'It's takes some time to get the bone handle correct. I had to file out a hollow to allow the tang to fit snugly,' he offers, already extending the blade and the hilt towards me. I step closer, forgetting in my haste Hedrek holds a pointed blade towards me. But I needn't fear. His eyes are only on the blade, satisfaction playing on his lips. I appreciate Hedrek's truly pleased with what he's discovered.

Once more, Madog holds the blade, weighting it, and then making some experimental moves with it. He pauses, and winces, and meets Hedrek and Terricus' interested gaze.

'I cut myself,' Madog mutters. Terricus grimaces. Hedrek looks perplexed. 'On the blade.'

'I hadn't considered that,' Terricus admits, eyes narrowed, and grabs the blade. 'Ah,' he mutters. 'Another piece can be added to stop the wielder from doing that.' I watch all this, nodding, but I'm secretly beyond pleased. The fitting of the hilt, and whatever else needs to be done, is a much more simple matter than forging the iron to make the blades needed. Madog will have blades. Terricus will forge them. And, it appears, Hedrek will earn his freedom by becoming involved in the process as well, just as Sian already is.

'I'll leave you,' I comment, but none of the three notice me. I allow a smile to touch my lips as I stride back towards Marchell, a bounce to my steps. I'll tell her of this. She'll be as satisfied as I am to have finally achieved success. When my father's blade is remade, and Madog carries it at his waist, the Eorlingas will truly be a mighty tribe once more.

32

WÆRMUND OF THE GYRWE

It takes longer than I anticipate. Indeed, three days pass with no sign of Isarninus, although there's a great deal of interest in the knives we have to trade.

Dewi and his men return more than once, eager to gaze upon the remaining long knives. I sense the other warriors would like a blade but must lack the ability to barter for it. Maggenræd grows ill-tempered at the extended delay. I'm not far behind him.

'If you're not careful,' Osfyth growls at me during the heat of the day, 'you'll be recognised.' Sweat's been beading down my face, the weather unseasonably warm for so late in the season. I realise I should be pleased, but I'm not. My beard and moustache itch from the walnut hull dye in them. I'd welcome removing the cloak from my head.

'I'm being careful,' I mutter at her, angrily kicking a half-starved dog sidling too close to the cook pot, only to take pity on the poor creature and bend to offer him some of my chicken. So engrossed in making amends to the dog, I don't realise until I hear his voice that bloody Isarninus has finally decided to make an appearance when I'm not at all prepared.

'What do we have here?' Isarninus announces arrogantly. He has warriors with him, six of them from what I can tell, looking over my shoulder to eye him. Isarninus stands proudly, bursting with conceit, his weapons belt filled with weapons, although whether any of them could cut a loaf of bread, I wouldn't like to say. He wears a shimmering copper breastplate, which I'm sure makes more of his chest muscles than we'll find when we cut through it and take it from his lifeless corpse.

'Good blades,' Bucge offers, ensuring she rolls her words in the ways of those Diseta grew up with, only her eyes visible beneath her hood. I wince, but think she manages it well enough. Anyway, Isarninus' focus is only on the blades, and not on the people who have them to sell. No doubt, he has no fear we'll return to take our vengeance. He's a damn fool.

Slowly, I stand, encouraging the dog to come with me. A moment ago, I kicked the poor creature, now I'm wary of him becoming another victim of our endeavour to gain revenge against Isarninus. I take the dog to where the horses shelter, my back to the figure of the man I despise. I won't be the one to draw attention to myself.

'They're passable,' Isarninus states leisurely. I shake my head as I secure the dog with a stray piece of hempen rope left behind by previous people using the shelter. I also offer him more chicken, and he sets to it with relish. My actions are slow, measured, but all the time I'm listening to the conversation. I breathe slowly, reducing the staccato of my heart. I reverse from the structure, seeking out the rest of my warriors as I do so.

Only Eastmund and Bucge stand close to our collection of knives for sale, huddled within their cloaks. The rest of us have been elsewhere, but never far. Just far enough that Eastmund and Bucge, despite the blades for sale, don't appear too threatening to Isarninus.

'Where did you steal these from?' Isarninus quips, evidently determined to infuriate the traders. Perhaps, I realise, he thinks to cause an argument and steal the knives while his warriors brawl. We're not going to do that.

I finally allow myself to look at Isarninus fully. His face is so familiar to me from haunting my dreams, but still, I startle to realise he's before me. I need only hold my nerve, and he'll be dead.

Quickly, I catch the eye of Heafoc and Maggenræd. The three of us slip through the market. Many people are already packing up and preparing to move to wherever the next market might be. The celebrations of the Christian holy martyr are over. Some say the next market will be in Londinium where there's another martyr to revere, but others think to travel further east, saying Londinium's a shadow of itself and not worth making the effort to reach. They deride the martyr. I've no thoughts on the matter because we'll not be traders for much longer. We certainly have no interest in offering prayers to whomever the grave belongs to and about which figures similar to Gildas and Iamcilla have been weeping and wailing beside at all times of the day and night.

Avoiding stray sheep and small children, the three of us emerge outside the remnants of the surrounding wall once more. My eyes alight on a collection of horses that must belong to Isarninus. Three men stand watch over the ten or so animals. Two of the

creatures have sacks hanging from their saddles. Isarninus intends to travel back to his eyrie with many
goods.

But the three men stand alone. Everyone else is
focused on their own business, and while people are
preparing to move on to the next market site, their
movements are slow. After all, if they take enough
time, they can spend another night here, and not on
the road to wherever their destination is.

'One each,' Maggenræd hisses to me.

'One each,' I confirm. 'And then we hide the
bodies.'

Pretending to a nonchalance I don't feel, we move
forwards, as though meaning to join the roadway behind them, but instead we turn back towards the
three. I have my new blade at the man's throat before
he can so much as whimper a warning to his allies. I
easily slice open his neck with my blade, the smell of
him noxious. I grimace as I lower his sagging body to
the ground.

With little care, I drag him behind the remains of
a tumbled-down wall, while Heafoc and Maggenræd
hurry to do the same. Then I release the horses from
ropes binding them, a gentle nudge forcing them on
their way. Only then, and first checking none of us
have blood on our clothes, do we make our way back

to our allies, ensuring our faces are covered. Looking at the man I hate as much as my father, I'm astounded he doesn't recognise us. Our attempts at concealment are really not that difficult to see through.

Isarninus laughs so raucously, I hear him before I see him. His voice is loud and filled with scathing humour directed at Eastmund and Bucge. How they don't attack him, I don't know. I would. But we all have a part to play here. Ensuring Isarninus is unable to call on the assistance of others is an important element. Now, with his allies dead, we need only contend with the six warriors with him, if they are warriors, and Isarninus himself.

It would have been good if he'd travelled with fewer men at his side, but at least this way our force is equal.

'You think this feeble blade is worth the same as these silver bracelets?' I hear. His words thrum with forced amusement. He wants what we have. He doesn't wish to offer the recompense they're worth.

'No.' I hear Bucge now. 'A single blade is worth twice as much.'

'Twice as much.' I hear Isarninus gargle with delight. 'What are they made from? Pure silver?' I know he means the blade.

'As you know, they wouldn't be much good if they

were,' Eastmund replies. 'Silver wouldn't be strong enough to kill your enemy with.' I finally see the scene laid bare before me. Many of the traders have paused all activity, and now watch, not daring to speak, the events taking place far down the row of stalls. I'm sure they're pleased we settled down there. They needn't fear for their own goods when this gets nasty. They don't need to worry they'll get caught up in whatever's about to unfold, because certainly, something's about to happen.

As silently as possible, Heafoc, Maggenræd and I return to Eastmund and Bucge. Bægmund and Osfyth are also nearby. I nod towards them, and even catch Eastmund's eye over the shoulder of one of the guards with Isarninus. The man's huge, but I remember he's not much of a fighter. Indeed, if any of these men were good warriors, they wouldn't have needed us to battle their enemy for them. Or to keep us captive in fear we might turn our skills on them.

'They're worth no more than two of these, combined.'

'They?' Bucge states.

'Yes, yes, I'll take the long knives you have left. All of them.'

'Eight of them for two silver bracelets, if they even are silver?' Bucge's reply is scathing. I sense the original warriors, led by Dewi, who paid so much more for their pieces, settle, where they stand just far enough away it's evident this fight isn't theirs. Mind you, they might get involved when the blades come out.

'Are you saying my payment isn't good? Don't you know who I am?'

'I'm saying your payment isn't enough,' Bucge clarifies firmly.

Isarninus is all wounded pride as he turns to his warriors. 'I think we can take them for nothing,' he calls, hand resting on his warriors belt, although I'm aware he's slipping back through the two ranks of warriors with him. He's a craven bastard. More and more, I realise he was all show and no substance. He's what my father would have termed an ambitious arse, but bugger all use at fighting. There was a time my father would have said the same about me. He wouldn't now. Gwladus and Heafoc have taught me a great deal.

Almost as one, the six others slip their hands to blades, and pull forth knives I know have about as much chance of giving a clean cut as Isarninus' face.

'We'll take those,' Isarninus calls, pushing one of his men forward, the intention evidently to steal the blades. As he does so, Isarninus moves further back, unaware Bucge and Eastmund aren't alone.

Osfyth's not far from the back of the warriors. Any moment now, Isarninus will be within striking distance. I wish I was the one to be so close, but I'm not. Instead, my place here is to ensure he doesn't get past us, and slip through the market to escape where he thinks his horses await him.

Bægmund does the same to the other side. He'll stop Isarninus from disappearing into the street of ruined dwellings. Eastmund and Bucge will attack from the front, while Osfyth and Maggenræd take the rear. It's all been planned. All of it. Mostly. What we didn't know was how many warriors Isarninus would have with him, only that we thought he'd leave some of his men outside. It's pure luck our strength matches.

The man's hand hovers over the knives Isarninus means for him to steal from us. I sense everyone holding their breath, even those for whom this fight means nothing. Maybe they hope Isarninus will prevail against us. Perhaps they believe we'll leave him bloodied and bruised. I doubt many of them expect us to kill him. But we will.

Everything seems to slow. I wait, calmly, preparing, and then it happens.

The man's hand curves around the hilt of one of the finest blades on display and Bucge advances more quickly than I've ever seen a person move, and despite her limp. Before the man's hand can close around the hilt, he's shrieking, his hand skewered to the wooden board with the knife next to the one Isarninus so admired.

A shriek of metal, and every warrior there's shouting, hands removing blades from weapons belts, while Isarninus can be heard above all else.

'You'll pay for this,' he shrieks. 'I'm the lord here.'

So intent on shouting, Isarninus is unaware of his warriors surging forward, leaving him with no protection as Osfyth moves closer, her hand also on one of the new blades. This one has been made to exactly fit her clenched hand. It's weighted to take advantage of how she strikes.

With a smile curving my lips, I watch her sidle up to Isarninus, her other hand reaching for him, and I know we have him. Here, now, we'll seek vengeance, and Isarninus will be dead.

Only then, he rounds on Osfyth, knife to hand, blood sheeting from a cut on her arm.

'Bitch,' he roars, but Maggenræd's close. He slashes towards Isarninus, so he veers backwards, almost losing his balance.

And then I don't have time to watch any more, because there are men who need killing. I grip my hilt, feeling the comforting shape of the bone handle. It's been fitted to my hand, perfectly. While some of the others like their weapon to be weighted from lower down the blade, I like it firmly balanced, so that, late at night, I can rest it on my extended fingers, carefully, and have both the hilt and the tip lie flat without so much as a wobble.

Now I thrust it towards one of the men. He's slow to turn, not realising there are more than four enemies to fight. I don't stab, not with this blade, but rather slash it across the man's face, his chin dropped low, so a well of blood appears, his beard sheering to the ground.

'Bastard,' he roars. I retrace the action, only slightly lower, and now a bloom of blood erupts from his neck. He shrieks, his own blade wavering, as his fingers dip into his life fluid. He's dead before he can see how much he bleeds, my blade impaled in his throat so he garbles his last breath around the metal blade.

A quick look towards Osfyth and I realise she and Maggenræd are making short work of Isarninus. As I suspected, he's not the warrior he claims to be. Heafoc's busy battling the huge warrior, the man who uses his weight but not his mind to place blows. With a giant fist clenched, he's beating against Heafoc's chest while Heafoc slices and stabs with his blade. Already, splatters of blood dot the stone floor, and a random hen pecks at what she believes is food.

I turn to Eastmund. He has the table of knives between him and the enemy. Almost sluggishly, he scoops up the blades, and uses them to stab down into the enemy warrior's hand, where one of them rests on the table. Blood's already bubbling from those fingers. The other warrior has removed the blade skewering him but howls in agony.

That leaves Bucge and Bægmund. Bucge's battling fiercely, her eyes flashing with fiery resolve as she counters two of Isarninus' warriors. I don't miss that in distancing himself from his warriors because he's craven, he's left himself exposed.

I struggle to see Bægmund, and when I do, I dash towards him. He's on the ground, a warrior leering over him menacingly. Bægmund's not moving. I'm unsure why until I get close enough, and then I see what's befallen him.

'Fighting a man who's insensible,' I glower, noting the smear of horse shit on the ground which must have fouled my warrior.

I fling myself onto the man's back, desperate to get

the blade and his fist away from Bægmund. Belatedly, I catch sight of the man who brought the two blades. I eye him. Dewi stands, hands on his fists.

'Help him,' I huff. 'Three blades in it for you.'

Not that I have time to see if he accepts my bargain or not. The man I'm gripping bolts beneath me, running forwards, trying to jostle me free. I quickly determine his intention. At the last moment, as he turns, meaning to knock me into the wall and wind me, I jump free, twisting my feet but managing to land on one knee and one foot with a huff of pain.

'Bastard,' my enemy glowers. I grin to see the slicing laceration I've scoured down his face. He bleeds, and blinks furiously, the cut so close to his left eye blood burbles into it.

But he's on me quickly, before I can secure the grip on my knife. He punches me. My head rebounds backwards, my nose erupting in a welter of blood. I taste the tang of iron and rust and duck aside from his following punch, using my knees and then surging upwards so I face his back. Now I hack into him using my blade, scoring three hits into his back before he can round on me.

Ignoring the streaming blood and his reduced vision, he comes at me with his elbow, forcing me to duck again to avoid him. I thought having better blades would make this easier, but this man isn't going down without a bloody fight. I slash towards him, but my cloak, so helpful until now, tangles my arm, and my aim falls short.

He's on me again, using both fists to pummel my arms and body. I absorb the impact, spitting my blood into his face, but he doesn't so much as grimace as my pink saliva joins his bleeding cut.

'I know you,' he roars angrily.

'And I bloody know you,' I reply, for in that moment I've realised who this man is. The very one who fed us while we were captives and, I'm sure, offered his piss to drink instead of water.

'I'll kill you,' he rages.

'I don't think so,' I retort, using my left hand to punch into his wound, and to give me the time I need to remove my cloak. I step back, cutting through the fabric close to the brooches which hold firmer than I think possible. I stab forward, aiming for his throat, only he jerks backwards, but all of my weight's balanced on my front foot. I can't redirect my strike. Not that I need to.

The blade grates through his open mouth, cutting his lips, severing the flesh all the way up to his nose as he howls in pain before my blade impales the back of his mouth and he chokes.

Hastily, I retrieve my blade, in case I need to strike again, but he's dead on his feet. A waver and he crashes to the floor. Only then do I turn to check on the rest of my warriors.

A shriek erupts from my mouth, my heart thudding loudly in my chest, my eyes sweeping over the scene of this fight. There's blood and gore everywhere, but somehow Isarninus still stands. He is, however, surrounded by all of my warriors apart from Bægmund.

I growl low in my throat. I need to end his life. I suspect the others know this as well. Maggenræd stands back, Bucge hobbles nearby. I have eyes only for Isarninus.

With an incline of my head for my warriors, I walk towards him.

Isarninus, blood on his beard, pants heavily. His mouth curls on seeing me.

'I know you,' he calls, fingering his blade. 'I know you,' he repeats, and he surprises me by smiling. 'You've come seeking vengeance, have you?'

'Vengeance, and the return of my treasures, yes.' I don't much wish to speak to him, but I do want him to know I'll kill him.

'Then I wish you luck with that,' he calls. Abruptly, his eyes narrow, and he licks his lips. 'You're

god-cursed, so I've been told by those who know you.'
I don't deny the news unnerves me, but for now my
focus is on Isarninus.

I point to my cheek, admittedly covered in dye
and my beard.

'I'm not god-cursed,' I delight. 'I'm marked by my
god to be a fine warrior.'

Isarninus chuckles, giggling almost, and I think
him quite mad. I realise only half of those watching
this understand our words.

'I'm Woden-marked,' I repeat, slowly, walking towards him, my breathing under control. But still Isarninus chuckles.

'They told me you were deluded. I realise now
how right they were.' And with no more words, and
no time for me to consider who this 'they' might be,
Isarninus leaps towards me, blade extended. I'm
aware of Heafoc shuddering, as though to intercept,
but he doesn't, bloodied Osfyth holding him back. I'm
grateful. This is my fight.

I flick my blade to counter the blow, considering
whether I might need a shield or not, but Isarninus,
as I suspected, is far from the warrior he believes himself to be. His movements are flash and showy,
sweeping the air with his blade, but there's no substance behind them. With a graceful movement, I

meet his strike, holding him off easily, and then I go from defending myself to attacking him, moving closer and closer to him, my new blade swirling so quickly I hear it cut the air. Isarninus skips back, and then back again, the amusement draining from his face. I smell his fear, and grimace, but hold my anger in check that he's always been little more than a small man dressed in the garb of a warrior.

With precise movements, I cut his chin, shearing away his beard, and then flick upwards, cutting his lower lip. He desperately tries to evade my blows, lifting his blade to counter my attack, but the weapon he holds can't sever and cut as mine can. I allow it to hit my back, but not to distract me.

Another flick, and now he bleeds along his collarbone. Another slice, and a slither opens on his exposed belly. Only then, I really have had enough.

'You will die,' I menace. 'You will die, as all those you've killed before. Cowering in your own shit and filth.' And with that, I retract my blade, redirect its perfect balance, and slice it through his mouth, quickly. I don't intend to prolong his death. That's not the sort of man I wish to be.

He gags on the blade, blood sheeting across my weapon and down his front. And then he falls, heavily. I realise I should have asked him who 'they' were, but there's no longer the opportunity.

I gasp, a quick glance to ensure Bægmund's well, and then a murmur of sound increases to a roar, and I turn to eye those still watching this. Some are fearful, stepping back from the fight hurriedly, but others are cheering, smiles on their faces, and the man who first brought our blades walks forward, grinning from ear to ear.

'That bastard needed to die many summers ago,' Dewi chuckles, kicking Isarninus, and then lowering his trews to piss on his face. 'I only wish I'd been the one to bloody do it.'

33

MEDDI OF THE EORLINGAS

The weather's cool, but I feel warm beneath my cloak and with the heat from the huge fire blazing just far enough away from the villa I needn't fear it catching alight. All the same, we have buckets of water to dampen down any stray sparks, and the youngsters under the command of our old warrior have been tasked with being alert to that happening.

It would be a terrible portent if such were to happen. I don't believe it will. The Eorlingas have triumphed.

Madog, his wife, with their daughter in her arms, and son, weave a steady path through all those assembled within the enclosure of our villa. Tonight we'll feast and drink and generally make fools of ourselves one more time before the dark times arrive and life becomes much more of a struggle. We'll celebrate the excesses the summer has brought us.

I note, with a pleased eye, the men who aren't on guard duty at the entranceway walk confidently, with new blades at their waists, sheathed for now in a variety of scabbards, for there's no need to use them. Unless, of course, there are problems with those invited to attend this feast provided by the Eorlingas.

The rich aroma of cooking beef fogs the air. Not one cow but two have been butchered for this coming together and celebration. Even with the Eorlingas grown to such a large number now we've been restored to our villa, that's far too much food for us to consume in one night. Instead, we've invited guests to join us. It's the first time Madog's felt comfortable to do so since he became our leader.

Those invited are our friends, and allies. I've already spoken with Padern of the Husmeræ. He informed me of Cadwysti's recent death. I'll ensure rites are said to remember her in the coming days, but not now.

'Did you ever find her?' Padern questions me, his eyes a little glazed from too much ale and probably mead as well. Not that he's insensible. Not yet.

'Alas no, but we did find my father's sword. And a great deal of blood. It must be assumed she's dead.'

'Well, it couldn't happen to a nicer individual,' Padern grunts.

I incline my head to him and then lean closer. 'If your new seeress ever needs any aid, please, send for me or Marchell. We'll do all we can to help her.'

At this Padern turns immediately more serious, and then nods, just once, revealing he's not as far gone on his ale as I thought. 'She's already wise beyond the winters she's lived, but I'll inform her of your very kind offer. She may well need some aid with a few of the older men and women more used to Cadwysti.'

I smile, and nod. It's ever the way with the oldsters and a new seeress. 'I experienced the same,' I offer as a reassurance.

Padern moves to intercept Madog, both of them embracing as though long-lost brothers, although I know Padern's keen to become a closer ally of Madog yet. I've seen him examining the fine blades the warriors now carry on their weapons belts.

I stop and adjust the brooches on my dress. The catch on the one's slowly becoming undone. I knew I should have chosen a different one, but the image of the twin horse-headed brooches is a powerful one, even beneath my cloak.

I look up and feel my forehead furrow.

'Mistress.' The woman bows towards me. I summon a smile. I'd not expected to see her here, although the invitation was extended.

'You're well?' I offer, recalled to the day at the beginning of the summer, when I returned the dead seeress to Ladus of the Stoppingas and was sent away, the body unclaimed.

'It's been difficult,' Ladus admits. I notice the ravages of her face in the dancing firelight. It's not yet the winter and, already, I suspect she and her people suffer without their warriors to provide for them. 'It'll be good to eat beef for the first time this year.'

Despite those words, she stands tall, proud, and I notice the shimmer of a golden torque around her neck, not dissimilar to the one I possess.

'We'll be well. The summer has been filled with problems. But we've much in store for the coming winter, despite appearances. The men were never good with the land and our resources. Next summer, we'll flourish.'

I nod, pleased to hear that.

'Tell me, did you ever find the woman?'

Uneasy at another unwelcome reminder I never

did discover Elen's body, I shake my head, and drink deeply from my beaker. 'Alas, no. But, it's believed she's dead, and her corpse lost in a river.'

'An unwelcome find for someone,' Ladus muses. 'But of course, food for the fish.' I grimace at the thought of pale, fish-nibbled flesh. She surprises me by laughing. 'It'll do someone some good, one day.' And then she too merges with the men and women talking too loudly as they celebrate the end of the growing season and the bounty of our harvest.

I find myself strangely distanced from it all. I've laboured to ensure the Eorlingas have what they need to survive the coming winter. Marchell and I have pots of unguents and dried herbs to treat winter colds and coughs. The horses and six foals are all strong and will survive with the good hay and oats grown and stored for them. I've tended to cuts and bruises, to women with child, and the oldsters, with backs riddled from their summers of scratching a living from the poor soil the Eorlingas had when banished from the villa throughout Edern's tenure. I've welcomed Madog's daughter into our tribe.

Yet a niggle of unease remains. Both Padern and Ladus have reminded me of the problem I shouldn't allow to fester in my mind.

Is Elen dead? Has her interference in my existence

finally come to an end? I'd like to know for certainty, but I'm never to have it. Marchell accepts it as accomplished. I wish I could do the same. For all I'm healed, there's a part of me hungering to know for sure my sister's definitely and absolutely dead.

'Seeress.' My brother recalls me to the here and now, the heat and the thrum of conversation, to the celebration this is intended to be. He smiles. I catch sight of the blade at his waist. He wears it proudly. Yes, it's not the sword of my father, but at its core is the heart of that blade.

'Madog,' I reply, swept along by the wide smile on his face.

'This is a fine feast, and Padern of the Husmeræ is most keen to know more about Terricus' work.'

'I'm sure he is,' I muse, not that it entirely surprises me.

'And those from the Færpingas are being respectful.'

'That pleases me, although I'm grateful we have the sharper blades here.'

Madog nods in agreement. I see him sway a little. Perhaps he's the one who's partaken of too much ale and mead.

'I've spoken with their leader, Prasto. He assures me the rumours of an attack were just that. Rumours.

He doesn't know how they developed. Perhaps too much ale consumed, when our trader was present. Some of the warriors do like to brag.'

'I imagine someone said something to the wrong person, as tends to happen.'

Madog nods again.

Maccus runs towards him, his face flushed and alight. 'Da, look at this.' He holds up something I take to be a small wooden stick. I can't see why the child is so keen to show it to his father. All smiles, Madog takes it into his hand, and pretends to examine it as he's done with Terricus' blades.

'It's a fine blade,' he tells his son. Maccus giggles, the sound vibrant and rising above the deeper voices of adults talking too loudly, against the crackle of the fire and the noise of so many people in one place all trying to talk at once.

'Madog,' Rhian calls to her husband. He places the wooden stick in my hand and turns to join her. I hold the small stick, watching my brother and his wife and children, a broad smile on my face, the tension from being reminded about Elen disappearing, as though a spark in the night air, jumping free from the fire only to be immediately quenched.

I turn aside, keen to check on Marchell who sits to the side of the feast, swaddled in thick cloaks, with

Sian for company. This coming winter, she'll live within the villa, with the benefit of the warmed floor to keep her moving. I'll not be as cruel as last winter. I owe her so much more, and it's about time I made that evident to her.

'How is she?' I murmur to Sian, from beside Marchell.

Sian grins at me, the winters drawn back from her face by the aid of the leaping shadows from the fire. 'She's well. Happily ordering all and sundry to do as she asks, summoning Padern and others to speak to her as though she were the leader of the Eorlingas.'

I nod. Smile as well. Marchell deserves this. I'm the seeress of the Eorlingas, but I know what I know thanks to her. It's good to see her restored to such a revered position amongst the people of the Eorlingas, and those who've been invited to join our feasting. Three days ago, Madog journeyed to the Husmeræ and indulged there. Seven days ago, he travelled to the Færpingas, and now he presides over a feast three times larger than any he's enjoyed, or so he assures us all. In such ways are our bonds with neighbouring tribes reaffirmed and strengthened. There will have been talk of unions between some of the younger men and women. Like the horses, there's a need for good breeding stock between our peoples.

We share so much and yet aren't quite the same. I know the Færpingas revere a different god to the ones we do. I know the Husmeræ grow different crops to us. The Stoppingas have few men left alive, and the younger women will need to breed with those more alike to them in age if the children brought forth are to be strong and hale. Old seed will only produce weak offspring, or so Marchell informs me.

It's only right our feast is larger than these three other peoples. We have more than them. We have the best horses. The most cattle. The best bull. The largest collection of hay and grains for the winter. And, of course, sharp blades with which to defend our largesse. Not that there's truly a need to fear here inside the protective double-ringed ditch surrounding Villa Eorlingas.

'What's that?' Marchell questions me as her eyes focus on what I'm holding, and she points to my hand.

'Maccus was pretending it was a blade of the finest iron,' I chuckle. Marchell nods, but the humour leaves her face as an insistent hand reaches for it.

I know a flicker of worry as she moves her hand up and down the stick, feeling the indentations in it, while the humour flees from her face. She goes to stand, but is restricted by the furs covering her to keep the cold from her body.

'Marchell, what is it?' I demand, hurrying with Sian to stop her from falling.

'This, go and look at it in better light,' she demands, her voice wavering with fury, thrusting Maccus' stick towards me angrily. I look at it, but really it's too dark to see much.

'Stay here,' I urge Marchell and Sian, and quickly make my way inside the main villa building. Within, there are silver plates heaped with good food and enough light from candles reflecting on the washed walls, I can see much more. My fingers quest over the stick, or what I thought was simply a wooden stick, my forehead furrowing as I hurry my steps. By the time I'm within, I know why Marchell's so angry. To see the lines carved into the wood is shocking.

'Surely not,' I mutter to myself, turning and hurrying back towards Madog. I almost collide with Urien as my feet cross the familiar mosaic laid into the floor, depicting the horses so important to us. His hands reach out to stop me from falling.

'Seeress,' he begins, but then he sees my face. It must concern him. 'What is it?' he demands.

'Have the men prepared. I fear we're to be attacked from within, not without.'

I thrust the stick towards him, and immediately comprehension covers his face as he also sees the careful lines carved into it. To most, they would be little more than a collection of marks, perhaps tally sticks. But that's not what they are. Not at all. The wood is from a silver birch, and that makes the green-tinged marks even more noticeable.

This is the oldest form of a declaration of hostilities, usually situated before the entrance to a settlement. The fact it was placed into Maccus' hands worries me more than anything. And if not gifted into his hands, then found by him. He's a nosy child. He gets into everything. He might just have given us valuable time to prepare.

'I'll alert the men. Tell Madog. Get everyone somewhere safe,' he shouts to me. I sense eyes on me from those gathering food to eat and drinking deeply of the ale and mead. I need to seek calmness.

'People of the Eorlingas, find what you can to protect yourself, anything, even these silver plates, and take yourself into the back room, the one with the door that can be closed and barred.' I see shocked eyes looking my way, and confused ones from Padern's people. I make a hasty decision, one I hope I won't regret. 'Take Padern's people with you, and

Ladus',' I order, some new and old friends already turning to do just that.

Before the words have left my mouth, I hear a rumble from outside, one of outrage that could have come from the sky above, and a chill runs down my spine, cold sweat sheeting my forehead. Everyone within that room stops and looks at me because I'm still within the doorway.

'Go, now,' I roar, and follow Urien outside, into the flame-lit night.

I don't know who's betrayed us, or even why. But I'll see every single last one of the bastards dead.

34

WÆRMUND OF THE GYRWE

We're bloodied and bruised, but as one we take our horses towards Isarninus' hilltop site, the dead flung over the backs of the mounts that originally brought live men to the market. We're joined by the five warriors, with Dewi as their leader, and they all now benefit from good blades. It seemed a small way of repaying them for their aid with Bægmund, and then with those who were angered because we killed in the sanctuary to this damn holy martyr. I lead the horse with Isarninus' dead body on it. I'm pleased to have finally taken the life of a genuine enemy. Admittedly, I wish I knew if he'd truly sent word to my father. I'll never know. Now.

We all ache from our exertions, but there's still

more to do, and we intend to do it before leaving Verulamium. I hope never to return here, although what I'll do now Isarninus is dead, I'm unsure. One thing I do know, I'll not settle here. I don't wish to rule the people who were once beholden to Isarninus. No. I think we'll return to Uriconium. I believe my future, and hopefully that of the rest of my warriors, lies far away from here. And from my father's reach, in the east.

Our unlooked-for allies are loud and raucous, more buoyed up on what we accomplished than my warriors. Bægmund's wounded, but he rides with us. If we have to fight to gain entry to Isarninus' stronghold to reclaim our lost treasures, he'll be no good to us. I'll contend with that shortly.

For now, blood and sweat dries on my face, making me itch once more, although I can finally scrub the crushed walnut hulls from my beard, moustache and hair. I don't need to hide any more. I can wear my wolf-shaped birthmark proudly.

In no time at all, we're almost level with the entrance to Isarninus' stronghold. I see the gated enclosure is open. All the same, I pause. This could still be a trap. They might know of Isarninus' death and there could be more warriors within who'll fight us. It might have been easy enough to overwhelm those accompanying Isarninus to the market, but there could be better warriors within.

Smoke from cook fires floods the air, as does the smell of baking bread, and the aroma of the penned cattle. There are many cattle now. Isarninus gained a great deal when he stole from the Hicca last summer. He took us and our treasures as well as the cattle.

'What now?' Osfyth questions. She's bound her wounded arm. I eye Heafoc. His keen gaze assesses our likely welcome. I feel my hand reaching for my new blade, while my leg bangs into my shield, re-moved from its storage sack and visible for all to see. The emblem there, that of a wolf like the one marking my face, speaks to who I am. I've become a wolf war-rior, using stealth to steal what I need to feed my blade.

My fellow warriors are daubed with the same em-blem. Admittedly, some depictions are better than others. Bucge might be good at many things, but painting isn't one of them. It caused much amuse-ment when Gwladus advised us to decorate our shields to mark ourselves out and to ensure we recog-nised one another in the heat of battle.

'We wait,' Heafoc suggests, bringing his horse to a halt before us. We don't stop the other animals though, with their grizzly cargoes. Indeed, I en-

courage them through the entranceway. I eye Isarninus' bleached-white face with a smirk. In death, he's
nothing. I see now much of who he was had more to
do with the way he held his body and walked, and his
arrogance, rather than any huge bulk or ability to
fight well.

Not for the first time, I consider how he came to
be the leader of these people. He said he was *comitatus*. I doubt that. I don't see how a man such as him
could ever have fought against the enemy and won. I
think he used stealth and subterfuge to get what he
wanted.

The first shriek from within jolts me from my
thoughts. My hand once more reaches for my blade,
and I sense the five other warriors doing the same.
Perhaps I shouldn't have allowed them to escort us.
Maybe, I realise, I should have discovered their true
identities before having them come with us. After all,
Dewi is so happy Isarninus is dead he pissed on his
face, but perhaps he means to replace him.

More and more cries flood the air, accompanied
by the wailing of women and small children. Still, I
don't order us on. Heafoc holds up his hand when
Osfyth's horse shuffles forwards.

'We wait,' I order. Our new friends are tense,
waiting to run through the gateway, and kill

whomever is within – if there's anyone but women and small children, and those too old to protect themselves, that is.

And still we wait. I agree with Heafoc. There's something we need to witness, or hear, and then we'll know it's safe to enter.

Instead, a roar of male outrage floods the enclosure, accompanied by a gabble of voices.

'We should go,' Eastmund complains.

'No, we wait,' I caution again, remaining mounted.

It's then a collection of warriors emerge through the gateway, one of them leading the others. I consider who he is. Maybe Isarninus' battle commander.

'You did this?' he demands, indicating the horse with Isarninus' corpse on it which he's led outside. I nod, and indicate my fellow warriors.

Behind him, I see the others sharing worried looks. Some are armed with little more than an eating knife or axe for chopping wood. A few have old and bashed copper breastplates, but most don't. However, the warrior who leads them has everything he might need to fight us.

There's a shield, a spear in his other hand, and around his waist are more blades. He even has Isarninus' white-haired helm on his head. For all he looks the part, I can tell from his stance he's no warrior, or if he is, not a very good one.

'Who are you?' I demand.

'I'm the leader here, now you've killed Isarninus. We'll have our revenge against you.'

'Will you?' I question, sitting back on my horse, casually. 'I don't think you could skewer the spot on the end of your chin,' and I realise I'm taunting him. It's akin to what my father used to do to me. Perhaps I should be grateful his derogatory remarks were always so well aimed. I've a large collection of them to fling at this boy who thinks to be a man. I sense the five new warriors chuckling at me. My warriors don't. In fact, Heafoc flicks me a quick look.

'We'll take our revenge and leave your bleeding corpses for the crows,' the boy shrieks, voice breaking because he shouts so loudly, and also because he's really but a boy.

'We don't have to fight,' I murmur. 'All I want is my treasures and the animals stolen from the Hicca. Then we'll leave here. Our argument was with Isarninus.'

'No,' the boy cries.

'What's your name?' I question quickly.

'I'm Iuti, son of Isarninus. I remember you, you bastards.'

'I remember you as well,' I menace, the horse picking up on my deepening tone. 'Your father coddled you,' I retort, reminded too keenly of my father and brother. Waga was about as much use as this arsehole before me. 'If you fight us, we'll win,' I state confidently.

'No, you won't,' he rejects, chin raised defiantly, although I can hear the spear pinging off his breastplate because he's shaking violently. 'You think these are all the warriors we have?' Now I still. I bloody did think that was all the warriors he had, and about as much use as a spindle beater for scything through the crops, the lot of them. I sense a shiver of unease along my body, and somehow, I realise, I'm not at all surprised when Cenbryht steps forward from those who surround him.

'Wærmund,' Cenbryht sneers, gaze assessing. I've not missed the bastard. He was the last and most important member of my initial warrior band who decimated my brother and his village. I always suspected him, but it was Wædel who betrayed me first. But Cenbryht's been missing since we escaped from Isarninus' hill fort. 'Your numbers aren't what they once were,' Cenbryht comments lightly, reminding me of the many we've lost at the end of a blade or because they were traitors. 'I have a few more with me.' And now I see seven of my father's warriors joining Cenbryht while the men and women of Isarninus step backwards, as though this is their task done and finished with. 'It's serendipitous you're here. Your father sent us to find you. We'd only tracked you as far as Isarninus'. From here, we had no idea where you'd gone.' I hold my fury in check. I doubted Cenbryht from the beginning. I was right to do so. He has, indeed, returned to my father and told him where I am.

'Well, we're here now, and happy to end your lives, as we did Isarninus'.'

'There's really no need for that,' Cenbryht states. 'We didn't come to fight you, but to take you back to your father.' I'm aware of Heafoc's unease at this unlooked-for turn of events. Bægmund's groaning weakly. The five other warriors look perplexed.

'You know these men?' Dewi calls.

'I do, alas. They're men of the Gyrwe. Warriors from my homeland. There's nothing to fear from them.' But I suspect there's a great deal to fear from them. I thought we'd overwhelmed Isarninus and would simply stroll in and take back what was ours. I should have been more circumspect. I should have considered one full summer and winter wouldn't make my father forget what I did to Waga and his

people. And the others we also killed when they attempted to murder us.

'Now, little Wærmund, you can come quietly, and
we can let the women go, or you can fight, and then
you'll all die.'

I'm eyeing the warriors. We killed many of my father's men last summer. I know we can overawe them
once more now we have such good blades. But we're
already tired and bloodied. If we were fresh, it
wouldn't be a problem, I'm sure of it.

'Come on, hurry up and make your decision,'
Cenbryht comments conversationally, while Isarninus' son looks on, his stance belligerent.

'We won't come quietly, as you ask,' I call to Cenbryht, aware my heart once more thuds loudly in my
chest. My sluggish limbs are stirring to life, the sweat
beading my face becoming less of an irritant, as I
reach for my shield, and slip from my horse, a slap on
the animal's backside to have it move away from us.
My fellow warriors copy me, and even Dewi and his
men who brought our blades stand close to me.

I look to them.

'We fight together in a shield wall. If you want to
join us, then do so at either end of the shield wall. We
have our own ways of aiding one another.' I sense a
flicker of unease on the men's faces. After all, three of

them have only just been given good fighting blades. They weren't expecting to face warriors of the calibre my father has always demanded.

'We'll do what we can,' Dewi affirms. 'We won't get in your way.'

'My thanks,' I murmur, and then turn to my warriors, even Bægmund, who've dismounted, and prepare to face an enemy we weren't expecting to see this day.

I offer them a smile, and ram the helm gifted to me by Gwladus over my head, while I test the weight of the shield and spear in my hand. We've not fought an enemy over the summer, well, not for many weeks, and not at all in an actual fight to the death. Now we face fighting twice in one day and this battle will be our ultimate test.

We simply can't fail.

Not now.

Not when we've come so far together and accomplished so much. We've become a true warrior band, a real *comitatus*, forged from iron and muscle, sinew and respect for one another.

'Right, let's kill the bastards,' I roar.

35

MEDDI OF THE EORLINGAS

The night's ablaze, or so it feels. Urien's dogged ahead of me. I intend to follow him but then remember Marchell and Sian. I can't abandon them, and Marchell won't be able to win free from her furs, let alone take herself to safety. Nothing must happen to her, not when we've achieved so much in a short space of time. Not when we're united as mother and daughter.

'Go on,' I urge Urien when he falters, realising I'm not following him. 'Get to Madog. Protect him and his children. I'll get Marchell.' There are people everywhere. Some still so filled with the joyfulness of this feast they've oblivious to anything untoward. Yet others, the people of the Eorlingas, dash towards where they know to seek protection. I force my way through the crush of women, children and the oldsters able to propel themselves towards the villa itself, to where I left Marchell.

My breath is harsh in my throat. A horrible fear threatens to stick my feet to the ground, making me useless. I fight off the terror and sudden fatigue. I just need to get to Marchell and Sian.

Already, I see people on the ground, bleeding from wounds, or trampled into stillness. My breath hitches once more, and then I reach Sian. She looks at me, all competent and assured, Marchell already standing, as though awaiting me.

'What are you doing here?' Marchell demands with the authority that's deserted me. 'Get away. Find your breastplate. Help the men. We'll be well,' she assures, but then stops, and reaches out to grip my arm. 'Meddi, you can do this. Protect your people. Protect your brother. Protect the Eorlingas. You know how.' Around us, the chaos fades away. I focus only on the flashing core of Marchell's eyes, the flames of the rapidly escalating fire reflected there. 'Do this,' she urges me. And then swallows. Her next words are wrenched from her and I know how much she grieves for events of the past. 'Don't let your people down. Don't do what I did.' And with that, she releases my hand, and moves aside, with more speed than I anticipate. I watch her for the blink of an eye, and then I'm running, to my workshop, to my breast-plate and copper blade, to all I am and all I must be.

Hastily, I thrust the breastplate in position, the catches tangling so I have to stop myself from rushing and focus on what must be done. Only then I hear the shriek of my favoured mare. It's not terror. No, she calls to me through the carnage of this fight. The walls of my workshop do nothing to stop the sound permeating.

On feet that move more quickly than I think pos-sible, I hurry towards the stables. They're far from the fire, as is right. There are people everywhere. The shadows are filled with the promise of the enemy, but here, to the rear of the villa complex, I know my way easily, and there are only people of the Eorlingas for me to shout to and surge through.

'Get within,' I urge those I see. 'Take Padern and Ladus' people with you,' I also shriek. It's hard to have myself heard over the roar of the flames, the strangled cries of those being cut down, and the increasingly agitated neighs of the horses. Smoke's starting to foul the air as well, making my eyes sting. I close my mouth, holding my hand before it to try and stop my-self from coughing.

The closer I get to the stables, the fewer people I see. Quickly, I dart inside, rushing to my mare, but aware of the terrified cries of the foals and their mothers. I don't know what to do with them. Is it better to allow them to run free, and not be contained if the fire spreads? I'm unsure. We can't risk them being injured, or killed.

I look to my mare, and then to the kicking mothers and their foals. The smaller animals are wide-eyed even in the dull light. The thickening smoke threatens to send them wild. I swallow down my reservations, and move quickly through the barn, releasing wooden catches and even freeing the oxen. The two animals are just as valuable as the horses. I'm grateful the sheep are still grazing, and the pigs comfortable in their stinking sty to the far, far end of the enclosure, as well as the cows that remain after the slaughter.

Some of the animals move, others don't, the noise from outside as terrifying as the smoke. I've done what I can.

Hurriedly, I mount my mare, patting her shoulder, and directing her towards the open doorway. It's difficult to see, but we both know the way. We know where to avoid the dips in the pathways and how to reach where I suspect my brother will be standing and fighting with his allies.

I don't look back to the horses. I hope they'll leave. I mutter a prayer to my god to keep them safe, but for now it's my brother and my people that consume me. I must protect them from whoever thinks to kill us.

I shouldn't have allowed this feast. I should have realised the Eorlingas still had many enemies. It's no great tactic to make overtures of friendship and then turn on those who believe you're an ally. But I banish such thoughts and, from atop my horse, I survey my home.

'Come on,' I urge my mare. She obeys me without flinching from the smoke or the screams.

In the dancing orange flames from the celebratory fire, I see the rest of the villa remains undisturbed. Whoever these people are, they want Villa Eorlingas intact, just as Edern once did.

A horrifying memory of that day surges into my mind, crashing into my head, and I shudder, and then swallow. Marchell trusts me to do this, and I must do it.

'This way.' We move quickly towards where I hear the crash of iron and wood, to the side of the villa, not far from the fire. The enemy mean to have light with which to see. They've given this a great deal of thought.

I can see much more from my horse's back. Quickly, I scour the landscape. My brother and his men – ably assisted by Urien, Tudwal and Kenal – are fighting a concerted attack by about twenty enemy. I can't see everything in the smoke. There are already some lying unmoving on the ground. I swallow against my sudden grief. I find myself hoping Terricus lives. So close. We can't lose him when we've rediscovered the lost magiks of how to forge iron into blades that can kill with a slicing cut and not just a stabbing motion.

I also see Padern, and his warriors. They fight with my brother. They aren't the enemy then. I knew in my heart they weren't. I was correct to protect his people.

Instead, my eyes focus on the shields being used against my brother's warriors. It's difficult to make out the details, but I'm sure the enemy are the Færpingas.

Staying back from the front of the fighting, I take a calming breath, and then, confident my horse understands my intentions, I begin to murmur, building to a thundering bellow. The words are so loud even I can't hear them, but all eyes look my way briefly. The lull in the fighting is audible briefly before it resurges. In that moment, I hope they see me for what I am, a seeress at the height of her abilities and able to call upon her ancestors and gods to protect her people.

I see a condescending smile on the face of the lead warriors amongst the Færpingas, but I know they lack a seeress and, instead, ascribe to a different religion. They'll see the error of their ways.

My hands are busy, my words meaningful, my cloak swept back so my breastplate is visible to all. In both hands, I carry the spangles of my craft, using them to take me away from here, driving the rage and fury of this slaughter to the back of my mind.

Closing my eyes, I concentrate on my words and actions, on finding the calmness and understanding I first experienced beneath the trees when returning from hunting for Elen. When I was healed. I know my people will not be abandoned by their horse god. For too long, we've protected our animals and lived with them in a special relationship. I know our god will aid us. She showed me the way to make the knives we need to protect ourselves. She healed me. She'll not abandon us now.

I perceive it. Before me, although my eyes remain closed, I sense the arrival of something else. The fighting continues to be bloody and brutal. I hear my brother urging his warriors on, the cries of those using all their strength to defeat a lethal foe.

Abruptly, my eyes open. I glower down into the taunting eyes of one of the Færpingas. He's a tall man, hair stringy, a dull blade flashing in his hand, a breastplate covering his chest, as he comes towards me, lips twisted with disdain.

I shudder, recalled to the here and now when I was on the cusp of something else. A startled gasp erupts from my mouth. My horse moves backwards, hooves clattering loudly over the stone surface. The blade comes close, too close, my hands too busy with my spangles to bring my shield in front of me and my horse. At the last possible moment, Kenal erupts from the smoke-filled air, his blade seeking my enemy's back. I think he'll score a direct blow and the foeman will falter, but my foe's more alert than that. He turns and counters the attack. I watch with horrified eyes as he lands a heavy blow against Kenal's shield, only just raised in time to prevent him being cut.

But it's enough. For now. Confident Kenal will protect me, I close my eyes once more, summoning the strength I fleetingly felt. Only my heart pounds too loudly, my breathing ragged. I seek the serenity I experienced before this attack. Tudwal's frantic cry rips at my resolve. I swallow my fear for him. For all of us. I can only do one thing at the moment, and it's the only way we can live through this and keep hold of Villa Eorlingas.

The night's a riot of crashing iron, thundering wood and the anguished cries of those who are wounded or bleeding their last.

The only constant is the horse beneath me, the animal I've known for much of my life. I focus on her. On the lifeblood thrumming through her, on the solid presence of her, banishing thoughts of my brother, my mother, my warriors, Terricus and Rhian.

I sense my god once more, and hold on to the steadiness required. My hands again run the spangles through them, my words are quiet, and then bellowing. I open my eyes, sight the stars above my head, shimmering brightly above the haze of the thickening smoke. And then I see her. And I know what I must do.

'Come on, girl.' I lower my hand to run it over my horse's shoulder. I feel the shuddering beat of her lifeblood there. She quivers, but her legs are firm.

She leaps forward, obeying my command, into the mass of swirling men, into the crashing of iron and wood, salt and rust, into the melee of the enemy and our warriors.

A crash, a snap, a howl of outrage and we're

through the collection of enemy warriors. I seek out my god, and see her, taking form in the swirl of mares who are standing, eyes wide, chests heaving, to the front of the villa. I allow a smile to touch my lips.

'Come on, girl.' I take my horse to the other mares. She nickers in greeting, and we turn, facing the back of our enemy. There's a gaping hole in the attack through which my horse cantered. I see shattered limbs and hear howling men, broken by my horse's hooves.

Without a single word of command, I bend low over my horse's neck. She leads the mares towards the fight. We crash into them once more. There are enough of us to direct our paths towards every single one of the standing enemy. A sharp snap of fracturing bones, a brief vision of a flailing limb. When it's almost too late, my horse bunches her back legs beneath her and soars over where my brother abruptly ducks lower, his eyes wild with shock, his face covered in the grey of the ash and smoke of the fire.

I hear the shriek of one of the animals and know a moment of fear, but the confusion caused by the unexpected attack seems to be working. The enemy's much reduced. The collection of fighting warriors has narrowed. I see Kenal, his lips red-rimmed, I think in the glow from the fire, and he's breathing heavily, but the man who thought to attack me is unmoving on the ground.

I turn the horses, prepared to lead them once more, into the sea of fighting, the sharp blades of the warriors rising and falling as though a rough sea, although the sound from the wounded and dying is as far from peaceful as it's possible to be.

I bend, and again run my hand over my horse's shoulder. I sense the stink of burning hair, and reach over to smack back flames running along another of the animal's manes, thinking nothing of the discomfort. The animal turns pain-hazed eyes my way but stands firm.

Before me, the fighting's turning in the favour of the Eorlingas. But I don't allow myself to luxuriate. No. There might be more of the bastards. I consider the men on guard duty and call to Kenal.

'We must go to the entranceway,' I urge him. He gulps, nods and turns to run that way. 'Take one of the mares,' I urge him, seeking out Madog in the mass of fighting. I see him. His blade is busy, severing flesh as easily as he did the cooked chicken when Terricus was first successful at forging the sharp edges of our blades.

My horse crashes through the enemy, an abrupt crack assuring me there are still some of the enemy to kill. The other horses follow once more, but my focus is now on where other foemen might be fighting more of our men.

As we move further away from the fire, darkness coats the land. The smoke begins to clear, allowing me to see more. My horse is sure-footed, and I'm aware more than Kenal keeps me company. Tudwal's also there, and even Urien. I hope my brother hasn't been entirely abandoned by his warriors, but then I see him as well, also mounted on one of the mares.

We thunder towards the entranceway, but not far from it, I appreciate the small fire lit there has been extinguished. The unmistakable aroma of burning flesh singes my nose.

I cough, eyes trying to see.

'Be wary,' my brother calls, asserting his command over our unruly advance. 'Be wary,' he reiterates, forcing his horse in front of mine. He doesn't look at me.

'Lord,' a familiar and fatigued voice calls.

'Idnerth, what happened here?' my brother barks.

'They tried to come through. We blocked the passage as best we could. It's good to see you alive, my lord.'

'You sent no warning.'

'I couldn't.' Urien's dismounted, and hastily removed some of whatever was blocking the fire. Flames leap upwards and now I realise why Idnerth could send no warning. He's trapped. A piece of the heavy gate has fallen over him, his legs held firmly in place by it. He bleeds badly from somewhere, his upper body sheeted in dark fluid.

I swallow against my sudden grief for him. He won't survive this.

'Spread out,' my brother commands. 'Two warriors together. Ensure the enemy are all dead. Take brands with you,' he also orders. 'Urien, Kenal and Tudwal, remain here with me and the seeress.'

A shuffle of horses, and I'm aware there are fewer of us now.

'Help me,' Madog commands. Together, the four men heave on the broken-down gateway and release it from Idnerth's body. I dismount as well, rushing to Idnerth's side, but while I'm aware of my brother and his fellow warriors returning the gate to the gateway, shoring up the defences to keep them blocked, I hold the hand of our dying warrior.

'You're a brave man,' I urge him, on my knees, unheeding of the smell of his bowels and the blood covering everything.

'My family,' he mutters, as his head falls backwards, the strength leaving him.

'Will be protected and cared for,' I promise.

'Seeress.' His words are little more than a whisper. 'I see her,' he states, wonder in his voice, and while I don't see her any more, I certainly feel her, close by. The god of the Eorlingas has come to take one of her people to the afterlife.

'Go speedily,' I urge him, and feel his body slacken. Tears sheet my face as I bow my head and offer more words for his safe travels.

Only when I sense the scrutiny of others do I look up.

Madog eyes me with fury on his familiar face, tears dripping down his ash-coated cheeks.

'Now, we hunt down the bastards, and make sure they're all dead.' And with that, he beckons Tudwal and Kenal to his side. 'Urien, stay here and protect Meddi and the gates. Ensure no one gets in or leaves. If more come, build the fire higher to warn us. And Meddi, restrain the rest of the mares. We can't lose them.'

36

WÆRMUND OF THE GYRWE

Our shields clash together, one over the other, the rippling effect reassuring me no matter how tired we are, how spent our bodies, we'll fight as brothers and sisters, determined to overawe these men who still think so little of my abilities they believe I'll capitulate and be easy to beat.

I observe the enemy. My father's men have done the same. I eye their weapons and shields. The shields are good, I admit. The weapons I doubt. They don't have the keenness of our blades, which we've shown can split the air, if we've a mind to do so.

'Advance,' I bellow, grateful to feel the strength of Heafoc to one side of me and Eastmund to the other. Next to Eastmund is Bucge, and then Maggenræd and

Bægmund. Beside Heafoc fights Osfyth. We're uneven now. I'm no longer protected by the same number of my warriors to either side as once. But I don't need them. Three of the other men have already slid into position there, and the other two to the side of Bægmund.

With steady steps, we crash against the enemy, shields extended before us, our blades in hands. Some of my father's warriors have spears, and they try to slip between our shields, but have no success. Those spears will be little use to them. I slither my knife between my shield and that of Eastmund's. The blade shimmers with the lifeblood of men I've already killed, including Isarninus. I smirk to see it, and jab forwards, determined to land first blood.

Unsurprisingly, Cenbryht faces me. He knows how we fight. Or he thinks he knows. He's been gone from our company for a long time. Throughout the summer, we've trained and practised with our new blades with the aid of the Wreocensætan. We must fight differently with them. No longer do we use the weight of the blades, but instead the fine cutting edge.

At the last moment, Cenbryht jerks his head away from my reach, but not before a shimmer of his cut hair falls to the ground.

'Bastard,' he huffs, breath hot in my face. I know

to fear Cenbryht. He was one of my father's chosen warriors. He's evidently wormed his way back into my father's favours. But I'm not the arsehole of last year who thought he could fight. No. I've honed my skills, and so have my allies.

I retract my blade, and thrust once more, at the last moment, slashing to my right, and severing the cheek of the man who fights there. Bright eyes flick my way, but Eastmund's also attacking him. He can't fight me and Eastmund. Cenbryht, sensing my distraction, crashes his shoulder into his shield, thinking to disturb my balance, but it fails. Heafoc and I are wedged so closely together, he and Eastmund keep me upright, no matter Cenbryht's intentions.

I can hear the shiver of our knives in the hands of my warriors, and the new men. Our enemy have nothing as good. But they do have rage. And their confidence. It won't better us.

Once more, I slip the blade between the two shields. This time, I lower my shield, watching Cenbryht as he hammers his blade against my shield. This time, I aim for his ear, and at the last moment, he detects the stealthy movement, and moves aside, but in the process he offers me the side of his neck instead. A much better target.

Blood wells from his sliced neck before he can so

much as move aside. It pools quickly down, sinking into his tunic, a howl of outrage on his lips, shock in his eyes.

I spare a thought for my fellow warriors, and realise they're having the same success as me. We all stand firm. We fight together. I'm aware of Heafoc to my left and Eastmund to my right. And a bleeding Cenbryht before me. I offer him a smile.

'Not a bad blade,' I suggest, and then thrust my shoulder against the shield, exerting all of my force against him, my head lowered beneath the curving edge of the protection.

His knife clatters against the reinforced rim of the shield, the sound loud and twanging, but he mistimes the action and his blade slips from his grip.

'Bollocks,' he roars. I sense his attention being diverted as he tries to reach for a new blade.

Quickly, I raise my head, and take a risk on leaning straight over. But Cenbryht's looking down. I have his head as a target, not his neck or face. He must sense my attention. He glances up, and that's when I slice the blade into his eye, cutting like a hot knife through butter, as he gargles and ineffectively tries to stop it with his hand. His hand's immediately cut, his grip failing him. While he howls in pain, I retract my knife and slide it into his open mouth, until he's gargling. He falls dead with a whimper. I almost overbalance and follow him down.

I just keep my feet and clutch my blade. Behind him, I see the frightened eyes of Isarninus' people as they hurry back inside the defences. They thought this would be their victory but it's not going to be.

Beside me, Heafoc's foeman is also on the ground. Eastmund's making short work of his opponent. Indeed, the huffs of a fight to the death are growing fainter.

I take a deep breath, and meet Heafoc's gaze. He's bleeding from his nose, licking the madder-red away. I glance further along the shield wall, to where Osfyth's almost overwhelmed her enemy and where the other men, which were three in number, are now, I'm sure, only two, but they're fighting well.

I'd go to their aid, but to do so would unsettle the shield wall. Instead, I fix my gaze on Isarninus' people.

'Get my treasure, or you'll be next,' I roar. Three women fall over themselves in their hurry to get away from me. I sense Eastmund's foeman fall, and realise our victory is near, only then a huge man barrels his way through the screaming, shrieking women. I feel the smile slip from my face.

I know this man. He's long been one of my father's

preferred warriors. Not because he can fight with skill or precision but because he's so tall, and so powerfully built, enemy warriors have never been able to get near him with their blades.

'Wærmund, you piece of shit,' he growls, taking in the fight and the state of his fellow warriors, mostly all dead now. 'I should have done this myself,' he grumbles, coming towards our shield wall, lacking a shield, but with a breastplate hammered to shape him that will do that work for him. He's accompanied by two other men. His sons. They're not as tall as him, but they're as broad, and they have chests as rippled as the breastplates. If they took their breastplates off, they'd still look as well formed.

'Bollocks,' I explode.

'Hold firm,' Heafoc reassures. 'For men with heads that huge, they're as slow-witted as sheep.'

I consider Heafoc's words, the sheep reference in particular, and then I understand.

'As one,' I roar to my warriors who're still standing. We've lost one of the five new men, and Bægmund's also absent, but he was already wounded. 'Push them,' I urge. We meet the attack of the three men with all of our strength. Those who lack shields slip into place behind us, using their vigour to reinforce ours. It's not a moment too soon. As we clash, I feel my feet slipping on the bloodstained grasses, my shield so tight against my chest it's an effort to take a deep breath.

With the aid of those behind me – Heafoc, Osfyth, Eastmund, Bucge and Maggenræd – we first get some distance between my body and my shield, and then, with my feet more firmly held on the ground, we begin to move against them.

This isn't about having the best blades. This is all about the strength in our arms and legs, my ability to keep hold of my shield, and my desire to overwhelm the enemy.

Slowly, so slowly I don't even realise I'm moving my feet, all the weight on my back leg, and then my front one, taking small, shuffling steps closer and closer, the three enemy warriors are forced to retreat. I sense their confusion. I realise Heafoc was correct to suggest this. What an incredible weakness to have. These men, so used to having only their strength to use against an enemy, struggle to retreat, just as sheep never wish to move backwards, their focus always on getting through whatever tangle of hedgerow they've become caught up in.

'Keep it up,' Heafoc roars. I feel sweat on my forehead. I sense the strain in my arms and legs, pushing me to accomplish more than I ever have before, and the shield wall moves again.

'Come on,' I shriek when I can catch a full breath. 'Come on, this is bloody it.'

And it is. Our enemy are shouting one to another, confusion in their voices. And now is the time to take advantage.

'Now,' I scream. I lower my shield, as do the rest of us, and we face our enemy, feet shuffling backwards, faces twisted, and despite my foeman's bulk, and his muscles, and his breastplate, I slide my blade into the exposed area on his lower belly. His skin opens up like a pig's gut, his innards tumbling to the ground as he roars in shock. Heafoc stabs him higher, angling the blade beneath his breastplate to where his heart should beat. He stills, and drops, the force of him sending a shiver of wind up my sweating legs.

All three of the bastards are dead. As is Cenbryht, and all the other bastards who thought to get in our way.

'Get my treasure,' I roar at the few remaining men and women who've not retreated inside the protective walls of the enclosure.

I expect my treasure to be handed to me immediately, by Isarninus' son, as I turn to face my warriors, desperate to be reassured they're all well and hale. My battle joy fades immediately to grief, for Bægmund's on the ground. He's not moving, a spear impaling his shoulder.

I rush to him, but Bucge beats me to it, her face blood-smeared, her movements laboured, her limp intensified by the fighting we've endured.

'Is he?' I ask, hardly daring to ask the question, but her sagging shoulders tell me all I need to know.

Angrily, I turn back to face the embankment of our enemy, desperate now to seek more vengeance for Bægmund's death. But my anger dies on my face. For they've not brought my treasure. Far from it.

My mouth drops open in shock at seeing the woman before me. She's much changed. Her hair is no longer lustrous. She walks with the aid of a stick, and Isarninus' son supports her, but for all that, she's regal. Her lips are downcast, as she runs her hands through the metal objects hanging from the girdle of her dress.

'Elen,' I whisper, the sound of hands seeking blades assuring me my allies see her as well as I do. I hear a hissed intake of breath amongst my warriors but keep my gaze on Elen.

'Wærmund.' She inclines her head towards me, surveying the paling bodies, nose wrinkling at the sharp stink of so much shit and piss, blood and pain.

'I'm pleased you're here,' she offers, her smile broadening despite everything, speaking in my tongue. 'These people are now mine. I'm their seeress.' It seems she's taken the time to learn to speak as I do throughout the summer. I consider how. Had Cenbryht been here all along?

I shake my head, astounded she's alive after Bucge's fight with her, and so very far from where that fight took place. There was so much blood. I'd like to ask her how she lives. But now isn't the time. Instead, a quick glance towards Bucge, and I'm reassured Osfyth and Heafoc have her restrained from hasty actions against the woman who wounded her so badly. But the expression on Dewi's face surprises me.

'Ah, you thought I was dead,' Elen chuckles.

My silence is telling.

'Not only do I live, young Wærmund, but I assure you, I've some very strong allies as well. Stronger than these men.' Her eyes graze the corpses of my father's dead warriors. I feel a shudder of unease. There are so few of us now. We left the land of the Gyrwe twelve strong, there's now half of that number, unless, of course, the four surviving warriors, led by Dewi, join me.

I swallow heavily, my joy in our victory evaporating like water over the blades Katourn forged for us.

'Your father will be here shortly. He'll recompense me handsomely now I can tell him where you are. And when he kills you, I'll have that fine blade you wear at your waist,' she announces, confidence oozing from her. 'I suspect it might belong to me, anyway.' I sense her gaze wavering towards Dewi and his warriors, but then she glowers at me.

I swallow once more, uncertain how to respond, having to work to keep my feet in place and not try and end her life right now, no doubt wasting mine when I can't hope to better her right now when I've already fought so many foes.

Despite everything we've endured, despite our better blades, I fear my father's vengeance for killing my brother, and the many warriors of his who've also fallen beneath our blades.

'Don't go far,' she calls over her shoulder, back turned arrogantly towards me, as she hobbles back into the stronghold that once belonged to Isarninus.

It seems, in seeking retribution against Isarninus, we've walked directly into a trap of our own devising, with an enemy we thought long dead. I swallow uneasily. Despite our blades, despite our successes, we are too few to overwhelm the combined might of the people of the Wæclingas, and the Gyrwe.

are too few, however, even the combined might of the
people of the V... village, and the Cyrne

37

MEDDI OF THE EORLINGAS

I close Idnerth's eyes, and with Urien's aid, manage to stand upright. Exhaustion has me shaking. That and shock for what's befallen us, tonight, as we gathered to celebrate our bounty with those we thought were the allies of the Eorlingas.

Padern rushes to Urien, followed by six of his warriors, armed, I realise, with a collection of Terricus' blades. My brother has decided, wisely, to share what should be our advantage.

'What by all the gods?' Padern questions, eyes appraising the scene as the flames from the fire now highlight the immediate area.

'We were attacked, from within,' I explain.

Padern nods, his lips downcast. 'We were promised hospitality,' he complains.

'As were we. It's a reciprocal arrangement,' Urien huffs, but I shake my head.

'We're all astounded by this. We shouldn't argue amongst ourselves,' I urge them. 'Now, protect the gateway. I'll gather the horses, as Madog suggested.'

'Seeress.' The men bow towards me, but I can smell the anger on them. All the same, it pleases me to see Padern helping us. He's a good ally. We'll treat him well after this. The blades, I'll argue, should return with him when the enemy are all dead.

'What did they hope to accomplish?' I hear Urien asking Padern. The two men stand close together, voices breathless. The words trouble me. What did our enemy hope to achieve? Why did they declare war against us using the oldest means possible?

'Terricus,' I call to Urien abruptly, my thoughts forming before me. 'Terricus,' I repeat, shock making it difficult to voice my concerns.

It's Padern who determines my worries and answers.

'He's well. He's the one who gave us the blades. He had two men guarding him and the blades, and his slave was also there. I assure you, they don't have him.'

I nod, relieved, and return to my horse. The animal's no longer placid. Her eyes are wild, and she paws at the ground. Not only that, but the other horses are acting in the same way. I narrow my eyes, walking confidently towards her. If I can calm her, the others will quickly follow.

'Come on, girl,' I murmur, and other nonsense streams from my mouth. Her long nose sniffs my hand but then she dances backwards quickly, and I understand my mistake. 'I smell of blood, don't I?' I realise, instead reaching for her with my other hand. It's a mark of our long friendship, that she sniffs my other hand instead. She wants to be calmed. I rub her head, up towards her ear, keeping her gaze fixed on mine, aware the horses with her are also starting to show less unease. 'Good, good,' I call, and then move to her side, and mount up. The smoke's growing increasingly thick. I need to find the foals before they injure themselves. And before they're wounded or taken by our enemy, who, I'm sure, remain within the enclosure. I hear Madog's distant voice shouting orders to his warriors, and there's an uneasy peace in the immediate area. I'd think the enemy were all dead, but I don't believe that. Somewhere, there are others. We need to find them, and kill them as well.

I squint into the gloom. It's difficult to see in the

darkness, especially as I move away from the glow of the burning fire, and the small blaze close to the gate.

'Mistress,' Urien calls to me. I should have him at my side. Alone, it would be easy for one of our foes to attack me.

'Come with me,' I urge him, but he doesn't materialise from the gloom. Instead, it's Padern who comes towards me. His lips are pale but sheeted with blood.

'He thought it best to hold the gate,' he explains, without a trace of rancour for being sent about as though a young man who's not yet bloodied his blade. And, for not being trusted to hold the entranceway to Villa Eorlingas, even though he's evidently bled for us.

'I need to find my foals before they're injured. Do you want to ride?' I indicate one of the other horses, following mine.

'I will, yes. Better able to see when mounted,' Padern confirms. I listen for the noise of him making a friend of the horse and mounting. 'Where did they go?'

'I don't know. We'll look where I think they'll probably be. In their grazing field.'

I don't see him nod, but I hear the chink of his blade and shield. I'm not sure if it's his own, or one he's taken from the dead enemy.

'How did this happen?' Padern muses. It's not a question I can answer.

'We had some warnings earlier in the summer they were planning something. But nothing materialised, and they welcomed overtures of friendship. Only a few days ago, Madog attended their feast.'

'Were they set against your people by that woman you were seeking?' Padern questions. I feel my head swivel before I can stop it.

'Elen?' I hiss. I'd not considered that. I thought our foemen had come for our blades, Terricus' knowledge, and perhaps our horses. But if Elen is involved, that's entirely different. 'She's dead,' I huff through tight lips, my hand unconsciously straying towards my previously scarred cheek. Only the smoothness of it beneath my touch assures me I'm healed. I've somehow assumed that could only have happened when Elen and Edern were both dead. But what if that's not the reason for it?

'Is she?' Padern questions.

'Why do you say that?'

'Something Cadwysti said before she died.'

'And what was that?'

I sense him shaking his head. 'She was with the gods in her mind before she was with her body. She mumbled of a coming conflict, I think. Blood, fire, blades. It made no sense at the time. I don't think even she knew what it was all about. But, then, she shouted Elen's name aloud. I only now made the connection,' he mutters. I can barely breathe. These words should have been told to me before, but I can hardly blame Padern for that. Men are never clever where the gods are concerned.

Ahead, I sense movement, and grip my blade tightly, and my mare's mane, but it's the foals. A collection of wild, whirling eyes greets me. The mothers rush to their offspring. I dismount, counting beneath my breath. Only when I'm confident the six foals are all there, having walked amongst them, and secured them within the gated enclosure, do I turn to Padern as I mount once more. He's right behind me, but I don't see his eyes.

'What is it?' I whisper, immediately alert to some fresh danger. He doesn't reply. My heart thuds too loudly, the roar of my life pulse loud in my ears so I can hear nothing above that beat and my breath.

'I don't know. Something still isn't right.'

I narrow my eyes, peering into the gloom, away from the blaze, which does seem to be dying down although it shimmers, yellowish against the swell of smoke isolating us from everyone else. My eyes switch towards the gate, but the fire is no bigger than it was before. The enemy aren't there.

I swallow, but remain alert, as the thudding and rushing in my ears slowly ebbs away. I feel as though I've run from one end of the villa to the other.

And then I hear it. A sharp cry. A terrible noise. I look to Padern. He meets my gaze, and his lips are downcast. He bends low over the horse, urging the animal to great speed. I follow behind, fear having me gasping all over again.

Somehow, I know what I'm going to find, and my heart stills.

I can't believe it. It can't possibly be true. But it is.

I dismount before my horse has come to a stop, and my knees buckle on meeting the ground, again, unheeding of the congealing blood surrounding Marchell.

I touch her, and see Sian nearby, sobbing desperately, bloodied as well, while Madog stamps from one end of the fire to the other, protecting Marchell in death as he couldn't in life.

I want to howl. I want to keen. I want to beseech our god to bring her back to me.

But there's no point.

Marchell is dead, and the only comfort is that the man who killed her lies just as sightless beside her, his bloodied blade slack in his hand. I don't know who he is. But I hate him.

I don't know why. I don't know how. But one of the Færpingas has murdered my mother.

It can only be the work of that bitch, Elen. Her own daughter.

'I'll hunt her down and find her,' I promise my god, even as tears streak down my face, and I hold my mother's hand as her body begins to cool. 'I will hunt her down and end her life,' I reaffirm, and with Madog's hand on my shoulder, I know I won't be alone in my determination. Not this time.

38

WÆRMUND OF THE GYRWE

'Bollocks,' I roar, unable to stop myself. Fear has me in its grip. I don't want to look along the path we've taken to reach the crest of the hill on which Isarninus' settlement sits, in case my father is surging upwards to find me.

'Who is your father?' Dewi questions me, warily.

'Wihtlæd of the Gyrwe.'

Dewi's unexpected response drives the panic from me. 'Never heard of the bastard.' He shrugs his wide shoulders.

I suddenly grin, gaze sweeping over Bægmund's body, and then to my surviving warriors, Heafoc, Bucge, Eastmund, Osfyth and Maggenræd. They're bruised and bleeding, but we accomplished almost all of our intentions this day. They stand proud, defiance writ into the lines of their bodies.

'But, I know who that bitch is, well enough.' I feel my forehead furrow, but Dewi's nodding fiercely. 'I know who she is. I'd like to see her dead.' His voice thrums with rage.

'Are you with us?' I demand from our new-found allies, absorbing the news he knows Elen. He shows no fear about facing my father, but his hatred of Elen is clear to see.

'What, against this Wihtlæd, and her?' I'm asked by Dewi, a scowl on his lips as he alludes to Elen, while the three other men look to their leader.

'As part of our *comitatus*?' I state.

'Yes,' is Dewi's immediate response. 'I wish to see that bitch dead for all she's done to my people.'

I nod, pleased to see he hates Elen as much as I do. 'Good. Welcome, all of you, to my *comitatus*. I'm sorry about your friend.'

'Nyfed was an arse.' One of the others shrugs. 'He only joined us because he couldn't do anything else. But, I'm sorry about your man. He was a fine warrior.'

I nod at that. 'He was, yes. We won't leave him here.'

With the gateway slammed behind us, I fear no

further repercussions from those within, not until my father arrives, and so hurry to Bægmund.

'Help me get him on his horse,' I order my warriors. It's Heafoc who hastens to help me.

'What are you thinking?' Heafoc whispers to me, as we bend to gather together the still-warm body of our dead friend.

'We have allies, far from here. Elen might live, and she might know we went to Uriconium to get our blades as she was leading us there, but she won't know of our friends amongst those people. We go there, and then we make our way further west, but I intend to bring more warriors to our *comitatus*. Then, we'll return and counter my father and that bitch when there are more than ten of us to do so.'

Bægmund's a heavy load, and the horse is skittish. Only with the aid of Eastmund do we manage to secure his body.

'A fine idea,' Heafoc surprises me by saying. 'You've become a better leader than you think,' he confides. I'd take pride in that, if I weren't hoisting the corpse of one of my beloved warriors onto a horse to take it away from a fight we should have won easily.

'I will be,' I vow with determination, and then turn to those of my warriors of the Gyrwe who yet live: limping Bucge, fearless Osfyth with her blood-streaked arm, brave Eastmund, tall Heafoc, red-haired Maggenræd, as well as the new men led by Dewi. I meet the gaze of each of them, tight chest slowly easing from my exertions. 'We ride from here. Retrace our steps to Uriconium. We'll grow stronger and then,' I vow, 'we'll beat my father, and need never fear him and his warriors again. We will also,' I incline my head towards Dewi, 'see Elen dead.'

So spoken, I mount up, and with a last glance at the enclosure that once belonged to Isarninus and now to his son – or, rather, Elen – I direct my horse, and Bægmund's mount, down the steep hillside, un-surprised when the dog, more alike to a wolf with his black, white and grey markings, I met earlier comes to my side, head and tail down as he creeps closer, des-perate to be at my side but unsure of his welcome. He's been hiding all this time, but evidently he means to align himself with us as well, if I'll have him.

'Come on, boy,' I call, and his head also rises, yellow eyes meeting mine. I take that as a comfort. I might feel weak in this moment, but we've killed many men and found new allies in the most unex-pected of places, even if one of them is this wolf-like dog. I don't miss he's my birthmark made flesh. There's something at work here, something I don't yet understand. Something that even Bucge doesn't comprehend.

We're far from done. We're far from finished.

We'll have our vengeance against Elen, and my bastard father, and his warriors.

* * *

MORE FROM MJ PORTER

Another book by MJ Porter, *Shield of Mercia*, is available to order now here: https://mybook.to/ShieldofMerciaBackAd

HISTORICAL NOTES

As is so often the case, I have decided very serendipitously to locate this series in an area that offers me more archaeology than even I realised. I mean, I wanted to tell the story of the early kingdom of the Hwicce (based at Gloucester/Glevum, and at this time potentially comprising the tribes of the Eorlingas, Beansæte, Stoppingas, Husmeræ, Weogoran and a tribe centred around Winchcombe, according to the Tribal Hidage.) (If you want to drive yourself a bit bonkers, spend a few hours on the web trying to find some consistency for these tribal identifications. Indeed, almost every book I consulted also seemed to have differing interpretations as well as spellings.) But even I didn't know there was *so much* there. Gloucestershire is home to the remains of at least fifty-two Roman villas, some of which are still standing, others of which have long since been buried and are now being rediscovered by archaeologists.

While the home of the Eorlingas is entirely fictional, I've made use of the archaeological site report for Frocester Roman Villa when devising what their home might have been like, and how the farming landscape worked. This report contains a rich vein of information, not all relevant to me, but I did welcome the work undertaken to determine how many animals such a villa could have supported at this time. That of the Husmeræ is based on Great Witcombe Roman Villa, situated just below the Cotswold escarpment. It was a rich and well-endowed settlement, although how much was still standing at this era is difficult to ascertain.

The date of composition for Gildas' *On the Ruin of Britain* is much debated (anywhere from the mid-fifth century until the mid-sixth), but speaks to a period before this story (although I've included him as a character because I've wanted to write about him for a decade – he was the subject of one of my earliest historical fiction short stories, and that character has very much influenced how he's presented in this trilogy). Gildas' account does, according to historians, reflect very much events in southern, western and south-western parts of Britain, so not necessarily where these stories are set. However, we don't know where Gildas was based. We don't know a great deal about him other than his fiery diatribe that survives, and which famously named five tyrant kings, as well as alluding to a sixth. These are the names with which this slightly earlier period resounds: Constantine, Vortipor, Aurelius Caninus, Cuneglasus and Maglocunus (not Arthur).

If you'd like to know why Arthur is absent from this tale, it's because I don't believe an 'historical' Arthur ever existed. However, the allure of Arthur has led to some fabulous archaeological endeavours which have added a huge wealth of knowledge to what is known about 'The Dark Ages.' His influence shouldn't be underestimated, even if readers need to understand the ongoing allure of the legend is being manipulated to achieve the ends of archaeologists (or at least it was to fund excavations in the 1970s and 1980s). Arthur's legend is still being constructed, even to this day, based on almost nothing. Gildas, famously, doesn't mention him in his writings, although he does reference some of the battles later attributed to Arthur. The first time the name Arthur appears is in the *Historia Brittonum*, once attributed to Nennius, a ninth-century Welsh source, surviving in an eleventh-century copy (so, yes, a record from 300 years later, only surviving in one that's 500 years after the events it describes – think about that in terms of us rewriting the affairs of Tudor England, and the following century in this day and age). It's no longer attributed to Nennius, although many still mention him as the author.

Non-fiction titles used during writing this novel were *Pagan Britain* by Ronald Hutton, *Treasures from Sutton Hoo* by Gareth Williams, the site report from *Frocester* by Eddie Price, *The First Kingdom* by Max Adams, *Felix's Life of St Guthlac* trans. B. Colgrave and the *Wroxeter Roman City* English Heritage guidebook by Roger H. White. There is genuinely no other book than Max Adams' *The First Kingdom* which tries to tackle this period in a very engaging and informative manner for a non-specialist reader approaching the period from a more 'historical' perspective. For those with more interest in archaeology, then Robin Fleming's *Britain After Rome* is the book for you, although alas, it only seems to be available in paperback. It is a fabulous and concise account of what was happening in Britain at the time and does not shy away from making sense of seemingly incompatible elements. I loved discovering this book.

I must also give a shout-out to Max Adams' *In the Land of the Giants: A Journey Through the Dark Ages*, which I made use of for recreating the landscape around Wroxeter, as well as visiting the ruins of the settlement, which are also well worth a visit, if only to walk through the reconstructed villa building.

Throughout these novels, my aim is to 'fuse' the cultures that are known to have been within Britain at this time, and in this location. As such, there are Iron Age elements for the Eorlingas/Meddi, including the sigils that have survived from the earlier period, boar, bear and the horse. For Wærmund, with his Saxon heritage and as a worshipper of Woden, and descendant (as was claimed in the later genealogies), I've chosen wolves. Gildas, as a Christian, and a writer of Latin (and it must be assumed a speaker of it), represents the legacy of Rome, if not its gods. I've found there is no room for the Roman gods, although it's unsure whether they were abandoned or not at this time. K. R. Dark has argued for there being a Christian element to the break with Rome in the early 400s:

Prior to the official Imperial withdrawal in AD410, the mainly pagan secular aristocratic elite of Late Roman Britain was replaced by a

Christian administration, with low-status origins. After the failure of Constantine III, the
new administration still sought to maintain
Roman modes of administration and cultural
values. It adopted a British political structure
(the only available alternative to Imperial
Roman rule) based on kingship. This change
resulted in the termination of many aspects of
elite culture, notably at villas and temples,
while the withdrawal of the Roman army ter-
minated activity at fort sites.

— *CIVITAS TO KINGDOM*, 1994

It must be remembered Christianity had been the
official religion of the Roman Empire before the
break with Britain.

As well as all the books I've read, and online lec-
tures I've attended to give me a feeling for this period,
I would like to thank the bladesmith I met at Jarrow
Hall in September 2024 who answered all my questions, and very confidently assured me that what I
wanted to do with this story to begin with concerning
the broken sword could never be done. Thank you,
sir. I'm sure I've avoided many complaints by following your fabulous advice. And speaking of that

day, I've also made use of *The Perfect Sword* by Paul Gething and Edoardo Albert when trying to determine how a blade and hilt might have been made and fitted together. It has become just another of those things that I thought I knew, but had no idea about.

With regard to the final feast, a single cow would consist of 200 kilograms of meat, and so rather than feasting being the exception, Robin Fleming has made the argument that it was also entirely necessary to be able to consume so much meat and not have it go to waste.

As ever, thank you to my readers for joining me on this journey to the real 'Dark Ages' (a term everyone knows I don't apply lightly). I hope you're finding it as fascinating as me, while also appreciating that, actually, the Arthurian legend perhaps masks what was an even more fascinating (and sophisticated) period than we could possibly have imagined.

ACKNOWLEDGEMENTS

As ever, my thanks must be extended to my editor, Caroline at Boldwood Books, and the whole team who support my stories, especially Amanda, Claire, Nia, Wendy, Ben and everyone else in the background, including Kate (I hope I haven't missed anyone out). And a special shout-out to my fabulous copy editor Ross who catches all my mistakes, picks up every time I misspell a character's name (often) and generally keeps me on track to make sure this story is as good as possible for my readers to enjoy without any pesky typos. And to Shirley, who has the unenviable task of double-checking everything Ross and I have done to the manuscript.

I would also like to extend my thanks to the narrators of this series, Antonia Beamish and Simon Mattacks, and also to Christine Rauer, who very kindly provided a recording of how many of these character names should actually be spoken (as opposed to the way I think they should be said which is wholly incorrect). It's a privilege to hear these names as they would have been spoken at the time.

A huge thank you to all the experts who work in this field, from historians to archaeologists to re-enactors to guides at historical sites. I'm so excited to see what else is discovered in the future about this period. One thing is certain, the story of this time is far from set in concrete. Who knows what the future will bring with regard to the past?

Special thanks to my other half, who took well to being dragged around many, many Roman sites which I can't pronounce even though I write about the Saxons. It's been quite a sea change.

And to my readers. Thank you for joining me as I work my way backwards through the Saxon period. I've always been a little chaotic in my approach to writing.

ABOUT THE AUTHOR

MJ Porter is the author of many historical novels set predominantly in Seventh to Eleventh-Century England, and in Viking Age Denmark. Raised in the shadow of a building that was believed to house the bones of long-dead Kings of Mercia, meant that the author's writing destiny was set.

Sign up to MJ Porter's mailing list here for news, competitions and updates on future books.

Visit MJ's website: www.mjporterauthor.com

Follow MJ on social media:

X x.com/coloursofunison
📷 instagram.com/m_j_porter
BB bookbub.com/authors/mj-porter

ALSO BY MJ PORTER

The Eagle of Mercia Chronicles

Son of Mercia

Wolf of Mercia

Warrior of Mercia

Eagle of Mercia

Protector of Mercia

Enemies of Mercia

Betrayal of Mercia

Shield of Mercia

The Brunanburh Series

King of Kings

Kings of War

Clash of Kings

Kings of Conflict

The Dark Age Chronicles

Men of Iron

Warriors of Iron

WARRIOR CHRONICLES

WELCOME TO THE CLAN ✕

THE HOME OF
BESTSELLING HISTORICAL
ADVENTURE FICTION!

WARNING:
MAY CONTAIN VIKINGS!

SIGN UP TO OUR
NEWSLETTER

BIT.LY/WARRIORCHRONICLES

Boldwood

Boldwood Books is an award-winning fiction publishing company seeking out the best stories from around the world.

Find out more at www.boldwoodbooks.com

Join our reader community for brilliant books, competitions and offers!

Follow us
@BoldwoodBooks
@TheBoldBookClub

Sign up to our weekly deals newsletter

https://bit.ly/BoldwoodBNewsletter